TEAM YANKEE

'Stunning. A powerful story, told with a breakneck pace.
This book is so real, you can smell the smoke.'
TOM CLANCY, author of *Red Storm Rising*

'A good and convincing picture of how war can be at
company level . . . which, in my opinion, is the battle
that really matters.'
GENERAL SIR JOHN HACKETT

'I found it absorbing, exciting, and was literally unable to
put it down. A first rate talent.'
W.E.B. GRIFFIN, author of the bestselling series
Brotherhood of War and *The Corps*

'Hard-hitting . . . One of the handful of "can't put down"
war novels.'
Yorkshire Evening Post

'Illuminating insight into the next war.'
Books

'Flawless writing, fluently presented, entertaining.'
JAMES A. COX, *The Midwest Book Review*

'Reeks of authenticity'
Today

'A realistic story . . . slam-bang finale.'
Washington Post

'Coyle captures the stress, exhilaration and terror of combat.'
Cincinnati Post

'Dramatic . . . frank and compelling.'
Christian Science Monitor

'Alarmingly realistic . . . a thrilling book that will pull you in and leave you amazed and exhausted.'
South Bend Tribune

TEAM YANKEE

A novel of
World War III

Harold Coyle

A STAR BOOK
published by
the Paperback Division of
W. H. Allen & Co. Plc

A Star Book
Published in 1989
by the Paperback Division of
W. H. Allen & Co. Plc
Sekforde House, 175/9 St. John Street,
London, EC1V 4LL

First published in the United States of America by Presidio Press, 1987
First published in Great Britain by W. H. Allen & Co. Plc, 1988

Copyright © Presidio Press, 1987

Printed in Great Britain by
Cox & Wyman Ltd, Reading

ISBN 0 352 32325 6

To Patricia,
my friend, my lover, my wife.

*Dulce Et Decorum Est**

Wilfred Owen
(1893–1918)

Bent double, like old beggars under sacks,
Knocked-kneed, coughing like hags, we cursed through
sludge,
Till on the haunting flares we turned our backs
And toward our distant rest began to trudge.
Men marched asleep. Many had lost their boots
But limped on, blood-shod. All went lame, all blind;
Drunk with fatigue; deaf even to the hoots
Of tired, outstripped Five Nines that dropped behind.

Gas! GAS! Quick boys! An ecstasy of fumbling,
Fitting the clumsy helmets just in time,
But someone still was yelling out and stumbling
And flound'ring like a man in fire lime. –
Dim through the misty panes and thick green light,
As under a green sea, I saw him drowning.

In all my dreams, before my helpless sight,
He plunges at me, guttering, choking, drowning.

If in some smothering dreams, you too could pace
Behind the wagon that we flung him in,
And watched the white eyes writhing in his face,
His hanging face, like a devil's sick of sin;
If you could hear, at every jolt, the blood
Come gargling from the froth-corrupted lungs,
Bitten as the cud
Of vile, incurable sores on innocent tongues, –
My friend, you would not tell with such high zest
The old Lie: *Dulce et decorum est*
Pro patria mori.

* *Dulce et decorum est pro patria mori:*
Sweet and fitting it is
to die for the fatherland

Contents

Calendar

Day   1 : First Battle
        2 : orders for the attack/relief in place
        3 : attack and the defense of Hill 214
        4 : defense of Hill 214 and relief
    5–8: reconstitution
        8 : reserve/road march
        9 : attack
     10 : night battle/cross attachment
     11 : across the Saale
     12 : defense
     13 : movement to contact/defense
     14 : cease-fire

Foreword

Since the end of World War Two, the confrontation between the United States and the Soviet Union has dominated world affairs. While it can be argued that the issue is one of freedom versus dictatorship, capitalism versus communism, NATO versus the Warsaw Pact, in the end, the confrontation is between the two main antagonists. Issues change, locations change, supporting players change, the means of warfare change. The only fixed constant is the two main players, the United States and the Soviet Union.

There is much debate on what the final outcome of this confrontation will be. At one end of the spectrum there are the optimists who believe that the two great nations will learn to coexist and find peaceful means of resolving their disputes. At the other end are the cynics who believe that the two superpowers will destroy not only themselves, but the rest of the world as well, in a nuclear holocaust. Both nations possess the means to accomplish either.

It is not the purpose of this book to debate the great issues, nor to predict how the confrontation will end. My goal is simple: to tell a story.

The story is of the men who would be called upon by the United States to decide the issue if the United States and the Soviet Union sought resolution of their difference by force of arms. More specifically, it is about one company, or team, in such a war. It is called Team Yankee, a tank-heavy combat team in West Germany. At the start of the story the Team consists of eighty-four men and a mix of modern, high-tech weaponry as well as tried and true, if somewhat old, equipment. Although the Team is a tank-heavy company team, it is attached to a mechanized infantry battalion.

The main character is Capt. Sean Bannon, commander of Team Yankee. Through his eyes, and those of his subordinates, a view of what modern war would look like in Europe from the standpoint of the American combat soldier is created.

Bannon is a typical American officer of the mid-1980s. Having been graduated from college and having obtained a commission through the ROTC programme, he has served as a tank platoon leader, a tank company executive officer and a battalion staff officer. His military education has consisted of the Armor Officer's Basic Course and the Armor Officer's Advanced Course, both at Fort Knox, Kentucky. He is married, 27 years old, has three children and a degree in history and probably will never be promoted above the grade of lieutenant colonel.

The men in Team Yankee are products of the society from which they came. It was said many years ago that the soldiers of an army can be only as good as the society that produces them. This holds true in today's army. The American soldier today is a product of his society. In the next war, as in past, he will be forced to exist in a nightmare environment of mud and extremes of temperature, subsisting on cold, dehydrated meals and little sleep, faced always with the possibility of death from any quarter. These are the people who will, in war, decide its outcome and the shape of the world tomorrow.

The scenario for this fictitious war is borrowed from General Sir John Hackett's books, *The Third World War* and *The Third World War: The Untold Story*. It is the scenario of a conventional war fought in the mid-1980s. In General Sir John Hackett's books the emphasis is on world politics and strategy. This book concerns itself with life at the other end of the spectrum: war as seen from the tank commander's hatch and the soldier's foxhole.

The characters are likewise fictitious. Any resemblance they have to real people is purely coincidental. The events and units involved are, of course, fictitious. Most geographical locations, towns, and areas mentioned are fictional and are not meant to resemble real places or locations. The exceptions to this are the Thüringer Wald and the Saale River, located in the southern portion of East Germany, and Berlin.

This book does not and is not meant to represent current U.S. Army doctrine, policy, plans, or philosophy.

Acknowledgments

In writing this book, I owe a great deal to three soldiers and their books. The first and most influential is Charles MacDonald and his book, *Company Commander*. MacDonald was an infantry company commander in the 23rd Regiment, 2nd Infantry Division, during World War Two. After the war he wrote of his experiences as a small unit commander in that war. This excellent book has served me well in my military career and in my efforts to write this book. His assistance, kind words, and guidance have made this book possible.

The next two books, both written by Gen. Sir John Hackett, are *The Third World War* and *The Third World War: The Untold Story*. From these books I received the impetus to write *Team Yankee* and a scenario into which I could place it. The most interesting part of both books to me, as a junior officer, was Sir John's description of the war from the soldier's viewpoint. I have, with Sir John's permission, expanded upon his books, telling the story of one company team from the beginning to the end of the war. I also owe General Sir John Hackett my everlasting gratitude for reviewing the manuscript, providing me guidance, and giving me encouragement to carry on.

The fourth book, *Heights of Glory*, written by Brig. Gen. Avigdor Kahalani, provided me with an excellent description of modern armoured warfare as experienced by a tank unit commander. General Kahalani commanded the 77th Tank Battalion, Israeli Defence Forces, during the Yom Kippur War in October 1973. This battalion held the critical sector of the Golan Heights overlooking the Valley of Tears.

NATO MILITARY SYMBOLS

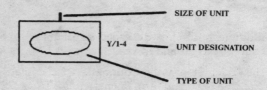

SIZE OF UNIT

UNIT DESIGNATION

Y/1-4

TYPE OF UNIT

UNIT SIZE

• • •	PLATOON
I	COMPANY
∏	TEAM
I I	BATTALION
∏	TASK FORCE
I I I	REGIMENT
X	BRIGADE
XX	DIVISION
XXX	CORPS
XXXX	ARMY
XXXXX	ARMY GROUP

UNIT TYPE

⊂⊃	ARMOR or TANK
⊠	MECHANIZED INFANTRY
⊘	ARMORED CAVALRY
⊙	ARTILLERY, SELF PROPELLED
⊏	ENGINEER
⊠	INFANTRY, STRAIGHT LEG
•	ARTILLERY, TOWED
⋈	ARMY AVIATION
⌒	AIR DEFENSE ARTILLERY
▭	UNITS WITH A BORDER ARE WARSAW PACT

Glossary

A-10: A U.S. Air Force jet designed specifically to provide close air support to ground forces.

AH 1: The designation of the Cobra attack helicopter. There are several versions and armaments range from 7.62mm miniguns up to TOW antitank guided missiles. The TOW provides the main punch of the Cobra.

AK: Short for AK47 or AK74 rifle, the standard assault rifle of the Soviet infantryman.

Armed Forces Network: The official radio and television network of the U.S. Armed Forces, serving American military forces deployed overseas.

Assembly Area: A location normally behind friendly lines where a unit closes into a tight circle in order to rest, rearm and prepare for further operations.

Autobahn: The German equivalent to our interstate highway system, the autobahns, in fact, inspired and acted as a model for our interstate highway system.

Auxiliary Radio Receiver: Sometimes referred to as the AUX, it is simply a radio receiver, unable to transmit. Command vehicles normally carry a radio that can receive and transmit set to the radio frequency of the commander's unit and an auxiliary radio set to the radio frequency of his commanding officer.

Basic Load: A prescribed number of rounds or amount of supply carried by a combat vehicle or individual soldier.

BBC: British Broadcasting Corporation.

BMP: A Soviet fully tracked infantry-fighting vehicle mounting either a 73mm gun or a 25mm cannon (in the BMP-2 version), an antitank guided missile, and 7.62mm machine gun. The BMP carries a crew of three and a nine-man infantry squad. The BMP provided the prime motivation for the design and production of the Bradley fighting vehicle.

BTR: A designator identifying any one of several types of Soviet armoured personnel carriers from the four-wheeled BTR-152 of World War II vintage to the BTR-70, an eight-wheeled armoured personnel carrier now being fielded.

BTR-60: A Soviet eight-wheeled armoured personnel carrier. This vehicle comes in several versions, from the original, which has an open top, to the BTR-60PB, which is completely enclosed and carries a small turret mounting a 14.5mm and a 7.62mm machine gun. In addition to the personnel carrier version, the BTR-60 serves as a command and control vehicle, close air support vehicle, and other such uses.

Bradley: An armoured fighting vehicle that comes in two versions, the M-2 mechanised infantry fighting vehicle version and the M-3 scout version. Both have a two-man turret that mounts a TOW missile launcher, a 25mm chain gun, and a 7.62mm machine gun mounted coaxially with the 25mm gun.

CEOI: Short for communication and electronic operating instructions. The CEOI contains all radio frequencies, radio call signs, signal information and passwords and countersigns.

CEV: Short for combat engineer vehicle. This vehicle is a specially modified tank that carries a large calibre demolition gun used for reducing obstacles, a dozer blade for digging positions or clearing debris, and a boom and winch.

Chemical Alarm: A small portable device the size of a bread box that samples the air and alerts its users when a chemical agent, gas, is detected.

CINC: Short for commander in chief, the term is pronounced 'sink'. In this case, it is referring to the four-star general in command of all NATO forces in Europe.

CO: Short for commanding officer.

COAX: Short for coaxially mounted machine gun. This

weapon is normally a 7.62mm machine gun mounted next to the main weapon of a fighting vehicle.

Cobra: Nickname of the AH 1 attack helicopter. The Cobra is also referred to as a 'Snake'.

Cupola: A small, freely rotating turret on top of a tank turret or personnel carrier that incorporates a hatch, vision blocks, and usually a weapon such as a machine gun.

CVC: Short for combat vehicle crewman's helmet. This helmet provides protection to the tracked vehicle crewman's head as the tank bounces around the countryside. It is also wired to the vehicle's radio and intercom, allowing the crewman to hear what is being broadcast and to broadcast over the radio and intercom.

Division Rear: Military units occupy terrain. The terrain that the unit occupies is called a sector and is normally subdivided into sectors with subordinate units responsible for the sector they occupy. The division rear is that part of the division's sector that is to the rear of the forward-deployed combat brigades. The division rear is normally managed by the division's support command, called DISCOM, and contains most of the noncombat support elements such as supply units, maintenance units, medical units, etc.

DPICM: Short for duel-purpose, improved conventional munitions. This is an artillery round that contains many small submunitions or bomblets that are capable of defeating the thin armour located on top of armoured vehicles as well as being effective against personnel and other 'soft' targets.

Dragon: A medium antitank guided missile launcher. Man-portable, the Dragon is the infantry's medium-range antitank weapon, with a range of 1000 metres.

Executive Officer: The second in command of a unit. In a company, the executive officer, or XO, is a first lieutenant; in a battalion, he is a major. Traditionally the XO is responsible for handling the administrative and logistical matters in the unit.

45: Short for the calibre .45 M1911A1 pistol, the standard side arm for the U.S. Army. This weapon has been in the Army's inventory since 1911.

Field phone: Simple telephones that are powered either by sound (TA-1s) or D-cell batteries (TA-312s) and connected by two-strand wire called WD-1.

Fighting positions: The location or position from which a soldier or fighting vehicle fights. This position is usually improved to provide protection to the soldier or vehicle and camouflaged to hide the position until the soldier or vehicle fires.

First Sergeant: The senior NCO in a company, normally a master sergeant or E-8. In combat, the First Sergeant assists the executive officer in handling the administrative and logistical needs of the company.

FIST: Short for fire-support team. This team is headed by an artillery lieutenant and co-ordinates all requests for artillery and mortar fires as well as close air support. The FIST team consists of four to six men and travels in an M-113, normally within arm's reach of the company commander.

FSO/FSE: Fire-support officer and fire-support element. The fire-support officer is responsible for co-ordinating all indirect fires, i.e. artillery, mortar, and close air support, for the battalion or brigade to which he is attached. The fire-support element is located at the battalion or brigade command post.

Gasthaus: A small German neighbourhood restaurant and pub that may also include a hotel.

GB: A chemical agent.

Gun Mantel: The armour that protects a tank's main gun and its cradle.

Halon Gas: A gas used to extinguish fires in the M-1 and Bradley vehicles. Automatic fire sensors detect fires and release the halon gas within milliseconds of activation.

HEAT: Short for high explosive antitank, a round that

depends on a shaped charge explosion to penetrate an armoured vehicle's armour. Because the round contains high explosive, it has a secondary role as an antimaterial round.

Hind: Nickname of the Soviet MI-24D attack helicopter.

Improved TOW Vehicle or ITV: A modified M-113 armoured personnel carrier that has an antitank guided missile launcher mounted on a small rotating turret. TOW stands for tube-launched, optically-tracked, wire-guided antitank guided missile. The TOW is currently the heaviest antitank guided missile in the U.S. Army's inventory capable of hitting a tank-sized target out to a range of 3700 metres with a 90% hit probability.

Intercom: Short for intercommunications system. The intercom links all tracked vehicle crewmen together and allows the crew to talk amongst themselves.

LAW: Short for light antitank weapon. The current U.S. Army LAW contains a 66mm antitank rocket that has an effective range of 300 metres. The LAW comes in a collapsible tube that is discarded when the rocket had been fired.

LBE: Short for load-bearing equipment. This is the web gear worn by soldiers that includes suspenders and a web belt to which equipment is attached, such as ammo pouches, the soldier's first-aid pouch, canteen, grenades, bayonet, pistol holster, etc. LBE is designed, in theory, to evenly distribute the weight of this equipment on the soldier's body.

LOGREP: Short for logistics report. Submitted to higher headquarters to inform them of the current status of ammunition, fuel, maintenance and supply of a unit.

LP: Listening post. A listening post is an outpost that is used during periods of limited visibility to provide security and early warning to the unit that it is covering. As its name implies, the LP relies on hearing the approaching enemy.

M-1: This is the current main battle tank of the U.S. Army. It has a crew of four, mounts a 105mm main gun, an M2 calibre .50 machine gun and an M240 7.62mm machine gun. The 63-ton tank is powered by a 1500 horsepower turbine engine and is capable of 45 mphs. The fire-control system incorporates a laser range finder, a solid-state computer, a thermal imaging sight, and other electronics that allow the main gun to fire while on the move with a high degree of accuracy, day or night.

M-3: The scout version of the Bradley fighting vehicle. See Bradley for a description.

M60: A 7.62mm machine gun that is the mainstay of the U.S. Army's infantry squad. It had an effective range of 900 metres.

M-113: Until recently, the M-113 was the primary armoured personnel carrier. Weighing 13 tons, it has a crew of two, driver and commander, and the capacity to carry an entire infantry squad. The M-113 is normally armed with a calibre .50 M2 machine gun located at the commander's position. Because infantry cannot fight while mounted, the M-113 is being replaced by the M-2 Bradley fighting vehicle. The M-113 still remains a mainstay in the U.S. Army, performing support roles on or near the front.

M-577: A specially configured personnel carrier used as a command and control vehicle at battalion and brigade level.

Mech: Short for mechanised, or in the case of this book, mechanised infantry.

MI-24D: A Soviet attack helipcopter similar to the U.S. Army AH 1. The MI-24D, named Hind, is heavily armed with an automatic cannon and antitank guided missiles and is well armoured.

Mine Roller: An attachment to a tank that clears a path through a mine field for an attacking armoured force. The rollers are nothing more than large metal wheels that are pushed ahead of the tank and set off mines as they run over them.

MOPP Level: short for mission-oriented protective posture. MOPP levels prescribe how prepared individuals are to be to meet a chemical attack. In MOPP level I, soldiers simply carry or have their protective gear available. In MOPP level II, soldiers will don the chemical protective suit and carry their protective masks, gloves and boots. MOPP level III requires the soldier to wear the chemical protective suit, gloves and boots. MOPP level IV, the highest level, requires the soldier to wear all his protective clothing and his protective mask.

MRE: Short for Meal, Ready to Eat. MREs have replaced the age-old, C-rations as the standard combat ration in the U.S. Army. MREs are a combination of dehydrated and ready-to-eat foods that come in plastic pouches.

MTU: A Soviet tank-mounted bridge that can be laid under fire across obstacles such as antitank ditches or small streams.

NATO: North Atlantic Treaty Organisation. Founded in 1949, it is a military alliance whose expressed purpose is to prevent Soviet expansion in Europe. Today, NATO consists of Norway, Great Britain, Denmark, Belgium, The Netherlands, Luxembourg, the Federal Republic of Germany, Portugal, Spain, Italy, Greece, Turkey, Canada and the United States. France is still a member but does not actively participate in NATO manoeuvres or exercises.

NBC-1 Report: An initial chemical attack report.

NCO: Short for noncommissioned officer or sergeant. NCO ranks are: E-5 or buck sergeant, three stripes; E-6 or staff sergeant, three stripes and one rocker or lower stripe; E-7 or sergeant first class, three stripes and two rockers; E-8 or master sergeant, three stripes and three rockers; and E-9 or sergeant major, three stripes, three rockers with a star between the stripes and rockers.

Night Vision Goggles: Night vision devices that amplify available light and provide the user with a visible image.

OH-58: Designation of the U.S. Army's current scout or observation helicopter.

OP: Short for outpost or observation post. An outpost is placed well forward of a unit's main position and is intended to provide security and early warning for the unit. An OP can be manned by two or more dismounted personnel or armoured vehicles.

Panzer: German for armour.

Panzer Grenadier: The German term for mechanised infantry.

Platoon Sergeant: The senior noncommissioned officer in a platoon, normally an E-7. The platoon sergeant is the second in command of the platoon and performs the same duties that the executive officer does at company or battalion level.

PRC-77: A small man-portable FM radio used by the infantry.

Protective Mask: Gas mask.

REFORGER: A peacetime exercise that practises the redeployment of U.S. forces from the continental U.S. to Europe.

Remote Box: Part of the track's radio system, it allows the track commander to change frequencies from his position without having to climb down into the vehicle.

RPG: Short for rocket-propelled grenade. The RPG is the standard Soviet infantryman's antitank rocket, the equivalent to the U.S. Army's LAW.

S-1: The 'S' is for staff. The S-1 is the staff officer responsible for all personnel matters in the battalion or brigade.

S-2: The staff officer responsible for gathering, analysing and producing intelligence on enemy activities and intentions.

S-3: The staff officer responsible for planning, co-ordinating, and monitoring combat operations of the battalion or brigade.

S-4: The staff officer responsible for providing and co-ordinating for supply, maintenance and non-combat transportation needs of the battalion or brigade.

SABOT: The word is actually French for shoe. Here, it is the name of an antitank round. SABOT is short for armour-piercing fin-stabilised discarding sabot. The round consists of a small tungsten alloy or depleted uranium penetrator that has a diameter smaller than the diameter of the gun tube. To compensate for this, the penetrator is seated in a boot that is the same diameter as the gun. This boot, called the SABOT, falls away after the round leaves the gun, leaving the penetrator to continue to the target.

SHELLREP: Short for shell report. Used to report the impact of enemy artillery.

SITREP: Short for situation report. Subordinate commanders use the SITREP to update their superiors on the current activities, location, and condition of their unit.

SOP: Short for standing operating procedures. A unit SOP prescribes set actions to be taken given in a given situation.

Spot Report: A short, concise report used to provide information on the sighting of enemy activity. At a minimum, the report provides information on who has made the sighting, when the sighting was made, where the enemy was observed, how the enemy was equipped, and what he was doing.

Stand-to: A set time, normally before dawn, when all members of a unit are awake and manning their weapons and fighting positions.

Stinger Team: The Stinger is a man-portable short-range anti-aircraft heat-seeking missile. Stinger teams are two-man teams that are stationed well forward with combat units to provide air defence.

T-55 Tank: A Soviet tank with a four-man crew and mounting a 100mm gun and a 7.62mm machine gun. This tank is considered obsolete by today's standards but is still found in Warsaw Pact inventories.

T-62 Tank: A Soviet tank with a four-man crew and mounting a 115mm smoothbore gun, a 12.5mm and a 7.62mm machine gun. Though considered obsolete, it is still very capable and found in many Warsaw Pact units.

T-72 Tank: A Soviet tank with a three-man crew and mounting a 125mm smoothbore gun, a 12.5mm and a 7.62mm machine gun. The elimination of the fourth crewman is achieved by using an automatic loader for the main gun.

Special armour and a sophisticated fire-control system make it a powerful foe that is difficult to stop.

Task Force: A combat battalion that has both tank and infantry companies. Under U.S. Army doctrine, battalions seldom fight as pure tank or infantry units.

Team: A company-sized unit that includes both tank and mechanised infantry platoons. Unlike a peacetime company, the number and type of platoons in a team can vary according to its assigned mission. In the case of Team Yankee, the Team initially has two tank and one mechanised infantry platoon as well as two improved TOW vehicles.

Thermal Sight: A sight that detects the heat emitted by an object and translates that heat into a visible image for the gunner or tank commander.

TOC: Short for tactical operations centre. This is where the staff plans future operations and monitors the current battle. The TOC receives and passes reports, relieving the commander of that responsibility so that he may run the current battle.

TOW: Short for tube-launched, optically-tracked, wire-guided antitank guided missile. The TOW is the U.S. Army's current heavy antitank guided missile with a range of 3700 metres. The guidance system provides a high probability of hitting a tank-sized target out to its maximum range.

Trains: A term used to describe the collection of support and service elements that support military units.

Two-and-a-half Ton Truck: A medium cargo truck with a hauling capacity of two and a half tons. This truck is also referred to as a deuce and a half.

VC: Viet Cong, another war.

Vulcan: A 20mm multi-barrelled short-range anti-aircraft gun. The extremely high rate of fire, 4000 rounds a minute, results in a chainsaw-like sound when firing.

Warsaw Pact: A military alliance founded by the European

Communist countries to counter NATO. It consists of the Soviet Union, Poland, the German Democratic Republic, Hungary, Czechoslovakia, Bulgaria and Rumania.

WD-1: Two-strand wire used to connect field telephones or other communications equipment.

ZSU 23-4: A Soviet anti-aircraft gun. It has four rapid-firing 23mm guns, (hence 23-4). It is very capable and serves the same mission as the Vulcan in the U.S. Army. The ZSU, sometimes called 'Zoo' for short, accompanies the first echelon attack elements to provide air defence for those elements.

Prologue

Associated Press news story, 15 July: 'Escalation of the Persian Gulf War continued today when Iranian aircraft attacked two oil tanks just outside the territorial waters of Bahrain. A ship of Dutch registry was reported sunk early this morning shortly after leaving port. At this time there is no report of survivors. The second ship, registered in Panama, was inbound to Bahrain when it was attacked by two Iranian war planes. Casualties are reported to be high ...'

Television news story, 22 July: 'Despite condemnation by the UN, Western European nations, Japan, and the U.S., Iran has pledged to continue attacks on any vessel that enters the Persian Gulf, now declared a war zone by that country. Outside the Straits of Hormuz, entrance to the Persian Gulf, the number of tankers sitting at anchor, waiting for a break in the deadlock, continues to grow. The ships' owners and their captains feel that this deadlock will not last long. As one ship's captain stated, 'They have tried this before and always backed off. They need us too much to keep this up for long.'

State Department press release, 26 July: 'The attack by Iranian war planes on commercial vessels in the international waters of the Indian Ocean yesterday is a threat to the security of the free world. The United States and the free world cannot allow such acts of deliberate terrorism to go unpunished. While the United States continues to pursue all available means to resolve this issue peacefully, military options are being considered.'

Department of Defense press release, 27 July: 'The destroyer U.S.S. *Charles Logan*, while on patrol in international waters off the Straits of Hormuz, was rammed, then fired upon by a Soviet Cruiser of the Gorki class this morning. U.S. forces returned fire. Damage and casualties on either side are not known at this time.'

TASS news release, 28 July: 'A meeting of the Warsaw Pact ministers ended today with a pledge to stand together in the face of threats and increased war preparations on the part of the United States. Representatives from Poland, the German Democratic Republic, Hungary, Bulgaria, Czechoslovakia, and the Soviet Union released a joint statement pledging to meet American aggression against any member state with retaliation in kind.'

White House press release, 28 July: 'In view of the current crisis, the President has issued an order federalising 100,000 Army Reserve and National Guard personnel. Personnel and units affected have been notified and are reporting to their mobilisation stations.'

Vatican press release, 29 July: 'A request on the part of the Holy Father to travel to Moscow to talk to the Soviet premier in an attempt to find a peaceful solution to the current crisis was denied. The Holy Father calls for both sides to remember their responsibility to their people and to the world and again offered his services in any future negotiations.'

BBC news release, 30 July: 'A stormy session between the French president and the Soviet foreign minister in Paris today ended when the Soviet foreign minister warned the French president that the national interests of France would best be served if that nation did not involve itself in the current crisis between the Soviet Union and the United States. In a statement immediately after the meeting, the president announced that France would stand by her treaties and do her part to defend Europe against aggression from any quarter. The president went on to announce that the French military forces, with the exception of its strategic nuclear forces, would actively co-operate with other NATO nations during the current crisis.'

2

Television news story, 1 Aug: 'We interrupt this programme for a special announcement. Unconfirmed reports from Brussels, headquarters for NATO, state that the NATO nations have ordered their armed forces to mobilise and commence deployment to wartime positions. While there is no official word from Washington concerning this, announcement of an address to the nation by the president at seven o'clock this morning, followed by a joint press conference by the secretaries of state and defense seems to add credibility to these reports.'

Chapter One

STAND-TO

The noise and the metallic voice sounded as if they came from the far end of a long, dark corridor. There were no other feelings or sensations as he drifted from a dead sleep through that transitional period of half-asleep – half-awake. An inner, soothing voice on the near end of the corridor whispered, 'It's not important, go back to sleep.' But the radio whined back to life again and the metallic voice called out unanswered, 'BRAVO THREE ROMEO FIVE SIX – THIS IS KILO EIGHT MIKE SEVEN SEVEN – RADIO CHECK – OVER.' The inner voice was silent this time. Duty called and further sleep had to be abandoned.

As Captain Bannon began the grim process of waking up, other senses began to enter play. First came the aches and pains and muscle spasms, the result of sleeping on an uneven bed of personal gear, vehicular equipment, ration boxes, ammo boxes, and other odds and ends that tend to clutter the interior of a combat vehicle. A tumbled and distorted bed made up of paraphernalia ranging from soft, to not-so-soft, to downright hard does cruel things to the human body. Only exhaustion and the desire to be near the radios whenever possible allowed Bannon to survive the ordeal of sleeping like that.

While still sorting out the waves of pains and spasms, he opened his eyes and began to search the interior of the armoured personnel carrier in an effort to re-establish his orientation. The personnel carrier, or PC, was dimly lit by a dome light just above his head. It bathed everything in an eerie blue green light that reminded him of a scene from a Spielberg movie.

First Lieutenant Robert Uleski, the company executive officer, or XO, was sitting in the centre of the crew compartment, on a box of field rations, staring at the radio, waiting for it to speak to him again. Cattycorner from where

4

Bannon was perched was the PC's driver, Sp4 James Hurly, huddled up and asleep in the driver's compartment. For a moment Bannon stared at Hurly, wondering how the boy could sleep in such a godawful position. A twinge and a spasm from one of his contorted back muscles reminded him of his accommodations. Perhaps, he thought, the driver wasn't in such a bad spot after all.

A static crackle, a bright orange light on the face of the radio and the accelerating whine of a small cooling fan heralded the beginning of another incoming radio call: 'BRAVO THREE ROMEO FIVE SIX – BRAVO THREE ROMEO FIVE SIX – THIS IS KILO EIGHT MIKE SEVEN SEVEN – RADIO CHECK – OVER.' Without changing his expression or moving any other part of his body except his right arm and hand, which held the radio hand mike, Uleski raised the mike to within an inch of his mouth, pressed the push-to-talk button, and waited a couple of seconds. The little cooling fan in the radio whined to life. When the fan reached a steady speed, he began to talk, still facing the radio without changing expression.

'KILO EIGHT MIKE SEVEN SEVEN – THIS IS BRAVO THREE MIKE FIVE SIX – STAY OFF THE AIR – I SAY AGAIN – STAY OFF THE AIR – OUT.' Releasing the push-to-talk button, Uleski allowed his hand to fall back slowly into his lap. He continued to stare at the now silent radio as if he would pounce and attack it if it dared to come to life again. But it didn't.

Bannon's first effort to speak ended in an incoherent grunt due to a dry mouth and a parched throat. After summoning up what saliva he could, his second effort was slightly more successful. 'Is that 3rd Platoon again?'

Still staring at the radio with the same expression, Uleski provided a short, functional, 'Yes, Sir.'

'What time is it?'

Uleski raised his left arm in the same slow, mechanical manner as he had used when answering the radio. Looking at his watch, he considered for a moment what he was looking at and in the same monotone he simply stated, '0234 hours.'

It wasn't that Lieutenant Uleski was an expressionless

automaton without feelings. On the contrary, 'Ski,' or Lieutenant U, as the enlisted men called him, was a very personable man with a good sense of humour, a sharp wit, and an enormous capacity to absorb Polish jokes and retaliate with appropriate ethnic jokes aimed at his opponent. It's just that in the very early morning, everyone falls into a zombielike state. The requirement – to sit on a hard surface for hours on end, in a small, cold aluminium armoured box called a PC, with two sleeping bodies as your only company, with nothing better to do than stare at a radio that you did not expect, or want, to come to life – only added to one's tiredness. Uleski was not an exception. Nor was Bannon.

Considering for a moment the information his XO had given him, Bannon slowly plotted his next move. The PC was quiet and Uleski had gone back to watching the radio. Slowly, his mind began to come alive and it became apparent that sitting there, watching Uleski watching the radios was definitely nonproductive. Besides, Bannon was now in too much pain to go back to sleep and movement was the only way he was going to stop the aches and spasms. It was time to make the supreme effort and get up. Besides, the Team would be having stand-to within the hour and he needed some time to get himself together. While it was permissible for everyone else to look like he had just rolled out of bed at stand-to, the Team commander, at least, had to give the appearance that he was wide awake and ready to deal with the world. The night, if four hours of sleep on a pile of assorted junk could be called a night, was over. It was time to greet a new day, another dawn, the fourth since Team Yankee had rolled out of garrison and headed for the border.

★ Long before the tanks rolled out of the back gate towards the border, Pat Bannon knew that Sean was involved in more than another exercise. After eight years of marriage and life in the army, Pat could read her husband's moods like a book. At first, there was little change. The sinking of the oil tankers in the Persian Gulf by perpetually warring nations was just another story on the Armed Forces Network evening news.

Life in the military community continued as usual, as did Sean's comings and goings.

It was the closing of the Straits of Hormuz and the commitment of a U.S. carrier battle group to the area that began the change. The husbands began to spend more time at their units. The normal twelve-hour day that commanders and staff officers put in stretched into fourteen and fifteen hours. They tried to shrug off the extra hours as prep for an upcoming field exercise. But the wives who had 'been in the service' a while knew that the new routine was not the norm.

Some wives became upset and nervous. They didn't know what was happening but felt that, whatever it was, it was not good. Others talked about nothing else, as if it was a challenge to find out what the big dark secret was. During the day they would gather together with the rest of the 'grapevine' and compare notes in order to pool information they had gleaned from their husbands the night before. Pat chose to follow the lead of the older wives in the battalion. Cathy Hill, wife of the battalion commander of 1st of the 4th Armor, went out of her way to carry on as if everything was business as usual. So did Mary Shell, the wife of the battalion S-3. Pat and many of the wives followed their lead, not asking questions or nagging. They agreed that, whatever was happening, nagging wives would not help the situation.

It was the public announcement that the Soviets were sending a naval battle group to the Persian Gulf to 'assist in maintaining peace in the Gulf' that destroyed the last pretence of normalcy. When Pat told Sean the news after he came home from morning PT, he simply replied, 'Yeah, I know.' His attitude convinced Pat that he had already known about the incident and probably more. The feeling of dread and foreboding became more pronounced when word spread around the community that the training exercise for which the battalion had been preparing for months was suddenly cancelled. In their two-and-a-half years in Germany, that had never happened before. To make matters worse, cancellation of the exercise did not change the new fourteen-hour day routine.

Over the next few days every new deterioration in the world

situation seemed to be matched with further preparations by the battalion. One night, Sean brought home his field gear and took out his old worn fatigues and clothing and put some of his newer fatigues in. The next day, while returning from the commissary, Pat saw trucks with ammo caution signs on them in the motor pool, dropping off boxes at each of the tanks. Even the community dispensary began to pack up. The news that a U.S. and Soviet warship in the Gulf had collided and then exchanged fire, silenced the last optimist.

Pat wasn't ready for this. It suddenly dawned on her that her husband might be going to war. The possibility was always there. After all, Sean was a soldier and soldiers were expected to fight. As Sean would say on occasion, that's what he was paid for. Pat knew that someday it might come to that but had never given it much thought. Now she had to. It was like a great dark abyss. She had no guidelines, no idea of what to do. The Army spent a fortune training and preparing Sean for this moment but not a penny to prepare her, the wife of a soldier. Pat decided that the only thing she could do was to make this period as comfortable and as easy for Sean as possible.

Besides Sean, there were the children. Little Sean, the eldest, already knew something was not right. For a child of six, he was very perceptive and picked up on the tension and fear that both his mother and father were trying to hide. He didn't talk about it but would show his concern by asking his father each morning if he was going to come home that night. Little Sean would stay awake until his father did come and then would get out of his bed, run to his father and hug him with no intention of letting go. Sean had to carry his son to bed, lay him down and talk to him for awhile. Kurt, at three, was hell on wheels and just the opposite of his older brother. Their daughter Sarah, at one, was fast growing up by trying to do everything her brothers did: her busy schedule of exploration and mischief kept her from noticing a break in routine.

The transition from home and family to field and prep for war boggled Bannon's clouded mind. It was almost as if he had been moved into a different world. Pondering such deep thoughts, however, was getting him nowhere. He had to get

8

moving and live in the present world and hope for the best in the other.

New pains and spasms were Bannon's reward for placing his body in motion. Slowly and with care, he moved each appendage of his body. Once in the sitting position, he stopped, rested, and considered his next move. These things can't be rushed. Minds work just as slowly as bodies do at 0234 hours.

'Well, I guess it's time for Garger's early morning ass chewing,' Bannon said, more to himself than to Uleski. 'You would think that after getting beaten about the head and shoulders for the same damn thing three days in a row he would learn. Oh Lord, save me from second lieutenants.'

For the first time Uleski's face showed expression as a small grin preceded a chuckle and his retort, 'Yeah, especially this one.'

'Don't be so smug, Ski. The only reason I like you is because I never knew you when you were a second lieutenant.'

Uleski faced Bannon, still grinning. 'I *never* was a second lieutenant. Wouldn't have any part of it and told the ROTC recruiter so. Naturally, once they found out who I was, they agreed. So here I am, a full-grown U.S. Army first lieutenant, guarding the frontiers of freedom and making the world safe for democracy.'

Bannon smirked and shook his head. 'God, the sun isn't even up and already the bull is getting deep in here. I better get out before I'm drowned.'

They both chuckled. It's amazing what soldiers find humorous and amusing at 0234 hours.

'I'm going over to 3rd Platoon first and give Garger his early morning lecture on the meaning of radio listening silence. Then I'm going to swing by the Mech Platoon and see how they're doing. I expect to be back for stand-to. When was the last time you checked the batteries?'

'About twenty minutes ago. They should be good until stand-to.'

'You better be right. I don't want to have the track that both the CO and XO occupied be the only one that has to be slaved off in the morning. Bad for the image.'

9

With a feigned look of surprise on his face, Uleski shot back, 'Image? You mean we're going to start worrying about our image? Do you think the men can take it?'

'At ease there, first lieutenant. XOs as well as platoon leaders can get jacked up in the morning too, you know.'

Hunching his head down between his shoulders and putting his hands up in mock surrender, Uleski repeated 'Yes sir, yes, sir, don't beat me too hard, sir,' as he turned back towards the radio with a grin on his face.

Digging through the pile of junk that had been his bed, Bannon pulled out his gear and started to get ready. Field jacket, protective mask, web gear with weapon and other assorted items on it, and, of course, the helmet. Putting on this gear always reminded him of a bull fighter preparing for the arena. All the gear that the well-dressed American soldier was supposed to wear was definitely not designed with the armoured vehicle crewman in mind. Bannon was reminded of this when he exited the PC through the small rear troop door. Climbing through this four-foot door was always a challenge. In the dark, with all one's gear on, made it that much more interesting. But at that hour in the morning the last thing he needed was a challenge.

It felt good to Bannon to be able to stand upright and stretch his legs. The chill and early morning mist were refreshing after being in the cramped PC for hours. It reminded him, however, more of an April or early May morning back in Pennsylvania than August – the German weather in August was more like a New England spring.

The chill cleared his mind and it began to turn to matters at hand. Yesterday had been hot and sunny, and with as much moisture as there was in the air, they were bound to have a heavy fog throughout most of the morning. That meant moving a listening post down into the valley to the Team's front, even though the cavalry was still deployed forward. This was the Mech Platoon's job and although they would probably do it automatically as soon as they saw the fog rising, Bannon intended to remind them when he got there. The old saying, 'The one time you forget to remind someone of something is the one time he forgets and it is the one time it really needed to be done,' kept buzzing through his head.

Bannon's eyes were becoming accustomed to the darkness. He could now make out images of other nearby vehicles like the headquarters PC he had just exited pulled into the tree line. One track, an Improved Tow Vehicle or ITV, attached to the Team from the Mech Battalion (to which Team Yankee was attached), sat forward at the edge of the tree line. Its camouflage net was off and the hammerhead-like launcher and sight was erect, peering down into the valley below. This track was one of the Team's OPs, or observation posts, using its thermal sight to watch the Team's sector of responsibility through the dark and now through the gathering fog.

Bannon walked over to the ITV to make sure the crew was awake. He stumbled over roots and branches that reached up and grabbed his ankles while low branches swatted him in the face. He stopped for a moment, pushed the offending branches out of the way and began to go forward again, remembering this time to pick up his feet to clear the stumps and using his arm to clear the branches. As he proceeded, Bannon decided that rather than fight the underbrush and roots on his way over to 3rd Platoon, he would skirt the tree line. This was not a good practice, but as it was dark and hostilities had not been declared yet, he decided to do it, one more time.

When he reached the ITV, the launcher's hammerhead-like turret slowly moved to the right, indicating that the crew was awake and on the job. Knowing that the crew would have the troop door combat-locked, Bannon took out his buck knife and rapped on the door three times. As he waited for a response, the shuffle of the crewman on duty could be heard as he climbed back over gear and other crewmen to open the door. Struggling with the door handle, the crewman rotated the lever and let the door swing out. Bannon was greeted by a dark figure hanging halfway out of the door and a slurred, "Yeah, what ya want?'

'It's Captain Bannon. Anything going on down in the valley?'

Straightening up slightly, the ITV crewman realised whom he was talking to. 'Oh, sorry, sir, I didn't know it was you, sir.

11

No, we ain't seen nothin' all night 'cept some jeeps and a deuce 'n a half going up to the cavalry. Been quiet. We expectin' something?'

'No, at least not that I've heard. The cavalry should give us some warning but just in case, I need you to stay on your toes. You checked your batteries lately?'

'Yes, sir, 'bout an hour ago we cranked her up and ran it for twenty minutes.'

'Ok. Keep awake and alert. Let the XO over there know if something comes along.' After a perfunctory 'yes, sir,' the crewman closed his door and locked it as Bannon turned away and walked out to the edge of the tree line. It bothered him that he didn't know the crewman's name. Bannon had only seen that ITV crewman for the first time three days ago after the Team had pulled into its positions. That's the trouble with attachments. You never know whom you're going to get and you never get a chance to know them. Except for the fact that he was the CO and the Team headquarters track was parked nearby, the ITV crewman didn't know much about him either. And yet, very shortly, they might have to take orders from him in combat. Bannon hoped that the ITV crewmen trusted his ability to command in battle with the same blind faith that he trusted their ability to kill Russian tanks with their ITV.

As he trudged over to the 3rd Platoon, he reviewed the Team's dispositions and mission. The Team had gone over it often enough using map exercises, terrain walks, battle simulations and field training exercises, or FTXs, on similar ground. But Bannon was still not totally satisfied that they were in the best possible positions to meet all eventualities. Team Yankee was deployed on the forward slope of a large hill overlooking a river valley. The forest where the Team was located came halfway down the slope until it reached a point where it dropped all the way down onto the floor of the valley. That point was the Team's left flank and it was where 2nd Platoon was positioned. From there the platoon could fire across the face of the slope, into the valley or across the valley, towards the high ground opposite them.

In the centre was the Team's headquarters section, consisting of Bannon's tank, the XO's tank and two ITVs from the Mech Battalion's antitank company. From there they had a good view of the valley, a small village situated in the valley to the right front, a road, and a separate small valley that ran along the Team's right flank. This constituted the limit of the Team's battle position.

It was on the right that the Team had the greatest concentration of power, the 3rd Platoon and the Mech Platoon. The Mech Platoon was equipped with M113 armoured personnel carriers and Dragon antitank guided missiles. This Platoon had been scheduled to receive Bradley fighting vehicles, but that kept getting put off since procurement of those powerful fighting vehicles had slowed down. The Mech Platoon was split into two elements. The dismounted element, led by the platoon leader, consisted of most of the infantry men, two Dragons and three M60 machine guns. This element held a walled farm in the small valley on the right. The mounted element, led by the platoon sergeant, consisted of the Platoon's PCs, their crews and two more Dragons. They were above the same farm on the slope in the tree line. From their positions, the Mech Platoon could block the small valley and keep anyone from exiting the village if and when the other people got in there.

The 3rd Platoon was located a little further behind and higher up on the slope from the Mech Platoon. The 3rd Platoon could fire into the main valley, the small valley to the right, the village, or across the valley at the opposite heights. The platoon would also cover the withdrawal of the Mech Platoon if and when that became necessary.

Bannon was not comfortable with the idea of defending on a forward slope. Should a withdrawal under fire be necessary, all the Team's vehicles would have to go uphill, at times exposed to observation and fire from the enemy on the other side of the valley. In addition, the only positions from which most of the Team would be able to fire were immediately inside the tree line. This position was so obvious it hurt. Bannon could visualise some Soviet artillery commander plotting likely targets and coming across their hill during his terrain analysis. Glee would light up on the Russian's face as he told his trusted subordinate, 'There, there they will defend, in this tree line. Make sure we target that area with at least five, no six, battalions of artillery, comrade.' Bannon had been over it all before and if they came out of this deployment without going to war he resolved that he would go over it again. But for now, he, and Team Yankee, were obliged to fight on the ground where they sat.

As Bannon approached the 3rd Platoon's position he heard a slight rustling followed by the two low voices. He had reached the 3rd Platoon's OP/LP. 'Halt, who goes there?' came the challenge in a voice that was a little too loud and sounded surprised. Bannon had no doubt caught the soldiers manning the OP half-asleep and had startled them. The voice that had issued the challenge sounded like Private Lenord from the 32 tank. The sentry repeated his challenge, 'Who goes there?' It was Lenord.

'Captain Bannon.'

'Oh, okay. You can come on in then.'

While this homey invitation was a refreshing change of pace from the less-than cheerful thoughts Bannon had been pondering, it was definitely not the way to do business while on guard. As he approached, he could hear a second soldier telling Lenord that he had screwed up. When Bannon was no more than arm's distance from them, the two men quietly stood up to face their commanding officer. As they were just inside the tree line, none of them could see the other's face. But Bannon was reasonably sure there was a pained expression on Lenord's face. Not knowing which of the two forms facing him was Lenord, Bannon directed his comments to both. 'Is that the proper way to challenge someone?'

'No, sir, it's not, sir.'

'How are you supposed to challenge a stranger when he approaches your position, Lenord?'

Without hesitation, and as if he were reciting from a book, Lenord went through the correct challenge and password procedures. With a plaintive voice and a few expletives, Bannon asked Lenord why he hadn't used the correct procedures. 'Because you said you were the CO and I

14

recognised your voice, sir.' The answer was honest but wrong. Bannon explained that everyone gets the full treatment. Lenord didn't seem to understand the logic in this but promised that he wouldn't forget the next time. As Bannon walked away towards the 32 tank he could hear the second soldier tell Lenord, 'See, I told you so,' as they settled down into their positions again.

Upon reaching the 32 tank, Bannon started climbing up on the right front fender but stopped halfway up when he heard the cocking of a .45 and a low, firm 'Halt.' The voice belonged to SSgt Joelle Blackfoot, a full-blooded Cherokee Indian and tank commander of 32. Bannon had no doubt that there was a .45 cocked, loaded, and aimed at him. 'Who goes there?'

'Captain Bannon.'

'Advance and be recognised.'

Bannon finished climbing up and moved slowly to the edge of the turret, now able to make out the figure in the cupola with an outstretched arm holding a .45. In a lower voice just audible to him, Blackfoot gave the challenge, 'Wrinkle.'

'Bait,' was Bannon's reply.

Satisfied with the answer, Blackfoot raised his pistol and slowly let the hammer down. 'When's the war going to start, Captain?'

Pulling himself up onto the top of the turret so that he was lying across the length of it with his head near Blackfoot's, Bannon spoke to Blackfoot about Lenord's failure to challenge properly and how things were going with the crew's preparations for combat. Being the thorough NCO that he was, Blackfoot was not happy with the crew drill between him and his gunner. Blackfoot explained that his gunner was slow to pick up targets that he had acquired and on which he had laid the main gun. He wanted some time on a road or someplace where they could move the tank and practise their crew drill. Bannon explained that for security reasons all vehicular movement had to be kept down to a minimum. Blackfoot, like everyone else in the Team, would just have to do the best he could from a stationary position. Blackfoot replied that he knew that but he saw no harm in asking.

After getting the weather prediction for the day and his best guess as to when the fog would lift, Bannon climbed down and proceeded to Lieutenant Garger's tank, the next in line.

As he approached the 31 tank, Bannon began going over the 'counselling' he would use with Garger this morning. Garger wasn't a naturally bad lieutenant. In fact, he was no different from any other second lieutenant, including himself, that Bannon had known. It took time, training, and a lot of patience to develop a good second lieutenant tank platoon leader. For only having been in the country for three weeks, Garger wasn't doing half bad. But while half bad was all right on a training exercise, it wouldn't hack it in combat. The time and opportunity to teach the lieutenant everything he needed to know just wasn't there anymore. The Team was about to go into combat and Bannon had no faith in Garger's ability to perform.

The platoon sergeant, SFC Gary Pierson, a veteran of Vietnam and an outstanding trooper, had been doing his best to train the lieutenant when Bannon wasn't. Pierson was also trying to cover for Garger so that the platoon didn't look bad. But Pierson couldn't do it all. Either the lieutenant had to perform or he had to go. At this late stage of the game, Bannon wasn't about to put lives in the hands of a lieutenant who had, so far, screwed up most of the tasks given him. He intended to talk to the battalion commander about the matter later that day. But first, there was the business at hand.

Climbing up onto the right front fender of the 31 tank, he was stopped as he had been on Blackfoot's tank with a 'Halt, who goes there?' Only instead of using a .45 to keep the unknown intruder at bay, the figure in the cupola tried to crank his M2 machine gun down and in Bannon's direction. As the firing mechanism is part of the gun's elevation handle and is easily activated, a brief moment of panic swept over Bannon. He considered whether it were better to jump, scream, or hope for the best. Fortunately, inept handling of the machine gun's controls frustrated the figure in the cupola and he decided to go to his .45 as an alternative. As the figure fumbled for his pistol, Bannon identified himself and finished climbing on board. Abandoning all hopes of covering the intruder with a weapon, the figure simply finished the challenge and password procedures in a dejected and apprehensive voice. Lieutenant Garger was running true to form this morning.

Bannon crawled onto the turret and propped himself up on his elbows so that he was less than a foot from Garger. 'Well, what shall we talk about this morning, Lieutenant Garger?'

Garger paused for a moment, not knowing if he was expected to answer or if the Team commander was simply going to lay into him. Hesitantly, he replied in a half-question, half-statement, 'RTO procedures, sir?'

'No, no. Close, but a no-go. How about radio listening silence? You remember our discussion on that subject yesterday morning?'

'Yes, sir.'

'THEN WHY IN THE HELL DID YOU BREAK RADIO LISTENING SILENCE AGAIN TODAY? ARE YOU FUCKING STUPID OR JUST SOFT IN THE HEAD?' While waiting for his answer, Bannon did his best to pull himself back and calm down. He had a tendency to become excited and abusive. He had told himself time and again that it wouldn't do to get this cranked up; he had to be calm and logical. But habits are hard to break, especially so early in the morning. There would, no doubt, be plenty more reasons for getting excited later today.

Falteringly, Garger replied. 'No, sir. I just wanted to make sure the radios worked since we changed frequencies and all.'

With his composure regained, Bannon continued, 'Did your radio work yesterday before I chewed your ass out for breaking radio listening silence?'

'Yes, sir.'

'And did your radio work the day before yesterday just before I chewed your ass out for breaking radio listening silence?'

'Yes, sir.'

'Then why did you do it again? I mean, by now even *you* should be able to figure out that, *a*, your radio works every time you use it and *b*, every time you use it I am going to come

17

down and jump in your shit. Do you understand what I'm telling you, I mean, do you really understand?'

'Yes, sir, I do, it's just that, well, I ...'

'One more time, I swear, one more time ...'

Without finishing or waiting for a response,, Bannon slid himself back off the turret and climbed down the same way he had come up. To stay any longer would not do him or his nervous system any good. If the point hadn't been made by now, it never would be.

Bannon hadn't walked ten metres from the 31 tank when Pierson's low, firm voice startled him. 'This is starting to be a regular routine, isn't it, Captain Bannon? I'm going to start setting my watch by you.'

Bannon stopped, turned toward Pierson's figure, and leaned against a tree for support. He still hadn't calmed down from his discussion with Garger and Pierson's sudden appearance had scared the hell out of him. As he collected his wits, he thought to himself, 'The sun isn't even up and it is building up to be a real peachy day.' Looking at the dark figure approaching him, he asked, 'Are you looking to give me a heart attack or is this some type of leadership reaction course?'

'No, sir, I just wanted to come over and save our favourite lieutenant before the wolves got him. But from the roar, I figured I was too late so I decided to wait for you here.'

'You know, I could charge you with attempted murder.'

'You wouldn't do that, Captain. Then, who would you find to whip this collection of derelicts and criminals you call a tank platoon into shape?'

'You're right Sergeant Pierson. No sane man would take the job. I guess I'll have to keep you. But I'm not too sure about your lieutenant. After stand-to and breakfast I'm going to talk to the Old Man about pulling Garger out. If I give you Williams as a loader do you have a gunner who can take over the 31 tank and a loader that can move into a gunner's seat?'

'Sergeant Pauly could handle the tank and I have a couple of loaders who are ready to gun. But do you want to start screwing around with crews at this late stage? I mean, the lieutenant may not have all his stuff together yet but given a little more time, I'm sure he'll catch on. You know how it was your first time out.'

'Yes, Sergeant Pierson, I know what it was like. I really wasn't much better than Garger. But this is different. When I screwed up as a young platoon leader the worst I got was an ass chewing from the CO, a lot of smirks from the men in the platoon, and a sick feeling in my stomach. If the balloon goes up in the next couple of days and Garger blows it, he not only stands a damn good chance of losing his own behind and his crew's, but a failure on his part could cost me the whole platoon and more. I feel sorry for the kid and I wish I could do more for him. But I have a whole company to look out for and I'm not going to take any chances that I don't have to.'

Bannon and Pierson stood for a minute and stared at each other, neither of them able to see the other's facial expression. Both knew that what the other said was right, to a degree. Pierson hated to admit defeat, the defeat of not being able to train his new lieutenant. Bannon felt the same. But they also knew that there simply was no time left, that they had to deal with bigger issues than pride. Garger might do well once the shooting started. There was no way to tell. Bannon didn't want to take the chance. His mind was set. If he could swing it, Garger would go.

The two men exchanged a few more remarks, mostly about the condition of the platoon's vehicles, plans to improve the positions, and the training that needed to be done that day. Then they parted, Bannon proceeding around the hill to the Mech Platoon while Pierson started rousing his platoon for stand-to. The war, or at least the preparations for war, went on.

By the time Bannon had worked his way down to the walled farm and to the dismounted element of the Mech Platoon's positions, it was getting light. Not that you could see the sun. In fact, the rising fog made it almost impossible to see anything beyond twenty metres. The Mech Platoon, led by 2nd Lt. William Harding, was already moving into its position and preparing for stand-to. Bannon decided to stay with them until after stand-to.

This platoon was good. They had an unusually good

combination of platoon leader, platoon sergeant, and squad leaders. Harding and the platoon sergeant, a SFC Leslie Polgar, had been together for almost a year and they complemented each other. Harding did the thinking, gave the orders, and led the platoon while Polgar led the training and did the motivating and the ass kicking, which to Polgar were all one and the same.

It was easy to see that the soldiers were well trained and confident in themselves, their weapons, and their leaders, Bannon thought as he watched them. The men moved into the positions with hardly a word, checked their weapons, situated themselves to cover their assigned areas, ready for the enemy or stand down, whichever came first. By the time Bannon had arrived at the farm, Harding had already sent a squad into the village to establish a listening post, or LP. The men manning the LP had taken two Dragons with them. Harding kept his other two Dragons with the mounted element.

As he leaned against the farmhouse wall, looking out of the window across from Harding, Bannon kept thinking how worthless he would be here if the other people came boiling out of the fog. Without his sixty-one-ton tank wrapped around him, he wouldn't be much good to anyone in a fire fight armed only with a .45 pistol that was probably older than he was. Not that the .45 was a bad weapon. It's just that in a real fire fight Bannon wanted to have the ability to reach out and touch someone. Hand-to-hand combat, eyeball-to-eyeball brawls with the enemy might make great war movies, but it simply wasn't his idea of doing business. At the first opportunity, he resolved to secure himself an M16 rifle. It might be a pain to carry around, but an M16 provides its owner with a much greater sense of security when he is fumbling around in the dark alone.

By 0500 it was as light as it was going to get and there were no Russians, or anyone else for that matter, in sight. Bannon told Harding to maintain the squad in the village until the fog lifted and to stand down the rest of his platoon. He also reminded Harding of the 0730 platoon leaders' meeting and the weapons inspection for the Mech Platoon at 0900 hours. Bannon knew that by the time he returned to the platoon all weapons would have been checked for cleanliness, functioning, headspace, and timing by either Harding or the platoon sergeant or both. But it was part of the routine that had been established, and it gave him a chance to learn more about the men in the platoon and a chance for them to see him. It was important that the attached units know that their commander had high standards when it came to important items like weapons, positions, camouflage, and all those things that separated the quick from the dead.

On his way back, Bannon walked from track to track, greeting each crew as they prepared for breakfast and another day on the border. He made some corrections, a few comments, listened to a complaint or two, and generally let himself be seen. Only around the 31 tank was his presence greeted with a proper but chilled reception. The other crew members of 31 were in a depressed mood, for they, like Pierson, did not want to be defeated by the loss of their lieutenant. But they were far less sanguine than Pierson about fighting for his retention. The crew knew that if Garger screwed up in combat they would be the first to pay for it. Unlike a dismounted infantry squad where every man can go off on his own if something gets screwed up, a tank crew is a joint venture where one's fate is welded to the actions of the other crew members. The sixty-one tons of steel that enclose them silently bind their collective fates together. So there is a strong self-serving motivation that causes tankers to work together and ensures that each member of the crew can perform his job. Pride was running a distant second to survival for most of the 31 crew.

Uleski, the tank crews of the two headquarters tank and the ITV crews were either washing and shaving or squaring away their tracks by the time Bannon finished his morning rounds. The ITV that had been at the edge of the tree line had pulled back into its hide position and was camouflaged. Uleski was squatting next to the PC, stripped down to his waist, washing himself from a small pan of water. Looking up as Bannon approached, he grinned, 'I knew you would be back by stand-to. I just didn't know what day. Do you have a murder to

21

report and an emergency requisition for a second lieutenant platoon leader to submit?'

'Come on U, I'm a nice guy. Do you for one moment think that I would bring any harm to that poor young man over in 3rd Platoon? I mean, do I look like a mean person?'

Standing up and squinting his eyes as he looked Bannon over, he replied, 'Oh, sorry. I thought you were my CO, the one who isn't worth a damn in the morning until he's eaten a second lieutenant.'

'Yeah, it's me alright. Only this morning a second lieutenant wasn't enough. Now I'm looking for a first lieutenant for dessert.'

Uleski looked to his left, then to his right, using exaggerated movements, then turned back to face Bannon. 'Ain't seen any o'them 'round here. Y'all might try over in yonder hill cuntree,' pointing east to the border.

With the second round of poor humour decided in Uleski's favour, the Team commander and XO got down to the morning's business while Uleski finished washing and Bannon dug his shaving gear out and prepared to wash up. Uleski had a long day ahead and Bannon wanted him to get started. There were maintenance problems that needed attention, and spare parts that had to be requested, borrowed, or scrounged. The laundry point needed to be located and arrangements made to turn in the company's laundry. Batteries for field phones and wire to replace some which had been torn out by a cavalry track that had wandered into the Team's area had to be found. These and many small but important tasks were required to keep the Team in business. Once the first sergeant came up to the position with breakfast, he and Uleski would divide up the list of tasks between them and go about the day's duties.

The Team wasn't in bad shape. The last tank that had fallen out of the line of march during the movement to the border had finally closed in yesterday afternoon, giving Team Yankee a total of ten tanks, five M113s, and two ITVs. Two of the tanks had problems with their fire control system but nothing that would take more than another day to repair. In fact, the vehicles were in better shape than the people were.

Not that they were falling apart. However, life in the field wears away at soldiers unless simple creature comforts such as food, clean dry clothes, and other such necessaries are provided. Added to the problems of living in the field, the tension caused by the alert and move to the border, followed by the flurry of almost panicked activity during the first twenty-four hours in position, followed by three days of waiting and there is potential for a disaster. This was made worse by the lack of solid news from the outside world and the concerns of the married personnel, including Bannon himself, about the evacuation of the dependants back to the States. To top it off, many of the men had not brought extra fatigues and some hadn't even brought a change of underwear. After three days of hot weather and hard work, the company was getting funky.

Efforts to secure reliable news from the outside world had failed. The rear areas were in a state of panic as German civilians ignored their government's call to stay in place and instead took to the roads leading west. The Office of Public Information, in a less than brilliant move, had taken the Armed Forces Network off the air. Censorship of the BBC and German radio only told the men in Team Yankee that NATO forces were mobilising and deploying, something they already knew, and negotiations between NATO and Warsaw Pact representatives were still going on at a secret location. So the men were in the dark, not knowing much more than what was going on within their platoon position and unable to find out from anyone whether they were going to go home tomorrow or be part of the first act of World War III. The longer this situation lasted, the more it tended to erode the men's morale.

While there was nothing that Bannon could do about news or settling the dispute that started the whole thing, he and the rest of the Team's leadership could do something about the physical well-being of the men. The first sergeant, Raymond Harrett, had found a *Gasthaus* where the men could wash up and rinse out some underwear. A schedule and transportation had been set up to rotate everyone through the first sergeant's comfort station, now being run by the company supply sergeant. The battalion had switched from dehydrated field rations that came in little brown bags, called MREs, to two hot meals a day, breakfast and dinner, and only one meal of MREs. A work and training schedule, which would allow the Team to improve positions, work out any last-minute crew co-ordination problems, and rest the men, had been instituted. In effect, the leadership was keeping the men as busy as possible doing constructive things without wearing them out. This kept their minds off the grim situation they were facing while preparing them to meet it. It was all that could be done.

Just as Bannon finished washing up, the first sergeant arrived with breakfast. His arrival at the headquarters position meant that the rest of the Team had finished breakfast, as headquarters tanks and ITVs were always the last to eat. When the men on the position had been served, Harrert, Uleski, and Bannon served each other breakfast. Standing around the hood of Harrert's jeep, they ate their cold powdered eggs, rubbery bacon strips, and soggy toast as they listened to the latest news the first sergeant had from the rear.

Most of Harrert's news was bad. The evacuation of dependants, which had started only yesterday, was going slowly. German military and civilian police had set up checkpoints to stem the flow of refugees and clear roads. The opposite was happening as monumental traffic jams became worse. Newspapers were scarce and none was making it farther forward than Division rear. Nor was the delivery of mail straight yet. Finally, there were no batteries or WD-1 wire to be found anywhere in the brigade.

The good news was limited but welcome. Harrett had located a quartermaster field laundry. The men would be able to exchange underwear. Uleski commented that the Environmental Protection Agency would be glad. The maintenance contact team working for the Team had located a new laser range finder for the 23 tank and would be up to install it that morning. While only a few problems would be solved, any forward progress was welcome. The three agreed that, given two more days of peace, the Team would have all the big problems squared away and would be one hundred per cent ready.

As they finished up their working breakfast, they were joined by the platoon leaders coming up for the 0730 meeting.

24

The group moved over to the PC where Bannon sat on the lowered ramp with Harrert and Uleski sitting on either side of him. The platoon leaders dropped down on the ground facing the three men, taking off their helmets, unbuckling their LBE belts, pulling out notebooks and pencils as they did so. The meeting had no sooner started when the first sergeant nudged Bannon and pointed to the left, 'Here comes the Old Man.'

Driving up through a logging trail that ran behind the Team's position came the battalion commander's jeep. One could always tell Lt. Col. George Reynolds's jeep. Four antennas that were never tied down were whipping wildly as the jeep rolled down the trail. The jeep had no top and a big infantry blue licence plate mounted on the front fender displaying the silver oak leaf cluster of a lieutenant colonel with a black '6' superimposed on it. This violated every security measure the Army had, but '6' didn't give a damn. He was the battalion commander, and he wanted to make sure everyone knew it. Bannon turned the meeting over to Uleski, telling him to find out what the platoons needed as far as fuel and supplies were concerned. He then got up, put on his gear, and walked over to the trail to greet Reynolds.

The jeep hadn't stopped rolling before the colonel jumped out and started heading toward Bannon. They met halfway and exchanged salutes. Instead of 'Hi, how are you?' Bannon was greeted with a gruff 'Well, Bannon, how are those overpriced rattletraps of yours this morning?'

'Sir, they're ready to kick ass and take names. When are you going to send me some Russians?'

Falling in on the colonel's left, he and Reynolds walked up to the gathering of platoon leaders despite Bannon's best efforts to steer him clear so that Uleski could go on with the meeting. Everyone stood up, dropping notebooks and maps while they put their helmets back on. Salutes, greetings, and some one-sided small talk ate up about five minutes before Bannon could pry the colonel off to the side and let Uleski carry on.

As they walked to the tree line, Bannon informed Reynolds of his intention to replace Garger. The colonel took the same position that Pierson had. War was imminent, and it didn't seem like a good idea to switch platoon leaders. As Bannon was going over his reasons and justification, they both stood at the tree line and watched a two-and-a-half-ton truck drive down from the far side of the valley. The fog had cleared by now except along the river. The sun was bright in a cloudless sky and getting hot.

The colonel was about to reply when the earsplitting screech of two fast-moving jets flying at treetop level cut him off. The two officers turned in the direction of the noise just in time to see two more jets come screaming into the valley from the east, drop down lower, and fly up the small valley on the right of the Team's positions. Bannon didn't recognise the aircraft type, aircraft recognition wasn't one of his strong points. But it wasn't necessary to identify the exact type. A glimpse of the red star on the fuselage told him everything that he needed to know about the two jets. The waiting was over. The balloon had gone up. Team Yankee was at war.

★ Despite his best efforts to give the impression that the current situation was nothing to worry about, Sean quietly had begun to make sure that the family affairs were in order. He saw to it that Pat had her emergency evacuation kit ready with food and blankets. He packed a special envelope for her containing the important family documents. All the little details were reviewed and listed. These efforts, while possibly reassuring to Sean, were disquieting to Pat. But she said nothing, listened intently to Sean's instructions, and prayed that all this wasn't going to be necessary.

Pat had known it would be the last night when Sean came in. In his eyes was a look of disbelief that all this was happening. She saw the same thing in her own eyes every time she looked in the mirror. When little Sean ran up to his father, rather than taking him to bed, Sean carried him to the sofa, pulled out the family album, and began to leaf slowly through the pages. The two sat there quietly looking at the pictures until little Sean fell asleep. With great reluctance, Sean put his son to bed. After fifteen minutes, he came out of his son's room with red and moist eyes. For a moment he looked at Pat, then simply said that he was tired and was going to go to bed. Pat went with him.

The phone rang. Sean was up and out in a flash, as if he had never gone to sleep but had been lying there waiting for the call. When he came back, Pat watched him for a moment in the shadows of the dark bedroom as he gathered up his uniform and boots. When she spoke, she startled him. 'Are you going in already?'

'Yes. Gotta. Wouldn't look good for the CO to be late, would it?'

'Will you be home for breakfast?'

'No, I won't.'

'Should I hold supper for you tonight?'

'No, no need to.'

Pat knew. And Sean knew Pat knew. After eight years of marriage, it's hard to hide secrets and harder to hide feelings. Sean came over to the bed and sat next to his wife. 'Pat, the battalion is moving to the border in an hour. I don't know when we will be back.'

'Is everyone going?'

'Everyone. The NATO ministers and their governments are mobilising. Everyone is going, including you.'

'Are they really going to evacuate?'

'Starting this morning at 0900. That was going to be announced anyway. Now, there's no doubt.'

As he finished dressing, Pat dressed. There was much to do. Sean was in the children's bedroom. She watched him for a moment and then went to the kitchen where she fixed her husband a bag lunch. As she was finishing it, all the restraint she had exercised and all her efforts to give Sean a cheery face and smile when he left collapsed. She began to cry. Her husband was going out the door in a minute to fight World War III, and all she could do for him was fix him a bag lunch.

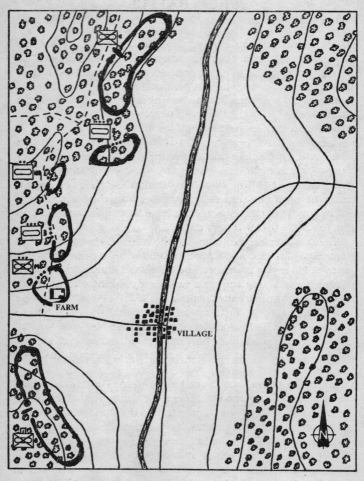

FARM

VILLAGE

MAP 1: TEAM YANKEE'S POSITIONS

Chapter Two

FIRST BATTLE

Both Colonel Reynolds and Captain Bannon stood there transfixed, staring at the point where the two Russian jets had disappeared up the valley. Bannon's mind was almost numb. He kept trying to convince himself that maybe he hadn't really seen two Russian jets. Maybe he was mistaken. It had to be a mistake. The thought, 'We can't really be at war. That isn't possible,' kept running through his mind.

They both snapped their heads back towards the east as a crash and rumble like distant thunder rolled over them. They could only see the hill across the valley. But neither man needed to see to know what the distant noise was. The endless chain of distant crashes and rumblings, caused by hundreds of guns, could only be the Soviets' preparatory bombardment on the cavalry's forward positions.

Bannon turned and looked at the colonel. He continued to stare east as if he could look through the hill across the valley and see what was going on. The numbness and shock Bannon had felt was giving way to a sickening, sinking feeling. They had failed. The primary purpose of the U.S. Army in Europe was to prevent war. Deterrence. That's what was supposed to happen. But it had failed. Something terrible had gone wrong, and they had failed. Now they had to fight. They were at war. And at that moment Bannon felt very alone, very unsure of himself, and very scared.

Reynolds turned and looked at Bannon. The colonel's face hadn't changed expression. If he were feeling the same things, he wasn't showing it. Reynolds studied Bannon for a moment, sensing the shock and uncertainty that showed on the captain's face. He had seen it before, in Vietnam, so Bannon's reactions didn't surprise him. 'Well, Captain, let's see if those buckets of bolts you always brag about are worth the money the government spent on them. Get your company in MOPP level II, stand by to occupy your fighting positions, and stay on the

29

net, but don't call me unless you need to. I expect the cavalry will come screaming back through that passage point like a whipped dog. Be ready to cover them and get them out of the way as fast as you can. You got any questions?'

Bannon took in what the colonel was saying. What was there to question? This was what all the training was about. All their preparations were for this moment. Now all they had to do was put it into action. 'No, sir, no questions.'

'Well then, get moving and good hunting.' Without waiting for a response, the colonel turned and began to move back to his jeep with a quick, purposeful pace. He did not look back. Reynolds was setting the example, and he expected Bannon to follow it.

As Bannon turned back towards the PC where he had left the platoon leaders, a new series of artillery concentrations began to impact closer to the Team's positions. Additional Soviet artillery units were joining in, hitting the cavalry's rear positions. The latest series impacted just behind the hill on the other side of the valley. 'Hell, the colonel could be cool and walk,' Bannon thought. 'This is my first war and I damn sure don't care about impressing anyone with my calm right now.' He broke out into a slow run, weapon, protective mask, and canteen bouncing and banging against his body as he trotted through the trees to the PC.

As he neared the PC, Bannon could see the platoon leaders, Uleski, and the first sergeant watching the colonel's jeep go tearing down the logging trail, throwing up stones and disappearing in a cloud of dust. They had heard the jets and the artillery. Bannon slowed down to a walk, caught his breath, and moved up to them. All eyes turned to him.

'All right, this is it. The Russians are laying into the cavalry and when Ivan finishes with them, we're next. I want everyone in MOPP level II. Leave the nets over your tracks but clear them away from the front so that you can move forward into position quickly. First Sergeant, take the PC and fire team from the Mech Platoon that are designated to man the passage point and get down there. Lieutenant U, you'll stay up here with the ITVs and fight them with 2nd Platoon if necessary. I'm going to move my tank down to the right of 3rd Platoon and fight from there. Other than that, we do it the way we trained and planned. Stay off the air unless you have something really critical to report. Anyone have any questions?'

He looked into each man's eyes, just as the colonel had done to him. He saw the same dark thoughts he had reflected in their expressions. Only the first sergeant, also a Vietnam vet, wore the stern, no-nonsense look he always did. For a few moments there was silence, broken only by the continuous crash and rumble of the artillery in the distance. 'All right, let's move out and make it happen.' Without waiting for a response, Bannon turned and began to walk towards his tank. As the colonel had done for him, he was setting the example for his people. He suspected that they would do the same with their tank commanders, and their TCs would, in turn, get their people moving. At least, that's what he hoped would be happening.

The drumbeat of the impacting Soviet artillery continued, growing louder but less intense. The Russian gun crews must have been getting tired of humping rounds by now, and the rate of fire was slowing down. The distant rumble was joined by the noise of Team Yankee coming to life. The PC's driver cranked up its engine, revved it up, and began raising the rear ramp. The crews of the ITVs and of Bannon's tank, 66, also cranked up their engines.

As he neared his 66 tank, Bannon could see Sgt. Robert Folk, the gunner, in the cupola. Folk had his combat vehicle crewman's helmet, or CVC, on and was manning the M2 machine gun, ready for action. Bannon tried to yell to him to dismount with the rest of the crew so they could tear down the net. The noise of the engine, the muffling of outside noise through his CVC, and Folk's preoccupation with trying to see what was going on to his front frustrated Bannon's efforts.

It wasn't until Bannon started climbing up on the front right fender that Folk noticed his commander. 'Let's get this net off! You and Kelp get out here and help me with this net. We're moving.' Without waiting for a response, Bannon dropped down to the ground again and began to pull down the support poles and spreaders that held the net up. Whether Folk heard him or not was unimportant. As soon as he saw his captain tear at the net, Folk took off his CVC, leaned over towards the loader's hatch, and, with his left hand, slapped Kelp, the loader, on top of his CVC. Kelp looked up at Folk who pointed to Bannon, who continued to tear at the net. Getting the message, Kelp also removed his CVC and climbed out to help.

'Let's get this net down and stowed, just like we do during training. Only let's do it a little faster this time, OK?' Neither man answered. The expression on their faces was the same that had been on the platoon leaders' – stunned disbelief.

Folk dropped to the ground and circled the tank, pulling up the net's stakes as he went. Kelp started to pull down the supports and spreaders that were on the tank. With the stakes out and the poles down, the hard part began. The net caught on everything, including the crewmen taking it down. Tugging seldom did any good. One had to find what the net was caught on, pull it free, roll it up a little until it caught again, and repeat the process. Trying to hurry only seemed to make it worse. Despite the delays, the crew finally gathered the net up into a pile on the bustle rack and secured it. They hadn't done the neatest job of stowing it, but it was probably one of the fastest.

Before they climbed in, Bannon told his crew to get their chemical protective suits on. This was MOPP level II. As Folk and Kelp dug their suits out of their duffle bags, Bannon walked forward to the driver's compartment and told Pfc. Joseph Ortelli, the driver, to climb out and get his suit on. As Ortelli reached over to kill the engine, Bannon stopped him, not wanting to run the risk of screwing something up. The last thing he needed was a tank that wouldn't restart. It was running, and he didn't want to mess with anything that was working properly.

As Bannon pulled his chemical suit on, the crew watched him. He took his time to ensure that he didn't fumble and fall. He had always been told that calm, like panic, was contagious. Now was a good time to find out. Besides, it had been a long time since they had trained in their chemical protective clothing and he had to figure out where all the snaps and ties

32

went. The heavy protective clothing was a necessary evil of modern war.

When Bannon was finished, he turned to Folk. 'We ready to roll, Sergeant Folk?'

Folk looked at him for a moment. 'Yes, sir. We're ready.' Folk's tense expression relaxed slightly.

'Are all weapons loaded and on safe?' Bannon's second question caused the relaxed look to be replaced by one of embarrassment as both Folk and Kelp stopped pulling at their suits and looked at each other. 'I take it that that's a big negative on my last question.'

Sheepishly, Folk replied that it hadn't occurred to him to do so because they were in an assembly area with cavalry still out in front. All the range safety briefings and all the times the men had been harangued about keeping weapons clear and elevated except when on a live fire range were coming home to haunt them. Bannon couldn't blame the men. In their first battle, he could only expect them to do what they were taught in training, no better, no worse.

Stopping for a moment, Bannon leaned back on the side of the turret and looked at his crew. 'Alright, guys, here it is. We're really at war. I don't know what's happening yet, but from the sound of that artillery you can bet the Russians are letting the cavalry have it. The cavalry is out there to buy us some time and let us get our shit together. That's what they get paid for. When the Russians finish with the cavalry, we're next. What I want you to do is to calm down and start thinking. Remember what we did in training and do it now. Only think! There are a couple of habits we picked up in training that you're going to have to forget about. Do you understand what I'm saying?'

With a nod and a glance sideways at each other, they gave their tank and team commander a subdued but nervous, 'Yes, sir.' 'Alright, finish getting your suits on. We're going to move over to the right of 3rd Platoon and take up a position there. If nobody has any questions, let's get moving.'

By the time the crew of 66 was finished and mounted, the rest of the crews and tracks in the headquarters position were in their chemical gear and mounted. The first sergeant, now mounted in the headquarters PC with his jeep following, had already pulled out of position and was moving down the logging trail. Bannon noticed that all the tracks were running. Everyone was cranked up and ready to move. As the cavalry's covering force battle would take hours, possibly a day, there was no sense in leaving the tanks running. All that would do was burn diesel, something the M-1 was very good at, and create a tremendous thermal signature, another trait of the M-1. The savings in diesel would be worth a small violation of radio listening silence. Besides, it might be good for at least the leadership of the Team to hear their commander issue an order and give some advice. Unless the Soviet radio direction-finding detachments were fast, it would do no harm.

Checking first the remote box to ensure that the radio was set on the Team net, Bannon keyed the radio and paused for a moment to let the radio come up to speed. 'ALL BRAVO 3 ROMEO ELEMENTS – THIS IS ROMEO 25 – IT IS GOING TO BE AWHILE BEFORE THOSE OTHER PEOPLE GET HERE – SHUT DOWN AND SETTLE DOWN – CHECK YOUR SYSTEMS AND LOCK AND LOAD – ACKNOWLEDGE – OVER.'

The platoons checked in and acknowledged. Uleski, in the 55 tank, simply stood up in its cupola, turned towards the 66 tank and waved, indicating that he understood. The ITVs did not respond but shut down. With nothing more to do there, Bannon turned around in the cupola and faced to the rear. Locking the push-to-talk switch on his CVC back so he could talk to the driver on the intercom and hang on with both hands, Bannon began to back the tank onto the logging trail. As he leaned over to the right side of the cupola, watching the right rear fender as 66 moved back, Kelp popped out of the loader's hatch and leaned over to the left, watching the left rear fender. Once on the trail, the tank made a pivot turn to the right and started forward towards 3rd Platoon.

The drive down to 3rd Platoon was a short one, only about 700 metres. But it felt good to be in the tank and moving. Standing in the TC's hatch of a tank, rolling down a road or cross-country, was always an exhilarating experience for Bannon. He never tired of the thrill. Despite all the pain, misery, and headaches tanks could give him, it was fun being a tanker. It is the little joys in life that keep one going, and right now Bannon needed a little joy.

As they moved along the trail Bannon watched to the left, catching an occasional glimpse of the 3rd Platoon tanks. Their nets were still up but were propped up clear of the exhaust to keep them from melting. When 66 cleared the last of 3rd Platoon's tanks, Bannon ordered Ortelli to turn left into the forest and move down a small trail cut by a combat engineer vehicle that had dug the Team's positions. As they had not planned to fight from here, 66 was taking one of the alternate firing positions from the 33 tank, now to their immediate left at about seventy-five metres. The 33 tank would now have only its primary position to fire from and one alternate firing position to its left. The 66 would not have an alternate. If 66 were detected and fired at while in this position, the best Bannon could do would be to blow smoke grenades, back out of sight, and hope that whoever had shot at them gave up before 66 reoccupied its firing position.

Rather than stay back and hide in the forest, Bannon eased the tank into the firing position where he could observe the village, the valley, and the hills across the valley. The walled farm was just off to the right, out of sight in the small valley. Satisfied with his position, he ordered Ortelli to shut the engine down and to get out with Kelp to cut some camouflage. Folk came up to the TC's position to man the M2 and monitor the radio while the rest of the crew camouflaged the tank.

Ortelli took the axe and began to cut some branches as Kelp and Bannon draped the camouflage net over the rear of the turret and back deck. They didn't put up the supports or stake it down; all Bannon wanted to do was to break up some of the tank's outline. Finished with the net, Kelp and Bannon began to place the branches dragged over by Ortelli on the side and front of the tank not covered by the net. They were careful to ensure that the gunners' primary sight was not blocked and that the turret could be traversed some without knocking off the camouflage. When they were finished, Bannon stepped back a few metres to view their handiwork. The 66 looked like a tank covered with branches. Someone looking hard would be able to see it, no doubt about that. But, with a little luck and some harassment from the air defence artillery, the Russian pilots would be moving too fast to take a hard look. Satisfied that they had done the best they could, the crew remounted and waited.

Bannon stood in the turret and watched to the east, taking off his CVC and laying it down on top of the turret. The radio was turned up so he could hear any traffic being passed. He began to listen to the noise of the battle to his front. The massive bombardment continued but had died down some. The noise of the impacting artillery had been joined by new sounds and faint cracks of new high velocity tank cannons firing. The cavalry probably was returning artillery and tank fire. That meant the enemy was out and coming. There was no way to find out what was going on out there. For a moment Bannon was half tempted to switch his auxiliary radio receiver over to the cavalry's frequency. But doing so would have meant leaving either the battalion or the Team net. Were he still up on the headquarter's position, that would not have been a problem because Uleski could have covered the vacated net. Thinking hard, but not coming up with a solution, he resigned himself to the fact that until the battalion started to pass information down, he would be in the dark. He felt it was more important to be near 3rd Platoon in case Garger blew it than to know what was happening.

Now the waiting began. It wasn't even 0830 yet. The last hour had gone fast but had been emotionally draining. Everything had changed that morning. Wars, once started, take on a life of their own, and what occurs and how they end are seldom controllable by either side. World War I, World War II, Korea, and Vietnam all took twists and turns no one foresaw. Bannon had no reason to think that this one was going to be any different. Those thoughts were disquieting. His mind needed to be diverted to something less ominous and more comprehensible.

He put on his CVC, muffling most of the noise of the unseen covering force battle. He locked the push-to-talk switch back

36

into the intercom position. 'Sergeant Folk, have you run a computer check yet this morning?'

'No, sir, we haven't.'

'Well, let's make sure we don't get any surprises during the first engagement. I intend to go home a veteran and collect some of those benefits Congress is always after. How about you, Kelp?'

Kelp stood on the turret floor and looked up out of the loader's hatch at Bannon with a grin. 'I'm with you. My uncle was in Nam an' he's always tellin' me how rough it was. By the time we get done kickin' ass on Russian tanks, I'll be able to tell 'em what a real war was like.'

Bannon left the CVC keyed to the intercom position so that the rest of the crew could hear their conversation. 'Well, if Ortelli can keep this beast running and Sergeant Folk can hit the targets I find him, you and I should do pretty well, Kelp.' Both Ortelli and Folk chimed in, vowing that they were going to be the ones waiting for Bannon and Kelp. After a couple more minutes of banter, Bannon judged that they were in a more normal state of mind, and he started them on the crew checklist. He read the list, item by item, and watched as the crewman responsible performed his check. Like an airline crew preparing for flight, the crew of 66 prepared for combat.

He began to feel more comfortable, and the crew seemed to be less tense. For the first time this morning he felt at ease. It would be possible to relax awhile, both physically and mentally.

Bannon took his CVC off again. To his front he could see pillars of black smoke rising in the sky, joining together high above the horizon, and drifting away to the east. Burning tanks. A lot of them. No doubt about that. Hundreds of gallons of diesel together with ammunition, rubber, oil, and the 'other' burnable material on a tank provides plenty of fuel when a penetrating round finds its mark.

The noise of the battle was more varied now. The initial massive bombardment was replaced by irregular spasms of artillery fire. The artillery batteries shifted their fires to hit targets of opportunity as they presented themselves. Irregular cracks, booms, and thuds were joined by a rapid chain of booms as an artillery unit fired all its guns simultaneously. He began to wonder how long the cavalry could maintain the tempo of the battle they were involved in.

Modern war consumes ammunition, material, and, worst of all, men at a frightening rate. Rapid-fire tank cannon coupled with a computerised fire control and laser range finders were capable of firing up to eight aimed rounds per minute at tank-sized targets at ranges in excess of 2000 metres. Guided munitions, fired from ground launchers or helicopters, had a better than ninety per cent probability of hitting a target at 4000 metres. Soviet multiple rocket launchers could fire hundreds of rockets in a single volley and destroy everything within a one-by-one kilometre grid. Chemical agents produced by the Soviets were capable of penetrating exposed skin and attacking the body's nervous system, crippling the victim in seconds and killing him in minutes. All the implements of war had become more capable, more deadly. All were designed to rip, crush, cripple, dismember, incapacitate, and kill men faster and more efficiently. In all the armies arrayed across the continent, the only thing that technology had not improved was the ability of the human body to absorb punishment.

Such thoughts were disquieting. The mind, left free, tends to wander into what might be and what could happen, as frightening as the Ghost of Christmas to Come was to Scrooge. A diversion from these thoughts came from the east.

Two dots, growing rapidly into aircraft, came screaming towards the small valley from the east just as the others had this morning. Bannon hoped the Team would abide by the standard operating procedures, or SOP, and not engage them. With only machine guns, they stood little chance of hitting fast-moving jets. The only thing that would be accomplished by firing would be to give away the Team's positions.

A Stinger team somewhere in the cavalry's sector had no hesitation about engaging, however. Bannon watched as the white smoke trail of a Stinger surface-to-air anti-aircraft missile raced up after the second jet. But it did not find its mark. The Soviet pilot dropped small flares and made a hard turn and dive. The missile detonated harmlessly in midair as the second jet turned to join the first, and both disappeared up the small valley. The ripping chainsaw-like report from a Vulcan 20-millimetre anti-aircraft gun somewhere behind the Team's position revealed that problems for the Russian pilots were just starting. The air defence system was now alert and in action.

As if to underscore that point, two more dots emerged from the east. Apparently the Soviets liked this air approach and were sending their aircraft through four at a time. Their heavy use of the small valley cost them this time. Two Stinger missiles raced up to greet the Soviet jets. The pilot of the trail jet in this pair was not as quick or as lucky as the other pilots had been; one of the Stingers found its mark. The missile detonated, causing the jet to tumble over as if kicked from behind, then disintegrate in a rolling orange ball of fire. The first jet kicked in his afterburners, dropped lower, and kept flying west, to the waiting Vulcan.

Kelp, who had been watching the engagement, let out an 'Ah, neat! Hey, Sarge, you missed it!' as if he were watching Fourth of July fireworks instead of the destruction of a pilot and a multimillion dollar aircraft. Kelp then described, in his own colourful way the action to Folk. As Bannon reflected on Kelp's reaction, he, too, had to admit that it was kind of neat.

★ Announcement of plans to evacuate the dependants was on the TV before AFN went off the air the morning Sean had left. The radio station stayed on the air but didn't provide much information. About the only news the radio provided was the closing of the commissary and the PX and the movement of all U.S. families living off post onto U.S. installations.

Pat Bannon prepared for their departure. Fran Wilson, the wife of the commander of Team Charlie came over later in the morning. She had to be with someone. Fran had sat alone in her quarters waiting for word on when to leave and where to go. When word didn't come, she gave up and sought some company. Sitting alone with her fears and nothing to do but think about what was happening was driving her crazy – she needed someone to talk to and be with. Fran's coming caused Pat to remember that Sue Garger, the wife of one of Sean's platoon leaders, was still staying alone in a German *Gasthaus* in town. The Gargers had been in the country less than a month and were waiting for quarters. Pat had met Sue only once and was afraid that Sue might not have heard the news and, because she was new to the unit, might have been overlooked. She called the number listed for Garger on Sean's alert roster. A German answered. Pat's attempt to talk to him in her broken German amused Fran but finally got results. As they talked, Pat could tell that Sue was lonely and nervous. When Pat invited Sue to stay with her Sue jumped at the offer. Like Fran, fear and loneliness had made the deplorable situation worse for Sue. Leaving Fran to watch the children, Pat took off to pick up Sue.

At the entrance to the housing area there was an MP road-block. Pat was halted and told she could not leave the area. She tried to explain to the MP that she had to pick up a wife that was living in town. The MP held his ground, insisting that she turn around and go back. Pat decided to escalate and told the private she wanted to speak to his superior. The MP went over to his sergeant and spoke to him a moment. The sergeant came over. 'I'm sorry, miss, you can't go off post.'

Pat was used to dealing with the military by now and seldom took no for an answer first time out. She had also learned that there were ways of dropping Sean's rank without being pushy or obvious. 'Sergeant, like I explained to the other MP, the wife of one of my husband's platoon leaders is at a *Gasthaus* in town and has no way of getting in. I'm simply going to get her. Now, unless you or your commander will go get her, I have to.'

The sergeant thought about it, then told Pat to wait while he checked with his platoon leader. After a few minutes, he came back and told her to go straight to the *Gasthaus*, pick up the other wife, and come straight back. She was not to stop for anyone or anything else and she was to check back with him when she returned. The speech and precautions worried Pat and made her wonder if this was such a good idea. But she was committed, and Sue Garger was depending on her.

40

Even for the families of servicemen, the old Army rule of hurry up and wait applied. While Pat was gone, Cathy Hall had called and passed on the word that the evacuation probably would not start until the next day. The Air Force needed some additional time to gear up. To maintain the appearance of normalcy, preparations for the evacuation of dependants had been delayed to the last possible moment. Some of the older wives compared the situation to Iran, where the families were pulled out only at the last minute. Pat was not at all pleased that she and her children had been retained in this country just for appearances but kept her own council. No need to cry over spilt milk now.

As the day wore on and it became apparent that the families were not, in fact, going to go anytime soon, the wives began to visit each other and let the children out to play. Cathy Hall put out the word that she was going to host a potluck dinner for the battalion wives. Most of the wives, with children in tow, showed up. Even though the conversations were guarded and there was a pall on the whole affair, anything was better than sitting alone and worrying. There was some comfort in collective misery.

By the end of the first day, Pat was physically and mentally exhausted. It seemed that so much depended on her now. With no husband to help her along, she felt uneasy and under pressure. Pressure to be mother and father. Pressure to set the example for Sue and the other wives. Pressure to make sure all was ready to go when the word came. Pressure to tend to the children and ease them through this crisis. Sean had always been around whenever there had been a big crisis in the family or a major decision to be made. But now he was gone and could not help with the biggest crisis Pat had ever faced. Having Sue Garger in the quarters helped. Sue had calmed down some and proved to be a big help with the children. But Sue was as lost as Pat was and still was learning about being in the Army. So Pat bottled up her fears and apprehensions and continued to stumble along the dark and mapless trail that her family was going down, alone.

The second day dragged along like the first. AFN TV came

41

back on but spent most of the time making public service announcements and broadcasting news that really didn't tell anyone anything. Rain in the afternoon made the dark and apprehensive mood of the community worse. Word that evacuations would start momentarily kept circulating along with a blizzard of other rumours.

But it wasn't until that evening that official word and instructions for the evacuation of the community came down. It was like a vent had been opened to relieve some of the pressure. At least now they knew what to do and when it would happen. For the sixth time in two days Pat went over the evacuation kit that had been sitting by the door. Blankets, food, water, cups, diapers, a small first-aid kit, a change of clothes for the boys, two for Sarah, a pocket knife, colouring books for the children, and other 'essential' items.

It was telling the children that Pat dreaded the most. She had put this off for as long as possible in the hope that some sanity would prevail and the whole affair would blow over. But there was no more putting it off. She assembled her children on Sean's bed and sat down with them. She told them that tomorrow they were going to leave Germany and visit Grandma's. Kurt was overcome with joy. He jumped up and down and began to ask what toys he could take. Sarah simply looked at Pat and tried to say Grandma, a word she had heard but could not associate with an object since she had never seen her grandparents.

As anticipated, Sean was the tough case. His first question was about his father, 'Is Daddy coming with us?'

'No, Daddy's not coming with us.'

'Why?'

'Daddy has to stay here and work. Remember I told you he went to the field? Well, he is still in the field with his company. He can't come with us this time.'

'When will we see Daddy again?'

'Daddy will come and join us when he is finished in the field.'

'When will that be?'

Pat was fast becoming exasperated. The boy was concerned, and she felt sorry for him because all that was going on so dwarfed him. But the line of questions only heightened her own fears and apprehensions. Before she lost her restraint and began to cry, Pat cut short the question-and-answer period and told Sean that his father would be home as soon as he could. This didn't satisfy Sean, but it was the best Pat could do.

The morning continued with little change. The heat of the day was turning the tank into an oven. The chemical suits only made things worse. Bannon began to let two men out at a time to stretch, smoke, cool off, and eat. During his break he walked over to check on the 33 tank. The TC was also rotating his crew out. Just after noon, Polgar came over to 66 from Mech Platoon's mounted element to report.

Bannon and Polgar were joined by the battalion commander and S-3, who came rolling up the logging trail in their M-113. Apparently, they were also bored and getting a little antsy with nothing to do but watch and wait. While the colonel went to visit his Mech Platoon on foot, the S-3, Maj. Frank Jordan, brought Bannon up to speed on the status of the covering force battle.

The cavalry was taking a beating and wouldn't last much longer. They had fought the first attacking echelon to a standstill and had badly weakened it. But they had paid for that success, as the parade of ambulances and evacuation of damaged vehicles, coming down the opposite hill through the village and down the small valley to the rear, indicated. Brigade was anticipating a passage of lines sometime in the late afternoon. The cavalry wanted to hold on until night in order to withdraw under the cover of darkness. But the bets were against them. The colonel rejoined the others, made some small talk, and then left with the S-3.

Rather than waiting out the afternoon doing nothing, Bannon decided to visit the platoons. The battalion commander had just been by and it was going to be a while before the cavalry came through. This was as good a time as any to show his face, to check on the rest of the Team to see how they were adapting to war, and to pass the word to be prepared for the passage of the cavalry. He told Folk where he was going to be; if a call came in on the battalion net, Folk was to drop to the company net and tell the XO to respond if he hadn't already done so. With helmet, pistol, and LBE, Bannon started his tour.

As he had that morning, Bannon went from tank to tank, working his way to those elements on the left first. When he reached the 31 tank, Bannon went over the information that had been passed to him and reviewed the status of 3rd Platoon with Garger. Then they reviewed the Team's and the platoon's actions during the passage and the conduct of the defence. Bannon was pleasantly surprised to listen to Garger go over each phase of the pending action and line out clearly those actions required of his platoon. Either Pierson had been working overtime with the lieutenant or the boy was catching on. Regardless of how, at least he had the concept of the operation straight in his mind. There was still the question, however, of whether he could make it work.

Even in the shade of the forest, tromping up the hill in the chemical protective suit and the floppy, loose-fitting chemical overshoes was brutal. By the time Bannon reached Uleski's tank, he was beat and needed a rest and a long drink of water. As he settled down in the shade next to 55, Uleski reached down and handed him a can of Coke, a cold can of Coke. Bannon had no idea where it could possibly have come from. He probably didn't want to know, either – something that good had to be illegal somehow. As he rested, Bannon went over not only the plan for the Team but also the battalion with Uleski. If he became combat ineffective, a subtle way of saying wounded or killed, Uleski, the XO, would have to be able to fight the Team within the framework of the battalion's battle plan as effectively as Bannon. In the Army, everyone was supposed to be expendable and replaceable. While it was not a comforting thought, it was part of the job and, in theory at least, universally understood.

Finishing with Uleski, Bannon toyed with the idea of letting the XO go over to 2nd Platoon to check them and pass on the word about the cavalry. It was tempting. But 2nd Platoon was the one platoon he had not seen that morning. It was only proper that an effort should be made to visit them. As with 3rd

44

Platoon, Bannon stopped at each tank, checked on their readiness, and exchanged small talk. When he reached the platoon leader's tank Bannon passed on word about the cavalry and reviewed the Team and platoon plan with him. No sooner had they finished when the hills across the valley erupted in a thunderclap of explosions and flames. The Soviets were committing their second echelon. It would not be long now. Bannon tromped on back to the 66 tank as fast as his floppy chemical overshoes would let him.

The cavalry had not lasted as long as had been expected. The fresh battalions of the Soviet's second attacking echelon broke the worn and severely weakened cavalry like a dry twig. Thirty minutes after the second echelon struck, it was obvious that the covering force battle was over, and it was time for the cavalry to pass through the Team's positions. The lazy, boring late morning and early afternoon gave way to a steady buildup of tension as the cavalry began the process of handing off the battle.

The first elements through were the support elements: medical, maintenance, and supply vehicles. These were followed by artillery units and headquarters elements. The passage was not the neat paradelike processions practised during training. Vehicles would come down singly, in pairs, sometimes in groups as large as fifteen. Some were dragging damaged vehicles. Some were limping or wobbling along like drunks, all showed some sign of damage. Trucks had their canvas tops shredded. Tracked vehicles that had had gear stowed on the outside now had it scrambled and tossed about on top, with articles of clothing hanging from the sides. There were even a couple of trucks running on tyre rims, unable or unwilling to stop to change tyres. If there was any semblance of order to the cavalry unit passing through the Team, it was not evident from where Bannon was watching.

During the passage, a scout helicopter, followed by two attack helicopters, came weaving down through the valley from the north. The three slowed to a hover, with the scout across from 66 and and an AH IS Cobra attack helicopter on either side. The OH-58 scout slowly rose until it was just barely

45

peering over the trees on the opposite hill. Its tail-boom moved slowly left, then right, as it scanned the landscape on the other side of the hill. Like a bird dog alerting, the scout froze, pointing to the northeast. The Cobra on the left rose slowly to treetop level, hovered there for a moment, orienting in the same direction as the scout. With a flash and a streak of white smoke, the Cobra let fly a TOW antitank missile. The Cobra remained in place for about fifteen seconds, then dropped down and flew a few hundred metres north to another position, preparing to fire again.

The second Cobra rose into position as soon as the first had fired. The second also fired, remained locked on target for about fifteen seconds, and then dropped down and moved to another position just as the first had done. By that time, the first Cobra was ready to pop up from his new position and fire again. After each Cobra had fired two TOWs, they flew back up the valley behind their scout to find a new firing position.

The thought that the Soviet lead elements were now close enough to be engaged by TOWs from across the valley startled Bannon. That meant that the enemy was now within five kilometres. To add weight to that point, friendly artillery from a unit behind the Team's position came whistling overhead to the east. The adrenalin started to pump. Across the valley the first undamaged cavalry combat vehicles came racing back from the opposite hill. M-1 tanks and M-3 Bradley cavalry vehicles, mixed together, their guns to the rear and their orange identification panels flapping as they moved, came rolling through the lanes marked in the Team's minefields and into the village. These vehicles looked worse than those that had preceded them.

The ordeal for the cavalry wasn't over yet. As the first vehicles entered the village, the streets erupted into a ball of flames and explosions. The Soviets were firing at least a battalion's worth of artillery against the town. The initial impacts were followed by a steady stream of artillery shells impacting every few seconds. Bannon had no idea of the calibre of rounds they were using nor how many were impacting. Not that he needed to know. Without doubt, the battalion commander was able to see it from his position.

Bannon's immediate concern was his first sergeant and the fire team, who were in the village in the middle of all that fire.

'ROMEO 25 – THIS IS MIKE 77 – SHELLREP – OVER.' Garger was on the ball. Reporting per the Team SOP, the lieutenant was calling to inform him of the artillery barrage to their front. Garger hadn't considered that Bannon, from his position, would be able to see the same thing. The fact that he was at least thinking of the SOP and had the presence of mind to report, however, was encouraging.

'ALL BRAVO 3 ROMEO ELEMENTS – THIS IS ROMEO 25 – I CAN OBSERVE THE ACTION AT 179872 – NO NEED TO REPORT THAT.' Bannon let the CVC push-to-talk switch go for a few seconds to frustrate Soviet direction-finding attempts, then started again. 'OCCUPY YOUR FIRING POSITIONS NOW – I SAY AGAIN – OCCUPY YOUR FIRING POSITIONS NOW – THE RUSSIANS WILL BE RIGHT BEHIND THOSE PEOPLE COMING THROUGH – ACKNOWLEDGE – OVER.' The platoons rapidly responded. The tracks to the left and right of 66 cranked up and pulled forward. In their excitement, some of them forgot about their camouflage nets. Bannon watched the 33 tank as the net supports tumbled and the net stretched forward as if it were a large spider web stuck to the tank. Once the stakes were yanked free, the net trailed the tank limply. In a belated plea, Bannon called over the company net to remind the platoons to remember the nets. Then he and Kelp jumped out, dragged theirs in, and jumped back into position.

The battalion net now came to life as the battalion Scout Platoon began to report sighting, then contact with the lead enemy element. As Team Yankee's artillery fire-support team, or FIST, was detached to the Scout Platoon while they were deployed forward, Bannon listened intently, hoping he wouldn't lose that valuable combat asset. The Scout Platoon's mission was to cover the withdrawal of the last of the cavalry, engage the enemy's lead elements in an effort to deceive them as to where the covering force area ended and the main battle area, or MBA, began, and then withdraw through Team Yankee. Their fight was to be short but important. Once they started firing, the battle had passed from the cavalry to the battalion. Though it still had to roll through sporadic artillery fire impacting in the village and up the little valley to the Team's right, the cavalry's battle was over. Team Yankee's first battle was about to begin.

The radio on the Team net came to life as First Sergeant Harrert called, 'ROMEO 25 – THIS IS ROMEO 97 – OVER.' He was still in the village and still alive.

'ROMEO 97 – THIS IS ROMEO 25 – WHAT KIND OF SHAPE ARE YOU IN? – OVER.'

'THIS IS 97 – I HAVE ONE WHISKEY INDIA APLHA – THE NOVEMBER 8 TANGO ELEMENT HAS COMPLETED PASSAGE – WAITING ON THE TANGO 9 FOXTROT ELEMENT NOW – OVER.'

'THIS IS 25 – DO YOU NEED THE BANDAID FOR THE CASUALTY? – OVER.'

'THIS IS 97 – NEGATIVE – HE CAN WAIT – OVER.'

'THIS IS 25 – THE TANGO 9 FOXTROT ELEMENT IS NOW IN CONTACT – I EXPECT THEM TO START BACK WITHIN THREE ZERO MIKES – HANG IN THERE – OVER.'

'THIS IS 97 – WILCO – OVER.'

So far everything was working according to plan. In their haste to occupy firing positions, the Team had probably screwed up most of its camouflage nets. But right now, that was the least of Bannon's worries. He continued to listen to the Scout Platoon's fight, now being joined by reports from Team Bravo. Team Bravo occupying the hill across the small valley from Team Yankee, was under fire from several battalions' worth of Soviet artillery. The initial and frantic report from the Team Bravo commander over the battalion radio net was cut off in mid-sentence. Attempts by the battalion S-3 to re-establish contact with Team Bravo failed. That meant that either its command track had had its antennas blown off or it had been hit.

The 1st Tank Platoon of Team Yankee was attached to Team Bravo. The 1st Platoon was probably in the middle of the impact area, judging from the fragmented report Bannon had monitored. Although he was concerned that some of his people were under fire, there was nothing that he could do. The thought 'Better them than me,' flashed through his mind. For a moment, Bannon was ashamed that he could harbour such a selfish thought. However, he immediately was able to rationalise by reminding himself that he was only human. With that, he turned his attention to more immediate and pressing problems.

Reports from the scouts continued to come in. One of the scout tracks had been hit, and contact with another had been lost. From the reported locations of the enemy's lead element, the scouts weren't slowing him down. Finally, the scout platoon leader requested permission to displace. Realising that leaving the scouts out there wasn't going to do the battalion any good, the battalion commander gave his permission to withdraw.

Unfortunately, this permission had come too late. The barriers and artillery that were supposed to slow the Soviet advance and allow the Scout Platoon a chance to pass through Team Yankee didn't slow the enemy. Ignoring losses inflicted on them by mines, artillery, and the Scout Platoon, the Soviets pushed forward. They were hell-bent for leather to break through and intended to do so regardless of the price. The Scout Platoon leader informed the battalion commander that rather than try for the passage through Team Yankee, he was going to withdraw to the south and cross at an alternate passage point.

This was not a good turn of events for the Team. With the scouts went Team Yankee's artillery FIST Team. Bannon had never been keen on the idea of letting his FIST go with the scouts, pointing out that they might not be able to rejoin the Team. But he had always been reassured that the FIST track would be back long before Team Yankee had any contact. This was one time he was sorry he had been right. Not only did he have to fight the Team, now he also had to play forward observer. Contacting the battalion S-3, Bannon asked him if he had any bright ideas on the subject. Major Jordan informed him that Team Yankee now had priority of artillery fire and all calls for fire would be directed to the battalion fire-support officer, or FSO. Jordan also informed him that Team Bravo had taken a lot of casualties, including its commander, who was dead. The battalion commander was going over to Team Bravo to attempt to rally the survivors. In the meantime, battalion was writing off Team Bravo as combat ineffective. Both the S-3 and the battalion commander were depending on Team Yankee to carry the fight.

Two company teams fighting a motorised rifle battalion would have been no problem. But one company team, even with priority of artillery fire, would have a hard time. Bannon contacted the battalion fire-support officer and made sure he had all the Team's preplanned artillery targets. The FSO had them. Quickly they reviewed his plans for fire support.

Bannon intended to let the Soviet lead elements reach the valley floor. When that happened, the Team would engage them with both tank platoons and the ITVs simultaneously. The 2nd Platoon would engage the lead element, the 3rd Platoon would hit the enemy still on the opposite slope, and the ITVs would engage supporting vehicles on the far hill. He wanted the artillery to impact along the crest of the opposite hill at the same time the Team began to fire. First, DPICM, an artillery shell that scattered many small armour-defeating bomblets, would be fired in order to take out as many Soviet PCs and self-propelled guns as possible. Then the artillery would fire high explosives, HE, and smoke rounds, laying down a smoke screen to blind any Soviet antitank system or artillery observers that might take up position there to engage the Team. That would leave the Team free to slug it out with only a portion of their force isolated from the rest. The FSO assured Bannon the artillery could handle the mission. All he needed was the word.

A sudden detonation in the village followed by the hasty retreat of a lone PC out of the village back to the Team's positions reminded Bannon that the first sergeant hadn't been told to blow the bridge in the town and withdraw. In the scramble to sort out the artillery fire plan he had forgotten the first sergeant. Fortunately, either Harrert had monitored the battalion net, figured out what was going on, and taken the initiative, or Uleski had ordered him out after hearing that the scouts would not be returning on the planned route. Either way, it worked out, and the first sergeant was headed back.

'ROMEO 25 – THIS IS MIKE 77 – SPOT REPORT – 5 T-72 TANKS MOVING WEST – GRID 190852 – CONTINUING TO OBSERVE – OVER.' Bannon snapped his head to the left. There was no need to use a map. There was only one place where the Russians would be, and that was on the hill 2200 metres away. All the training, planning, and preparations were over. Team Yankee was about to learn if the Team's seventy-nine men and twenty-five million dollars worth of equipment could do what they were supposed to do: close with and destroy the enemy by fire, manoeuvre, and shock effect.

The five T-72 tanks began their descent into the valley in a line with about 100 metres between tanks. One of them had a mine roller attached to the front of its hull. He would have to be taken out in the first volley. As soon as the tanks started down, a line of Soviet armoured personnel carriers, BMP-2s, appeared on the crest of the hill and followed the tanks down. There were fifteen of these personnel carriers deployed in a rough line about one hundred metres behind the tanks. The tanks and the BMPs moved down the opposite slope at a steady and somewhat restrained pace, as if they really didn't want to go into the valley, or they didn't want to get too far ahead of follow-on elements.

A third group of follow-on vehicles appeared. These were a gaggle of dissimilar armoured vehicles. As they reached the crest of the hill, they paused for a moment. Just before they started their descent, the tanks and the BMPs in front made a sharp oblique to the left and headed for the north side of the village. With one BMP, a T-72, a BTR-60, followed by an MTU bridge tank and a ZSU 23-4 anti-aircraft gun, this could only be the battalion command group.

The scene before Team Yankee was too good to be true. For some unknown reason the Team had not been hit by artillery yet. The Soviets were rolling forward as if they were on manoeuvres, not attack. Their change in direction offered most of the Team flank shots. And the actions by the

51

command group had telegraphed who they were. If luck held for another minute or two, it would be all over for this motorised rifle battalion.

'ROMEO 83 – THIS IS ROMEO 25 – DO YOU SEE THAT LAST GAGGLE COMING DOWN THE HILL – OVER.'

'25 – THIS IS 83 – ROGER – OVER.'

'83 – THIS IS 25 – THAT IS THE COMMAND GROUP – I WANT YOU AND THE TWO TRACKS YOU HAVE UP THERE TO TAKE THEM OUT – THE BMP AND TANK FIRST – OVER.'

'THIS IS 83 – WILCO.'

Uleski considered this last order before he relayed instructions to the ITVs. He paused for a moment and watched the advancing Soviets. The 55 was silent except for the hum of the engine. Uleski could feel the tension build up in himself and his crew. In the past, he had always been able to crack a joke or say something funny to lighten the pressures of a tense moment. But he couldn't, not this time. It suddenly dawned upon him that this was real. The tanks and BMPs were manned with real Soviets and they were coming his way.

Despite the heat of the day, Uleski felt a cold shiver run down his spine. His stomach began to knot up and he felt as if he were going to throw up. It was real, all real. In a minute, maybe two, all hell was going to break loose and he was right in the middle of it. Uleski's head, flooded with disjointed thoughts, began to spin, with one thought coming back over and over, 'Oh God, please make this go away.'

When Bannon had finished with Uleski, he switched to the battalion net and instructed the FSO to fire the prearranged artillery barrage. When the FSO acknowledged the request, Bannon went back to the Team net, 'ALL BRAVO 3 ROMEO ELEMENTS – UPON IMPACT OF FRIENDLY ARTILLERY, YOU WILL COMMENCE FIRING – MAINTAIN FIRE DISTRIBUTION AND GOOD SHOOTING – ROMEO 25 OUT.'

This last message neither upset nor unnerved Garger. Without bothering to acknowledge the commander's orders, Garger switched to the platoon net and issued his own. The clear, sunny day, with the sun to the 3rd Platoon's back, made it all too easy. All the BMPs were exposed to the entire platoon. Garger ordered Pierson and Pierson's wingman, the 33 tank, to engage the right half of the BMPs. Garger instructed his own wingman, Blackfoot, to begin to engage the far left BMP and then work his way towards the centre of the line. He would begin in the centre and work his way to the left. In this way, the platoon would avoid killing the same BMP.

With nothing to do but wait for the artillery, Garger leaned back and considered the scene before him. This was easier than the Armor School at Fort Knox. It couldn't be that simple. There had to be a catch. The Soviets were coming at them as if the Team wasn't there. Garger tried hard to think if there was something he had missed, an order to be given. Something. But there wasn't. All seemed to be in order. All was ready. 'What the hell,' he thought, 'Might as well relax and enjoy the moment.'

In the Mech Platoon's positions Sergeant First Class Polgar grasped the hand grips of his M2 machine gun as he watched the Soviets. He was amazed. When he was a young private, Polgar had been in Vietnam two months before he had seen his first VC, and they had been dead VC. In the first day of this war, he was looking at all the Soviets he cared to see. He looked to his left and then to his right at his PCs. The four M-113s with him weren't going to do a hell of a lot if the tanks in the Team fell flat on their ass. As the Soviets drew near, Polgar tracked the Soviets with his M2 and thought, 'Those dumb-ass tankers better be as good as they think they are, or this is going to be a damned short war.'

The Team was charged and ready. Bannon could feel it. Now, he prepared to fight his own tank crew.

He grabbed the TC's override and traversed the turret to his intended victim, yelling out the fire command without switching on the intercom, 'GUNNER – SABOT – TANK WITH MINE ROLLER.'

'IDENTIFIED.' Folk had the target in his sight.

'UP.' Kelp had armed the main gun and was clear of the path of recoil.

Bannon knelt down on top of his seat, perched above the gunner and loader, watching through the extension as Folk tracked the T-72. They waited. The enemy continued to advance. And they waited. The line of tanks was now beginning to reach the valley floor. And they waited. The sweat was rolling down Bannon's face and he was beginning to lose nerve. And they waited.

'SPLASH – OVER.' The FSO's call on the battalion net heralded the impact of the artillery. Across the valley, the crest of the far hill erupted as hundreds of small bomblets impacted and went off. On target!

'FIRE!'

'ON THE WAAAAAY!'

The image of the T-72 disappeared before Bannon's eye in a flash and cloud of smoke as Folk fired. The tank rocked back as the gun recoiled and spit out the spent shell casing. Kelp hit the ammo door switch with his knee, causing it to slide open with a bang. He hauled out the next round, loaded the gun, and armed it before the dust and obscuration cleared. When it did, the T-72 with the mine roller was stopped, broadside to 66, and burning furiously.

'TARGET – CEASE FIRE.' They had drawn their first blood. 'STAND BY GUNNER.'

Bannon popped his head up to get an overall picture of what was going on. Just as he did, the 33 tank fired a HEAT-T round at the BMP. He watched the tracer streak towards the target and impact with a bright orange flash and black ball of smoke. The BMP lurched forward another few metres then stopped, quivered, and began to burn. Bannon scanned the valley floor and opposite slope watching that scene repeated again and again. When the first round missed a BMP, the BMP would turn away from the impact. This manoeuvre, however, only added a few more seconds to its life because the second round usually found its mark. He watched as two BMPs, scrambling to avoid being hit, rammed each other and stopped. This calamity only made it easier for Team Yankee's gunners, and both BMPs died within seconds of each other, locked together.

The crest of the far hill had disappeared from view. The smoke and DPICM were doing their jobs. So far, nothing had followed the Soviet command group down. The command group had scattered, but it, too was suffering. The BMP from the command group was lying on its side, a track hanging off and burning. The tank that had been with it had been hit but had only shed its right track. It stood, immobile but defiant, returning fire towards the headquarters position. This uneven contest, however, did not last long. In return, the T-72 received a TOW missile that detonated at the turret ring and ripped the turret off with a thunderous explosion.

'I have a BMP in my sights, can I engage.' Folk was impatient.

Bannon knelt down, glanced at Kelp to ensure he was clear, checked that the gun was armed, and gave the command to fire. Folk gave an on-the-way and fired. The rock and recoil shook the tank. A glance in the extension told him that Folk had been on the mark again. Another BMP crew and infantry squad had become heroes of the Soviet Union, posthumously. 'Sergeant Folk, find your own targets, if there are any left, and engage at will. Just make sure you're not killing dead tracks.'

'Yes, sir!' His reply had a glee in it that reminded Bannon of a teenager who had just been given the keys to the family car. Bannon popped up again to survey the battlefield.

The devastation in the valley was awesome. Over twenty armoured vehicles lay strewn there, dismembered, twisted, burning hulks. Folk had nothing to engage. The lead echelon of the motorised battalion had been annihilated. Six T-72 tanks, sixteen BMPs, a BTR-60, a ZSU 23-4, and an MTU bridge launcher, along with almost two hundred Russian soldiers, were gone. The engagement had lasted less than four minutes. Team Yankee had won its first battle.

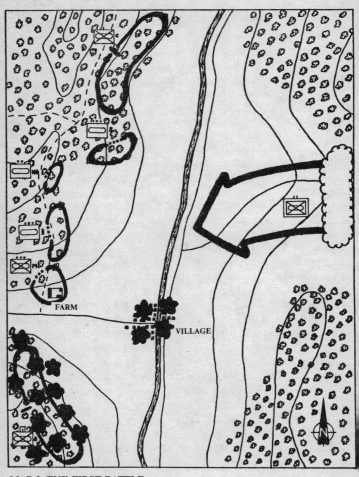

MAP 2: THE FIRST BATTLE

Chapter Three

CHANGE OF MISSION

When the decision to evacuate military dependants from Europe was finally made after countless delays and hesitations, there was a rush of frantic and seemingly uncoordinated activity to get it done before hostilities broke out. The drive to Rhein-Main, which normally took one hour, on that evening took nearly four. There was solid traffic on the autobahn from the time Pat Bannon and the others left the housing area until they pulled into the Air Base. The regular German police, reinforced with military personnel, had established checkpoints along the route. At every checkpoint the NCO on the bus had to present his paperwork before being cleared through. Pat noticed that the Germans were retaining some people at one checkpoint. There was a stationary car riddled with bullet holes on the autobahn's median. Next to it a white sheet with red blotches covered a mound. No one could imagine what offence could have caused such a response by the Germans. Whatever the reason, the fact that the Germans were ready to use their ever-present submachine guns highlighted the seriousness of the situation.

The last checkpoint was at the main gate of Rhein-Main. Before the bus was allowed to enter, Air Force security personnel boarded the bus and checked everyone's ID card. They, too, had their weapons at the ready. Two more security personnel had the bus driver open the baggage compartments of the bus. While one of the security officers checked them and the driver, the other stood back and covered the driver with his weapon. The German police on duty at the gate with the U.S. personnel were questioning two women off to one side. Pat guessed that they were German nationals trying to get out with the U.S. families.

The Air Base was swarming with activity. At one of the intersections, the bus was stopped while a line of trucks rolled by, coming up from the flight line and heading to a back gate.

In the trucks were U.S. troops, reinforcements from the States deployed under the REFORGER programme. Pat guessed that the dependants would fly back on the same planes that were bringing these troops in. Maybe this nightmare was almost over. At least they were now at the last stop on this side of the Atlantic.

Instead of going to the terminal, however, the buses dropped them off at the post gym. There were already a large number of people there. On the gym floor, rows of cots with blankets were set up. As at the post theatre, the families were grouped by unit. Some of the women from the battalion who had come up on the first group of buses had established an area for the families from each of the units. The new arrivals were told that since the terminal was already overflowing with evacuees, they had been sent to the gym until it was their turn to go. Pat was told that the Air Force personnel running the evacuation were better and more helpful than the Army community personnel but were having difficulties dealing with all the incoming families that were being dumped at Rhein-Main. One Air Force officer had told them that the people in the gym probably wouldn't leave until the morning.

This depressed Pat. She, like the other wives and mothers, was ready to go. They had finally geared themselves up for the final leap. Now, they had to spend a night in an open gym with hundreds of other dejected and anxious people. It seemed that every new move only added more stress and pressure. The situation, however deplorable, had to be endured. Pat decided that she could hold out a little longer. She had to. A little group was beginning to depend on her. And it was growing. Jane Ortelli, the wife of Sean's tank driver, joined them. She was nineteen years old and had never been out of the state of New Jersey until she came over to Germany. Jane stood at the side before boarding the bus, clutching her four-month-old baby as she would a teddy bear, for security and comfort. Pat went over to her and insisted that she join them since they were all going on the same bus. Jane was thankful and relieved.

A little girl named Debby had also joined the group. Debby's only parent was a medic who had been deployed to the border with everyone else. Fran Wilson had volunteered to escort the eight-year-old girl back to the States where her grandparents would meet her.

Pat and her group established themselves a little area by taking eight of the cots and pushing them together. The four adults stationed themselves on the corner cots and put the children in the middle. Jane kept her baby with her, not wanting to part for a moment with the only thing of value she had on earth. Sarah, overcoming her fears, insisted on having her own cot, just like her brothers. Sean and Debby stayed together. Sean, despite being a year younger, took over the role of big brother and helped Debby. He tried to explain everything to her like his father had to him, even though he had no idea what he was talking about. Debby would listen intently to every word as if it were gospel, then ask Sean another question. But at least Debby was talking now and seemed to be more at ease. Kurt insisted on staying near his buddy Sue. He was enjoying all the attention Sue was giving him.

There was little rest that night. Fear, apprehension, discomfort, and a desire to get on with the evacuation kept the adults awake while the adventure of the trip kept the children alert and active. Some of the adults talked in hushed voices, seeking company and escape from their fears. Others simply withdrew into themselves, no longer able to cope with the grim reality they found themselves in. Pat prayed that all this would end tomorrow. It had to. There was only so much more that she could give and hold back. It had to end, soon. Only exhaustion allowed her to get a few hours sleep.

Movement to the terminal began early. Groups left in the order in which they arrived. Pat and her little group had time for breakfast before their turn. Everyone was tired. It had been nearly impossible for anyone to get a good night's rest. Cold meals, little sleep, overcrowded conditions, wearing the same clothes they had slept in, and the trauma of the whole ordeal had worn women and children down to the point of exhaustion. Pat could not remember a time when she had been more tired and miserable. The ride to the terminal was a quiet one.

The passage of thousands of evacuees before them had left its mark on the terminal. The clean, modern building that had greeted Pat and Sean on their arrival in Germany was now strewn with litter and discarded blankets and clothes. Those who had left the gym before them were inside the terminal mixing with the evacuees that had spent the night there. Looking around as they entered, Pat decided that, though the gym had been miserable, staying here would have been worse.

At the door, an airman took their names, gave them a roster number and directed them to the second floor where they would wait until their numbers were called. From the second floor at least they could look out onto the airfield and watch the aircraft coming in. To one side of the flight line there were trucks and buses waiting to pick up the newly arrived troops arriving from the States. Pat and the children watched as a large C-141 transport taxied to a stop. Its large clamshell doors opened, reminding Pat of an alligator. As soon as the cargo ramp was down, troops began to double time out and fall in on their NCOs, forming squads and platoons. Once formed, they began to move to the trucks and load up.

While the troops were still deplaning, Air Force personnel scrambled out to service the aircraft. A fuel tanker lumbered up and began to refuel the aircraft. Everyone seemed anxious to get the C-141 turned around and on its way.

A female voice began to call out roster numbers over the PA and give instructions. None of Pat's little group heard their numbers called. So they stayed where they were and watched the lucky ones move onto the airfield, form into two lines, and move out to the C-141. The ground crew finished up and moved into position to service the next aircraft that was already coming in, a huge C-5. The sight of that plane caused excitement. Fran turned to Pat and said she was sure they would be able to get on that one. Inside, Pat prayed that would happen.

For a moment there was almost total silence in the valley in front of Team Yankee's positions. It was a dull, numb silence that comes after you have endured prolonged exposure to a deafening noise. The crackle and popping of small arms ammunition igniting in the burning Soviet tracks, with an occasional rumble as a main gun round cooked off, was all the noise that rose from the valley. Distance and CVCs hid the moans and screams of agony of those wounded or burning to death in their disabled tracks.

The report of a machine gun from the right alerted Bannon to the fact that not all the Soviets were hors de combat. He watched as a stream of tracers struck short, then climbed into a group of four Russians trying to make their way back up the hill. As soon as the firer found the range, he let go a long burst in the centre of the group. While some rounds kicked up dirt, a few found their mark, causing the Russians to either spin around, drop and roll back downhill, or simply plop down.

For a moment he thought of ordering the firing to stop. The Russians had suffered enough. But quickly this humanitarian thought gave way to cold, practical, professional considerations. If these survivors were allowed to live, they would only fall in on equipment in storage or being produced. Team Yankee would never see them again, but another NATO company would. They were at war, a war the Soviets had started. The Soviets must pay.

Reports started to come in over the company net as other tanks began to search out and destroy the Russian fugitives. Both tank platoons reported in with no losses, a total main gun expenditure of thirty-seven rounds, and inflated kill reports. Only the launcher on one of the ITVs had been hit and destroyed. The ITV crew was untouched and the track was still operational. But without its launcher and sight, the ITV was worthless to the Team. Bannon instructed Uleski to have that crew pass all the TOW rounds that it could handle to the operational ITV, then have the damaged ITV report back to the maintenance collection point. He then called the battalion S-3 and passed the Team situation report, or SITREP, to him.

With the reports and status of the unit in hand, Bannon ordered the Team to cease fire and move to alternate firing positions. The smoke screen along the crest of the far hill was lifting, and the third company of the Soviet motorised rifle battalion was unaccounted for. The possibilities of where it was and what it was doing ran through his mind. The lead units, instead of having eight tanks and twenty BMPs, had had only five tanks and fifteen BMPs. Perhaps the Soviet moto-rised battalion had suffered so many losses in their fight with the cavalry that it had merged all its companies into two weak, composite companies. Or perhaps, listening to the demise of the rest of the battalion had convinced the third company commander that he stood a better chance against the KGB than against the Americans. Or perhaps the Soviet company commander decided to stop on the crest of the hill and engage his yet-unseen opponent on a long-range duel once the smoke cleared and while he waited for reinforcements. Whatever the case, it was now his move. The Team prepared to parry that move.

While Bannon was pondering the larger tactical questions, Kelp stood up in his hatch. Using the binoculars, he surveyed the carnage he had helped create. As Kelp looked, Folk slowly traversed the turret, doing likewise. Ortelli, because the valley was hidden from his view by the berm that protected 66's hull, asked the other two crewmen to describe the scene. Talking in hushed voices so as not to disturb their commander's train of thought, Folk and Kelp described the scene in a gruesome, if colourful manner. Folk was particularly proud of 'his' destruction of the T-72 with mine roller and made sure that Kelp identified it.

Ortelli wanted to come up and see what it looked like but knew better than to ask. He dropped hints but received no response. At times, it was difficult to be the crew of the Team commander's tank. Bannon was seldom there to help in the maintenance of the tank or weapons. Yet the tank, radios, and gear always had to be ready whenever he came running up and climbed aboard, or there was hell to pay. And the crew had to be straighter and more correct than the crews in other tanks. It's not that team commanders are ogres. Commanders share an easier and closer relationship with their crew than they do with other tankers in the company. But the commander is still the commander and this thought is never far from the crew's, or commander's minds.

Uleski was only beginning to calm down. He felt drained, physically and mentally. It was all he could do to lift his canteen and take a mouthful of water. Swishing this around for a moment, he spit it out over the side of the tank. The taste of vomit still lingered, but it wasn't nearly as bad. After replacing his canteen, he sat there for a moment and watched the crewmen from the ITVs move from one track to the other, carrying rounds to the undamaged vehicle. It was late afternoon, the sun was softly filtering down through the trees. Except for an occasional pop or bang from ammunition cooking off in the valley below, all was quiet, all peaceful. The XO thought about how nice it would be if it could be over, just for a day, just an hour, just enough time for him to pull himself together.

A blinding flash and an overwhelming blast struck Uleski and knocked him back. Instinctively, he allowed himself to drop down to the turret floor as the soft green image of the forest disintegrated into flames and explosions.

★ The Soviet major was completely flustered. Nothing, absolutely nothing had gone right that day. First, the traffic regulators had misdirected their column before the attack. They had almost crossed the border before the scheduled attack time. It took the rest of the morning to get them turned around and back to their proper place. Then the resistance of the American cavalry was far greater than expected. The division's second echelon, to which the major's battalion belonged, had to be committed before the division's first objective was reached. The delay required a complete revision of the plan, a plan that had been drilled and practised for months. Artillery units were now in the wrong place and did not have the detailed fire plans needed to support a break-through attack properly. And to top off the whole day, the major's battalion commander had managed to get himself killed, leaving the major in command.

The major was in a dark mood. Not even the sight of burning American equipment cheered him. He had already seen far too much destroyed Soviet equipment. His orders and mission kept running through his mind. They were simple enough – cross a major valley, advance up a small side valley, and seize the regiment's objective, an intersection where two autobahns met. But the major had not been given any time to plan properly, recon, or co-ordinate for artillery support. The regimental commander, under pressure from his commander, merely told the major to move as rapidly as possible and that all the artillery planning would be taken care of for him. Even the battalion's political officer balked when they were told that a battalion, attacking in the same place earlier, had failed.

There was, however, nothing to do but to follow orders and hope for the best. The major put all his faith in the effects of the chemical weapons being used and his attack from an unexpected direction. As they neared the line of departure, he took one more look around at the mass of vehicles huddled near his and then closed his hatch.

Bannon's wandering thoughts were jarred back to the present by the impacts of artillery to his left on Team Yankee's hill. He could not see anything but had no doubt that the headquarters position and possibly the 2nd Platoon position were under fire. A second attack was starting.

'GAS! GAS! GAS!' The muffled cry by someone in a protective mask on the Team net electrified the crew of 66. As one, they tore open their protective mask cases and scrambled to mask. First, the CVC came off. Then the mask, chin first, emplaced. Once on securely, the hood had to be pulled over. Next, the CVC placed back on and the protective mask's mike jack plugged into the CVC. All this had to be done in less than twenty seconds.

'ROMEO 25 – THIS IS TANGO 77 –SHELLREP – OVER.'

'TANGO 77 – THIS IS ROMEO 25 – SEND IT.'

'THIS IS TANGO 77 – HE AND GAS IMPACTING FROM 190896 TO 199893 – CALIBRE AND NUMBER OF ROUNDS UNKNOWN – OVER.'

From the co-ordinates given, Bannon knew that the 2nd Platoon leader, who was making the report, and his platoon were safe. But the XO and the ITVs were catching hell. Because the Soviets were only firing up the hilltop and not at the actual positions of the Team's two tank platoons, it was obvious that they did not know for sure where the Team was. The Soviets were firing blind. While that was good for the Team overall, Bannon had no doubt that that thought was cold comfort for Uleski and his people. Provided, of course, that Uleski was still alive.

'TANGO 77 – THIS IS ROMEO 25 – I NEED AN NBC-1 REPORT AS SOON AS POSSIBLE – OVER.'

'ROMEO 25 – THIS IS TANGO 77 – WE'RE WORKING IT UP NOW – OVER.'

The Team had not been informed by battalion that the Soviets were using chemical weapons. It may have been an oversight on their part. Just in case, Bannon needed to pass on information about the attack as soon as possible. This new aspect only promised to make their existence more intolerable. Bannon decided not to wait for the complete report from 2nd Platoon before informing battalion. This information caused a great deal of concern on the battalion net. Judging from the pitch of the voices and the excited chatter, Team Yankee had been the first unit within the brigade to be hit by chemical weapons. The snap analysis was that the Soviets were anxious to make a breakthrough and were getting desperate. The chemical attack, the massive artillery barrage, and the loss of contact with the XO and the ITVs seemed to signal a change in the Team's fortunes.

The shadows in the valley were getting long. Early evening was upon them, and there was no end of the Soviet attack in sight. The barrage on the hill had been going on unabated for ten minutes without let up. The 2nd Platoon sent up its NBC-1 report indicating that the Soviets were using GB, a nonpersistent blood agent. While that particular agent would not last once the attack was over, GB broke down the protective mask filters rapidly, making them useless. The Team would need to change filters quickly or suffer mass casualties in the next chemical attack.

To Bannon's surprise, another Soviet artillery unit began to lay down a massive smoke screen just in front of the Team's positions. They were going to attack, soon. Bannon had expected the Soviets to wait until night to attack. But apparently they were being pushed by their commanders to break through and could not wait. Not that night would have made much of a difference. The gunners in the tank platoons and those manning the Dragons in the Mech Platoon were already switching to their thermal sights. The smoke screen the Soviet gunners were arduously building would offer the attacking force scant protection, if any.

The 2nd Platoon reported the new attack first. At a range of 2500 metres, the Soviet vehicles appeared as green blobs in the thermal sights. The Soviets were emerging from the tree line on the hill to the Team's right front, across from Team Bravo. They were either going to go straight into the village or through Team Bravo's position. Bannon informed the battalion S-3 of the enemy's appearance and direction of attack. The S-3 replied that Team Bravo was in no shape to fight. With only two functional tanks and three Dragon teams, Bravo would be pressed to protect itself, let alone stop a determined attack. Team Yankee would have to do the major portion of the fighting again.

Because of the range and the quality of the image produced on the thermal sight, it was impossible to distinguish which of the attacking blobs were tanks and which were BMPs. Bannon ordered the 2nd Platoon to engage the lead vehicles with SABOT, assuming that the Soviets would lead off with tanks. The 3rd Platoon was to fire over the village at the centre and rear of the attacking formation as it came out from the tree line. They would engage with HEAT on the assumption that the BMPs would follow their doctrine. The Mech Platoon stood ready to catch anything that got through. With no time left for a co-ordinated ambush like the one the Team had used for the first echelon, Bannon gave the platoons permission to fire and then began to work on getting some friendly artillery into the act.

As the firing commenced, Bannon fumbled with map and grease pencil in the confined space in which a tank commander has to work. The rubber gloves and the protective mask only made it more awkward. As he searched his map for an appropriate artillery target reference point, the hose of his protective mask kept flopping down in front of him, obstructing his view of the map. He had to stop and fling the protective mask carrier, containing the filter, over his shoulder to get the hose out of the way. This succeeded in clearing his view of the map but now the weight of the filter pulled at the hose and kept pulling his head over to one side. That he was able to accomplish anything amazed him. But he succeeded in finding a suitable target reference point, contacted the FSO, and got the call for fire in.

The second attack had caught Garger by surprise. He had not expected the Soviets to be foolish enough to continue the attack in this sector. He had read that the Soviets never reinforce defeat. It was a practice in the Red Army to push everything into the attack that succeeded. They had not succeeded before, and Garger was confident they would not succeed now. Even the artillery impacting to his right, close enough so that the shock waves could be felt, did not alter his opinion. Garger listened to the Team commander's orders and acknowledged them. He sized up the Soviet force that he was to engage and issued his instructions to the platoon. Then he got down to the serious business of killing Russians.

With artillery on the way, Bannon had to catch up on the battle. He called each platoon leader for a SITREP. The 2nd Platoon reported destroying six vehicles but had been unable to stop five vehicles that had disappeared south of the village. Bannon assumed that these tracks were going to swing south, using the village for cover, and either try for the small valley or go up the hill where Team Bravo was. The Mech Platoon had to be ready to deal with them.

The 3rd Platoon, being at closer range, was enjoying a higher percentage of first-round hits. They had dealt easily with the tracks on the slope and were now playing a cat-and-mouse game with Soviet tracks still emerging from the tree line. Observing through his extension, Bannon watched as the 3rd Platoon allowed two or three Soviet tracks to emerge and start down the hill. When they were 100 metres or so from any cover, the whole platoon would fire. In a flash the Soviet tracks, still appearing as green blobs in the thermal sight, would stop, then grow greener as the heat of onboard fires provided a clearer, more intense thermal image.

A Spot Report from Harding, the Mech Platoon leader, alerted Bannon to the fact that the five Soviet tracks that had disappeared to the south of the village were moving up the small valley. The small Soviet force consisted of two T-72s and three BMPs. The platoon leader's voice betrayed no nervousness or confusion. Bannon felt more apprehensive than Harding. It would have been far better, Bannon thought, if there were some tanks in the small valley to deal with the T-72s. He had little confidence in the Dragons' ability to stop tanks.

★It was a disaster, a bloody disaster, and there wasn't a damned thing the Soviet major could do but carry out the insanity he found himself in to its final conclusion. A quick check revealed that only two tanks and two other BMPs had made it with him across the main valley to the small valley. He had no idea what in the hell he was going to do once he reached his objective. That plan had to wait for now. All he wanted to do was to get out of the Americans' kill zone and seek some cover. The major turned his small force towards a walled farm complex in the small valley in the hope he could find some protection there.

The Mech Platoon was ready. Using sound-powered phones connected in a loop, the platoon leader passed his instructions down to Polgar and the squad leaders. The two Dragons and the dismounted infantry in the farm would take out the two T-72 tanks. Polgar, with his two Dragons and the M2 machine guns, would take out the BMPs and provide suppressive fires. For good measure, in case a Dragon missed its mark, the infantrymen in the farm had light antitank rockets, called LAWs, at the ready.

They allowed the Soviets to advance to within 300 metres of the farm before the Platoon cut loose. At that range, it was very difficult to miss with a Dragon. They didn't. On Harding's order, every machine gun and Dragon launcher in the Platoon cut loose. The speed and accuracy with which modern weapons are capable of killing is as awesome as it is frightening. Had they survived the Dragons and the massed machine guns, the Soviets would have been impressed by the performance of the Mech Platoon.

The firing died away slowly. This last fight had lasted some twenty minutes from when the enemy first appeared to when the order came to cease fire. The Soviet artillery barrage on the headquarters position and to the Team's front had stopped. The clearing smoke screen revealed twenty-three newly smashed and burning hulks in the valley to the Team's right front. The eight T-72s and fifteen BMPs amounted to more than a company but less than a motorised rifle battalion. The why of this did not concern them just then. All that was important was that the Soviets had stopped coming. Like two fighters after a round, the opponents were both in their corners, licking their wounds and eyeing each other for the next round.

Reports started to come in from the platoons, but Bannon cut them off and tried to establish commo with Uleski. His calls received no response. Second Lieutenant McAlister, the 2nd Platoon leader, reported that his flank tank could see a burning vehicle to its rear. Bannon immediately contacted First Sergeant Harrert and instructed him to get up to the XO's location with the ambulance and the M-88 recovery vehicle. When the first sergeant acknowledged, Bannon pulled 66 out of position and headed up the hill to the headquarters position.

Enroute he checked in with 2nd Platoon to learn if there was still evidence of a chemical agent. McAlister reported that he had no indications of any agent at his location and requested permission to unmask. This was granted. The 3rd Platoon was instructed to do likewise after they had conducted a survey of their area for contamination. Because 66 was headed into the centre of where the chemical attack had been directed, the crew remained masked.

As they neared the position, the logging trail that had run behind the position ceased to exist. Shell craters and smashed and uprooted trees dimly lit by the failing light of late evening and small fires blocked their passage. Progress was slow as Ortelli carefully picked his way through the debris. Despite his skill, the craters and irregular pattern into which the trees had fallen threatened to throw one of 66's tracks as they proceeded. Through the shattered forest Bannon could make out a burning vehicle.

The condition of the three tracks that had occupied the headquarters position matched that of the shattered forest. One ITV was lying on its side, burning brightly. Its aluminium armoured sides were glowing bright red and collapsing inward. Burning rubber and diesel created a thick, black, rolling cloud of smoke. The TOW launcher of the second ITV was mangled; chunks of electrical components dangled down from the launcher on wires. Set back and in the centre of the ITVs was the 55 tank. Moving around on the right side of the tank were several figures. They were unmasked, so 66's crew unmasked as soon as the tank stopped.

Bannon dismounted and moved towards 55. Uleski was kneeling next to a figure on the ground. He looked at Bannon as he approached, then back at the figure. There were three men lying on the ground and two more sitting up next to 55. Even from where Bannon was, he could see that they were wounded, badly. Two of 55's crew, the gunner and the loader, were working on the wounded men. They were frantic in their efforts, not knowing where to start or how to deal with a body so badly ripped apart.

Bannon's attention was diverted when he stepped on a broken tree branch that gave way under his weight. He looked down, froze, then jumped back in horror. The tree branch was an arm, shredded, torn, and bloody. For a moment, he was unable to do anything except stare at the limb, unable to force himself to think or move. Only when Folk brushed him as he ran by with 66's first-aid kit was he able to proceed. Even then, he walked slowly and carefully, watching where he stepped. The Team's charmed life had run out. It had paid in blood for winning the second round.

After reaching the tank, he looked at each of the wounded men as the crew of 55 and Folk tore at clothing to expose wounds and began to work on them. One of the men had lost a foot. He was in horrible pain, his head rolling from side to side, his arms thrashing the ground next to him. Another soldier beside him simply lay there, not moving. It took a second look to see if he was still breathing. A check of the other three showed they all had their arms. Bannon turned for a moment and surveyed the shattered landscape. The thought that one of his people was out there, smashed and scattered, was repulsive and frightening. Whoever he was, that soldier was beyond help. There were those who needed more immediate attention.

Bannon knelt down beside the body on the ground across from Uleski. For the first time he looked closely. It was Sp4 Thomas Lorriet, the driver for 55. He was from a small town somewhere in Indiana. Lorriet was motionless. His right hand still grasped the hose of his protective mask. His mouth was opened as if he were gasping for air. His eyes were wide open but unseeing, his skin ashen white. He was dead.

Bannon looked up at Uleski who continued to stare at Lorriet. Uleski was shaken. Bannon had never seen him so despondent. After a few moments, the XO finally realised his Team commander was staring at him. He looked back, showing no emotion as he spoke.

'The ITV crews were transferring TOW rounds when the first volley hit. One minute it was quiet, the next all hell broke loose. They didn't know which way to turn. Some just flopped on the ground. Others tried for the tracks. One of the men lying over there was just wounded. He screamed for help but no one went for him. He just kept screaming until the gas reached him. The chemical alarm went off before it was smashed. We all buttoned up and waited. When there was no letup, I ordered Lorriet to back it up. He didn't answer. I started to scream, but he wouldn't answer. I cursed at him and called him every dirty name I could think of. The whole crew started to yell at him to get the tank out of here. The whole tank shook. Smoke and dust and gas seeped in. Shrapnell kept pinging on the outside, and each round sounded as if it was closer than the last. We all yelled at Lorriet till we were hoarse. He didn't answer.'

Uleski paused for a moment. He was starting to tremble. His

71

eyes were filling with tears. He turned away for a moment in an effort to regain his composure. Once he had settled down, he continued, 'After the shelling stopped, we found him like this. His hatch was pulled over but not locked down. He never got his mask on. All the time we yelled at him he was dead. We didn't know, we just didn't know.' These last words trailed off into silence.

The sound of the first sergeant's M-113 and the M-113 ambulance coming up broke the silence. Bannon reached out and grabbed Uleski's shoulder to make sure he was paying attention. 'All right, Bob, I want you to go over to the first sergeant's track and contact the platoons on the company net. I haven't taken any SITREPs from them yet nor have I reported to battalion. Once you've consolidated the platoon reports, send up a Team SITREP to the S-3 and a LOGREP to the S-1 and S-4. Do you have that?'

For a moment Uleski looked at the Team commander as if he were speaking a foreign language. Then he blinked and acknowledged the instructions and slowly picked himself up. Without another word, the XO headed for the first sergeant's track, turning and looking at Lorriet's body one last time.

As the medics, Folk and the loader from 55 worked on the wounded, Bannon grabbed Sergeant Gwent, the gunner on 55, by the arm. 'What's the condition of your tank?'

Gwent looked at him as if he were crazy. He repeated the question. Gwent slowly turned his head to look at his tank for a moment, then back at Bannon.

'I . . . I don't know. We were so busy with the wounded and all. I don't know.'

'OK, OK. I understand. But the medics and the first sergeant can take care of them. I need you to check out that tank and find out if it can still fight. The Russians may come back and the Team needs every track it's got. Get your loader and do a thorough check, inside and out. When you're done, report back to me. Is that clear?' Gwent looked at Bannon, he looked at the tank, then he gave his commander a 'yes, sir' and called his loader over. They both started to walk around the tank, checking the suspension and tracks in the gathering darkness.

As soon as the wounded were on board, the ambulance took off, making the best possible speed. Bannon walked over to the first sergeant and Folk as they watched the ambulance disappear in the darkness. When he closed up on them, Harrert asked about Uleski. Before answering, Bannon turned towards the M-113. He could hear the XO talking on the radio to battalion, sending up the SITREP, line by line. Uleski would be all right. Bannon then told Harrert to search the area for dead and to get a dog tag from each of the bodies, if he could find one. Folk was sent over to the ITV with the damaged launcher to see if it could be driven. As they turned to their tasks, Bannon walked back to 66.

Ortelli was walking around the tank, checking the suspension and tracks. Every now and then he would stop and look closer at an end connector or pull out a clump of mud to check a bolt. When he was satisfied that the bolt was tight, he would go to the next one. Kelp was perched in the commander's cupola, manning the machine gun and monitoring the radio. His eyes followed the first sergeant as he went about his grim task. When Kelp saw Bannon approach, he turned his head back to the east, watching the dark hill across the valley.

Bannon hadn't realised how tired he was until he tried to climb onto 66. He fell backwards when his first boost failed to get him on the tank's fender. He rested for a moment, one foot on the ground, one foot in the step loop, and both hands on the hand grip. With a hop and a pull, he managed to pull his body up. He stood on the fender pondering his next move for a moment. Decisions were becoming hard to make. He moved over to the turret and sat on the gun mantel with both feet on the main gun. He was dead tired, physically and mentally. So much had happened since the morning. His world and the world of every man in the Team had changed. They hadn't budged an inch from where they had been, but the scene before him now was foreign and strange. It was all too much for a tired brain to take in. The Team commander let his mind go blank as he sat there perched over the 105mm cannon of 66.

Folk startled him. For a moment Bannon lost his balance

and almost toppled off the gun mantel. He had fallen asleep. The fearful day had finally ended, and it was dark. The short nap only accentuated his exhaustion. The ITV that had burned was still glowing red, with small fires consuming the last of its rubber. Through the trees he could see smashed Soviet vehicles still burning. Some were like the ITV, red and glowing. Others were still fully involved, yellow flames licking at dense black clouds of smoke rising in the still night air. The shattered and skewed trees and tree trunks added to the unnatural scene.

'Captain Bannon, the battalion commander wants to see you.' First Sgt. Harrert was standing on the ground in front of the tank looking up. They looked at each other while Bannon collected his thoughts. 'Are you OK, Captain?'

'Yeah, Yeah, I'm OK. Give me a minute to get my shit together. Where is the Old Man?'

'He said he's back down where you last saw each other. He wasn't sure how to get in here and didn't want to throw a track finding a way in.'

'Are you finished here, Sergeant?'

'Yes, sir. The other ITV was still running. Newell is going to drive it down to the maintenance collection point. We'll turn it over to the infantry there. 55 is still operational. The only real damage was to the antennas. We replaced them with the spares we carry around and made a radio check. 55's good to go.'

'And bodies?'

'Folk and I moved them over out of the way and covered them with 55's tarp. The location has been reported to S-1. There's nothing more for us to do here.'

Harrert's last comment was more like fatherly advice than a statement of fact. He was right, of course. The hilltop had been a dumb place to put a position. It took three men killed to convince Bannon of that. He had no desire to invest any more here.

He stood on the front slope of the tank and stretched, then, squatting down closer to the first sergeant, he told him to pass word on to the XO to move 55 over to the 2nd Platoon position. Harrert was to follow the XO over. Once there, the first sergeant was to pick up the XO and the 2nd Platoon leader in the PC and bring them over to 66's position to the right of

3rd Platoon. A runner would go for the 3rd and Mech Platoon leaders. No doubt there would be some new information to pass out once he had finished with the battalion commander. There might even be a change of mission. Even if there weren't he still wanted to gather the leadership and assess the impact of the first day's battle on them and their platoons.

The 66 pulled out of the old headquarters position, carefully picking its way through the debris until they reached the logging trail. Once on the trail it only took a couple of minutes to reach their former position. They did not pull all the way up to the berm this time but stayed back in the woods about ten metres. The other tanks had also pulled back just far enough so that they could still observe their sectors without being readily visible to the other people across the valley. The battalion commander was waiting as 66 pulled in.

Bannon had been right on both counts. Colonel Reynolds was there to provide an update on the *big* picture and give him an order for a new mission. Colonel Reynolds had just come from brigade. Rather than pull all the team commanders back to the battalion CP, he was making the rounds and passing the word out himself. Besides, Bannon suspected that Reynolds wanted to gauge the impact of the first day's battle on his team commanders just as Bannon wanted to do with his platoon leaders.

The first item covered was a rundown on the battalion's current situation. Team Yankee had been the only team to engage the enemy within the battalion task force. For a moment, Bannon wondered why the colonel bothered to provide him that brilliant flash of the obvious. Team Bravo had been badly mauled by artillery, losing five of its ten PCs, two of the four ITVs that had been with them, and one of the four 1st Platoon tanks Team Yankee had attached to them. The destroyed tank had taken a direct hit on the top of the turret. The armour on a tank can't be thick everywhere and the top is about as thin as it gets. None of 12's crew survived. Of the remaining three tanks, one had lost a road wheel and hub but had been recovered and would be back up by midnight. Because of the losses, the trauma of being under artillery for so long, and the loss of its commander, Team Bravo had been

75

pulled out of the line. D company, the battalion reserve, had moved up to replace Bravo, to give them a chance to regroup.

C company, to the left of Team Yankee, had had an easy day. They hadn't seen a Russian all day and had not received any artillery fire. The battalion commander told Bannon that the C company commander and his men were chomping at the bit, waiting for a chance to have a whack at the Reds. In a dry and even voice Bannon told the battalion commander that if the gentlemen in C company were so fired up for action, they were welcome to Team Yankee's position, including the bodies. The cold, cutting remark caught Reynolds off guard. He stared at Bannon for a moment, then let the matter drop, moving on to the battalion's new mission.

In the colonel's PC, Bannon received his new orders. On the wall of the PC was a map showing the brigade's sector. The battalion task force was on the brigade's left flank. First Brigade, to the north, had received the main Soviet attack and had lost considerable ground. The attack against the battalion had been a supporting attack.

Bannon throught about that for a moment. The Team's fight had been a sideshow, unimportant in the *big* picture. As that thought rattled around in his mind, he felt like screaming. Here the Team had put its collective ass on the line, fought a superior foe twice, and had three men killed and five wounded in an unimportant sideshow. His ego and pride could not accept that. What was he going to tell Lorriet's mother when he wrote her? 'Dear Mrs Lorriet, your son was killed in a nameless, insignificant sideshow. Better luck next time.' He began to feel angry.

Slowly he became aware that the battalion commander and the S-3 were looking at him. 'May I proceed?' the battalion commander's curt question didn't require a reply. The 1st Brigade would be hard pressed to hold another attack. Intelligence indicated that the Soviet forces in front of 1st Brigade had lost heavily and were no longer able to attack. A second echelon division, the 28th Guards Tank Division, was moving up and was expected to be in position to attack not later than dawn tomorrow. The 28th Guards had been under attack by the Air Force most of the day but could not be stopped. Division had given brigade the mission to attack into the flank of the 28th Guards Division as soon as they were fully committed in the attack.

The Mech Battalion was given the mission of pulling out of the line on order, moving north, and spearheading this attack. The battalion commander was now giving Team Yankee, his tank-heavy team, the mission of spearheading the battalion's effort.

Bannon's mind again wandered off the matter at hand. Somewhere in the division's rear, several hours ago, while Team Yankee was still knee-deep in Russians, the division's commanding general had told his colonels as they surveyed the map: 'Attack there.' While the first sergeant and Sergeant Folk had been dragging the bodies of Team Yankee's dead to an out-of-the-way spot, the brigade commander had told the battalion commander: 'Attack there.' Now the executor of the plan, the lead element commander, the lowest ranking person in the U.S. Army to carry the coveted title of Commander, had his marching orders.

As he received the detailed instructions from the S-3 as to routes, objectives, fire support, and co-ordination instructions, they were joined by the Team's fire-support officer or FIST Team Chief, a 2nd Lt. Rodney Unger. He had finally made it back. He was already familiar with the concept of the operation so there was no need to go over everything. When the S-3 finished, he asked if there were any questions or anything that the Team needed. Bannon's request that the Team be pulled out of the line now to an assembly area for a rest was denied. According to the battalion commander, Team Bravo needed it more than Yankee did. As Team Bravo was going to be in reserve, Bannon requested that the 1st Tank Platoon be returned. That request was also denied. He then requested that an ITV section be attached to the Team to make good their losses. That request too was denied as the other companies without tanks needed some antitank fire power. Seeing that he wasn't going to get anything from battalion but a pat on the back and a pep talk, he stopped asking, and the meeting was over. The battalion commander and the S-3 left

Team Yankee to go down to C company to calm them down before they chewed through their bit.

Uleski had the platoon leaders and the first sergeant assembled in the PC when the battalion commander left. They were exchanging information and observations as Bannon climbed into the track. Before he discussed the new mission, he had each platoon leader update him on the status of his platoon and the condition of the men and equipment. They were all tired but confident. The first day's success had removed many of the fears and doubts that they had had in themselves and in their men. The Team had met the Russians, laser range finder to laser range finder, and found that they were not ten feet tall and could be beaten. Even Uleski was more himself. Bannon began to feel better. The negative thoughts that had kept clouding his mind in the battalion commander's track were fading. The quiet, calm confidence of Team Yankee's leadership gave its commander's flagging morale a needed boost.

According to the book, a leader is supposed to use one-third of the time he has available from when he receives a mission to when he executes it for the preparation of his order. That formula is a good guide, but it seldom works out in practice. Rather than keep the platoon leaders and FIST chief waiting while he came up with his plan, Bannon gave them what information he could. As the platoon leaders copied the graphics of the operation from the commander's map to theirs, Bannon considered his plan of action and quickly wrote some notes for his initial briefing. The briefing included the general situation, the enemy situation, the Team's mission, routes of movement, objectives, and a simple scheme of manoeuvre. The Team may have done well in its first fight, but it had been an easy one, conducted from stationary positions using a plan that had been developed for months. The new mission was an attack, a short notice one at that. He didn't want to do anything fancy or complicated. Simplicity and flexibility were what he wanted.

The Team would use standard battle drill and rely on their

SOP. Order of march out of the position would be the 2nd Platoon with 55 in the lead, followed by 66, the FIST track, 3rd Platoon, and the Mech Platoon. Bannon explained that they would travel with either the two tank platoons up and abreast and the Mech trailing or in column with 3rd Platoon overwatching the advance of 2nd. This scheme put the majority of the Team's combat power forward and left some flexibility to change formations rapidly with minimum reshuffling. Detailed instructions, the artillery fire support plans, and any new information would be provided prior to the move.

After his briefing, Bannon made a quick check with the platoon leaders to answer any questions concerning the new mission. He reminded them to ensure that their platoons stayed alert and on the radio. He also stressed the need to make sure they rotated with their crews when it came to sleeping. He wanted wide awake, alert leaders when the Team went into the attack. With the platoon leaders dismissed, he went over the needs of the Team and the support plan for the attack with Uleski and Harrert.

The news the first sergeant had was not good. The heavy fighting to the north had consumed huge amounts of ammunition, in particular tank main gun ammo. Because the corps ammo resupply point was still being set up, division ordered the brigades to send whatever tank ammunition they had to the 1st Brigade. All the rest of Team Yankee's basic load of ammunition that was supposed to be in the battalion trains area was gone, headed north in the Team's trucks to someone else's tanks. Bannon was too tired to work himself into a rage. The battalion commander and the S-3 had been there for over thirty minutes and had neglected to inform him of this 'minor' point. He began to wonder whose side the battalion commander was on. It almost seemed as if this was some kind of test to see how far Team Yankee could go on its own.

The good news was that the Team would still get a hot meal in the morning, provided there was no interference from the Russians. New protective mask filters would be passed out at that time. The first sergeant had been working on securing them since he heard the news of the chemical attack. He would have enough replacements for the entire Team. An additional day's worth of MREs would also be passed out to add to the two day's supply already on the Team's tracks. The Team was in good shape as far as fuel was concerned, but Bannon wanted to be sure. Harrert was to arrange for a top off right after breakfast, provided battalion hadn't taken the fuel too. The three of them exchanged a few sharp humorous remarks on that subject and, with a chuckle, broke up the meeting. The first sergeant returned Uleski and McAlister to the 2nd Platoon's positions before heading back to the trains area. Bannon headed back for the FIST track to finish the Team's plan.

Second Lt. Rodney Unger was a good FIST Team chief. He still had a lot to learn about tanks and infantry. But he knew about artillery and how to get it. When he was first assigned to the Team as the FIST nine months before, he still had a lot of funny ideas about what his role was and how he wanted to do business. It didn't take long to convince him that a lot of what he had been taught at Fort Sill was best left there. Once that was accomplished, Bannon taught him all the 'Bad' habits FIST chiefs use in the field.

While Unger worked up his initial fire plan based on what he had been given in the first sergeant's track, Bannon started to go over the scheme of manoeuvre in more detail. First he considered how the Soviets might be deployed to defend their flank. All likely locations and fields of fire were marked in red. Satisfied that this 'Russian' plan of defence was plausible, Bannon began to work on the details of how the Team was going to seize its assigned objective quickly and with minimum losses. This time, he methodically went over the actions the Team had to execute in order for it to get from where it was to its objective. Whenever Bannon came across a Soviet field of fire he had plotted, he determined the best way to deal with it. He wanted to bypass wherever possible. When it wasn't possible, he had to plan the best way to destroy the enemy without destroying the Team. This process continued until he had completed the entire route of advance.

Once Bannon finished, Unger superimposed his supporting fire plan over the scheme of manoeuvre. When there was a deficiency or Bannon required a special method of engagement from the artillery, he explained what he wanted, and Unger made the changes. As most manoeuvre commanders are prone to do, he asked for an enormous amount of artillery-delivered smoke. If he could have, he would have moved the Team through one huge smoke screen from where they were all the way to the objective. If every company and team commander were given all the smoke he asked for, all of Germany would have been perpetually shrouded in a dense smoke screen. But reality and the constraints of the artillery basic load reduced his demands. Satisfied with the soundness of the plan, he climbed out of the FIST track and returned to 66 while Unger rumbled off into the night to pass his plan on to the Battalion FSE.

The high-pitched whine of the FIST's modified M-113 faded into the night and was replaced by a stillness punctured at random intervals by distant artillery fire. The moon was out and full. Its pale grey light provided near-perfect visibility of the hill across the valley. Many of the smashed Soviet vehicles still glowed bright red. Fires in the village continued but had died down. Everything else was quiet and peaceful. The casual observer would have been hard pressed to find any sign of life in the valley. It was amazing how quiet hundreds of men, intent on killing each other, could be.

Folk was manning the fifty when Bannon reached 66. Ortelli was asleep in the driver's compartment, and Kelp was lying out asleep on top of the turret. The image of the severed arm and wounded men at 55 flashed through Bannon's mind. Looking at Kelp lying there, exposed to artillery fire and anything else the Soviets might throw at them, he regretted not requiring the tank crews to dig foxholes. He would have to see that that was corrected. At least Kelp had his protective mask on. If nothing else, he was protected from a surprise chemical attack.

He relieved Folk and told him to get a few hours sleep. They would then switch off until stand-to. If the lull continued after stand-to, he would issue his complete order during a working breakfast, then get some more sleep. It was a good plan and he prayed like hell he could implement it.

For the next two hours Bannon stood there alternately

fighting sleep and boredom. He had to change his position every five minutes in order to stay awake and semi-alert. Every hour on the hour 66 and the rest of the tracks would crank up their engines to recharge their batteries. They didn't all come up together but it was close enough. If every vehicle ran its engine on its own, the Soviets would be able to pinpoint every track by the sound of the engines. By running them together, that became more difficult. Once finished, Ortelli would immediately crash back into a deep sleep.

Bannon began to wonder what was happening on the other side of the hill. Even with the muffled rumble of artillery in the distance and the smouldering remains of combat vehicles in the valley before him, it was difficult to think that they were at war. From the Baltic Sea to the Austrian border almost three million men were facing each other, preparing to hack away at the enemy on the other side of the valley, or across the river, or in the next village.

He tried to imagine what the young Russian company commanders were doing in the 28th Guards Tank Division. No doubt they were going over in their minds how they would seize their objectives, trying to guess where their enemy would be and how they would deal with the U.S. forces once they were encountered. He knew enough about Soviet tactics to appreciate that their company commanders had few decisions to make. The regiment made most of the decisions. The battalions and companies simply carried out the orders using fixed formations and battle drill. That made it a lot easier on the Russian company commander. But, if the end results were attacks such as the two Team Yankee had smashed yesterday, Bannon wanted no part of a system like that. Even if he didn't get all the support he wanted, at least he had some control in deciding how to crack the nuts Team Yankee had been given. His only worry now was whether he had guessed right and come up with the best possible plan.

At about 0130 he woke Folk. The gunner needed a few minutes to get himself together. Bannon considered waking Kelp and putting him out as an OP, but that would have left him out there alone and it was a cardinal sin to place one-man outposts. The 3rd Platoon OP to the left and the Mech Platoon

OP to the right covered 66. Each tank was supposed to have half of its crew up and alert. But he saw no useful purpose in waking Kelp. In a moment of weakness, he let him sleep.

Once Folk was ready, they switched places. Rather than Folk rolling up his sleeping bag and Bannon rolling out another, they hot bunked with Bannon using Folk's sleeping bag tonight. It was a normal practice in a tactical environment. Besides, he was ready to crash and didn't feel like screwing around with gear.

With pistol at arm's reach, protective mask on, and the sleeping bag pulled over but not zipped, he could finally let his mind go. The enormousness of the events of the day quietly slipped away. But in their place, personal concerns crept in, concerns and thoughts that had been pushed aside by the needs of Team Yankee. Now, with Team Yankee's needs taken care of for the moment, Bannon's concern about the safety and welfare of his wife and three children could no longer be denied. Where was his family? Had they made it out? Were the air fields still open? Was someone protecting them and caring for them? When would he find out about them? Only sleep quieted the Team commander's troubled mind.

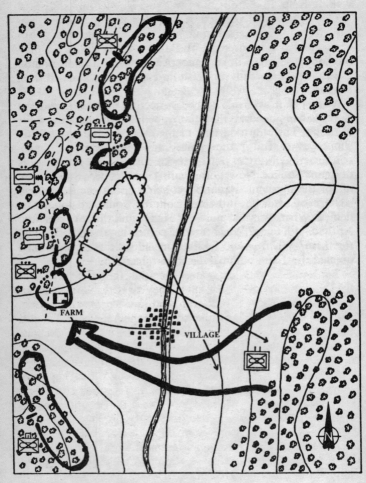

MAP 3: THE SECOND SOVIET ATTACK

Chapter Four

INTO THE VACUUM

★ The quiet chatter of the evacuees watching the loading of the C-141 was drowned out by the blast of air raid sirens. Everyone froze in place, looking at her companions to the left and right, not knowing what to do. An Air Force sergeant began to run up along the window yelling for everyone to get back and down on the floor facing away from the windows. The Air Base would be under air attack in a minute.

Like a deer in a forest fire, Pat turned and looked for a way to safety. She noticed that the stairs leading down to the flight line had a solid wall on both sides. While not offering complete cover, they would be protected from flying glass. Pat yelled to her group to follow her, grabbed Sarah, and ran for the stairs. At the top of the stairs, Pat told everyone to go halfway down and get against the wall on the airfield side. When everyone was accounted for and on the stairs, she followed.

The children huddled against the adult they were with and held their hands over their ears. They all had a look of sheer terror on their faces. Kurt, Sarah, and Jane's baby were crying, Kurt pleading with his mother to make the noise stop. Pat and the other women were barely able to hold back their screams.

From outside in the distance soft muffled explosions of air defence weapons could be heard above the wailing of the siren. The detonations grew closer at an alarming rate. They were joined by the pop-pop-pop of more anti-aircraft guns. Just outside the terminal the report of a gun that sounded like a chainsaw joined in. Then, the first bombs impacted.

A series of crashing explosions outside was mixed with the sound of shattering glass and screams of women and children on the second floor. Now all the children were crying and screaming. Fran pulled Sean and Debby in closer. Sue, tears running down her face, held on to Kurt, trying to cover his ears and face. Jane and Pat did the same with the babies. Just as the tinkling of glass and the screams from upstairs began to

85

subside, another series of bombs went off closer to the terminal, blowing out more glass and causing the screams to begin anew.

They were going to die. They were all going to die. This trip was no longer one of inconvenience and discomfort. It had become a life and death ordeal. Any second now the next series of bombs could hit the terminal and they would all be dead. Pat was horrified. What had she ever done to deserve this? What harm had her children ever done to anyone? What purpose would their deaths serve? It wasn't fair. It wasn't right. Pat began to weep and rock Sarah in a vain attempt to comfort her baby.

At the height of the bombing, an Air Force officer without a hat came running in from the flight line and began to run up the stairs. He noticed the group and stopped. He looked at them for a moment, then yelled, 'YOU PEOPLE, FOLLOW ME. QUICKLY!'

Pat looked at the officer, the other women looked at Pat. The officer reached down and grabbed Pat's arm. 'COME ON. FOLLOW ME. I'M TAKING YOU OUT OF HERE NOW.'

Pat thought anywhere would be better. There must be a shelter the officer was taking them to under the terminal. Pat got up and yelled to her group to follow the officer. Fran told him to carry Sean while she picked up Debby and began to follow. Pat waited to make sure that her group was in motion before she followed, taking up the rear.

Pat reached the bottom of the stairs and turned the corner. To her horror she saw that the officer had gone out of the door and was running out onto the flight line. The rest of her group was following obediently. What were they doing? Was that man mad? Why are we going away from shelter? After a brief moment of hesitation, she ran after them. She had to. The officer had Sean and Sue had Kurt. She had to go.

Once outside the pop-pop-pop, the detonations, and the gun that sounded like a chainsaw became louder. The giant C-5 that had been taxiing up to the terminal had been hit and was now burning and shaking from explosions, its huge wings drooping down to the ground like an injured bird. Together with the siren, it drowned out the officer's voice when he turned to scream something to them. Pat saw the C-141 beyond him. He was running straight for it. He was going to get them out of here. Pat's heart began to beat faster as she picked up her pace. A chance to survive. A chance to escape this madness. This was it. She would use whatever reserve she had left on this one last effort. All or nothing.

The group ran. The officer began to swerve to avoid a shell crater on the flight line. The line of women followed. As they swerved around the next crater, Fran suddenly stopped dead, causing Sue to ram into her from behind. The officer saw her stop, turned, and ran back. Pat caught up and looked down.

There in front of the women were the remains of several bodies tossed about the flight line. The brightly coloured clothing was civilian, not military. Some of the people headed for the C-141 before the attack had been caught in the open and killed. The officer had come back for more evacuees to take their place.

Pat looked up, saw the officer coming back with Sean. No, she wasn't going to let anything go wrong this time. Every step of the way during this evacuation had been screwed up. Now, when they were only a few feet away from their means of salvation, Pat was determined they were going to finish this trip. Pat pushed Fran and yelled at her to go. When Fran began to run, Pat pushed Sue along behind her. Jane followed. The officer stopped, let Fran catch up to him, then grabbed her with one arm and pulled her along.

The crew chief of the C-141 came down the ramp and helped the women up. Another airman inside pushed them over to some empty nylon seats arranged along the sides and middle of the aircraft's cavernous body. As soon as they were all on board, the officer handed Sean to the crew chief who threw the boy on a seat and buckled him in. The officer then ran down the ramp and back to the terminal. He was halfway there when the closing ramp shut out the view of the shattered flight line.

The crew chief and airman buckled in the new arrivals as the plane began to roll. The dark interior of the aircraft was full of women and children. Their sobs inside and the sound of the air attack outside were drowned out by the roar of the engines. It sounded and looked as it they were inside of a huge vacuum cleaner.

The plane picked up speed. The pilot was just as anxious to leave as Pat was. The lift-off was quick and steep, causing a chain reaction as everyone was thrown sideways into the person seated next to her. When the pilot quickly levelled the plane, everyone was thrown back towards the front. The climb hadn't been much. Pat turned and looked out a small porthole-like window behind her. The plane was skimming along at tree top level and moving fast. The pilot apparently didn't want to go high and become mixed up in the air battle.

Pat turned and surveyed her little group. There was a blank, emotionless stare on the face of every woman and child. They were drained, exhausted, listless. The climax of their ordeal had finally succeeded in beating the last bit of energy and emotion out of them. The long flight home was made in silence, only the steady drone of the engines filling the cavelike interior.

Bannon was not ready to wake. It was too soon, far too soon to end his retreat from reality and misery. Even with the protective mask on and lying on the hard turret roof, the sleeping bag was too comfortable to surrender without a struggle. It was too damned soon to get up. But Folk was persistent. As soon as he registered a muffled obscenity and some independent movement on his commander's part, he stopped shaking.

In less than thirty minutes it would be dawn. The second day of World War III; and just as difficult to greet as the first had been. The pain from sleeping on a hostile surface, the dullness of the mind from too little sleep, and the realisation that this day would be no better than the last was a poor way to begin the day.

Sitting up, he leaned forward and squinted at Folk, trying to see if he was masked. Satisfied that he wasn't, Bannon removed his protective mask, the cool morning air hitting his face. After sweating for two hours with the rubber mask against his skin, the air felt like a slap in the face. Looking around, he saw Kelp stowing his gear. Folk ordered Ortelli to crank up the tank. It was 0400. In the dark forest, the sound of other tracks doing likewise could be heard. At least some of the Team was awake and alert.

As soon as Bannon was ready to climb down to his position, Folk slid to the gunner's position. Still groggy but at least functioning, the crew went through their checks while they waited for stand-to and the new dawn. Computer checks. Weapon checks. Thermal sight check. Engine readings and indications. Ammo stowage and count. The 66 tank was ready.

Just before dawn, Lieutenant McAlister called. He and his platoon were observing a group of six to eight personnel in the woods across the valley from them. Early morning is the best time for detecting targets with the thermal sight because the ground and trees lack any warmth from the long absent sun. McAlister wanted to engage with the platoon's calibre .50s. Bannon vetoed that idea and opted to hit the intruders with artillery instead. That way they would cause the same amount of damage, or more, without having any of the Team's tanks expose themselves. His best guess was that the dismounted intruders were there in order to locate the Team and either call in and adjust artillery or engage with antitank guided missiles. Either way, they had to go.

McAlister contacted the FIST Team. Using a known target reference point to shift from, he provided Unger with the location of the target and what the target was. Bannon cut into the conversation and instructed Unger to fire at least three volleys of artillery with mixed fuse settings of superquick and delayed. The superquick fuse setting would go off as soon as the round hit the tree branches, creating an air burst effect and showering shell fragments down on exposed personnel. The delayed fuse setting would burrow into the ground, hopefully getting anyone in foxholes. The FIST replied that he would try. Bannon told him to try hard.

The call for fire took close to five minutes to process. At this hour, it was not surprising. Everyone waited impatiently, hoping that the Russians didn't leave before the artillery hit. It was almost as if they were preparing to spring a prank on another fraternity. They knew it was coming and the other people didn't. But this prank was deadly. In a very few moments, some of the other 'fraternity' brothers would be dead. The more, the better. Maybe they wouldn't come back.

To the rear of Team Yankee the low rumble of the firing guns could be heard as the FIST called, 'SHOT – OVER' on the Team net. McAlister replied, 'SHOT – OUT.' Unger's call of 'SPLASH – OVER' was drowned out by the detonation of the impacting rounds.

In an excited, high-pitched voice, McAlister called, 'TARGET – FIRE FOR EFFECT – TARGET – FIRE FOR EFFECT.' In the excitement of the moment, he forgot that they were, in fact, firing for effect. From 66, Bannon could see the impact through the trees. He wanted to move forward to observe but knew that would serve little purpose and unnecessarily expose 66. So he sat where he was, having to content his morbid curiosity by listening to McAlister's reports.

The guns to the rear boomed again, followed by another series of impacts. The rounds with superquick fuse settings burst high in the trees with a brilliant orange ball of fire. For a split second, it lit the surrounding trees and area like a small sun. Then it died as fast as it had appeared. Anyone staring at the blast lost his night vision. In the place of clear images there was only the fading after-image of the bright orange blasts engraved in their eyes. The final volley was no less spectacular.

As Bannon waited for the results, he began to hope that the results would be worth the efforts of the artillery. More was involved than merely the act of making the calculations, preparing the rounds, laying the guns, and shooting twenty-four rounds.

The firing battery now had to displace rapidly. If the Russians were alert, their target acquisition people would have picked up the flight of these incoming rounds. With some calculations of their own, they would be able to locate the guns and fire counter-battery fires. It was therefore important for the artillery to keep moving. Shoot'n scoot was a popular way of putting it. In modern combat you're either quick or you're dead. There is no middle ground.

After observing the area for ten minutes, McAlister reported that neither he nor any other tank in his platoon could detect any more movement in the target area or to the left or right.

Bannon therefore reported to battalion that they had engaged and probably killed eight dismounted personnel. Whatever those people had been doing or planning to do, they weren't going to do it to Team Yankee this morning. The efforts of the cannon cockers were rewarded.

The Soviets were also placing demands on their artillerymen early that morning. The American guns barely had fallen silent when the sky to the east was lit up with distant flashes, followed by the now familiar rumble of enemy artillery. At first, Bannon thought that it was counterbattery fire searching out the guns that had just fired for the Team. But the distant crash of the impacting rounds drifted down from the north, not from the rear. After watching and listening to the barrage for five minutes and unable to detect any sign of letup, it became obvious that this was more than counterbattery fire. In all likelihood, it was the preparatory fire for the attack of the 28th Guards Tank Division.

The night slowly gave way to the new dawn as the Soviet artillery preparation to the north continued. First Sergeant Harrert appeared with breakfast, passing the word to the track commanders to send half of their men at a time back for chow. At first Bannon was apprehensive about allowing the men to dismount for breakfast. He was fearful that the enemy would launch another holding attack against them as they had yesterday. If not a ground attack, he at least expected the Soviets to pin the battalion down with artillery. But nothing happened. Perhaps the Soviets didn't have any more units they could throw away in useless holding attacks. Perhaps the people the Team had hit with artillery across the valley were antitank guided missile teams or artillery forward observers who had the mission of pinning the battalion. Perhaps, perhaps, perhaps. As the platoon leaders began to gather for the early morning meeting, he gave up on the second guessing. No one was shooting at him or the Team right now and that was all that mattered.

The leadership of Team Yankee gathered around the rear of the first sergeant's PC, map case and notebook tucked under arm, breadfast and coffee in hand as they had done just twenty-four hours earlier. But this morning there was a difference. The nervous apprehension of yesterday was gone. There was a slightly haggard and dishevelled look from too little sleep and too much stress. That was to be expected. Today, however, there was also a look of confidence on everyone's face, a calm, steady look. In the words of Civil War veterans, they had seen the elephant and had changed forever.

It didn't matter that they had been incredibly lucky, that the task had been simple and straightforward. It didn't matter that the new mission was going to turn the tables around and expose the Team to the same punishment that it had given to the Soviets. What did matter was that they had won their first battle and any doubts as to equipment, leadership, and each individual's perceived ability to face combat had been temporarily put aside. The Team was ready to move forward and tackle its new mission.

The meeting started with a discussion of the previous day's action. Just as they had done numerous times after a training exercise, the leaders went over step by step what had happened. First the platoon leaders gave their account and observations. Then Bannon gave his. They briefly discussed what needed to be done better the next time. With that aside, Bannon issued the completed Team operations order that he had worked on earlier that morning. After he finished, Unger went over the fire-support plan in detail and answered any questions. Finished with that, Bannon informed the platoon leaders that he would visit each of them for a one-on-one brief back of their platoon plans. In the meantime, they were to prepare for the attack.

As he prepared to turn the meeting over to the XO and first sergeant so that they could cover the Team's admin and maintenance chores, a call from battalion put an end to his plan to catch up on some sleep. There was going to be a meeting in thirty minutes at the battalion CP to go over the new mission. Not wanting to move 66 out of position, he decided to use Harrert's PC. While the platoon leaders moved and the PC prepared to roll, Bannon quickly shaved and washed his hands and face. Cleaning up was going to make him late, but it was a matter of pride that he look as sharp as possible. He might be miserable, but he didn't have to look miserable. Standards had to be preserved.

The lack of change at the battalion CP struck Bannon as odd. He really couldn't say what should have been different. But something should have been. Back at Team Yankee he could feel the change that had occurred between yesterday morning and this morning. At the CP, all was still running as if a training exercise was being conducted. The M-577 command post vehicles were parked side by side with their canvas tent extensions set up and connected. A massive camouflage net covered the tracks and extensions. Around this was barbed wire with one entrance guarded by a soldier checking access passes as staff officers and other commanders entered the tactical operations centre, or TOC. Somehow, things should have been different.

While the outside was quiet and peaceful, the inside was utter chaos. There were staff officers and NCOs busily updating and preparing their maps and charts for the briefing. Team commanders were in one corner talking and joking. The battalion commander and his XO sat in the middle talking over maintenance and supply matters. All the running around, confusion, and last-minute preparation by the staff made Bannon wonder what they had been doing all night. But that wasn't really hard to figure out. The lack of haggard faces and bags under eyes betrayed the fact that late nights and little sleep were not part of their daily schedule. He wondered how long that would last.

Off to one side by himself was First Lieutenant Peterson, formerly the XO, now the commander, of Team Bravo. In sharp contrast to the staff and the other commanders, his uniform and gear were dirty and dishevelled, his expression gaunt and without emotion. Bannon watched for a few minutes while Peterson simply sat there, staring at his notebook. Everyone in the crowded TOC was making a valiant effort to ignore him, even to the point to taking the long way around if they had to go from one end of the centre to the other. He had been under fire and his team had been hit hard. Those who hadn't 'seen the elephant' yet didn't know how to treat him, so they left him alone. Ignored him was more correct.

Bannon felt sorry for Peterson. Yesterday had been an emotional nut roll for Team Yankee despite the fact that he had been in command for ten months and had been training for what happened. It must have been hell for Peterson to watch his team get ripped to shreds, then be given the job of putting the remains together again. The treatment the staff was giving Peterson was, Bannon felt, cold and inappropriate.

The battalion XO, Major Willard, began by going over the briefing sequence and then instructed the intelligence officer, or S-2, to start. With pointer in hand and every hair in place, he began to talk about the *big picture*. He talked about how the 'hostile forces' had 'initiated hostilities,' how this combined arms army was driving here and that combined arms army was pushing there and some tank army was moving forward ready to exploit the penetration to our north.

The situation in NORTHAG, or Northern Army Group, was grim. Soviet airborne forces had seized Bremerhafen. Soviet ground forces were making good progress and had broken through in several areas. In CENTAG, Central Army Group, the situation wasn't nearly as bad. Both forward-deployed U.S. corps were in CENTAG. While one could immediately claim that U.S. forces made the difference, anyone who understood the overall strategy knew better. The terrain in NORTHAG was more conducive to massed, mobile warfare than the hilly, heavily forested south. The North German Plain provided a natural highway for armies to flow from the east to the west through Germany into Holland, Belgium, and France. By luck of the draw and post-World War II agreements, the U.S. had the easiest and least important area to defend.

Bannon sat waiting patiently to hear about the enemy forces that were across the valley from the Team and the composition, locations, and strength of the forces in the area where the battalion was going to attack. He wanted to know about nuts and bolts, and the S-2 was lecturing on skyscrapers. When the S-2 finished and turned to sit down without mentioning a thing about the Soviet forces they faced or were going to face, Bannon half jumped out of his seat.

'Wait a minute! What about the people across the valley from us? What are they doing now and what do you expect them to do?'

For a moment, the S-2 looked at Bannon as if he didn't understand the question. 'Oh. Well, I don't think they will be doing much after the pounding we gave them.' He continued to his seat.

Bannon was livid! The pounding *we* gave them! 'What kind of bullshit answer is that? And what's this *we* shit? Except for a few shots from the scouts, I only know of one team that engaged the 'hostile forces yesterday.'

In a flash, the battalion commander jumped up and turned to face Bannon. With his index finger almost touching Bannon's nose and his face contorted with rage, he laid into him. 'That will be enough, Bannon. If you got a burr up your ass about something, you see me after this. We got a lot to cover and not a lot of time. Is that clear?'

Bannon had overstepped his bounds, lost his cool, and offended Colonel Reynolds and his staff. But he wasn't going to buckle under either. The S-2 hadn't given him a single piece of useful information that would contribute to the success of the upcoming mission. Bannon wanted that information. 'Sir, with all due respect, the S-2 hasn't told me squat about the enemy now facing me or those we will be attacking. I need to know what they are doing and where they are if we're going to pull this attack off.'

'With all due respect, Captain, I recommend that you shut up and pay attention.' The battalion commander had spoken, and the conversation was terminated. Without waiting for any sign of acknowledgement, he turned around and sat down, instructing the S-3 to proceed. Chances were the S-2 really didn't know what was happening anyway. Bannon dropped the matter.

The battalion S-3 stood up, prepared to present his portion of the briefing. Maj. Frank Jordan, the S-3, was an outstanding officer and a professional by any measure. He more than made up for the shortcomings of the other battalion staff officers and was the real driving force behind the battalion. Colonel Reynolds might make the final decisions and do the pushing in the field, but it was Jordan who developed the battalion's game plans and made all the pieces fit. He also was easy to work with. After waiting a moment until everyone was settled again, he began his briefing.

The organisation of the battalion, or task force, as a battalion with tanks and infantry companies combined is called, remained as it had been from the beginning. The friendly situation, or the mission of the units to the battalion's left and right as well as the mission of the battalion's higher headquarters, hadn't changed from what the S-3 had briefed last night. 'Our mission is as follows: Task Force 3-78 Mech will attach at 0400 hours Zulu 6 August to seize the town of Arnsdorf. The task force will then continue the attack to the north to seize the high ground south of Unterremmbach, north east to the bridge at Ketten am Der Hanna or west against objects yet to be determined.'

Jordan then began to explain the plan of how the battalion would carry out its new mission. It was basically the same plan that he had explained the night before. The main difference was that he tied together a lot of the loose ends and explained what would happen after the battalion got to Arnsdorf. They would be relieved in place that night by the divisional cavalry squadron starting at 2400 hours Zulu. One company at a time would pull out of line and begin to move north towards the new area of operations. Team Bravo, now in reserve, would lead the battalion. Team Yankee would be the first unit to pull out of line, followed by company C and company D in that order. Once the battalion was closed up on Team Bravo, it would move north. The route was not the most direct, as division wanted to deceive the Soviets as to the intent of the battalion and the point of attack for as long as possible. If all worked out as planned, they would arrive at the line of departure, or LD, on time and would roll straight into the attack without stopping.

The battalion would attack in columns of companies – one

company behind the other. When they approached the town of Kernsbach, they would leave the road and move cross-country. Just east of Kernsbach they would pass through the U.S. front lines and begin to deploy. Team Bravo would move to the high ground northeast of Kernsbach and take up overwatch positions in the northern edge of the Staat Forest, from which it would be able to cover the movement of Team Yankee. Major Jordan did not expect that Team Bravo would encounter any sizable enemy forces during this manoeuvre. If there were any enemy force, they would be reconnaissance and would give ground quickly. Once Team Bravo moved into position, Team Yankee would be in the lead.

Team Yankee, followed by company C and overwatched by Team Bravo, would first attack and seize an intermediate objective called Objective LOG located midway between the line of departure, Team Bravo's location, and Arnsdorf. Once Team Yankee had cleared Objective LOG, company C would turn west and seize the village of Vogalburg. Company D, the trail company, would close up behind Team Yankee once company C was out of the way. Team Yankee was not to stop but was to continue to move north to Hill 214, called Objective LINK. From the north slopes of Hill 214, Team Yankee would take up positions to overwatch company D, much the same as Team Bravo had done for Team Yankee before, and cover the attack of company D as they moved in and seized Arnsdorf. Once in Arnsdorf, the brigade commander would then decide where the battalion would strike. This would depend upon the situation at that time and the reactions of the Soviets to an attack into their flank.

There were aspects of the plan that made Bannon uneasy. The total lack of information on enemy strength and disposition was number one on his list. The seizure of Vogalburg by company C appeared to be unnecessary and dangerous. They would be out there alone, unable to receive support from other battalion elements. Their presence in Vogalburg would, however, protect the left flank of Team Yankee as it was moving to Hill 214. So he didn't raise any objections over that issue.

The issue he did object to was the lack of artillery

preparation on Objective LOG. That position was just too good a position not to be occupied by the Soviets. When the S-3 finished and asked for questions concerning the execution of the mission, Bannon recommended that a short but violent artillery prep followed by smoke be put on that objective. Both the S-3 and the colonel denied the request, stating that the element of surprise would be lost. Apparently, they expected the attack to be so fast that anyone there would be unable to react in time. Besides, they assured Bannon that Team Bravo would be in overwatch and artillery would be ready to fire if needed. Unger and he exchanged glances. After his tiff with the S-2, anything Bannon said was bound to be wrong, and he was not in the mood for another public flogging by the colonel.

The S-3 was followed by the battalion S-4, who briefed on the current status of supply and maintenance, supply routes, and a myriad of other details. As they were all covered in a written order that they had been handed, Bannon tuned him out. He began to go over the map sitting in his lap, looking at the operation again from beginning to end in an effort to make sure he understood all of the missions and tasks Team Yankee had to perform. There is nothing worse than to leave a battalion briefing, go back to the company, give an order, then have one of the platoon leaders ask a question on a point that had been missed. As they were playing for real this time, Bannon wanted to make damn sure that he didn't miss anything.

The colonel's rousing 'Let's go kick ass and take names' speech at the end of the briefing brought Bannon back to the here and now. Reynolds knew he had not been paying attention to the last portion of the briefing and especially to his 'go get 'em' speech. Bannon didn't really care. His Team was only an attachment, a very bothersome one at that, and therefore he was expected to be somewhat different and a bit of a maverick. Today had been a good case in point. With the company C commander chanting obscene ranger chants, the briefing broke up.

On his way out, Bannon briefly stopped in front of the intelligence map to see if there was any useful information he could glean from it. The S-2 watched him as if he expected

Bannon to turn and attack. After studying the red lines and symbols for a couple of minutes without being able to find anything of use, he gave up and left. Team Yankee would find out soon enough what was there, the hard way.

The balance of the day passed rather slowly. After arriving back at the Team position, Bannon made another analysis of the terrain they would be covering. Satisfied that he had gotten as much as he could from his map, he rewrote those parts of the plan that had changed because of the briefing at battalion and the second map study. In reality, not much had changed. A few new artillery targets, a better concept for crossing the stream west of the village of Lemm, and some more information on what would happen after Arnsdorf was all. With that finished, he sent Kelp with word to the platoon leaders that they were to assemble at 66 at 1300 hours for an update and further instructions.

Throughout the morning the Team had gone on about its business in a slow and deliberate way. After stand-to, the checks and inspections that had not been performed while waiting for the dawn were completed. All problems that turned up were reported to the platoon sergeants, who in turn reported them to the first sergeant, who in turn reported them to maintenance personnel. There were several tanks being worked on when Bannon returned from battalion.

Once the checks were complete, the weapons were cleaned. First, the crew-served weapons. Every tank and personnel carrier had one M2 calibre .50 machine gun, called a Ma Duce. It was the same heavy machine gun the Army had used in World War II and was still one of the best. This was the tank commander's weapon. Then there were two 7.62mm machine guns, M240s, on each tank. These were of Belgian design and were good weapons. One was located next to the main gun, mounted coaxially with it, hence its nickname 'COAX'. The second M240 was mounted on a free-swinging mount outside the loader's hatch. The loader had little need for a weapon as his primary job was to feed the main gun. But since the loader's M240 was interchangeable with the COAX, it had value.

Besides, it gave the loader something to hang onto when the tank was moving.

While some of the platoon were working on the machine guns, three or four of the men went around cleaning out the main guns with a twenty foot rammer staff topped with a bore brush. It took three to four men to manoeuvre the staff and then ram the tight-fitting brush down the gun tube. Rather than have each crew assemble its own staff, the platoon sergeant had one tank, usually his, put one together and then had one man from each crew on the detail. It was efficiency and teamwork in action.

After the tanks and the personnel carriers with all their crew-served weapons were squared away, each man's individual weapon was cleaned. For the tankers, this was a calibre .45 pistol for the tank commander and the gunner. The driver and loader each had a .45 and a calibre .45 M3 submachine gun. This last weapon also was a veteran of World War II, but it had not aged as well as the M2 machine gun. Some said the M3 was worthless. Bannon always considered that rating too generous.

Only after all the equipment had been squared away were the men free to tend to their personal needs and hygiene. The Team worked under the old cavalry principle, 'The horse, the saddle, the man.' The men understood this and for the most part abided by it. The majority on the second day wished they were elsewhere, but they were not elsewhere, and the war wasn't going away. They didn't know what was going to happen next, but they did realise that their best chance of survival was to stay with the Team. They knew what the Team was doing, and there was safety in numbers. What lay behind the hills to the front and rear was now a mystery that none was interested in exploring. They wanted to stay with the Team, and to stay with the Team, their track and weapons had to work. There was no false patriotism, no John Waynes, only tankers and infantrymen doing their jobs and surviving.

Except for some sporadic shelling by the Soviets, the afternoon passed quietly. The tank commanders and squad leaders kept half of their men on alert while the rest slept. After the 1300 hour meeting with the platoon leaders, Bannon was able to catch up on some personal needs. Washing from head to toe was a priority. After twenty-four hours in the chemical protective suit, he was ripe. The only reason no one else had noticed was because they were equally dirty and smelly. It had only been at the battalion CP that he had noticed how filthy he was in comparison to people who were not – the battalion staff. At battalion, however, he really hadn't cared if he had offended anyone. Once clean again, he let Uleski know that he was checking out the net and finally took time to get some sleep.

His sleep lasted exactly forty-five minutes. The cavalry troop commander and platoon leaders from the troop that would be relieving the Team that night showed up for co-ordination and a reconnaissance. They were from B troop 2nd of the 14th Cavalry, the divisional cavalry squadron. He had met the troop commander several times before so he was surprised when a tall, lanky first lieutenant introduced himself as the troop commander. Bannon asked what had happened to the man he had met and was told that he was missing in action.

The former troop commander had given the order for the troop to withdraw and after that was not seen again. He, his personnel carrier, and its crew had all disappeared while they were moving back to their next position. This put a chill on the co-ordination meeting and the recon. Conversation was limited to simple questions and answers as to the positions, enemy activities, and the lay of the land. As soon as the first lieutenant was satisfied that he had all the information he needed, he and his platoon leaders left.

Towards dusk the Soviets became really restless and began a massive shelling to the rear of the Team. Everyone either buttoned up in his tracks or made friends with the bottom of his foxhole as scores of shells screamed overhead, searching for targets in the battalion's rear. Their fears were only partially relieved by the fact that it could have been worse; those shells could be hitting the Team itself. They waited patiently, alert and ready for either a ground attack or a shift in the artillery fire onto their positions. Given a choice, the ground attack was the more inviting prospect. At least they could do something to the attacking troops. The enemy was in the open. He could be seen, hit, and destroyed. That wasn't true of artillery. Of course friendly artillery could direct counterbattery fires against the Soviet guns. But that wasn't the same. The Team, the target, would not be able to do anything but hunker down and pray. A ground attack would be better.

As it turned out, neither occurred. As the day finally ended, the Team began to prepare for the move. While the rest of the crew prepared, Bannon pondered the meaning of the prolonged artillery attack. Had the Soviets somehow gotten wind of the planned move? Had they destroyed the roads and bridges to the rear? Had Team Bravo been hit again, or had it been the turn of the battalion CP to see the elephant? Would Soviet artillery strike again while they were moving? He of course did not have the answers, and the silence on the battalion radio net remained unbroken. He therefore turned his efforts to a more useful pursuit, dinner.

At 2345 hours the Team started their engines and revved them up to as near normal operating RPMs as possible. As they were not going to have friendly artillery fire to cover the noise of the movement, they hoped that by running the engines all together, the Soviets might not notice any change in established habits. Chances of that working for long were slim, however; the highpitched squeak of a tank's sprockets and the crunching noise of the tracks in motion could not be covered. But it was worth a try.

The cavalry troop began to arrive on schedule for the relief in place. They came up along a small trail that ran west to east to the rear of the 2nd Platoon. The 2nd Platoon began the relief by pulling back from the tree line and moving south along the trail. As soon as the 2nd was out of its position and cleared the trail junction, the first cavalry platoon moved in where 2nd Platoon had been. As the 2nd moved farther down the trail, Bannon counted the tanks passing in the darkness. When the fifth passed, he gave Ortelli the order to move. The 66 fell into line behind the last 2nd Platoon tank. The movement of 66, followed by Unger's FIST track, was the signal for the 3rd Platoon to begin its move, and they too swung out onto the trail and began to follow. As with 2nd Platoon, as soon as the last 3rd Platoon tank pulled out, the second cavalry platoon began to move into 3rd Platoon's vacated positions. The process was repeated with the Mech Platoon, which followed the 3rd. In this way, two company-sized units changed places in the dark without a single word other than that between the track commanders and their drivers.

Uleski, leading the Team, hugged the tree line on the northern side of the small valley that the Soviets had tried so hard to reach. When he reached a point about three kilometres west of the village, he moved onto the road and slowly began to pick up speed at a predetermined rate. Had he gone too fast at the beginning, the Mech Platoon at the tail of the column would have been left behind, as they were still hugging the tree line. When the column finally reached the designated march speed, Bannon began to relax. So far, all was going well. The relief had gone off without a hitch and the Team had gotten out of the line without drawing fire. Now they were on the route of march about to hit the first checkpoint along the route on time. This was a good omen. If the rest of the operation went off this well, it would be a piece of cake.

The drive through the dark countryside was quiet and eerie. The only lights visible were the small pinpricks from the taillights of the tank in front and the blackout drive lights of the tank behind. The steady whine of the tank's turbine engine along with the rhythmic vibrations caused by the tracks had a hypnotic effect. Bannon had to make an effort to pay attention to where they were as the column moved along. Reading a map with a covered and filtered flashlight on a moving tank while trying to pick out terrain features on the darkened countryside was difficult but not impossible. Although Uleski was leading, Bannon needed to monitor exactly where they were at all times as a check on Uleski's navigation and in case something unexpected popped up. The platoon leaders and platoon sergeants were expected to do the same.

On board the tank all was quiet. Both the Team and the battalion radio nets were on radio listening silence. If the radios were used freely, Soviet radio direction finding units would be able to follow them and keep track of where they were going. Kelp was standing on his seat, halfway out of the turret and facing to the rear of the tank. He was the air guard. It was SOP that the loader would watch to the rear for air attack and any surprises from that quarter. Folk, in his seat, was fighting sleep. He was having little success. During a road march the gunner was supposed to cover his assigned sector of observation at all times. But when there is a whole column in front and little prospect of action, it is difficult to maintain a high state of vigilance. But Bannon knew that when he needed him, Folk would be on his sight and ready.

Every ten minutes or so Bannon talked to Ortelli. Marching in column like this is worst for the driver. Not only does he have to fight the hypnotic effects of the steady engine noise and vibration, but he must also keep alert to any changes in the distance and speed of the tank in front of him. Drivers moving in column had a tendency to stare at the taillights of the tank in their front and become mesmerised by them. When that happens, they are slow to notice a sudden change in distance. Rear end collisions are common under such conditions. Therefore, tank commanders tried to ensure that even if no one else was alert, the driver was.

As they moved deeper into the rear area, other traffic and friendly units began to appear. The farther back the Team went, the more numerous they became. At first, there were the combat support forces and the artillery units. Team Yankee went past a self-propelled artillery battery lined up but pulled off to the side of the road. Apparently they were waiting for the battalion to pass. Every now and then a single vehicle or a group of three or four trucks would pass headed in the opposite direction towards the front, probably supply vehicles of units still there. At road junctions, MPs directed traffic, alternately letting one vehicle from the battalion column go through, then one from another column on the intersecting road go through. Occasionally the Team would pass lone vehicles on the side of the road. Some were broken down. Some had been destroyed by artillery or air attacks.

The villages the Team passed were now populated with a new class of inhabitants. Signal units, headquarters units, and support units of every description had moved in and set up housekeeping. Night was the time when many of these units came to life to do the majority of their work, especially supply units. They were in a hurry to resupply their units for the next round and get back under cover before the new day brought out the Soviet birds of prey that feed on supply convoys.

It was just after passing through one of these busy little hubs of nocturnal activity that the Team hit its first snag. The 66 lurched to an abrupt halt without warning. At first, Bannon thought they had hit something. Ortelli informed him that they were all right, but that the tank in front had stopped. Bannon watched its dark form for a few minutes, expecting it to move out and continue the march. When it didn't, he became concerned and decided to dismount and walk up to the head of the column. Whatever was wrong, it wasn't serious enough to break radio listening silence. As he dismounted, Folk moved up into the commander's position, just in case.

Bannon was not happy about the disruption in the march but was thankful for the chance to walk around some, stretch his legs, and break the monotony. It was 0345 Alpha time. They had been moving for almost three hours and were scheduled to attack in another hour and fifteen minutes. As he moved up the column, he noticed a lot of activity in front of the Team and in the fields at the side of the road. There were lights on all over just a little beyond the head of the column.

Uleski was already dismounted and talking to some people when Bannon arrived. As he reached the group, he noticed that it was an engineer unit and that the people in front of the column and in the fields beyond were working on sections of a combat bridge.

'Well, Ski, what do we have?'

'Sir, this is Captain Lawson, commander of the 79th Bridge Company.' Uleski motioned to a tall captain across from him, then continued, 'His people put this ribbon bridge in earlier today. When Team Bravo crossed it, too many tanks got onto the bridge at once and did some damage. Captain Lawson has to close the bridge and repair it before we can pass.'

'Captain Lawson, Sean Bannon, commanding Team Yankee. How long is it going to take your people to unscrew the mess some of my tanks made?'

Lawson gave him an estimate and a brief explanation of what had to be done and why the work had to be finished before he would chance having any more tanks cross. He was hoping to be done within thirty minutes, barring any unforeseen problems. As Lawson seemed to know what he was about, and his people were hustling, Bannon asked him to keep the XO posted, excused himself and Uleski, and let Lawson get on with his work. Both agreed that except for the bridge, everything so far was going very well. Uleski was told to stay at the front and monitor the work on the bridge. Bannon was going to walk down the column and have the tanks disperse and shut down. This halt would give the people a chance to dismount, shake out their legs, and check their tracks. If the engineers finished before he returned, Uleski was to have his driver crank up 55 as a signal.

The crews were slow to respond. They were tired. Perhaps the halt was a good thing. It would give everyone a break. The tanks moved off the road, every other one on the opposite side, and all facing out at a forty-five degree angle. This was a formation called a herringbone, used by mechanized forces at times like this. By the time Bannon had reached the 3rd Platoon, he didn't need to tell the crews any more. The tank commanders began to move their tracks off onto the side in the alternating pattern when they saw the tanks in front of them do so. The entire centre of the road was cleared by the time he reached the Mech Platoon.

It was then that it occurred to him that something was wrong. Had C company maintained its time schedule, it should have been closing up behind the Team by now. But there was no one behind the Mech Platoon. The road behind Team Yankee was clear. When the last tracks had shut down their engines, he walked about a hundred metres down the road and listened for the whine of C company's personnel carriers. Still night air, an occasional rumble from distant artillery, and the pounding and yelling of the engineers working on the bridge were all that could be heard. After five

106

minutes, he abandoned his vigil and began to walk back to the head of the column. He really didn't know if there was in fact anything wrong. With radio listening silence in effect, he had no way of finding out. Of course, if something really terrible had happened to the rest of the battalion, he hoped someone would take the initiative to break radio listening silence and spread the word. But that was a hope, not a sure thing. Bannon had a bad feeling that things were not going well. Something was wrong, and there wasn't a damned thing he could do about whatever it was.

★ It took Pat's parents a moment to realise that their joyous welcome and enthusiasm wasn't evoking any response. Pat barely acknowledged their presence. She briefly looked at them, softly said, 'Hi Mom, Dad,' and then turned her head down to look at her children. Sarah hung around her mother's neck, making no attempt to move. Sean leaned against her side and wrapped both hids around the arm Pat held Sarah with. Kurt held her free arm and leaned against her on the other side, head tucked down, sucking his thumb. For an uncomfortable moment, her parents stood there, not knowing what to do or say. Pat's father offered to go get the suitacases while they waited there. Pat's simple response, 'There aren't any,' made her parents more uneasy. Her father gave her a look, then went to pull the car around to the front of the terminal.

When Pat and her children moved to leave, they moved as one, none of them wanting to let go of the other for the briefest moment. Pat's mother continued to stare, feeling less and less at ease in the presence of her daughter. As they left the terminal, an airman took Pat's name the children's names, her husband's name and unit, and Pat's destination. The final checklist and roster in their long odyssey.

Outside, Pat and the children climbed in the back seat. Even in the car they continued to hold on to each other. As they pulled away, Pat turned and watched the terminal. They were finally leaving military control. She thought about that for the moment. She thought about the other wives and their children. She looked at her parents in the front seat and began to wonder, Now what? The evacuation was over, but now what? There was nothing more to do. She was safe. Her children were safe. She was going back to her parents' home. But what then? Wait? Wait for what? For the war to end? For word to come about her husband? And what kind of word? Pat had listened to stories from wives who had waited while their husbands were in Vietnam. She wasn't ready. Even now, safe in the U.S. the dark abyss of the trackless future opened before her.

Like an earthen dam that had tried to hold back more water than it could, her resolve collapsed, and she began to cry. Her children silently tightened their grips on their weeping mother to comfort her and themselves. Her parents in the front seat stared ahead, not knowing what to do or say.

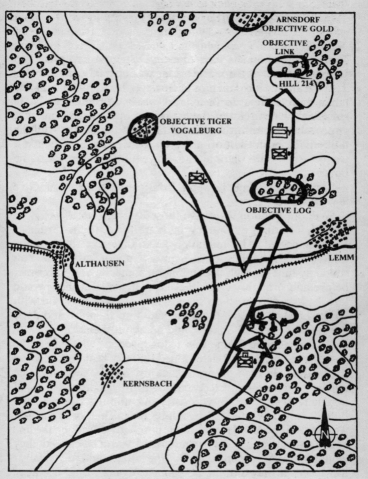

MAP 4: THE BATTALION PLAN OF ATTACK

Chapter Five

HUNTER AND HUNTED

Twenty-eight minutes from the time Bannon had talked to Lawson, 55 cranked up. The bridge was opened and ready for Team Yankee. The engineers, however, made sure that the tanks didn't screw up their work again. An engineer NCO stood at the near end of the bridge, stopping each tank as it approached the ramp. He would hold the tank there until the tank on the bridge got off on the far side of the river. when it was 66's turn at the on ramp, Lawson came up to the side of the tank.

'Right on schedule, Lawson. Your people done good. Give 'em an atta boy.'

'Will do, Bannon. You give those Russians hell.'

With a thumbs up and a grin, 66 rolled onto the bridge as Lawson waved. The military was strange like that. In the middle of the night you run into a major problem. You suddenly find yourself depending on someone you never met before and probably would never see again. But that person knocks himself out to do his job and helps you get on with yours. Lawson and his engineers had done their job and done it well. Now Team Yankee could go about theirs.

Crossing one at a time was a slow process. Uleski kept the pace down until he had determined that the Team had cleared the bridge. He then began to pick up speed slowly until he reached, then slightly exceeded, the former march speed. All together, Team Yankee was forty-five minutes behind schedule. It was now 0430 hours, Alpha time. The sky in the east was becoming light. They were supposed to be crossing the line of departure in another thirty minutes. Even at best speed, they would not be able to make it. But the tanks could not travel at top speed. If they did, the personnel carriers would not have been able to keep up. It would be useless to arrive on time without the infantry or the FIST. So the Team stayed together and made the best possible speed.

110

What concerned Bannon more than being late, however, was the failure of C company to close up at the bridge. Even as the Team left the bridge site, he kept looking back across the river in the gathering light, searching for a glimpse of anyone else in the battalion. But there was no sign of C company, D company, the battalion CP, or trains. C company was thirty-five minutes behind schedule for some reason. Perhaps the battalion had learned about the problem at the bridge and had diverted C company to another route. If that were the case, C company could be in front of Team Yankee. Or C company could be lost. Or they could be held up in a massive traffic jam in one of the small villages. Bannon didn't have any idea what had gone wrong, but he did know that Team Bravo was in front of Team Yankee, continuing with its mission. Without the faintest idea as to what was going on behind the Team, all he could do was to carry on as ordered. When they closed up on Team Bravo, he hoped someone would be there who knew what was going on or had some new orders.

By 0520 Team Yankee was only three kilometres south of Kernsbach at the point where they were to turn off the road and begin to deploy. But rather than turn off, the tanks to his front began to deploy into another herringbone formation on alternating sides of the road. Bannon turned, signalled the FIST track to pull off, and told Ortelli to drive up to the head of the column and find 55. As 66 came up to the XO's tank, Bannon saw Major Jordan standing on the side of the road next to his PC. To prevent a cluster of parked vehicles, Bannon pulled off on the opposite side of the road. At this point, they were only six kilometres from the line of departure, the front.

Jordan stood next to Uleski across the road, looking unhappy and impatient to be on his way. He began talking while Bannon was still in the middle of the road. 'There has been a change in plans. You're to pull your Team into an assembly area over there in the forest and await the word to move into the attack.' He motioned to the northeast where a road coming out of Kernsbach disappeared into a forest between two hills. 'The battalion column became separated

111

last night. I'm going on back along the line of march and see if I can find the rest of our people.'

'Any idea how long it's going to be before we move into the attack?'

'Not until, and only if, we get this jug fuck unscrewed. For now, no one in this battalion is going to do any attacking. Any other questions?'

'Yeah, where's Team Bravo and any other friendly units?'

'Team Bravo is in position now as planned. Team Charlie, Task Force 2nd and the 93rd Mech is in the tree line just west of Kernsbach. The Scout Platoon from 2nd of the 93rd is in that wood lot just to the north. If you need to, contact them by radio. I gotta be rolling. Good luck.'

Without waiting for further questions, Major Jordan climbed up onto his personnel carrier and took off down the road to the south as fast as his PC could roll. Bannon turned to Uleski, 'Bob, go get the platoon leaders and double time them up here ASAP.'

'On the way.'

While the XO was gathering up the platoon leaders, Bannon put out his map on the front slope of 55 and for a moment studied the area where the Team was to go. He decided quickly to put the two tank platoons on the west, one on each side of the road, facing out where they would have good fields of fire. The Mech Platoon would go through the woods to the east side and straddle the road. He wanted to get the Team under cover and deployed. As soon as the platoon leaders were gathered around the map, he gave his orders.

'There has been a delay in the attack.' The faces of the platoon leaders lit up as if the governor had just given them a last-minute reprieve. 'We are going to move into an assembly area to the northeast. Second Platoon, you deploy here to the north of the road and orient to the west. Third Platoon, you deploy here and orient to the northwest. That will give you two crossing fires. Be advised, there are friendly scouts and a friendly company team here. So don't shoot unless you're sure they're Russians. Lieutenant Harding, you will deploy your platoon here on either side of the road. The XO will deploy with you. Once we're under cover, check out your tanks and tracks, boresight your main guns, and feed your people. As there is no way of telling how long we'll be here, treat this as you would any defensive position. If there are no questions, let's roll.'

Garger stopped Bannon as he was about to pick up his map. 'I don't have a question, but I think you ought to be advised that 33 fell out about ten klicks down the road.' Uleski and Bannon stopped midstride and stared at Garger as he continued, 'Sergeant Pierson stopped to see if he could help. O'Dell told him he suddenly lost all power. They tried to restart 33, but the engine kept aborting. I have the grid location of where 33 is.'

'Give it to the XO when we get into the assembly area. Right now let's get off this road before some Russian jet jockey makes us all grease spots.' With that, the group scattered and remounted.

The woods of the Staat Forest were easy to move through. It was a typical German forest, with the straight, tall trees well spaced in neat rows. The forest floor was as clear of clutter as if it had just been raked. As the tanks jockeyed into positions and shut down, the forest and the hills on either side trapped the noise and caused echoes. When all were shut down, Bannon could distinctly hear the conversations of other crews as they dismounted, stretched, and went about taking care of their tanks. The routine called for Folk and Bannon to check out the fire control, while Kelp and Ortelli checked the track and suspension. When the fire-control system was finished, they boresighted the main gun and checked the weapons.

The other crews nearby were beginning to break out their morning meal of dehydrated MREs. Folk pulled out an opened case and began to pass one out to each man. Normally there would be complaining and haggling to secure a better meal, but they were all tired and thankful that the road march was over and they had a break. Bannon munched on his cold meal, popping bits of dehydrated peaches into his mouth, causing his lips to pucker as the peach drew every bit of moisture from his tongue.

He pondered his next actions. It might not be a bad idea to

go up to Team Bravo and do a visual recon of the area they were to cross. Objective LOG would be visible, as well as all the terrain the Team would have to cross. He finished all the MRE that he wanted, stuffed what he wanted to eat later in a pocket, and threw the rest into an empty sandbag tied to the side of the turret that was used for trash. Kelp was sent to fetch Lieutenant Harding and one of his PCs for the recon and to tell Uleski he would be in command while Bannon was away. Bannon went to gather up the two tank platoon leaders and the artillery FIST himself.

Once everyone was gathered and mounted in the PC, they moved out through the woods. Bannon didn't want to expose the PC in the open. He also didn't want to come storming up behind Team Bravo and get blown away by a nervous gunner. It took ten minutes to reach Team Bravo. As he had feared, when they sighted each other, there were several weapons of various calibres trained on the track. He immediately stopped and identified himself. This task was made easier by the fact that several of the people in Team Bravo recognised Harding and the PC driver. Once they were accepted as friendly, they dismounted, left the PC to the rear of the position, and slowly moved forward to the north edge of the tree line.

The last few yards were covered on their bellies. From where they stopped, the leaders from Team Yankee could see everything. The village of Lemm was to the right front, the hill that was Objective LOG was directly to the front, and the village of Vogalburg was to the left front in the distance. As they lay there, an infantryman from Team Bravo crawled up behind Bannon and slapped the side of his boot. When he turned to find out what he wanted, the infantryman whispered that the colonel wanted to see him. Bannon left the platoon leaders and crawled back.

'Bannon, what in the hell are you doing here? Where is your goddamned company? Why are you on this fucking hill and not that one over there?'

For a moment, Bannon was dumbfounded, just staring at the colonel, unable to understand why he was so excited. 'I don't understand, sir. My Team is in the assembly area where

114

we were ordered to move just south of here. I was waiting for the order to attack.'

'Waiting! Waiting! Who the hell told you to wait? We've been up here for the last hour and a half waiting for you.'

Bannon still wasn't understanding what was going on, but it appeared that there had been a disconnect between the colonel and the S-3. 'Sir, the S-3 told me to put the Team into an assembly area and wait until the rest of the battalion closed up.'

'I never gave such an order. The S-3 must have been mistaken. Now I want you to get your people moving and get up to LOG and Hill 214. IS THAT CLEAR?'

The colonel was beside himself with rage, while Bannon was equally angry at the implication that he had screwed up. But that was not the time or place to take up a point of personal honour. The colonel was yelling so loudly that Bannon was positive that his orders were clearly heard by all of the men in Team Bravo and every Russian in the area. 'Then I understand that I am to attack without C company behind me.'

'You let me worry about C company. You just get those people of yours moving. *Now.*'

With that, the conversation was over, and the colonel left. Things were going to hell in a handbasket, and the Team was right in the middle of a bad situation. The idea of starting the attack with only half of the battalion on hand was, in Bannon's mind, insane. He had, however, been given a direct order. The spectre of the 'Charge of the Light Brigade' and Pickett's Charge began to loom before him. He had to find an out fast.

As the PC moved back, Bannon's mind was racing a mile a minute, trying to find a way out or around this dilemma. An order had been given. In his heart and mind he knew that it was wrong for the Team to go all the way to Hill 214 on its own. Yet he couldn't get around the order. Not immediately. A partial solution slowly began to take shape. The Team could at least attack and seize LOG. Conditions for that part of the operation were still favourable. Team Bravo was in overwatch. The artillery could still support that manoeuvre. If the Team took LOG unopposed, they could then manoeuvre against Hill 214 in a slow and deliberate manner. The colonel told him to move, but he didn't say how fast. If the Team hit some, or a lot of resistance on LOG, he would be able to use his discretion as a commander and hold onto LOG until C company appeared or Team Bravo moved up to support. It was decided, then. Team Yankee would comply but with extreme caution. They were going to take this one step at a time and hope for the best.

Uleski and First Sergeant Harrert met the personnel carrier as it pulled up next to 66. 'First Sergeant, when did you get here? Is C company here too?'

'I've been here for about fifteen minutes. I haven't seen C company since last night. In fact, after I left the column, I didn't see anyone in the battalion until I came up to O'Dell and 33.

'What do you mean, left the column? Where are they? Why did you leave the column?'

'Well, sir, you see, it's like this. We weren't on the road an hour before the company we were following made a wrong turn. We began to go in circles, up dirt roads, down dirt roads, through side streets in villages where the M-88s got stuck, and on and on for two hours. At one of our halts while we were waiting for an M-88 to turn around, I went up to the captain leading the column and asked him if he knew where he was. When he showed me a spot on his map that was two map sheets to the west of where we really were, I tried to explain to him that he was wrong. Well, it had been a long, hard night for him, and he wasn't about to listen to an obnoxious NCO. He told me to get back to my track and get ready to roll. So I said to myself, "screw you, I'm going to find the company." I went back, pulled my track, the ambulance track, and the M-88 out of column and took off looking for you. That boy had his head so far up his fourth point of contact that I doubt he knows we left.'

'Well, I really wish you could have brought C company with you. Even so, it's good to have you here. You're the first good thing that has happened all day. Besides, you're just in time for the attack.'

Uleski, who had been eyeing the platoon leaders and

116

wondering why they were so glum, turned his head and exclaimed, 'Do *what?* Attack *now?* Without the rest of the battalion?!'

Bannon knew the platoon leaders had heard everything that had gone on between him and the colonel. They were waiting to see his reaction and how he was going to approach this nightmare. It would serve no one to bitch and moan. The last thing the Team needed right now was for the leadership to go into a potentially costly operation with a negative attitude. It would take a lot of finesse to convince the platoon leaders and Uleski that they could pull it off. But if Bannon could do it, they would have a fighting chance. With all the positive enthusiasm he could generate, given the mission, he began issuing new orders.

'Gather around and listen up, gents, while I tell you how we're going to skin this cat. The situation and the conditions for the first part of the operation, the attack on LOG, are still the same. If anything, we have improved the odds. We've had a break, bore-sighted the guns, checked the tracks, had breakfast, and got a chance to recon the area some. Team Bravo is in position and ready. So we will go as we had planned. Lieutenant Harding, you will start the move by bringing your platoon up the road. As before, your platoon will be in the middle with my tank hanging onto your far right track. The two tank platoons will start their move when the Mech Platoon comes up even to them. Both tank platoons will move out in an echelon formation. Second Platoon, you'll refuse your right. Third Platoon, you'll refuse your left. When we get out in the open between those two tree lines, the whole Team will pivot on 2nd Platoon, move through the gap and head for Objective LOG. As we move on LOG, I want to give the village of Lemm a wide berth, just in case the Russians are in there. So don't crowd the 2nd Platoon.'

'Lieutenant Unger, I want you to contact your guns and have them locked, loaded, and ready to fire on LOG the instant we receive fire. All you should have to do is yell shoot. Don't wait for me or anyone else to tell you, just do it.'

'Lieutenant U, as 3rd Platoon is short a tank, I want you to

117

team up with Pierson and play wingman. That way you won't be so obvious hanging out there all by yourself in the centre.'

'Once we're on LOG, we'll size up the situation before we roll on to Objective LINK. If no one comes up to cover our move, 3rd Platoon will take up positions on the far side of LOG and overwatch the move of 2nd Platoon followed by the Mech Platoon. We will move up onto LINK as planned, 3rd Platoon coming up on order. I'll be between the Mech and 2nd Platoon. Do you have any questions?'

The platoon leaders looked at him, they looked at each other, then looked back to their commander, and shook their heads negatively.

'All right then, Lieutenant Harding, I want you to start your move in twenty-five minutes. I have exactly 0835 hours. Let's roll.'

The platoon leaders saluted and went their separate ways. The XO and first sergeant stayed. Uleski was the first to speak.

'Are we going to be able to pull this off?'

'Well, Bob, like I said, as far as the first part of the attack, if anything, we're in better shape. It's the second part that's shaky. It's my intention to take my time going from LOG to LINK. The longer we take, the better the chances are that the rest of the battalion will close up. If we're hit hard getting onto LOG, I'm going to hold at LOG until the battalion commander either moves up Team Bravo to support or D company comes up. I think that's the only way we can play it.'

'Agreed. But once we're out in the open, the other people may not like us taking one of their hills and try to take it back. Those Russians get very possessive of land once they take it.'

'Yeah, well, that's why I said we are going to have to play it by ear when we get on top of LOG. I don't intend to jump out beyond LOG on our own unless I'm sure we can do so and talk about it tonight. And if you take over, I expect you to do the same. Use your discretion. Clear?'

'Clear, boss. Got any more good news?'

'No, none that I can think of. If I do, you'll be the first to know.'

With that Uleski turned and headed for 55. Bannon then turned to Harrert.

'First Sergeant, there are some people over there in those woods from the Scout Platoon of the 2nd of the 93rd Mech. Take your track, the bandaid, and the 88 over there and let them know what we're about to do. I doubt if anyone else has co-ordinated with them. If there are mines or some kind of danger that they know about, get on the radio and call me ASAP. Stay there until we get up on LOG, then close up on us on LOG if you can.'

'I don't have the 88 with me right now. I left it with 33. But I'll take the bandaid and get moving unless you have something else.'

'No, that about covers it all. See you on LOG.'

Bannon's positive attitude and confidence spiel did little to relieve the doubts and foreboding he had about the upcoming attack. He didn't know if he had sold anyone. He certainly hadn't sold himself. There were twenty-two minutes to go before the Mech Platoon began to move. Time to mount up and wait. As he did so, the crew of 66 watched him. They had heard the orders and didn't look very convinced. Bannon thought that the old saying, 'You can't fool all the people,' was true.

Now that the issues had been decided, and the wheels had been set in motion, Bannon was anxious to get on with it. There was still the gnawing fear that they were about to stick their collective neck out and lose their head. It wasn't going to be a peacetime training exercise. There wouldn't be the after-action critique to discuss who did well and who didn't. This was really it. The graves registration people, either Russian or U.S., would be the ones sorting out the winners from the losers this time. Still, there was also the possibility that the Team just might pull this off. He had to think positively. Be positive. They had to go out there and make things happen. Like the roll-call sergeant on 'Hill Street Blues' would say, 'Let's do it to them, before they do it to us.'

The Mech Platoon began to come even with the rest of the Team. As they broke out of the tree line, they began to deploy into a wedge formation. When their last track was in the open, Bannon gave Ortelli the order to move and joined the formation to the right and a little behind the far right personnel carrier. Unger and his track did likewise behind 66. The 2nd Platoon then began to deploy, each track always a little to the right and a little farther behind the track in front. When the entire Team was deployed, it formed a large wedge that measured 700 to 800 metres at the base and had a depth of 500 metres. In this formation they could deal with any threat that appeared to the front or to either flank.

When they began to pivot on 2nd Platoon and turn north, Bannon saw the first sergeant's track and the bandaid waiting in the tree line behind the scout platoon position. Harrert stood just out from the tree line alone and watched the Team deploy and turn. The first sergeant, whom he had known for several years, was reliable, steady, and a damned good tanker. He was a good man to have near in a tight spot. Bannon wondered for a moment what he was thinking of as he watched his company roll into the attack. Given the chance, Harrert would have traded places with anyone in the Team. His company was going into the attack, and he was staying behind. He turned to walk away, went a few paces, stopped, glanced over his shoulder one more time, then disappeared into the tree line.

★ The young Soviet lieutenant played with the remains of his breakfast. It wasn't fit to eat, he thought, so he might as well get some other pleasure from it. The men of his small unit sat around finishing their meals or simply enjoying the chance to rest. The entire company, or more correctly, what was left of the company, had spent all night preparing fighting positions on the small hill overlooking a town named Lemm. Since there had been no engineer support available, all the work had been done by hand.

On the first day of the war, the company had been with the first attack echelon. Heavy losses, including all of its officers except for the lieutenant, resulted in the company being pulled out on the second day. But instead of going into reserve, they had been sent to establish an outpost on the regiment's flank. The lieutenant didn't much care for the mission. With the exception of three tanks in Lemm, they were all alone. He looked at the collection of tired soldiers he had and decided if the fight did come, it wouldn't last long. Letting his mind wander, he thought that things could have been worse; the regiment could have sent a political officer with him.

As the Team passed between the two tree lines and crested a small hill, the terrain beyond opened up before it. The hill that was Objective LOG was directly in front about four kilometres away. The German countryside was lush and green on this August morning, just like any ordinary August morning. There wasn't anything to indicate the fact of a world war. The very idea that this quiet and beautiful landscape was a battlefield seemed absurd.

But it was a battlefield. As the Team moved out from its last cover, all eyes for kilometres around were turning on it. The Scout Platoon to the left, and Team Bravo on the right, watched Team Yankee as it rolled forward. The Team was ready for battle. Guns were oriented to cover their assigned sectors and all but the track commanders were buttoned up and ready for action. Team Bravo and the scouts watched in morbid curiosity, waiting to see what would happen next and thankful that they weren't the ones out in the open.

The other people, the Soviets, also watched. Their reaction was different. They began their scramble to meet the American movement. Reports were flashed to their commanders. Gunners threw down their mess tins and slid into position. Loaders and ammo bearers prepared to load the next round. A new battlefield was about to mar the much-contested Germany countryside.

Team Yankee had two obstacles that had to be negotiated. The first was a railroad embankment that ran across their front. Going over it wasn't the problem. All the tracks could do that. The problem was that it required the Team to slow down. It would break up the formation momentarily, and as the tracks went over it, their soft underbellies would be exposed to direct fire. If they were going to be hit, this is where Bannon expected it. The first track came up and began to go over. Bannon held his breath as he watched the PC crest the embankment, hang

121

there for a moment fully exposed, then drop down to the other side. Two more PCs followed and dropped down to the other side. Nothing happened. The PCs rolled on. Perhaps the Russians were waiting for the tanks. Perhaps they wanted to let the PCs go over and let the embankment separate the Team before firing.

Then it was 66's turn. Ortelli slowed 66 until it made contact with the embankment. As soon as the tracks bit into the embankment, he gunned the engine, and 66 began to rise up. Folk, by instinct, depressed the gun to keep it level with the far horizon. Bannon grabbed the commander's override, ready to elevate the gun once they were on the other side. If he didn't the depressed gun would dig itself into the ground as 66 went down the other side. As the tank crested the embankment and started down, Ortelli switched from accelerator to brake, and Bannon jerked the commander's override back, elevating the gun. Folk kept fighting for control of the gun but didn't get it back until 66 was level again. He then reoriented the gun and continued his search for targets.

As 66 continued forward, Bannon turned in the cupola and watched the rest of the Team come over the embankment two at a time. Satisfied that they were not going to be hit there, he turned back to the front and eyed the next obstacle, a stream that, like the railroad embankment, ran perpendicular to their direction of travel. The first PC was already down in the stream and halfway across when he turned around. The stream was small and shallow but years of erosion had created a ditch some twenty metres wide with embankments a metre high. Ortelli eased 66 down into the streambed, crossed and began to climb the far bank. They were halfway up when the shit hit the fan.

Several flashes from Objective LOG were followed almost instantly by a thud and the appearance of a column of dirt in front of 66. 'REVERSE! REVERSE! GET BACK IN THE DITCH!' The sudden change in direction threw everyone on 66 forward. Bannon reached for the smoke grenade dischargers and fired a volley. The six grenades launched and shrouded 66 in a curtain of white smoke as the tank settled back down in the streambed.

Grabbing the radio switch on the side of his CVC, Bannon

keyed the Team net. 'ALL BRAVO 3 ROMEO ELEMENTS – DEPLOY INTO LINE IN THE STREAMBED – BREAK – ZULU 77 – BRING YOUR PEOPLE BACK – THIS IS ROMEO 25 – OUT.'

Commanders are paid to make decisions. Sometimes, there is ample time to consider all the angles, to analyse the situation, develop several courses of action, compare each, and then decide which alternative is best. Then there are occasions when there is no time for all that – occasions when the commander must see, decide, and act in almost the same instant. This was one of those times.

'GUNNER, STAND BY TO ENGAGE.'

Bannon looked to his right and saw the FIST track halted next to his. The 2nd Platoon was entering the streambed and pulling up. He turned to his left and saw two of the PCs plop back into the streambed. They had also fired their grenade launchers. He turned back to the front. The smoke was beginning to dissipate. Off to the front left about fifty metres from 66, a PC was stopped in the open and on fire. There was a burning man hanging from the troop door in the back of the vehicle. Bright flames spilled out of the door and the hatches on top. The 66 had been exceedingly lucky. The PC hadn't been.

The turret of 66 suddenly jerked to the right as Folk yelled out an acquisition report without bothering to key the intercom. 'ENEMY TANK – TWELVE O'CLOCK.'

'GUNNER – SABOT – TANK.' Bannon dropped down to view through the commander's extension. He couldn't see the target.

'UP!'

'FIRE!'

'ON THE WAAAY!'

Tank 66 rocked back as the main gun went off. The view to the front was obstructed by the muzzle blast and dust it created.

Folk yelled out his sensing of the round he had fired. 'TARGET!'

Bannon put his eye up to the extension and confirmed Folk's sensing. The enemy tank he had not seen before was now clearly visible as it burned. But he had a Team to run. He had no time to play tank commander right now. He had to let Folk search for his own targets and engage them when he found them. 'CEASE FIRE – FIRE AND ADJUST.'

'ROMEO 25 – THIS IS TANGO 77 – ON LINE AND READY – OVER.' 2nd Platoon was ready.

'ROGER TANGO 77.'

'ROMEO 25 – THIS IS ZULU 77 – READY – OVER.'

'ROMEO 25 – THIS IS MIKE 77 READY – OVER.' The Mech and 3rd Platoons were ready.

'SPLASH – OVER.' The artillery.

The hill that was Objective LOG appeared to lift up as the artillery impacted. Bits of trees and fountains of dirt rose up above the tree line. 'BRAVO 3 ROMEO ELEMENTS – THIS IS ROMEO 25 – MOVE – MOVE – MOVE! LIMA 61 – KEEP THE ARTY COMING.'

As one, Team Yankee lurched forward. For the second time, 66 moved up over the stream bank. This time Ortelli had the accelerator to the floor. The tank flopped down on level ground with a bang and took off at a dead run. A line of three tanks and three PCs to the left of 66 were also out of the streambed and charging forward past the burning PC. The tank that had been to the right of 66 was stopped, half hanging out of the streambed. It was burning and shuddering as its on-board ammo blew up. Second Lieutenant McAlister was dead. The rest of the 2nd Platoon was out and rolling further to the right, firing as they moved.

Folk yelled out again. 'LOADER – LOAD SABOT – TANK!'

'UP!'

'ON THE WAAAY!'

Again 66 shuddered as the main gun fired, recoiled, and spewed out a spent shell casing. This time the obscuration didn't cling to the tank as 66 rolled through the dust cloud created by the muzzle blast. Bannon turned to see what Folk had been firing at but saw only a column of dirt. He had missed whatever it was. Not that it mattered. Another tank to the left got it. A brilliant flash and a shower of sparks marked the Soviet tank that had been Folk's target.

A quick survey of Objective LOG revealed four burning vehicles of which two were definitely tanks. The other two were partially hidden but emitting billowing clouds of flames and black smoke. Freshly dug dirt was now visible just inside the tree line. There were Soviet infantrymen dug in on the objective. Bannon had no intention of fighting it out with the Soviets on LOG. He did not want to dismount the Mech Platoon in the open. 'BRAVO 3 ROMEO – THIS IS ROMEO 25 – THERE ARE DUG-IN TROOPS ON LOG – WE WILL CONTINUE TO ATTACK THROUGH – DO NOT DISMOUNT OR STOP ON THE –'

His transmission was cut short by two huge explosions on either side of 66. The tank bucked violently from side to side. He lost his footing and fell to the floor. Kelp reached down to help him as he struggled to climb back up into the commander's cupola. Kelp yelled over the engine noise, 'ARE YOU OK?'

'Yeah. Get ready to man your machine gun!'

'Your face is bleeding.'

Bannon took one hand and touched his face. When he pulled it away there was blood on it. But it couldn't be too bad. He was still moving and talking. He had to regain control of the tank and the Team. With an effort, he boosted himself up and back into place. The scene outside was chaos. The explosions that had rocked 66 were from Soviet artillery. Tank 66 was on the verge of rolling out of the impact area. To the right there were still two tanks moving. One of the 2nd Platoon tanks was several hundred metres to the rear; just sitting there. The FIST track was also gone. To the left there were also two tanks still moving and closing up on 66. The missing 3rd Platoon tank was nowhere to be seen. The Mech Platoon PCs were falling behind and, as a result, were still in the middle of where the Soviet artillery was impacting. Bannon could make out only two PCs bobbing and weaving through the columns of flame and dirt. Seven vehicles. That's all the Team had left. Seven out of fourteen vehicles.

'TROOPS – TWELVE O'CLOCK! ENGAGING WITH COAX!'

Folk's call pulled Bannon's attention back to the front. They were now within three hundred metres of the objective. Several Soviet infantrymen had popped up to engage them head-on with RPGs. The total stupidity of that was beyond comprehension. They were now being cut down by the machine-gun fire from 66 and the surviving tanks without being able to hurt the tracks. An RPG just wasn't going to stop an M-1 head-on, regardless of how brave the gunner was. Tank commanders began to cut loose with the calibre .50, spraying rounds in wild arcs and patterns and, in general, adding to the mayhem. An American tank would fire an occasional HEAT round, adding to the effect of the friendly artillery that was still impacting on LOG. In another minute, the four tanks that were still with 66 would be on the objective.

The destruction of their tanks, the steady artillery fire, and the failure of their RPG gunners to stop the rush of Team Yankee were too much for the survivors. Just as the Team was about to enter the tree line, individual Soviet troops began to flee to the rear. To the right of 66, a hidden Soviet BTR-60 personnel carrier began to back up, seeking to escape. But its movement gave it away, and it was destroyed by a 2nd Platoon tank. Kelp was up on his machine gun, firing at individual Soviet soldiers as they fled helter-skelter to get out of the way.

Just as 66 entered the tree line, a lone Soviet soldier rose up out of a trench not twenty metres to the right of 66 and aimed an RPG straight at Bannon. He panicked. He tried to traverse the M2 to the right to engage the Soviet but he knew in his heart he wouldn't make it in time. The Russian calmly took aim and prepared to fire. He knew he had 66 and there wasn't a damned thing Bannon could do to stop him.

But luck hadn't given out yet. The Russian was suddenly kicked backwards as a stream of machine-gun rounds hit him in his chest. A 2nd platoon tank had come up, seen the RPG gunner, and fired. The relief Bannon felt was incredible. For the second time in a matter of minutes, 66 had been saved by the slimmest of margins.

★ The Soviet lieutenant watched the American tanks rumble by. He was overwhelmed by alternating rushes of fear, anger, and helplessness. All their efforts had been for nothing. The American tanks had ripped through his position as if he hadn't been there.

Catching his breath, the lieutenant began to survey the scene. Some of his men were coming up from the bottoms of their foxholes. Looking back over the field to his front, he saw several personnel carriers closing on his positions. 'Well,' he thought out loud, 'If we can't kill the tanks, we'll kill the American infantry.' With that, he grabbed an RPG from a dead man and bounded over to some of his men to rally them and continue the fight.

The five tanks of Team Yankee were now in a staggered line moving forward through the woods. Friendly artillery had stopped falling, probably as a result of a call from Team Bravo. After entering the woods a hundred metres, the tanks lost contact with the Soviets. There was also no sign of any other positions. Bannon decided to stop and wait for the Mech Platoon. 'ALL BRAVO 3 ROMEO ELEMENTS THAT ARE WITH ME – STOP AND FORM A COIL – I SAY AGAIN – STOP AND FORM A COIL – WE WILL WAIT FOR THE ZULU 77 ELEMENT TO CLOSE UP – OVER.'

The other tanks did not slow down. Bannon called again but got no response. The radio was keying, but for some reason the other tanks were not hearing his transmissions. Instead of stopping, they were, in fact, beginning to speed up. He called a third time with no luck. To make matters worse, artillery began to fall on them. He assumed it was Soviet but couldn't tell. This caused the other TCs to crouch low in their cupolas and orient to their front as they directed their drivers. Ortelli kept twisting through the woods, alternately trying to avoid artillery and pick a trail through the trees.

As the tanks emerged from the far side of the woods, 66 suddenly slid to the right and stopped with a violent jerk that knocked Kelp and Bannon over to the right. As they tried to regain balance, Ortelli gunned the engine. But 66 did not move. Bannon stuck his head out and saw that they had slid sideways into a shell hole. Ortelli tried again to drive out but failed. They were stuck. And to his front, Bannon watched the last of Team Yankee's tanks, all four, continue to roll on towards Hill 214, Objective LINK.

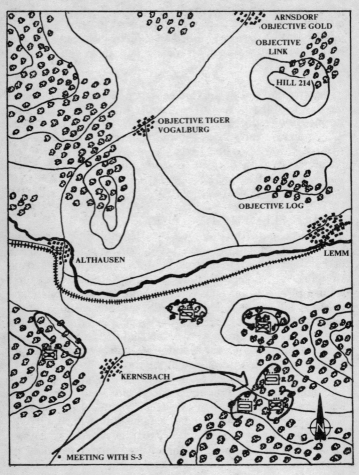

MAP 5: TEMPORARY ASSEMBLY AREA

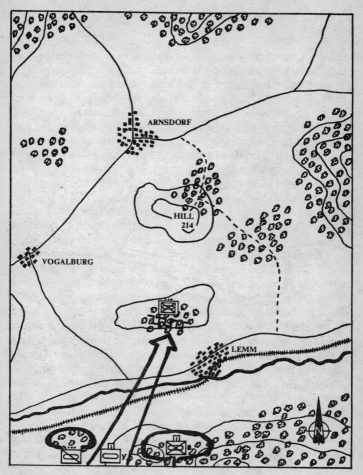

MAP 6: TEAM YANKEE IN THE ATTACK

Chapter Six

ON THE RAZOR'S EDGE

'Lay off the accelerator, Ortelli. We aren't going anywhere that way. You may be making it worse.'

Kelp and Folk turned and stared at Bannon wide-eyed and fearful. Ortelli's face, no doubt, was no different. They were waiting for their commander's next brilliant idea. 'Why me?' Bannon thought, 'Why in the hell *me?*' He felt lost. He had managed to lose half the Team and get 66 stuck in an artillery barrage in the middle of a battle. Now his crew was looking at him expecting him to come up magically with the right answer. Maybe there was no right answer this time. Then again, maybe there was.

'Right. Listen up. I'm going to go out and see how bad off we are. Kelp, cover me with your machine gun if you can. Sergeant Folk, be ready to give me a hand if I need you. Clear?'

They both nodded their heads. Bannon turned and opened the TC's hatch all the way and stuck his head out to check the situation. The 66 was just on the edge of the artillery-beaten zone. Another twenty to thirty metres and they would have been in the clear. So much for luck.

He ducked down, turned to Kelp, and asked if he were ready. Kelp's eyes were wide open and his face drawn in fear. But he was standing ready to leap into position when Bannon gave the word. He simply nodded yes. 'Alright, *let's go.*'

With that, Bannon jumped out of the TC's hatch, rolled down the side of the turret, and dropped to the ground. The drop was more than he had anticipated. He landed on his side with a thud, knocking his wind out. As he lay there struggling to get his breath back, he looked around. The neat German forest was now ripped and pockmarked by the artillery fire. Branches and trees were thrown askew and broken. Artillery rounds continued to impact around 66. Every now and then there would be a zing or a ping as a shell fragment from a near miss flew through the air or hit the tank. Bannon quickly became motivated to get on with his inspection. The track he was lying next to was still on all the road wheels and the drive sprocket. They hadn't thrown a track. Thank God for small miracles. He crawled along the track as close as he could for safety. He wanted to look between the road wheels. The other track was also on. When he reached the rear of the tank, he found mounds of loose dirt the tracks had been building up to their rear. Both tracks had obviously been spinning free. As he crawled around to the rear of the tank and looked under the hull, he could see the problem. The tank was hung up on a shattered tree that was still partially connected to its stump. As 66 had manoeuvred through the forest, it had straddled the shattered tree and driven itself up onto the stump. To make matters worse, there was a shell crater to the right of the tank that the right track had dropped into just as 66 had bellied out on the stump.

The solution to their problem was not going to be simple. If there was another tank around, it would have been easy to hook tow cables to the two tanks and pull 66 off. But all the remaining tanks had run off to Objective LINK. They could sit and wait. Eventually, if the rest of the battalion came along a tank in Team Bravo or an M-88 recovery vehicle could pull 66 off. But it seemed just as likely that the Russians would show up. Besides, Bannon was the team commander. He had to get back with the Team and regain control, even though the Team was now nothing more than a reinforced platoon. Also, simply sitting there and waiting to see what happened next was not his style. A solution had to be found. Throwing dirt under the tracks would do no good. The tracks would simply pile it up onto the mounds of dirt they were already building. It was too late to back out. Ortelli had hit the tree at a charge and driven 66 up onto it. Something substantial had to be shoved under the right track so that it could rise up and let the hull clear the stump. But to do that would have required all of them to haul tree trunks and other rubble over to 66. The artillery would surely get some of them. Bannon tried hard to remember what he had been taught at Fort Knox during the Basic Course in the vehicle recovery class. Why in the hell didn't I pay attention to what was going on in that class instead of kicking dirt clods and bullshitting at the rear of the group, he thought. The instructors had always said, 'Someday this may save your life.' Today was that day, but he couldn't remember the technique. There was something they could do but he wasn't sure if he remembered it all. What the hell, maybe it would come back as he went along. Something had to be done fast.

He climbed back up on the tank, staying as low and as near to the turret as possible. 'Sergeant Folk, get out here now.' As Folk was climbing out, Bannon pulled a hammer from a sponson box and threw it to the ground on the right side of the tank. Bannon then had Folk help get the tow cables off. The two men crouched down as they worked to free one tow cable, throw it to the ground near the hammer, then free the other cable and throw it down on the other side. They then leaped off the right side and took cover.

While they lay down on the ground next to the track, Bannon explained what they were going to do. The plan was to hook the tow cables together in front of the tank. They would then wrap the cables around the two tracks at the front of the tank so that the tow cables stretched from one track to the other. When Ortelli put 66 in forward gear, the tracks would move the cables back along the ground. In the process, the cables would catch on the stump. Hopefully, as the tracks continued to try to pull the cables back, they would stay caught on the stump and pull 66 forward and off the stump and tree. The plan was worth a shot.

Bannon took the hammer and used it to get the tow hooks off the front and back of 66 while Folk dragged the two cables to the front, crawling on his hands and knees and staying as close to the tank as he could. They used one of the tow hooks to connect the cables together. Then they wrapped one end of the cables around the track on the left side and used a second tow hook to connect the loop formed around the track, doing the same on the right side. Bannon put the fourth hook and hammer to the side in case a hook broke and a second try was needed. Folk got back in 66.

From the outside, Bannon signalled to Folk, who had Ortelli put the tank in low gear and slowly apply power. The cables were dragged under and caught on the stump as expected. As they caught, Ortelli applied more power. The slack in the cables was taken out, and they became taut. For a moment the tracks stopped and the engine began to strain. Bannon hoped the hooks could stand the pressure and not snap. If the scheme worked, 66 would be free.

Ortelli continued to apply power slowly. The tank began to inch forward, moaning and screeching as the hull scraped across the stump. The cables held. The 66 continued to move and rise up over the stump. Once the tank's centre of gravity was past the stump, the front of 66 flopped down. The tracks bit into the ground, and 66 began to roll forward on its own. Bannon signalled to Folk to have Ortelli stop. He crawled to the rear, disconnected the cables from around the tracks, then climbed back on. They were going to leave the hooks and cables behind. With luck, someone could get them later. There were far more important things to do, including getting out from under the Soviet artillery.

As Bannon was climbing back into the commander's cupola, he noticed for the first time that 66 had lost its antennas. Both were sheared off at the base. That explained why the other four tanks had not stopped when he had called them. The last order the Team had heard from him was to keep moving and not stop. Apparently, they had thought that he wanted them to keep going all the way to Hill 214. When they couldn't contact him, they simply carried on with the last order they had received. As 66 began to roll off the hill that had been Objective LOG, Bannon wondered how much that misunderstanding had cost the Team. Clausewitz called it the friction of war. Some called it Murphy's law. Right now, the thought of losing what was left of the Team to a simple misunderstanding was devastating. Sixteen men and four tanks lost because a damned antenna was broken.

Once in the open and out from under the Soviet artillery fire, Bannon had Ortelli move as fast as they could go. He had to find out if there were any tanks in the Team still on Hill 214. If there were, he would be able to contact battalion and find out what everyone else was doing and what the colonel wanted the Team to do. Not that there was much left to do anything with. If batallion couldn't be contacted, then the ball was back in his court. He had to decide what to do with the surviving tanks. Bannon was fast becoming tired of making these decisions. They were too expensive in terms of men and equipment. He wondered what he would lose first, the Team or his nerve.

Movement to Bannon's right diverted his attention. Three Soviet T-62 tanks were moving north on an intersecting course with 66. They must have come out of Lemm and were headed to hit the tanks on Hill 214 in the rear. Bannon grabbed the TC's override and jerked it over as far as he could, swinging the turret towards the threat.

'GUNNER – SABOT – 3 TANKS!'

Kelp dropped down and yelled, 'HEAT LOADED – UP!'

The last round Kelp had put in the chamber had been a HEAT round. Not as good as a SABOT round when fighting a tank, but it would do. There was no time to switch ammunition.

'IDENTIFIED!' The gunner had acquired the targets and was ready to take over. Bannon let the override go. At the same instant, the lead T-62 began to traverse its turret towards 66.

'FIRE HEAT – LOAD SABOT!' At least the next round would be right.

'ON THE WAAAY!' Folk fired.

As if it was all one action, the main gun recoiled, and the tank shuddered and bucked as if hit on its side by a massive hammer. The sound of the gun firing was replaced by a high-pitched scream of agony over the intercom and the hiss of the halon gas fire extinguishers discharging. The turret was instantaneously filled with the halon gas. The 66 jerked to the right and staggered to a stop; it had been hit.

'What happened? Why are we stopping?' Kelp was panicked and about to go out through the loader's hatch. Bannon could feel Folk grab at his leg to get by him and out. Ortelli was screaming. 'Shut up, Kelp. Everyone stay where you are. Crew report.'

'*We're on fire! Get out!*' Folk kept trying to get past.

'GET BACK IN YOUR SEAT AND PREPARE TO ENGAGE.' To make his point, Bannon took his free foot and blocked Folk's route out. For the briefest of moments Folk stared at him, then got back into position.

'KELP. IS THE GUN UP?' He looked at Bannon dumb-founded. 'LOADER – LOAD SABOT – NOW!' Kelp turned and grabbed the next round.

The screaming on the intercom had been replaced by a continuous moaning from Ortelli. He had been hit. Bannon had no idea how badly, nor could he find out at that moment. He popped his head back out to find out what the Russians were doing.

There was thick black smoke coming from the engine compartment and rolling over the tank. The fire extinguishers in the engine compartment had failed to put out the fire. Across the open field one of the T-62s was burning and shuddering from secondary explosions. The other two had just begun to move out again for Hill 214. Their gun tubes were pointed at 66. Apparently they thought 66 was finished.

'Sergeant Folk, can you see the other two tanks?'

'Yeah, I got them. They're at the edge of my sight.'

'Move your turret slowly and lay on. We don't want to let on that we're still functional. When you're on, fire. I'll hit the smoke grenades. That should cover us from return fire. Kelp, you up?'

Across the turret from Bannon, Kelp was standing against the turret wall. There was a look of terror on his face, but the gun was loaded and armed. 'Kelp, give me an up.'

'SABOT UP.'

'Anytime you're ready, gunner.' Through his extension Bannon watched the T-62s. The range readout digits on the bottom of the sight changed. Folk had ranged and gotten a good range return. 950 metres. God, they were close. The ready-to-fire indicator was also on. He put his finger on the smoke grenade launcher, ready to fire.

'ON THE WAAAY!'

As the gun fired, Bannon hit the grenades, covering 66 with a curtain of white smoke. 'SWITCH TO THERMAL!'

As Folk slid the sight shutter into place, the view of the smoke screen was shut out. But instead of the green thermal image, the sight remained black. 'The thermal is out!'

'Switch back to the day channel and look sharp. They're going to make sure we're dead this time so we have to get the f up?'

'UP.'

'STAND BY TO ENGAGE.'

The fire in the engine compartment was growing. The black smoke mixed with the white smoke from the grenades. Ortelli's moaning was softer and weaker now. Within the turret there was the smell of cordite from the spent shell casing, diesel from a ruptured fuel cell, the acrid smell coming from the engine fire, and the odour of sweat from the crew as they waited for the T-62's to reappear.

'IDENTIFIED!'

A T-62 was charging down on 66, gun aimed dead on them.

'FIRE!'

'ON THE WAY!'

Both tanks fired at the same time and both hit. The difference was that the Soviet round didn't penetrate the turret of 66. The 66's found its mark and with telling effect. There was the flash of impact followed in rapid succession by secondary explosions. The first series ripped off the turret of the T-62, flinging the fifteen tons of steel high in the air as if it was cardboard. The turret slammed into the ground and flopped over upside down. A quick scan of the area revealed that the other T-62 that 66 had engaged was smoking. Though it was not burning as the other two were, the body of the tank commander was draped over the side of the turret. Even at that range, the spatter of red on the Russian's black uniform was visible. That and the high angle of the gun tube told Bannon that it was dead. With no other threat in sight and the fire in the engine compartment becoming larger, it was time to abandon 66.

Ortelli had stopped moaning. Folk slowly traversed the turret until he reached the driver's compartment. Ortelli's crumpled form lay limp against the side. There was diesel and blood spattered all over him, his seat, and the compartment. While Bannon held him forward, Kelp lowered the seat back. They eased his body back onto the turret floor. The right side of his face had been torn open and burned. The chest of his chemical protective suit was shredded and soaked with blood and diesel. His right sleeve ended just below the elbow in a bloody tatter. Ortelli was dead.

Bannon's first thought was to leave the body and abandon the tank. But he felt they owed Ortelli better than that. He had been a good soldier and a loyal crewman. To just leave the body there and give it to the fire that would soon engulf 66 was unfeeling. If they survived, Bannon, at least, wanted to be able to tell his family that they had done all they could for him, even in the end. 'Let's get him out of here.'

Kelp and Bannon dragged Ortelli's body out of the driver's compartment and propped it up. Folk, kneeling on the turret roof, reached down and took Ortelli under the arms and pulled him out as the other two pushed from below. Bannon reminded Kelp to take his submachine gun and the ammo pouch before he exited. Bannon stayed behind to prepare 66 for destruction.

Though the engine compartment fire would probably finish off 66, he wanted to make sure that his tank was not going to be displayed in Red Square as a trophy. Bannon opened the ammo ready door and locked it open. He pulled one round out and put it halfway in the main gun's chamber, then placed several more rounds on the turret floor. He turned the radio frequency knobs off of the Team's frequency. As he really didn't know by whom they would be picked up, he took his CEOI that contained all the radio frequencies and call signs for the brigade and tore the pages out, spreading them around the turret. Satisfied that 66 was ready, he put two frag grenades and one thermite grenade in his pocket and climbed out.

Once outside Bannon threw his CVC down into the turret, put on his web gear, helmet, and binoculars and grabbed his map case. He ordered Folk and Kelp to head for the woods to their right. Once they were on the way, he took the thermite grenade, pulled the pin and dropped it in the loaders hatch among the shells on the floor. He leaped down on the right side of the tank and crouched low, waiting for the first explosion to make sure 66 would burn.

He landed next to Ortelli. While Bannon had been inside,

Folk and Kelp had put Ortelli into a sleeping bag and laid him a few feet away from the tank. There was a tag with his name and social security number attached to the zipper. They had placed his head so that the damaged side of his face was not exposed. Except for the tag, he looked as if he were asleep. Folk and Kelp had felt the same way Bannon had about their friend. Just as they had cared and looked out for each other in life, they had done so in death. When the first round went off, Bannon took off to catch up with the rest of the crew. Ortelli and 66 were gone. It was time to carry on.

Folk and Kelp were both lying in the tree line watching 66 burn by the time Bannon caught up. He plopped down next to them and began to watch, too. The tank was fully involved now, burning from front to rear and quivering as rounds cooked off and detonated. Off to the left the T-62s also were burning. He studied the four burning tanks. For the past three days he had thought of Soviet tanks as nothing more than objects, machines to be smashed, destroyed, or 'serviced' as the Army had once referred to the act of engaging targets. But in 'servicing' those 'things', they had killed sixteen men and had lost one of their own.

The whole scene began to seem unreal. Bannon felt detached from the horrors and the dangers that surrounded them. It was all like a bad dream. Not real. His head began to spin, and he became nauseated. He turned away and lay on his back, closing his eyes and letting his mind go blank. The nervous stress and the emotional strain, as well as the physical exhaustion, were catching up to him. He was thirsty but too tired to do anything about it. He needed a few minutes alone to get himself together.

The sounds of battle to the north from Hill 214 drifted down to their refuge. The boom of tanks firing their main guns rolled over them. Bannon listened for several minutes without thinking or moving. To the south the sounds of small-arms fire could be heard from Objective LOG. The battle there was still going on. The familiar pop pop of the M16 firing was answered by rifle reports that were not familiar to his ears. Probably

Soviet AKs. It was the high-pitched whine of two personnel carriers approaching that finally got him to move.

He rolled over onto his stomach and propped himself up on his elbows. Coming up along the same route 66 had taken were two PCs. As they approached 66 from behind, they slowed down, passing it, one on each side, checking out the area. They turned towards the wood line and headed for Bannon. He knew they hadn't seen him or his crew. They were going to get out of the open and hug the tree line for cover. At least 66's crew would be able to ride up to Hill 214.

Without thinking, Bannon began to stand up to wave down the PCs. Just as he was about to straighten up, the closest PC cut loose with a burst from its calibre .50 machine gun. The wild burst ripped through the trees above him, scattering splinters and pieces of bark all over. He dropped down like a ton of bricks. Folk let out a stream of obscenities while Kelp covered his head and curled up, 'JESUS CHRIST! THOSE FUCKERS ARE TRYING TO KILL US!'

Still on his stomach and with his face buried in the ground, Bannon raised his right arm and waved frantically. The shooting stopped. He looked up to see both tracks side by side headed for him, guns aimed and ready. He continued to wave as he slowly rose, ready to go down again if they fired. This time, they didn't. Once the PC commanders were satisfied that they were not facing Russians, they picked up speed and continued towards the tree line. Their guns, however, stayed aimed at Bannon. No one was taking any chances.

'Damn, sir, we thought you were dead!' It was Polgar, the platoon sergeant of the Mech Platoon. The two PCs pulled into the tree line on either side of them, turned around to face out, and stopped.

'Thanks to you we almost were. Is this all that's left of your platoon?'

'No, Sir. There are a few men back on LOG with the L. T. but they're mostly wounded, including the L.T. I got most of the 2nd and the 3rd Squads with me. The 1st Squad bought it on that first volley back at the stream. I see you got some before you lost your tank.'

'Yeah. We did. Have you been in radio contact with anyone else in the Team?'

'Yes, sir. The XO. He's up on Hill 214 with the rest of the Team. That's where we're headed now.'

Bannon felt as if someone had just removed a stone from the top of his heart. There still was a Team Yankee! Right now it didn't matter that it had lost so much. It didn't matter that they were in the wrong place. All that mattered was that there was at least something left. He hadn't pissed away the whole Team.

The crew of 66 mounted the PCs. Bannon boarded Polgar's track and stood up in the troop hatch behind the TC as they rolled out and headed for Hill 214. The PCs continued to hug the tree line until they were just across from the woods of Hill 214. Then the PCs dashed across the open area into the eastern side of the trees on Hill 214. After wandering cautiously through the forest, they came up to the four remaining tanks of the Team.

The four tanks were deployed along the tree line overlooking Arnsdorf, just as they should have been deployed to support the attack of D company. As the PCs came to a halt about fifty metres to the rear of the tanks, Bannon saw Uleski dismount one of the tanks in the centre. Even at that distance, he could see that Uleski was injured. Polgar and Bannon dismounted and met him halfway.

The XO had his right arm in a sling and splint. He saluted with his left hand and asked if anyone else was coming. Bannon replied that he had had no contact with battalion since moving out of the assembly area and was hoping Uleski had some news. Uleski shook his head and informed him that the battalion frequency was being jammed, making contact impossible. He had been trying to work through the jamming but had gotten nothing. Bannon and Uleski turned to Polgar and asked if he had made any contact with battalion before coming up to Hill 214. His reply was also negative. So, to the best of their knowledge, battalion had no idea where the Team was and what it was doing.

For that matter, Bannon didn't know for sure what was going on either. His next priority was an update on what had happened after the tanks had left Objective LOG, and what the enemy situation was. The three of them sat down in a circle, though Uleski had some difficulty doing so because of his arm. He then described how the four tanks had continued onto Hill 214 as Bannon had ordered. Once they had cleared the woods and the artillery fire on LOG, Uleski noticed 66 was gone. When attempts to contact 66 failed, Uleski closed up the remaining tanks, contacted the Mech Platoon, ordered them to follow up when they could, and pushed on.

The four tanks under the XO reached Hill 214 without further contact and began to sweep through the Objective. As the tanks crested the hill, they ran right into the middle of a Soviet artillery battery of towed guns preparing to move. The Soviet gunners were totally surprised. Since the tanks were still rolling and less than two hundred metres away, Uleski charged through the battery's position, destroying the guns and their prime movers as well as cutting down those Soviet gunners that were not quick enough to get away. Apparently, not many of the Soviets were able to make good their escape. After having watched so many of the vehicles in Team Yankee get hit, the tankers went on a killing frenzy, literally running down and over fleeing Russians. Everyone fired whatever weapon he could as they hunted the Soviet gunners down, sometimes one at a time.

Uleski related how he had watched four Russians run into the nearest house in Arnsdorf with a tank hot on their heels. The last man in closed the door as if that would keep the tank out. The pursuing tank drove up to the house, rammed its main gun through the door, and fired a HEAT round. This started a fire, and the tank backed up a few metres and waited. When two Russians came out, the tank cut them down. As he told this story, Bob Uleski's face was without emotion. His eyes were set in a steady gaze that went through Bannon as though he were reviewing the scenes he was describing in his mind's eye. His voice betrayed no regret or disgust. Three days of war had done much to harden this man. As Bannon watched Uleski's face and listened to his story, he wondered how much, if at all, he had done to stop the killing spree.

Uleski paused for a moment after finishing his report on the action against the battery and then continued. After the tanks were finished, they withdrew up the hill and occupied the positions they were currently in. There were several minor wounds that had required tending, of which his was the most serious. Ammo had been counted and was being redistributed. Main gun rounds were the most critical problem. Each of the four tanks now had less than ten rounds of SABOT and six rounds of HEAT on board. If and when the Soviets got serious about counterattacking, the Team would quickly run out.

The personnel side was better, but not much. The dead and missing included Unger and his entire FIST team, Sergeant Pierson and the 34 tank, as well as Lieutenant Harding, wounded on LOG. That left the XO with the 55 tank, Garger with 31, Sergeant First Class Hebrock with 24 and Staff Sergeant Rhoads with 22. The tanks had nineteen men, including the crew of 66. Polgar had his 23 track with Staff Sergeant Flurer and 2nd Squad and the 24 track with Staff Sergeant Jefferson and the 3rd Squad. Each infantry squad had the driver, track commander, and six men, giving the Mech Platoon seventeen men. Team Yankee was now down to four tanks, two PCs, two Dragons, and thirty-five men.

The enemy had not yet reacted to the loss of Hill 214. After destroying the artillery battery, the tanks had had no contact with the Russians. It was, however, only a matter of time. The presence of Team Yankee on Hill 214 or in the area had to be known. Why else would the three tanks that 66 had encountered have been pulled out from the front and sent back to the rear in the middle of a battle? Bannon doubted that the Soviets knew how much, or how little, was on 214. His guess was they they would send in a small element first to locate the Team, discover their size and composition, and pin them. Once they had done that, the Soviets would strike and strike hard. It was the way they did business.

While Uleski and Polgar gathered up the Team leadership, all the track commanders this time, Bannon pondered their options. They could withdraw. As there had been no contact with battalion since the attack had begun and there was little prospect of achieving contact now, withdrawal would be

142

acceptable. Team Yankee was obviously incapable of performing a Team-sized mission because of its losses. Ammunition was becoming critically low and Bannon had no idea when or even if battalion would link up. Although Polgar had informed him that LOG had been cleared, it could have been reoccupied by the Soviets. Only Harding and a few wounded had been left to hold that hill while they waited for Team Bravo to move up. That had not yet occurred when Polgar had left. To stand on Hill 214 and attempt to continue, knowing full well that the Soviets would be back, made no sense.

But neither did a simple withdrawal. While there was almost no hope of holding Hill 214 against a powerful counterattack with the Team's current strength, there was no guarantee that the Russians would, or could, counterattack in strength. There was the possibility that they were in just as bad shape as the Team and could not counterattack. They might have pushed everyone forward and left no one to reinforce the flanks. The fact that the three T-62 tanks had to be pulled off the front to reinforce the rear hinted at this. To withdraw and learn later that there had been no threat would ensure that the deaths of the men in Team Yankee had been in vain.

There was also the chance that the rest of the battalion would finally make it up and continue with the mission. It would be humiliating to be in the process of withdrawing against an imagined foe and run head-on into the rest of the battalion as it advanced up to Hill 214. Not that pride and humiliation were of prime concern to Bannon right now. It was just that such an occurrence was as likely, given his lack of information, as anything else. Besides, the order to seize Hill 214 was still in effect.

It was decided, then. Team Yankee had taken this hill and was going to keep it until ordered elsewhere or thrown off. Bannon began to appreciate the old philosophy that once soldiers had paid for a piece of ground with the blood of their comrades, the value of that land became greater and transcended what cold logic would otherwise calculate. For Team Yankee, this ground was important. They would hold.

Now that it was decided, he had to determine how to hold

Hill 214. With four tanks and two PCs, they could hold four to five hundred metres of front. But the Team was on its own and had to worry about its flanks and rear, not just the front. The Soviets might try a frontal attack once, but they would not do it twice. Besides, they might try holding the Team's attention to the front while manoeuvering infantry through the woods to hit them in the rear. Flank and rear security were therefore critical.

★ Lt. Col. Yuri Potecknov prepared to execute his new mission in the exact, scientific manner that he had been taught and had used in Afghanistan. It was a simple mission and well within the capabilities of his unit. A small probing attack by some American tanks had penetrated the thin security screen on the Army's flank and was threatening a critical town named Arnsdorf. Colonel Potecknov was to wipe out the enemy force and restore the security screen.

While Potecknov was unhappy that his motorised rifle battalion was being diverted from the main effort of the army, he rationalised that it was for the better. His troops were still untried by battle. They had followed around in reserve for the last three days, awaiting the chance to pour through a breach in the American lines that never came. By sweeping up the enemy force at Arnsdorf, the colonel could blood his troops. The cheap victory would help instill some confidence in the battalion and allow him to see how well his officers performed under fire. This would be nothing more than a live-fire exercise with a few targets that fired back.

With Team Yankee's leadership assembled, Bannon went over their current situation, how they were going to hold Hill 214 and what he expected the enemy to do. There wasn't a lot to work with. What they did have had to be stretched to cover threats from any direction. The result was not the soundest plan he had ever made. It violated just about every tactical principle. But, given the situation and time, it was the best he could do. Once the orders were out, the Team began to deploy and dig in.

The tanks still constituted their major firepower. Initially, they would fight from their present positions – for now, they were pulled into hide positions. A two-man outpost was established at the tree line to watch to the northwest. From that position, the tanks were prepared to defend against an attack from Arnsdorf. They also would be prepared to occupy two other positions. The first was on the eastern side of the woods covering the open space between Hill 214 and a wooded lot to the southeast. A Soviet commander could use the lot as a staging area and rush across the open area onto Hill 214. The second position was on the crest of Hill 214 facing south. The Soviet commander might decide to seal off the Team's routes of escape and reinforcement, then hit it from that direction.

The Mech Platoon was broken up into three elements. The two rifle squads dismounted and established an ambush along a north-south trail that ran through the centre of the woods north of Hill 214. This protected the Team from a dismounted attack from the north through the woods, provided the Soviet commander used the trail to guide on. The two PCs with only the drivers and track commanders under Uleski established an outpost on the crest of Hill 214 watching to the south. The third element was a two-man OP on the east side of the woods watching the southeast wooded lot. Bannon hoped that if the Soviets came from the south or from the east, the two OPs would be able to give the tanks sufficient warning and time to switch to the alternate positions.

It was the attack through the woods from the north that was, to Bannon, the greatest threat. Polgar had a total of thirteen men to cover that area. This number included Folk and Kelp as there were no vacant positions on the tanks. The distance from the west edge to the east edge of the wooded lot was just a little over one thousand metres. With two men per foxhole and ten metres between foxholes, the most Polgar could cover was sixty metres. That left a very large gap on either side that the Soviet commander could move whole companies through, if he knew where they were. In all likelihood, however, a commander conducting a night attack through unfamiliar woods would stick to or near the trail for no other reason than to maintain orientation. If that happened, Polgar was ready and waiting with one of their Dragons, two M60 machine guns, two grenade launchers, and the riflemen. To provide an additional edge, antitank and antipersonnel mines were deployed to the front and flanks of the infantry positions.

Command and control of the Team was simplified. First, there wasn't that much to command or control. Second, all radios were put on the company net. Bannon took over the XO's tank and stayed with the tanks. With his arm injured, Uleski could not fight 55. Besides, Bannon wanted someone dependable with the PCs covering the south. After the run-in with the T-62s in the morning, he was paranoid about the southern side of Hill 214. The OP in front of the tanks had a sound-powered phone running back to 55 so that the men at the OP could pass information back to the tanks. The OP on the east side was also using sound-powered phones to maintain contact. Their phone line ran back to Polgar who in turn maintained contact with Bannon via a portable PRC-77 radio on the Team net. With the exception of Polgar, who had to run his dismounted infantry using voice commands, everyone in the Team could contact everyone else.

The afternoon passed in a strange and unnerving silence. The distant rumble of artillery hitting someone else far away had become so routine that unless an effort was made, it wasn't noticed anymore. Everyone was nervous and on edge. At the slightest sound or movement out of the ordinary the men would stop work and grab their weapons. Since the war had begun no one in the Team had had much of a chance for a decent, uninterrupted sleep. In the last thirty-six hours, no one had had more than two hours sleep. While it was noticeable on everyone, this lack of sleep had its most telling effect on the leaders. Bannon found that he had to repeat orders two or three times. When the orders were being issued for the defence of Hill 214, one of the tank commanders had fallen asleep. Once, while Uleski was telling of preparations, he stopped in mid-sentence, unable to remember what he intended to say next. The only way Bannon kept going was by constantly moving around. Even then, he sometimes had to stop and try hard to remember what it was he had been doing. The Team could not go on like this for another twenty-four hours. By tomorrow, Bannon thought, they would be at the end of their ability to endure and function.

As he was going over this in his mind, he decided, despite his previous decision, that if they had no contact with anyone from battalion or brigade by 0300 the following morning, he would take Team Yankee off Hill 214 and, under the cover of darkness, re-enter friendly lines to the south. If someone was coming, they would be there by then. To try and hold on for another day would be beyond their physical capability. He could only ask so much of the men. During his rounds Bannon informed Uleski and Polgar of his decision.

It was during the last hour of daylight that the Russians came. A column of four T-72s and eight BTR-60PBs rolled down the road into Arnsdorf from the northwest. A motorised rifle company. Garger, Hebrock, and Bannon crawled out to the OP and watched them come. They drove down the road as if Team Yankee were a thousand miles away. The tanks led, followed by the BTR-60s. As this unit had T-72s, it was Bannon's guess that they were from a different regiment or possibly a different division than the Soviet unit the Team had overrun in the morning. The theory that the Russians had shoved everything forward and left their flanks weak seemed to be correct. Their coming from the northwest pointed to the fact that they were robbing the front line units to secure the rear areas. If nothing else, Team Yankee's attack had caused the Soviets to divert forces from their attack to the west.

As they lay there watching the motorised rifle company and tanks move into Arnsdorf, Bannon asked if anyone knew how many men a BTR-60 could carry. Without hesitating, Lieutenant Garger informed him that it could carry twelve passengers and had a crew of two. For a moment Bannon put down his binoculars and looked at the young lieutenant. In the past three days he had done exceedingly well. His performance had been on par with that of McAlister and Harding. The fact that he had made it this far was a testament to his ability as a tank commander. Bannon had often heard stories about men who were complete zeros in peacetime but became tigers in war.

Garger seemed to be one of them. He was glad that circumstances had prevented his replacing him.

They watched and listened as the motorised rifle company pulled into Arnsdorf and stopped. The vehicles cut off their engines. Orders given by the Russian officers could be heard as they dismounted. Chances were they would wait until dark before trying anything. Probably a dismounted recon and then an attack. The red setting sun seemed an omen of things to come.

★ From the edge of Arnsdorf, Colonel Potecknov, his deputy, his operations officer, and his political officer surveyed the hill to the southeast. They could see the debris of the artillery battery that had been caught in the open as well as the track marks gouged out by the American tanks. He tried to listen for any tell-tale signs of activity from the hill but could not because of the noise his men were making in the town. He had ordered one company to do so in order to attract the Americans' attention. If they were watching, which the colonel had no doubt they were, they weren't showing themselves. Turning to his operations officer, he said, 'Very well. If the Americans won't show themselves, we will go in and find them. Prepare a patrol.'

After the operations officer scurried to issue the necessary orders, the colonel turned back and continued to study the hill in the failing light. 'A simple exercise. Easy. We shall squeeze this hill like a grape and see what comes out,' he said, talking to no one in particular as he watched and waited.

While they continued to watch Arnsdorf in the failing light, 55's loader crawled up beside Bannon and informed him that Polgar had received a report from the OP on the east side that they had heard the sound of vehicles moving through the woods to the southeast. The Soviets evidently intended to hit the Team from both sides at once. As they crawled back, Bannon tried to figure out how to deal with the two threats. The Team could deal with one attack at a time from one direction, not two from entirely different directions. He began

148

to wonder if the show the motorised rifle company had put on while entering Arnsdorf was, in fact, a deception. Perhaps the real attack would come from the east. There was less open ground to cover from that direction. It made sense.

Once back at 55, Bannon radioed Uleski. He ordered the XO to move from the hilltop and go over to where the infantry OP was sited on the east side. He told him also that he was sending the two 2nd Platoon tanks over. Uleski was to organise the defence there but be prepared to send the tanks back if they were needed. Polgar and his men were to stay put for now, but he was told to be prepared to go either way to reinforce Bannon or Uleski. If the defence of Hill 214 failed, Polgar was to try to get back to his PCs or, if that was not possible, to escape and evade south on foot as best he could.

The odds were not good. They had at least four tanks and probably more supported by upwards of two hundred infantry. But it was too late to have second thoughts about fighting or fleeing. The Team was committed. With the last light of day gone, all that was left for the Team to do was wait for the Russians to come.

They didn't have long to wait.

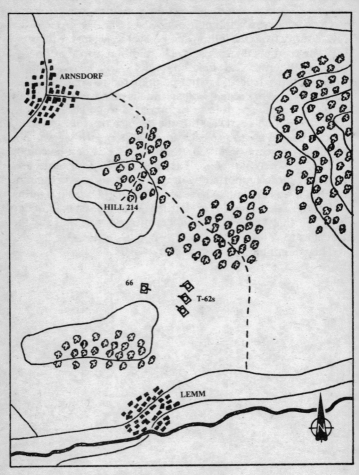

MAP 7: THE LAST BATTLE OF 66

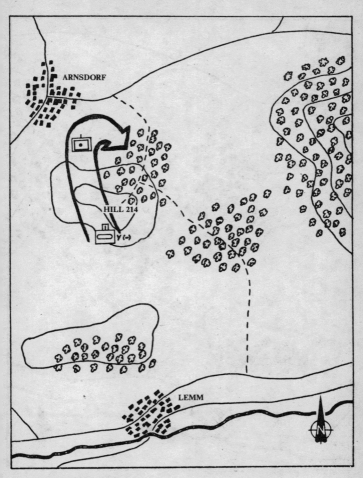

MAP 8: THE TANKS' REVENGE

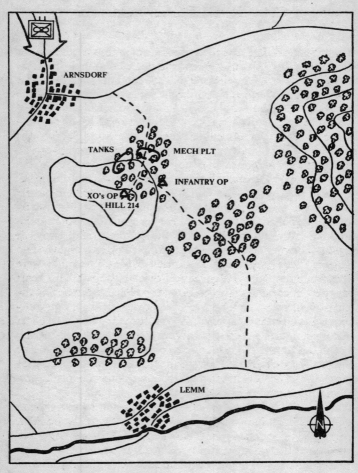

MAP 9: THE DEFENSE OF HILL 214

152

Chapter Seven

CHECK AND CHECKMATE

It was Sergeant Polgar and his thin line of infantry that were hit first. Just after 2300, movement was detected to their front. At first, it was just the faint rustle of leaves and the snap of a twig. Not enough to home in on or know for sure if there really was someone out there. But soon the infantrymen, using their night vision devices, could see a line of figures slowly advancing in a staggered column on either side of the trail. Polgar was pleased. Their formation and direction could not have been any better as far as he was concerned. He was going to let the lead man get to within ten metres of his foxhole before firing.

As he waited for them, Polgar's pulse began to beat harder and faster. The fear of premature disclosure of his position by one of his men increased his nervous anxiety, so he kept looking left down his line of positions, then right, then left again. The men, clearly visible through Polgar's night vision goggles, were ready and like himself, tense. When they were thirty metres from Polgar, the Soviets stopped. His heart skipped a beat. Had his men been discovered? Had he lost the element of surprise? The two lead Soviet soldiers, now fully exposed and clearly visible to Polgar, turned and looked back. Another figure, ten metres behind them, waved a pistol and pointed it forward, whispering a command of some type. The two lead soldiers turned back to the front and proceeded. They were the point element, and the one with the pistol was obviously the officer in charge.

When the lead Russian came to within ten metres, Polgar slowly released the safety on his M16, raised it to his shoulder, and fired. The single shot knocked the Russian back and unleashed the well-rehearsed and deadly ambush drill. Three of the infantrymen hit the antipersonnel mine detonators, causing thousands of small round pellets to rip through the Soviet column. The machine guns opened fire along set sectors with a withering cross-fire that knocked down those still standing after the mines had detonated. The grenadiers plunked out 40mm grenades in their sectors. The riflemen surveyed their areas and, like the grenadiers, marked their targets and took them out.

The violence and shock of the ambush were overwhelming. The Russian officer barely uttered a word before he was cut down. The deadly and accurate point-blank fire ensured that any movement by any Russian who survived the first volley was his last. The darkness, the violence of execution, the loss of their leaders, and the resulting confusion were too much. Those lucky enough to be in the rear of the column withdrew back down the trail, pursued by a hail of bullets. Some made it.

The order to cease fire could be heard throughout the woods. As quickly as it had started, the firing stopped and quiet returned.

Polgar's report to Bannon was matter-of-fact, accurate, and succinct. In his opinion, the Russians had been a platoon and were merely probing for positions and strengths. That discovery had been costly for the Russians. But they had the men available and could afford the price.

While the Team awaited the next Soviet move, Polgar shifted his men back several metres to a new line of positions. If the Soviets decided to hit the Team in all directions, the survivors would surely lead the next group back to the point of the ambush. The next group along the trail would be in attack formation. By dropping back, the next Soviet attack would hit an empty sack. If the Soviets didn't catch on to what was happening and milled around the old infantry positions, Polgar might catch them off guard and have the edge again. With so few men, he needed every advantage he could get.

About forty-five minutes after the fire fight in the woods, two of the tanks in the village of Arnsdorf cranked up and began to move slowly towards the north, to where the trail entered the wooded lot. The slowness of the move gave the impression that the Russians were trying to hide the move. Any movement of tanks, however, is very difficult to hide.

154

Bannon informed Polgar and told him to be ready for tanks. Smugly, Polgar simply replied, 'Send 'em, we're ready.'

As the tanks moved to the north, the OP in front of the Team Yankee's tanks reported that there was additional movement just inside of that part of the village facing Hill 214. When Bannon radioed to Polgar that he thought both tanks and infantry positions would be hit at the same time, Uleski also reported movement to his front. The Russians were putting on a full court press. The moment of truth was at hand. After ordering the OP back and telling Lieutenant Garger in 31 to move up as soon as he heard 55 crank up, Bannon wondered if the next move would be check or checkmate.

The incoming rounds simply began to explode. Instinctively, Bannon dropped all the way down into the tank and masked. Specialist 4 Newman, 55's loader, was already masked and looking at Bannon. In an almost matter-of-fact manner, as if he was discussing sports or the weather, he told Bannon. 'Those don't sound like the shells we were hit with the other day. There's no whine before they impact.'

'Mortars. They must be firing mortars. Probably 120mm mortars from the battalion's mortar battery. They can't do much to us.' At least, Bannon didn't think they could.

Once masked and hooked into the intercom, he had the driver crank up the tank and move up to its fighting position. As they moved forward, Bannon popped his head up and surveyed the scene. The mortar rounds were falling just to the rear of the tanks. The volume of fire was impressive but doing little more than creating noise. A check with Polgar and Uleski revealed that 55 and 31 were the only ones being shelled. Bannon guessed that the Soviet commander was attempting to draw their attention to the sector facing Arnsdorf.

Through their thermal sights, the crews of 55 and 31 watched a line of fifty or more Russian soldiers move out from the village and begin to advance towards the hill. They were followed by four BTR-60s and two tanks at a distance of twenty metres. Behind them came another line of troops followed by their BTRs. The Russians were coming in force this time.

Bannon ordered 31 to engage the T-72 on the left on order. Tank 55 would take out the one on the right. They would be firing at the T-72 with straight frontal shots. Bannon wasn't sure how well the 105mm rounds of the M-1 would penetrate the front slope of a T-72. He therefore instructed Garger to continue to engage until it burned. There was no time for second-guessing. He didn't want to have some Russian do to them what he had done to the T-62s.

Once the T-72s were destroyed, Bannon wanted 31 to suppress the infantry while 55 took out the BTRs. Not that a BTR was dangerous. With only a 14.5mm gun in its turret, it could not hurt an M-1. But the destruction of the tanks, the methodical destruction of the BTRs, and a steady stream of lead pinning them to the ground in the darkness and confusion of a night attack would have a severe psychological impact on the individual Russian soldier. Bannon hoped that it would discourage him from rushing forward to become a Hero of the Soviet Union.

Polgar came up on the net and reported that he could hear the tanks coming down the trail. He was ready and waiting. Polgar's transmission was followed immediately by Uleski, who announced that there were about one hundred dismounted soldiers advancing towards him in a column formation. The Russians were going all out this time. They wanted to hold the Team's attention in the front, pin those people they had discovered in the woods with a secondary attack, and sneak up behind. Team Yankee was in check.

It was the infantry that was first in action. The lead tank hit one of the antitank mines. The detonation was followed by a wild volley of small-arms fire from the accompanying Soviet infantry. They simply dropped down wherever they were and opened fire in whatever direction their rifles were pointed. Polgar managed to keep his men in check and quiet. He wanted to suck the Russians in.

When it became apparent that the lead tank was crippled, unable to move forward, and blocking the advance of the second tank, the Russian leading the infantry rose, gave a series of commands, and led his men forward in the attack. As the Russians advanced in a line straddling the trail, they fired from the hip and yelled in order to psych themselves up. Their firing was wild and of more danger to themselves than to Polgar's infantry. The firing by the Russians served only to keep Polgar aware of the progress of their advance.

The line of Russians came on. When they reached the line of deserted foxholes, the Russians began to throw grenades in the foxholes and increase their rate of fire. As it became obvious that there was no one there, the Russian officers began to shout orders and attempt to regain control of their men. It was while the Russians were milling about in an effort to reorganise and reorient for their next move that Polgar hit them.

As before, the infantry set off several Claymore antipersonnel mines followed by machine-gun and automatic-rifle fire. As the Russians were in a line parallel to the new infantry position, rather than perpendicular as the first group of Russians had been in their column formation, the effects of the volley were far more devastating. Most of the officers went down fast. The Russian soldiers dropped down and began to exchange fire with the infantry. The disabled tank attempted to support from where it was by firing its main gun, but it did little good.

There began a deadly game of hide and seek. The Russians, lacking night vision devices, waited until an American infantryman fired. When he fired his first few shots, the Russian would orient his weapon to the general location that he had seen the muzzle flash. If the American did not move before he fired again, the Russian would take final aim and fire a burst. Doing this, however, exposed the Russians to the same risks and results. So the infantry battle bogged down into a fire fight with sporadic and violent exchanges of gunfire followed by brief pauses as both sides tried to fix new targets, followed again by a new exchange of gunfire as someone found a mark and fired.

Just as the infantry fight reached this standoff, a volley of Soviet artillery hit the trail junction in the centre of the wood lot. Obviously, they wanted to isolate each element of the Team to keep it from shifting forces to reinforce an

157

endangered sector. In this manner, if one of Team Yankee's elements beat back one of the three attacks, Bannon would not be able to use the people thus freed to help defend against one of the other two Soviet attacks.

The Soviet battalion commander who had come up with this plan was good. He knew his business and was playing all of his pieces well.

As if the impacting artillery was a signal, the infantry advancing on 55 and 31 began to pick up their pace to a trot. As they were not masked, Bannon ordered the crews of 55 and 31 to unmask and prepare to fire when the T-72s were at 700 metres. He issued the fire command and watched as the gunner laid on the T-72. It was becoming quite large, taking up most of the sight. Hitting it would not be the problem. Killing it was his concern.

The gunner hit his laser range finder button with his thumb. The range return digits in the bottom of Bannon's extension showed 750 metres. They sat and watched the tank advance. It rumbled along, straining to hold back behind the line of infantry. The gunner ranged again. 720 metres. Almost there. The tank continued to advance. A large inanimate object whose sole purpose was to kill Americans. Team Yankee. Bannon. The gunner ranged again. 690 metres!

'FIRE!'

'ON THE WAAY!'

The flash, the recoil, and the blast broke the silence. Target! But the Russian kept coming, turning his gun towards 55. 'TARGET! REENGAGE – FIRE!'

'UP!'

'ON THE WAY!'

Again the flash, the recoil, and the blast announced the firing of a main gun round. Again 55 hit the T-72. Still it kept coming. Not only coming, but returning fire. The 55 shuddered in almost the same instant that the T-72 fired.

The loader looked and yelled, 'WHAT'S THAT?'

'NEVER MIND.' 55 had been hit. 'ARE YOU UP?'

'UP!'

FIRE!'

'ON THE WAY!'

The 55's efforts were finally rewarded. The third round found its mark. The tank commander's hatch on the T-72 was blown open. A fireball rose above the battlefield and was followed by a sheet of flame. The T-72 was dead. The range showing at the bottom of extension was 610 metres.

Bannon stuck his head out of the hatch to see what 31 was up to. Its T-72 was also burning. Steady streams of tracers from 31's COAX, loader's machine gun, and calibre .50 were raking the line of Soviet infantry. Already most of them had gone to ground, either dead or trying to keep from becoming that way. Two of the BTRs were starting to fire at 31. Bannon decided to take them out first. Grabbing the override, he slued the turret to the left.

'GUNNER – HEAT – TWO BTRS – LEFT BTR!'

'UP!'

'IDENTIFIED!'

'FIRE!'

The first HEAT round found its mark just below the small turret on the BTR. The impact and the internal explosions caused the BTR to swerve to the left and out of the battle. Both the gunner and Bannon yelled target at the same instant. Without waiting, the gunner laid his sights on the next BTR and yelled 'IDENTIFIED!' Once the loader gave an up, Bannon gave the command to fire, and another BTR was dispatched.

Garger surveyed the scene before him. This was becoming all too easy. Both 55 and 31 sat there as if they were on a gunnery range firing at cardboard and plywood targets instead of real people and vehicles. All three of his machine guns were firing, each one covering a different area. The flames from the burning T-72 provided more than enough light for him and his gunner to fire without the use of night vision devices. A move on the part of the Russians was rewarded by a hail of machine-gun fire. When he couldn't see any movement, he fired at the forms he saw lying on the ground. No doubt he was hacking away at men who were already dead.

When he became bored with that, he personally turned the calibre .50 on a BTR. It was something new and would be challenging. At Knox he had been taught that a calibre .50 could take out a BTR. Here was the perfect opportunity to learn if that was true.

As Bannon was preparing to engage his next target, he noticed that 31 was engaging a BTR with the calibre .50. The rounds were hitting but causing little damage. As a way of reminding Garger to get back to concentrating on pinning the infantry, he turned 55's main gun on the BTR that the lieutenant was trying to destroy with his fifty. One HEAT round was all it took.

Newman informed Bannon that 55 was out of HEAT and down to nine SABOT rounds. As he didn't want to waste those on BTRs, he ordered the loader to load a SABOT round but not to arm the gun. Then he ordered 31 to switch roles with 55. Garger was to work on the last of the BTRs, and 55 would pin the infantry. Garger's reply betrayed his joy. As 31 had, 55 divided its fire into sectors. The gunner engaged the troops to the front and right. The loader manned his machine gun and fired at the troops to the left. When his crew began to fire, Bannon called Uleski and Polgar for an update.

The infantry was still engaged in a standoff fire fight. Just as a Russian officer or NCO would get some of their troops moving, a volley of fire from the infantry would drive them to ground. The Russian leaders would have to start all over again. Polgar decided to break the deadlock. He sent his Dragon gunner on a wide sweep around the flank to destroy the two Russian tanks. Two other men, each carrying an extra Dragon round, also went to provide cover to the gunner. One of them was Kelp, who volunteered when he heard Polgar giving the order to the Dragon gunner.

The three-man team dropped back a short distance while the rest of the infantry line increased their fire to cover the move. The Dragon gunner, a specialist 4 named Sanders, led the other two as they circled around the fire fight, using the sound and the gun flashes to guide on. When the lead Soviet tank fired, Sanders would reorient himself on his objective and continue. They were going to go for the second tank first

because it was still fully capable and therefore more dangerous. The crippled tank could be dispatched at their leisure.

They closed in on the second tank from behind. It was
apparently wedged in between some trees and unable to move
forward or backwards. Sanders watched for a moment and
then moved to a spot where the trees and branches would not
interfere with his wireguided missile. He carefully set up his
weapon as if he was on a shooting range. When he had the
thermal tracker sighted in on the rear of the Soviet-tank, he let
the missile fly. The missile was launched with a flash and
whoosh followed by the igniting of the Dragon's rocket and
the pop-pop-pop of the small guidance jets. The impact lit up
the surrounding area and immediately ignited fires in the
tank's engine compartment. One Soviet tank was down with
another to go.

As he was manoeuvering against the crippled tank, a lone
figure stood up in front of Sanders at a distance of five metres
and fired his AK into his chest. Kelp levelled his submachine
gun and in turn cut down the lone figure. Both Kelp and the
other infantryman, a private as young as Kelp by the name of
McCauley, stood there frozen as they waited to see if any other
Russians would pop up. Once they were satisfied that the
Russian had been alone, the two knelt beside Sanders' body.

In the darkness Kelp felt for his pulse, first on his wrist, then
in his neck. There was none. 'He's dead.'

'How do you know?' asked McCauley.

'I know. He's dead.' At nineteen, Kelp was fast becoming an
expert on death. 'Do you know how to work that thing?'

'Yeah. We had a class on it once. I think I can do it. But I
ain't sure how we're going to get around to the other tank.
There may be more Russians.'

'You just get that thing and follow ole Kelp here. I'll get you
to the Russians' back door.'

With that, the two privates set out in the dark hunting for
the second tank.

The sound of the infantry's fire fight followed by the artillery
barrage and then the firing of 55 and 31 began to unnerve
Uleski. It wasn't easy to stand there in the dark, listening to the

161

sounds of a battle immediately to the rear while watching a hundred trained soldiers, whose sole intent was to kill you, calmly advance on your position. Not that Uleski had any doubt about the outcome. Unless there were tanks in the far tree line, the infantry would be no match for the tanks and PCs. Uleski was simply getting impatient. He wanted, as did everyone else, to get on with it. Now.

The nausea and fear that had crippled him during the first battle were not present this time. Instead, a hatred was welling up in him. As he watched the advance, he pounded the fist of his good hand against the roof of the PC. The image of the dead and wounded men scattered about 55 after the second attack on the first day flashed through his mind, flaming his hatred into an open rage. Quietly, the easygoing, fun-loving XO began softly to repeat, 'Come on, you mothers, come on and die.'

The column of Russian infantry began to deploy into platoon columns. Their advance was at a nice steady walk. They were in no hurry to join the chaos in the woods on which they were advancing. It seemed to Uleski as he watched that this group of Russians would be just as happy if they arrived in time to help with the body count and not a minute sooner. There was definitely a lack of gung-ho spirit here.

Uleski had his PC turned sideways in a depression near the tree line. One of the infantrymen who had been on the OP and the PC driver were standing up, hanging out of the cargo hatch, their M16s resting on the side of the PC. The PC commander had the calibre .50 over the side, locked and loaded. Several boxes of additional ammunition were opened and ready at an arm's distance. A loaded M16 lay on the roof of the PC next to Uleski's good arm. When the time came, he had every intention of joining the killing.

The other PC with the second man from the OP was also ready, in position to the left of Uleski. The two tanks were deployed to the right of the PCs, ready to engage the infantry or any tanks that popped out and surprised them.

When the Russians were about three hundred metres from the PCs, Uleski gave the order to fire. Eight machine guns and four M16s cut loose, unleashing a hail of tracers and lead that peppered the deploying Russians. For a moment they stood there transfixed, unable to comprehend what was happening to them. Uleski watched through his night vision goggles as some of the Russians first ran one way, then the other, before going to ground for cover. Officers would try to rally their men and drive them on, only to be cut down as the machine guns from the tanks and PCs raked the area with steady, measured bursts of fire. Uleski decided that this was a green unit and tonight was its baptism by fire. A smile came across his face. Quietly, he said to himself as he picked up the M16, 'So be it. You shall be baptised in blood.' Robert Uleski, good-natured Ski, had become a cold and hard man.

As with the infantry fire fight, once the Russians went to ground, an impasse seemed to settle in. The Russians stayed where they were while the PCs and tanks were unable to finish the prone figures off. Uleski was too impatient for this. After emptying the magazine of the M16, he decided to break the deadlock. He ordered the two tanks to move out and make a sweep of the area where the Russians were pinned. Hebrock protested that there could be tanks or antitank guided missile teams in the woods across the way. But Uleski would not hear of it. He wanted the Russians swept away and swept away now. Besides, if there had been tanks or antitank guided missiles in support of the attack, they would have fired by now.

Hebrock and the 22 tank cranked up and moved out. Swinging out wide and then turning north, the two tanks slowly began to advance side by side. They sprayed their machine guns to their front as if they were spraying for insects. The fury of their first fire and the irresistible advance of the steel monsters was too much for some of the Russians. They got up and began to withdraw, some without their weapons. The PCs watched, waiting for such targets. When the Russians got up, the riflemen and machine gunners cut them down. When the tanks reached the end of the area where the Russians had gone to ground, they swung around and went back through the area again, searching out those who had survived the first run. Most of those who were still alive played dead. They would wait till later to make good their escape.

With no more targets, Uleski ordered the tanks to their

alternate positions. He also moved the two PCs. Once his repositioning was finished, and quiet returned to his sector, he reported the status of his element to Bannon.

★ Potecknov was not at all pleased with the progress, or more correctly, the lack of progress that his companies were making. From the village he watched the destruction of the tanks and BTRs followed by the methodical massacre of his troops. Although he could see his officers attempting to get the men up and moving, it was to no avail. The officers were cut down, and the men, seeing that, decided that it was unwise to expose themselves.

Contact with the company on the far side of the hill had been lost after an initial and incomplete report had stated that they were in contact. Only the company commander in the woods reported progress. Potecknov could hear the report of the T-72's cannon and see an occasional flash. He decided that the attack from the north through the woods offered the best chance of success. Turning to his deputy, he ordered him to stay there with the political officer and try to reorganise the unit to their front. He would go around to the north and push the attack through the woods. Without further ado, Potecknov ran down the stairs and into the street to his vehicle. He was determined to win, regardless of the cost.

Uleski's report found 55 and 31 in the same type of stalemate that he had been in before the counterattack by 24 and 22. Bannon had monitored that action and pondered doing the same thing. Tanks 55 and 31 had destroyed six BTRs in addition to the two tanks. Two BTRs and some of the infantry in the second line had managed to pull back into the village. The surviving first-line infantry were on the ground and dispersed. Those near the burning vehicles attempted to crawl away from the light and heat created by the fires. Sometimes their efforts were rewarded by a burst of fire from either 55 or 31. Earlier in the fight a few stout-hearted souls had attempted to engage 55 and 31 with RPGs. Quick reaction ended these efforts.

While there was no longer any return fire from the line of pinned Russian infantry, Bannon knew there were many of them who were still alive. If they stayed out there or withdrew to the village, they would be of no immediate concern. But if some of their officers were able to rally a few men and slip around to the rear, 55 and 31 would be in danger.

The shifting of the heavy artillery barrage from the trail junction to the tree line where 55 and 31 were located, decided the next move. Rather than sit there and be pounded, 55 and 31 were going to attack.

'MIKE 77 – THIS IS ROMEO 25 – OVER.'

'THIS IS MIKE 77 – OVER.'

'THIS IS 25 – WE ARE GOING TO ATTACK – WE WILL ADVANCE ABREAST TOWARDS THE VILLAGE AT 10 MILES PER HOUR – ONCE AT THE VILLAGE WE WILL GO UP THE STREET THE BTRS WENT UP – FALL IN BEHIND ME AS WE GO THROUGH THE VILLAGE AND COVER OUR REAR – HOW COPY SO FAR? – OVER.'

'THIS IS 77 – GOOD COPY – OVER.'

'THIS IS 25 – ONCE IN THE VILLAGE WE WILL TURN RIGHT ON THE MAIN ROAD AND GO NORTH OUT OF THE VILLAGE – FROM THERE FOLLOW ME – I'M NOT SURE WHERE WE WILL GO – OVER.'

'THIS IS 77 – WILCO – OVER.'

'THIS IS 25 – LET'S ROLL.'

'THIS IS 77 – I HEARD THAT.'

Garger didn't have to tell his driver twice. He was just as anxious to get out from under the artillery fire as his tank commander was. As 31 broke the tree line, Garger could see 55 illuminated by the fires of the burning Russian vehicles. Both he and his loader increased their rates of fire and began indiscriminately to spray machine-gun fire before the tank as it advanced.

This was too much for many of the survivors still lying on the ground between the village and the tree line. First there had been the battle between the tanks, which their tanks had lost. Then there had been the accurate and deadly machine-gun fire that had cut down their comrades and officers and anyone who tried to stop it. Their BTRs had been destroyed one at a time and were now burning hulks incinerating their crews. Around them were visions of horror: burning vehicles, steady fire from an unseen enemy, apparent failure of their tanks and artillery, death of their comrades, moans of the wounded, screams of men burning to death, and the smell of burning flesh. And worst of all, the feeling that they were the only survivors, that every man around them was dead or dying. All this pushed the green Russian soldiers to the limit of their endurance. The appearance of the American tanks closing on them, spraying death, pushed them beyond.

The 55 and 31 had no sooner cleared the tree line and the incoming artillery when individual Russian soldiers began to jump up and flee. The driver kept 55 at a steady ten miles an hour. Bannon, the loader, and the gunner covered their sectors, engaging Russians as they made their appearance. The loader covered the left flank, the gunner the centre, and Bannon the right. Those who were smart and not in the direct path of the advancing tanks stayed put and played dead. There were few smart Russians that night.

The tanks converged on the village. At the edge of the village, 31 slowed down, let 55 take the lead, and swung its turret over the rear, continuously engaging soldiers who were attempting to flee the carnage. As 55 turned the first corner in the village, it was greeted by a BTR at a range of twenty metres. The BTR was frantically trying to back up and get out of the way. Both the BTR commander and Bannon looked at each other for the briefest of moments before they began to issue frantic orders.

'GUNNER – BATTLESIGHT – BTR!'

The shock of seeing a target so close caused the gunner to raise the level of his reply several decibels.

'IDENTIFIED!'

'SABOT LOADED – UP!'

'FIRE!'

At this range and with the speed of the SABOT round, firing and impact were almost simultaneous. Bannon felt heat of the impact on his face. The brilliant flash of contact and the shower of sparks lit up the street and momentarily blinded him. The SABOT round cut through the centre of the BTR and went flying down the street behind the BTR into a building. The BTR burst into flames and staggered to a stop.

For a moment, 55 stood there with its gun tube almost touching the BTR. All action seemed to stop, as if everyone had to pause to catch his breath. Carefully, Bannon guided 55 around the burning BTR and continued down the street. Tank 31 followed, Garger and his loader shielding themselves from the heat of the flames. The tanks continued into the town, searching for new targets.

Kelp and McCauley had finally managed to get themselves into a good position. The rear of the crippled T-72 was less than a hundred metres to their front. They had a clear shot. The burning hulk of the other T-72 provided just enough light for McCauley as he fumbled about fitting the thermal sight to a new Dragon round.

Kelp was getting impatient, 'I thought you said you knew how to use that thing.'

'I told you, I only had one class on it, and that was a long time ago. Give me a break, will ya? I'm doin' the best I can.'

'Well, do your best faster, damn it.' For a moment the situation reminded Kelp of many similar conversations between him and Folk. Folk was always on his back to do things faster or better. As he watched McCauley fumble with the sight and round, Kelp realised why Folk had been so hard on him. He owed Folk a huge apology.

'*Got it!* I think.'

'About time. Let's do it.'

McCauley set up the Dragon and braced himself as he had seen the other gunner do. Kelp got over to one side and scanned the area for Russian soldiers.

'Here goes.'

The shock of firing the weapon for the first time made McCauley jump as the missile launched. The missile flew a few metres and hit a tree, causing it to fall to the ground and spin around as the rocket motor burned and popped.

167

'SHIT! GET THE OTHER ROUND!'

McCauley scrambled to detach the sight from the expended round as Kelp rolled the next one to him. Kelp watched as a figure came up out of the T-72's TC's hatch and looked to the rear where the first missile was still burning. The turret began to traverse around. 'SHIT! HURRY OR WE'RE DEAD MEAT!' yelled Kelp.

Fear of death motivated McCauley. He managed to connect the sight to the new round the first time. Kelp kept glancing back and forth between the T-72 and McCauley. It was a race that would have horrible consequences for the loser.

Just as the T-72's long gun was about to lay on the two privates, it slammed into a tree and stopped. The tank commander yelled an order. The gunner swung the turret back a few metres and then tried to knock the tree down with the gun tube. But the tree was too big. They could not finish laying on the two privates. When the tank commander saw they were not going to get the turret around, he unlocked his 12.7mm machine gun, trained it in their direction, and fired.

The wild burst flew harmlessly over the heads of the two privates. Kelp brought his submachine gun up to his shoulder and fired an equally harmless burst at the Russian tank commander. It was then that McCauley let loose with the second Dragon missile. The flash and whoosh of launch, the burn of the rocket motor, and the detonation of impact ended the fire fight.

The small-arms fire to their rear and the destruction of the second tank took the last fight out of the Russians facing Polgar. One at a time and in pairs they began to drift back north along the trail. At first Polgar thought that they were thinning the line to form a group for an end run. But as the Russian return fire slackened, then ceased, he knew the truth. The shadows created by the Russians as they drew back past the burning tanks kept moving north. For the second time that night, the order to cease fire rang out through the wooded lot.

The firing began to slacken, then stop, as Colonel Potecknov moved down the trail. At first, he was elated. They had succeeded in breaking the American line. But the faint yells in

English, followed by the appearance of figures headed in his direction convinced the colonel that success had not been his. His men were retreating.

Potecknov was not about to give up. Picking his pace up to a slow trot, he began to wave and yell at his men, ordering them to turn around and go back.

The relief and elation over their victory against the T-72 were short-lived. Kelp and McCauley had just begun to move back to rejoin the rest of the infantry when several figures came towards them from the direction of the infantry positions. Both of them dropped down behind a tree, back to back. At first Kelp thought the Russians were sending men back to find them. But the figures went past them in a hurry. They were making no effort to search the bushes for the tank killers. It dawned upon Kelp that the Russians were retreating. That was good. Unfortunately, they were right in the middle of the Russians' path of retreat.

The two soldiers continued to huddle behind the tree, each facing out to one side with their weapons at the ready. Kelp watched as the number of Russians increased. It hadn't occurred to him that there were so many of them. It was amazing that the infantry had not only held, but had caused the Russians to retreat. As he was watching this flood of refugees from the front, a lone figure came running south down the trail, waving a pistol and shouting. Had to be an officer, Kelp thought. The dumb bastard was trying to stop the retreat. For a moment Kelp wondered if he should kill the officer. But that feat of heroism was not needed.

Kelp watched as this figure stopped a group of three retreating Russians and tried to push them back. To Kelp's surprise, one of the three levelled his AK, stuck it into the officer's stomach, and let go a burst. The officer flew back and sprawled over the trail like a rag doll. The one who had fired the AK said something in Russian. All three continued north, stepping over the dead officer. One of the party kicked the officer in the head as he went by. The Russian soldiers had had enough for the night.

Kelp's attention was suddenly drawn to his front as a

Russian stumbled and fell next to him. Kelp and the Russian stared at each other for a moment before they realised that they were looking eyeball to eyeball at the enemy. As the Russian opened his mouth to let out a scream, Kelp leaped on the Russian's chest, putting one hand on the Russian's throat and the other over his mouth. The Russian grabbed the hand Kelp had over his mouth with both hands and tried to pry it off. Kelp pushed down harder but felt his grip slipping.

Just as the Russian succeeded in prying Kelp's hand off his mouth, he went stiff and let go of Kelp's hand. Kelp turned around to see McCauley jab his bayonet into the Russian's stomach a second and third time. When the Russian went limp, Kelp let him go and grabbed McCauley's arm as he started to stab the Russian a fifth time. The two privates looked at each other, then resumed their back-to-back position behind the tree as the last of the Russians went by without noticing the small battle that had occurred in the silent and dark wood.

★ Colonel Potecknov lay there on the trail, unable to move. In the silence of the dark woods he could feel his life slipping away. There was pain, intense pain. He also began to feel cold even though it had been a warm summer evening. He was bleeding to death, and he knew there was nothing that he could do to stop that. In his last minutes, his thoughts were not on the fears of the unknown fate that awaited him or of the shame of failure. Rather, he was puzzled and bewildered. His battalion should have succeeded! He had done everything right. The plan had been a good one. It had been foolproof. What had gone wrong? Why hadn't it worked? The Russian colonel sought answers for these questions until darkness swept over his mind.

The 55 was just entering the village square when Bannon received Polgar's report that the Russians had broken contact and had withdrawn to the north. The run through the village so far had been quick and dirty. After the BTR had been destroyed, everyone and everything scattered up alleys or into houses. In the town square there were several trucks and two BTRs with soldiers scrambling to board them and get out. When 55 rolled into the square, the trucks began to roll with troops hanging half in, half out. One of the BTR drivers panicked and backed up over a group of soldiers that had run behind it for cover. A truck driver watching 55 and not paying attention to where he was going ran over an officer waving him down and crashed into a store window at the edge of the square. All this confusion was created just by 55's appearance and without a shot being fired. When 31 pulled up next to 55, and both tanks began to fire with main guns and machine guns, the situation really went to hell.

Satisfied that all the Russians were gone, Kelp and McCauley began to move forward cautiously towards the infantry positions. After what they had gone through, the last thing Kelp wanted was to get blown away by his own side. As he moved forward, Kelp stepped up onto a piece of metal. When he looked down, he was overpowered by a surge of fear. In the faint light from the burning tanks Kelp saw that he was standing on one of the antitank mines they had put out earlier. He knew he was dead.

But nothing happened. It finally occurred to him that he was not heavy enough to set off the mine. Even so, when he mustered the courage to remove his foot, he did so with the greatest of care. Sweat rolled down his face as he tried to regain composure before moving on. There were too many ways to get killed out here. Kelp wanted his tank back. This infantry shit was for the birds.

When he thought that they were close enough to the infantry positions, Kelp called out to let them know they were coming back. Polgar, unfamiliar with Kelp's voice ordered them to advance and be recognised. When they were in the open, Polgar gave them the challenge. Only after Kelp gave the proper password were the two tank killers allowed back into the fold.

Once the tanks were clear of the village, Bannon ordered 31 to move up to the right of 55. As they were starting to swing south to return to their positions, they ran into the Russian infantry that had just broken contact with Polgar. Apparently, the Russians had not heard of the run through the village by the American tanks and thought 55 and 31 were Russian. They simply stood aside to let them pass. When the tanks cut loose with machine guns, the last semblance of order evaporated and the Russians scattered to the four winds. Only the jamming of 55's last operational machine gun broke off the engagement. The battle for Hill 214 was over, for now. Checkmate.

As 55 and 31 moved south along the tree line in silence, Bannon radioed Uleski and Polgar. He ordered them to pull their people back to the trail junction and form a coil. Polgar and his men would cover the north, Uleski and his element would cover the east and south and 55 and 31 would cover the west. When everyone was in, they were to meet at the trail junction.

Bannon was the last to arrive. Uleski, Polgar, Jefferson, and Hebrock greeted Garger and him with nothing more than a nod. With not so much as a word of greeting, he simply asked, 'Ok, what do we have?'

Uleski had suffered only one wounded, a PC driver who had been hit in the shoulder during their fire fight and had lost a lot of blood but was in stable condition. Both the PCs and the 2nd Platoon tanks had ample ammo on hand. Polgar's dismounted element had suffered two killed, including the Dragon gunner, and four wounded, two of them seriously. Although his people had run low on ammunition while on the firing line, now that they were with the PCs, the men were replenishing their ammo pouches from ammunition stored on the PCs. The only casualty between 55 and 31 had been 31's loader. He had been hit in the face by a bullet during the run through the village. Though he was in a lot of pain, he would survive. For the price of two dead and six wounded, Team Yankee had held.

But the Team had reached the end of its rope. Even as they stood there, Bannon could tell that the stress and strain of this last fight had used up every man's final reserve of energy. They had done their best and done well. But there was no more to give. Besides the exhaustion, the tanks were down to a grand total of thirty-one main gun rounds and four thousand rounds for the COAX and loader's machine gun. Even if the men could hold up under another attack, which was impossible, the ammunition couldn't.

Bannon informed the Team's leadership that at 0330 they would leave Hill 214 and move south in order to re-enter friendly lines. There was no need to explain. There were no protests or speeches. Everyone understood the situation and knew there was nothing more to be gained here. Now the Team's mission was to save what was left for another day.

To prepare for the move, the wounded were loaded onto the PCs, three in each. Folk, who could drive a PC, took the place of the wounded PC driver. Kelp took the place of the wounded loader on 31. Uleski would command one of the PCs and half of the infantry while Polgar took the other PC and the other half of the infantry. The tank crews redistributed the ammunition between the tanks. When all was ready, the Team settled in to wait until 0330 and move out. Deep inside, Bannon wanted to believe that at the last minute the battalion would come forward and link up. He was going to give them another hour and a half. If they didn't get here by then, he was going to save as much of Team Yankee as he could.

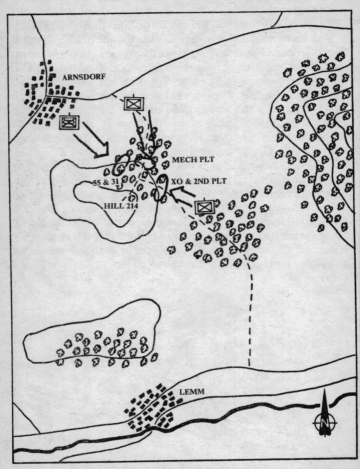

MAP 10: THE SOVIET ATTACK ON HILL 214

174

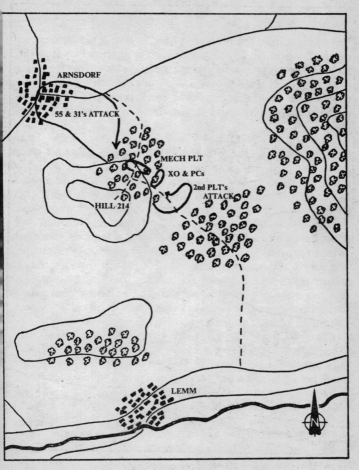

ARNSDORF

55 & 31's ATTACK

MECH PLT
XO & PCs

HILL 214

2nd PLT's
ATTACK

LEMM

N

MAP 11: THE TANKS COUNTERATTACK

175

Chapter Eight

R AND R

The damned fly kept bothering him. It wasn't the buzzing so much. Bannon could block that out. It was the fact that the bastard kept landing on the cut on the side of his face and irritating it. He'd no sooner shoo it away with a halfhearted wave of his hand than it would come back and land. How could he get any sleep with that damned fly bothering him. Sleep.

'SLEEP! MY GOD, I'VE FALLEN ASLEEP!' That thought stunned Bannon. His eyes popped open and were greeted by the morning sun. Almost instinctively, his arm shot up to check the time on his watch. 0548. The Team had missed its move-out time by over two hours! Now it was full daylight. Chances of slipping away under cover of darkness were gone.

Bannon looked over into the loader's hatch. Newman was sitting upright on his seat sound asleep. A scan of the tight circle of tank and PCs failed to reveal any sign of movement. Instead of being alert and watching their sectors, track commanders were slumped across their machine guns asleep. Infantrymen lay curled up on the ground asleep where they had fallen. Even the wounded were quiet. The calamity was complete. Team Yankee had collectively gone to sleep.

Bannon jumped down to awaken the crew of 55. The gunner was lying up against the main gun. 'Sergeant GWENT! Sergeant GWENT! WAKE UP!' Gwent sat up, shook his head, then jumped when he realised he had fallen asleep.

'*Oh shit*, sir. I fell asleep. Goddamn, I'm sorry.'

'Well, don't feel like the Lone Ranger. Everyone is asleep.'

Gwent suddenly realised what Bannon was telling him, and that it was light outside. His eyes grew big, '*You mean we didn't pull off that hill yet? We're still behind enemy lines?*'

'Target. Now get the rest of the crew up while I wake the Team up. AND DON'T CRANK THE TANK.'

Without waiting for a response, Bannon climbed out and

began to dismount the tank. The spaghetti cord connecting the CVC to the intercom jerked his head back to remind him to disconnect it before jumping off 55. Once disconnected and on the ground, he headed for the first leader he saw, Polgar. Polgar was asleep, leaning against the side of a tree with his M16 cradled in his arms. After being shaken a moment, his eyes opened into narrow slits, looked to the left, looked to the right, looked at Bannon, then flew wide open. 'SHIT! I fell asleep.'

'Well, Sergrant Polgar, you ain't alone. Wake up the XO and your people while I get the tank crews. Gather the leadership at 55 when they're up. AND DON'T START ANY ENGINES. Clear?'

'Clear.' With that, Polgar was up in a flash, hustling from body to body, waking each one up with kicks, shakes, and curses. Bannon trotted over to 31.

Garger was leaning over backwards, asleep, arms extended and stiff. He looked as if he had been shot. 'Gerry! Gerry! Lieutenant Garger WAKE UP!'

His eyes opened in tiny slits. Like Polgar, he looked at Bannon for a moment, then jumped upright. 'OH SHIT!' It occurred to Bannon that 'Oh shit!' was fast becoming the standard greeting for the Team instead of good morning. If their predicament wasn't so serious, this whole situation would have been comical.

'Gerry, get the rest of the tank crews up and have the TCs meet me over at 55. And tell the TCs not to crank the tanks.' As Bannon was getting off, Garger reached down and kicked his gunner in the back, telling him to wake up.

As he headed back to 55, Bannon began to work on a way out of this one. There would be no slipping away under the cover of darkness. If the Team moved, it would be in broad daylight, just like yesterday. That thought was disturbing. But staying here to face a new series of Russian attacks was equally distasteful. The collapse of the Team's security confirmed his belief that it was at the end of its tether. The Russians were sure to come back with more people and tanks. Bannon didn't dare face a wounded bear with a handful of punch-drunk soldiers. They had to pull out, the sooner the better.

Once the leaders were together, he issued his orders. The Team would go out the way they had planned. Since the Soviets had not hit them from the south, that was the direction the Team would take. The 55 and 31 would lead, travelling abreast once they were in the open. The PCs would come next, in the centre, followed by 24 and 22. The Team would move around the west side of the hill that had been Objective LOG and go back into friendly lines the same way they had come out. The only difference in the plan was that rather than creep along in an effort to sneak out, they would roll as fast as the PCs would allow. In addition, the tanks would fire up their smoke generators and blow smoke the entire way back. While 55 and 31 would be exposed to the front and flank, the PCs and the other two tanks would be hidden in a rolling cloud of smoke.

As they were about to break up and return to their vehicles, a volley of artillery fire impacted to the south in the vicinity of Hill 214. Everyone turned in that direction. When a second volley confirmed their fears, all eyes turned back on Bannon. They had been too late. The Russians were coming back.

'All right. Sergeant Polgar, you come with me. We're going to go up there and see what's going on. Bob, you're in charge while we're gone. Be ready to crank up and roll if the Russians come. Until then, stay alert and keep quiet. If the Russians come before we're back, leave without us. Move in the opposite direction until you're in the open. Then carry out the plan as we have discussed. Any questions?'

There was none. What else could they do? Bannon turned to Polgar, 'Do you have an extra M16?'

'Yes, sir. I can take one from one of the wounded.'

'Good, get me one, a couple of magazines, and meet me back here, pronto.' Polgar went over to one of the tracks. Bannon turned to Uleski. 'Bob, no heroics. If there's trouble, and we're not back, get out of here. Clear?'

'Clear.'

By the time he had his helmet and web gear on, Polgar was back with the rifle. After inserting a magazine and chambering a round, the two turned and started to head south. Polgar followed Bannon at a distance of five metres and a little to his right. The assembled leaders watched them for a moment before Uleski bellowed out the order to mount up and be ready to move.

After they had gone a hundred metres, the artillery stopped. He and Polgar paused and squatted down to listen for a moment. The sound of tracked vehicles could be heard to the south. Bannon motioned to Polgar. They continued on. As they were nearing the crest of the hill and the tree line, he saw movement to his front. Instinctively, he dropped into a prone firing position behind the nearest tree. Both he and Polgar watched and waited.

To the left Bannon noticed a movement. Then there was more to the front at a distance of fifty metres. As they watched, a line of figures approached the woods. He turned to Polgar and whispered, 'When I start shooting, run like hell back to the XO and tell him to go east out of here.'

Polgar thought about it. 'You're the Team commander, I'll cover you. You go back and tell the XO.'

'Damn it, Polgar, I gave you an order. You better be ready to move when I let go. Clear?' Polgar didn't reply. He only nodded.

Bannon turned back to watch the line of figures continue forward. Slowly he reached into his pocket and pulled out the two frag grenades he had taken off 66 before destroying it. He raised the M16 to his shoulder and began to sight in on the nearest figure. This was going to be a very short fight.

As Bannon watched the figure in his sight, it occurred to him that the uniform was very familiar. It was camouflaged. So far the Russians they had faced weren't wearing camouflage. Then he noticed the rifle. It was an M16. They were Americans. He turned to Polgar and whispered, 'Americans.' Polgar stuck his head up a little higher, looked, and then smiled.

Remembering the day before, he was a little more cautious in making contact. He let the line of infantry get within twenty metres and then bellowed out 'HALT!'

The line of infantry froze where they stood, ready to drop and fire. Their heads slowly turned to find the origin of the voice.

'Advance and be recognised.'

Their heads snapped as one in Bannon's direction. He slowly rose up to the kneeling position but kept his rifle trained on the nearest man. He began to move towards him. When he was close enough, Bannon repeated the order, 'Halt.' At that point, he was unable to recall the challenge and password. He had to do something fast before the people in front of him got excited and fired. 'We're Team Yankee, Task Force First of the Seventy Eight. We were cut off. Who are you?' Bannon kept his rifle aimed at the figure.

'What's the challenge?'

'I don't know. We were cut off yesterday. I'm Captain Bannon, the team commander.' The infantry was beginning slowly to spread out. Things were not working out well at all.

From behind, Polgar called out, 'Hey, Kerch. Is that your mob of dirt bags out there?'

The infantryman in front of Bannon straightened up, let the muzzle of his rifle drop some, and turned towards Polgar's voice. 'Polgar, is that you?'

'Yeah, it's me. Now tell you mob to ease up so the captain and I can get up.' With that, Polgar stood up and began to come over to where Sergeant First Class Kerch, A company 1st of the 78th Mechanised Infantry and Bannon had been holding each other at bay. Team Yankee had been relieved.

Polgar led Kerch and his people through the woods to where Team Yankee was located. Bannon went up to the top of Hill 214 where the battalion command group was. It occurred to him as he followed the trail to the top of the hill that he'd been here for over twenty hours, had fought for the hill and done his damnedest to hold it and had never been to the top of it. He was finally going to see what the Team had paid for so dearly.

At the wood line he passed the tracks from a platoon of the 1st of the 78th that had been attached to the 1st of the 4th Armor. They were waiting for word to go in and pick up the dismounted element he and Polgar had encountered. Just below the crest of the hill, two tanks and a PC sat, peering over the top towards Arnsdorf below. There were three figures standing next to the PC looking at a map board. When one of the figures looked up and saw Bannon approaching, he motioned. The other two looked up, put down the map board, and started towards him. They were the battalion commander, XO, and S-3 of the 1st Battalion, 4th Armor, Team Yankee's parent battalion. As he closed, Bannon saluted and, as nonchalantly as possible, greeted Team Yankee's saviours.

'Sean, Colonel Reynolds told us you had been wiped out last night.'

'Sir, the news of our demise has been greatly exaggerated. D company is reporting for duty.' Not that they could do anything but, what the hell, it sounded good.

Maj. Frank Shell, the S-3, looked him over for a moment, then turned to the battalion commander. 'If the rest of his people look as bad as Sean, the infantry was right, Team Yankee was wiped out.' Then he turned back to Bannon and, seriously this time, asked if the rest of the Team did look like him. Bannon's eyes were bloodshot and had dark circles around them. Every exposed patch of skin was dirty. He had two-days growth of beard. The cut on the side of his face had become swollen from infection, and there was dried blood on his face and neck and around his collar. There was also dried blood on the chest and sleeves of his chemical suit from pulling Ortelli from 66. This was mixed with diesel and oil stains. Bannon guessed he couldn't have looked much worse.

As they walked over to the PC, he explained the Team's situation and requested that an ambulance be sent imme-diately to the trail junction to bring out the wounded. The battalion XO got on it and had an M-113 ambulance rumbling down to the Team in minutes. They stopped by the tanks and looked down into Arnsdorf. There were still wisps of smoke rising from some of the burned-out Soviet vehicles. Scores of dead Russians littered the field among the smashed vehicles. The battalion commander looked at Bannon, 'I take it you did that last night.'

'Yeah. With a little help. Very little help,' he replied without turning away. It all seemed so remote now, so foreign. Bannon had difficulty equating the scene before him with the horror show that had been last night. He gazed up at the clear blue morning sky, across the valley to the green hill to the north, and then at the battalion commander. 'Yes, sir. We did that and more.'

After the battalion commander and XO left to go down into Arnsdorf and follow the attack, Major Shell updated Bannon on what had happened since yesterday morning and how 1st of the 4th had come into play. The Mech Battalion that Team Yankee was part of had become spread out all over the division's rear during the night road march. While passing through one of the villages at night, part of the column had taken a wrong turn. The people leading the two line companies, C and D, the battalion trains, and the battalion CP all realised their mistakes at different times and tried to get back onto the proper route separately. This led to confusion and more errors, just as the first sergeant had reported.

D company was the first to show up and join Team Bravo on its overwatch position at 1730 last night. C company went into the rear areas of the German panzer division that was to the south of the division, got turned around, and then ran out of fuel. It never reached its destination, being held in the rear as part of the division reserve. The battalion trains pulled in at night but never told anyone. Major Jordan found them by accident in the area where they were supposed to be. The S-4, in charge of the trains, thought the battalion was still under radio listening silence, never realising the net had been jammed, and the battalion had moved to another frequency. Team Bravo, which had been in position to support Yankee, moved up to LOG but was thrown off in the late morning by a dismounted counterattack from Lemm.

When all this had been sorted out by the battalion and brigade commanders, it was decided to pull the 1st of the 78th Mech out and throw in the 1st of the 4th Armor. As Team Bravo was combat ineffective, and everyone thought that, except for recovered tracks, Team Yankee was gone, the 1st of the 78th was sent to the rear to reconstitute and act as reserve. The 1st of the 4th relieved the Mech Battalion at 0300, just after the battle of Hill 214, and began its attack at 0530, just before the Team woke up. Major Shell told Bannon that he, the commander, and the XO were trying to figure out what had happened to all the Russians that the 1st of the 78th had reported and who had done all the damage in Arnsdorf when Bannon showed up.

The good news from this comedy of errors was that Team Bravo held LOG long enough for First Sergeant Harrert to gather up the Team's wounded and recover those tracks that had only been damaged. To Bannon's surprise, he found out that First Sergeant Harrert had four tanks and two PCs, including the HQ PC, in varying states of repair. In the attack against LOG, Team Yankee had had only two tanks totally destroyed, 21 and 66, one PC, the 1st Squad of the Mech platoon and the FIST track. For casualties, not counting the men who were killed on Hill 214, the Team had lost fifteen killed and six wounded. The number of killed seemed staggering and out of proportion. But as he thought about it, it made sense. Tank 21 and the infantry PC alone accounted for thirteen of the dead.

While Bannon pondered the Team's good fortune, Major Shell contacted brigade and received orders for Team Yankee. The Team was to road march to the rear and join the 1st of the 78th in reserve. He gave Bannon the location of the Mech Battalion's new CP in the rear and the route the Team was to use. Bannon asked for and received permission to stop by the 1st of the 4th's combat trains and pick up some diesel. With a battalion to run, the S-3 had to go. He told Bannon to get the cut on his face taken care of while the Team was refuelling at the trains and wished him luck. The S-3 mounted his PC, they exchanged salutes, and then he rolled down into Arnsdorf to join his commander. Bannon went back to Team Yankee, relieved in every sense of the word.

The formal portion of the morning briefing at the Tenth Corps Headquarters was over. The commanding general got up and walked over to the two maps that were displayed before him. On the large-scale map the overall situation in Germany was displayed. It was not good. In the NORTHAG, or Northern Army Group, area the Soviets were fast approaching the Dutch border. Hamburg and Bremerhaven had fallen. Though there had not been a breakthrough, several portions of the front were threatened with collapse. Already two corps commanders had requested the release of tactical nuclear weapons in order to break up concentrations of Warsaw Pact units. Follow-on Soviet, Polish, and East German units were moving towards the front to resume the attack.

The CENTAG or Central Army Group area, where the Tenth Corps operated, was much better. The terrain there was not the best for armoured warfare. In addition, French forces were readily at hand and beginning to reach the front.

Turning to his small-scale map that depicted the corps' area of operation and current situation, he began to run his finger along the front line trace of his units, stopping every so often to study Warsaw Pact forces that were opposing the corps. At one point, he stopped his finger on a group of Soviet units and turned to his intel officer. 'George, these people here, you said that they are continuing west?'

'Yes, sir. We expect them to be in the vicinity of Kassel by tomorrow morning at the latest unless we can get the Air Force to delay them.'

'What's coming up behind them, George? Who is going to be in the Leipzig area two to four days from now?'

'Well, sir, right now, no one. There is one Polish division here that could be in that area, but that's about it.'

Without turning away from the map and motioning with his hand, the general began to issue instructions to his operations officer. 'Frank, get your Plans people to work on an attack centred around the 21st Panzer Division. As soon as the French relieve it, I want the 21st to move here and attack north into the Thuringer Wald. The mission of the 21st is to breach the Soviet security screen and then cross the Inner German Boundary here. The second phase of the operation will be a passage of lines by the 52nd or 54th Division with orders to continue the attack north across the Saale River towards Leipzig. I want this operation to commence in three days. Have your people prepared to present me a decision briefing by 1800 hours tonight. What are your questions?'

The operations officer studied the map for a moment, then turned to the general, 'Sir, can I plan on using the 25th

Armored Division? Also how far do you want us to plan after we reach Leipzig?'

'Frank, I want your plan to use everything we've got. For planning purposes you will consider our axis of advance from where we are to Leipzig, Berlin, and finally the Baltic coast. If I can convince the CINC, we're going to go for broke.'

Without further ado, the briefing broke up, staff officers scurrying in all directions to prepare for the evening briefing.

The road march was uneventful. Team Yankee had forty-five kilometres to cover and could have done it in an hour had it not been for the traffic. As Team Yankee was going to the rear this time, and its road march had not been scheduled by the division's movement control centre, it was bumped by higher priority traffic going to the front or wounded headed for the rear. It was amazing how many vehicles there were driving around in division's rear. As they sat on the side of the road waiting for a convoy to go by before the Team could move again, Garger wondered if someone was really in charge of all this. There were long convoys of supply and fuel trucks, artillery batteries, columns of ambulances moving rearward, a field hospital moving forward, engineers all over, and equipment he had never seen before and whose purpose he had no idea of. That an army could bring order out of this apparent chaos, keep people fed, vehicles fuelled, and units arriving at the right place at the right time was a source of wonder to him.

The biggest problem Bannon had during the long pauses while the Team waited for a break in the traffic was waking everyone up when it was time to move. It seemed that each time they stopped, the men fell over asleep. Once, when a break in the traffic appeared, it took so long to wake everyone up that by the time they were ready to roll, a new convoy came by and the Team had to wait again. The men immediately went back to sleep.

The worst part of the march was seeing the suffering of the local Germans who had stayed. As the Team rolled past, if they acknowledged them at all, it was only with blank stares. Bannon shuddered to think what was going through their minds, especially the old people. This was the second time in their lives that they had seen war. As the Team passed through one of the villages, an old woman stopped pushing a cart and watched. Bannon could see tears running down her cheeks as they went by. He would never know for whom she was crying.

The children bothered him the most. During peacetime manoeuvres through the German countryside they would wave and laugh and run along the side of the tracks, yelling to the soldiers to throw them candy or rations. American soldiers often did. But now the children didn't come. Instead, when they heard the rumble of the tanks, they ran and hid. Only a few would peek to see whose tanks they were. Even when they saw that the tanks were American, there were terror and fear in their eyes.

Bannon began to understand why the pacifist movement had been so large in Europe. The children of the last war, who had witnessed his uncle's Sherman tank roll through their villages, had not wanted their children to experience the same horror. Unfortunately, the good intentions of the parents were no match for the intentions of the Soviet leaders. As had happened too often in the past, good intentions and desire for peace were useless against cold steel and people willing to use it.

Looking at these children caused Bannon to wonder about his own. They still didn't know if all the families had made it out before hostilities. After awhile, he began to turn away whenever he saw the children. The thoughts they brought to his mind were too painful.

Three hours after they started, Team Yankee finally rolled into the town where the 1st of the 78th was supposed to be. As the Team entered the town, they passed a group of American soldiers sitting in front of a house cleaning their weapons. They were stripped down to their T-shirts or bare chests, enjoying the weather and in no hurry to finish the tasks at hand. Some of the men didn't even have their boots on. Their PC was parked in an alley. Clothes and towels were draped on it to dry. A shirt was even hanging on the barrel of the calibre .50.

Bannon stopped 55 and signalled the rest of the column to

halt. Turning to the group of soldiers, he called out, 'Who's in charge here?'

A couple of the soldiers looked to the left and the right, then chattered among themselves. One young soldier turned and yelled back: 'Who the fuck wants to know?'

Garger later told Bannon that he had never seen him move so fast. When the soldier gave him that reply, he was out of the turret of 55 and on the ground headed for the man at a dead run, all in one motion. 'ON YOUR FEET, YOU SORRY EXCUSE FOR A SOLDIER! ALL OF YOU! YOU TOO!'

They suddenly realised that perhaps they were talking to an officer and began to stand up. Not that they could tell – the only thing different about Bannon since his meeting with the Tank Battalion command group that morning had been the cleaning of the wound on the side of his face. Regardless of who he was or how he looked, 'Who the fuck wants to know' is a poor reply, especially for a soldier.

'All right, soldier, I'll ask you one more time. And if you give me a smartass answer like you just did, they'll be sending your remains home in a very small envelope. Is that clear?'

Before answering, the soldier took stock of this godawful-looking and -smelling figure before him. Taking no more chances, he came to attention. 'Sir, our squad leader is not here.'

'That's not what I asked you, soldier. I asked you who is in charge. There is someone in charge of this gaggle, isn't there?'

'I guess I am, sir.'

'YOU GUESS! YOU GUESS! DON'T YOU KNOW?'

'Yes, sir, I am in charge, sir.'

'What unit are you soldier?'

Company C, sir.'

'Good, great! You wouldn't happen to know what battalion you belong to, would you?'

'Sir, the Fighting First of the 78th, sir.'

By this time, the tracks in Team Yankee had shut down and were listening to the conversation. When the soldier Bannon was dressing down came out with the fighting first comment, everyone in the Team broke out in uproarious laughter. From struggling with his rage, Bannon suddenly found himself struggling to hold back his laughter. He lost. The C company soldiers were enraged at being the object of laughter, but they said and did nothing. They were not about to tempt the wrath of a column of soldiers who looked as Bannon did. They simply stood at attention and bit their tongues.

After regaining control of himself, barely, Bannon continued, 'All right, soldier. Where is your battalion CP?' The soldier told him that it was in a school just down the street and how to get there. With that Bannon turned and climbed aboard 55, gave the hand and arm signal to crank up and move out, then led Team Yankee at a dead run to the headquarters of the Fighting First.

As Bannon and Uleski walked down the corridors of the German school, Bannon felt out of place. In the field he felt at ease. They belonged in the field. That was where they worked. But this was a school, a place where young children came to learn about the world and to prepare for the future. Bannon was a soldier whose job was to close with and destroy the enemy by fire, manoeuvre, and shock effect. In short, to kill. He had no business here, in a place of the future. The two hurried down the corridors in silence so as not to offend the spirit of the school.

When they entered the classroom where the battalion staff and company commanders were having a command and staff briefing, they felt more out of place. Though hard to imagine, the battalion staff appeared to be even cleaner than they had been two days ago, when the order to take Hill 214 had been given. It could have been that Bannon was just dirtier. Both he and the XO had gone tromping into the room like two men storming into a strange bar looking to pick a fight with the first man who said boo. They stood there for a moment, surveying the scene as the assembled group surveyed them. It reminded Bannon of a scene from a B-grade western. He looked at Uleski, who appeared to be thinking the same thing, and almost began to laugh.

It was Major Jordan who first came up and greeted them with a sincere smile and a handshake, as if they were long-lost cousins. The battalion commander and the other company

188

commanders followed. Only the C company commander hung back. Bannon imagined it was from embarrassment. When the greetings were over, Colonel Reynolds took him to the front of the group and sat him on the seat next to his, displacing the C company commander. This move shocked Bannon since Captain Cravin, commander of C company, had always been Colonel Reynolds's fair-haired boy. Whatever Cravin did was good and right. Major Jordan, who didn't think much of Cravin or his company, smiled at the sight of the colonel's fair-haired boy being taken down a notch.

As the meeting continued, Reynolds would stop, turn to Bannon, and ask what Team Yankee needed from the battalion motor officer, the S-4, the S-1, and so one. It quickly became apparent that the colonel was prepared to give Team Yankee first choice on whatever was available. Given the opportunity, Bannon grabbed it and ran. When the S-1 wanted to know about personnel needs, Bannon told him that the Team needed eighteen infantry men to replace Polgar's losses. The S-1 stated that it would not be possible to replace them now. Bannon turned to the battalion commander and told him that since C and D companies were still up to strength, if each of their squads gave up one man, Polgar could be brought up to strength. He had meant this as a cheap shot at the two companies. To his surprise, the colonel told the S-1 to see that this was done and to ensure that only the best soldiers went. He then turned to the S-4 and told him that if the S-4 couldn't get another PC for Polgar right away, C company was to turn one over to Team Yankee.

At the end of the meeting Bannon and Uleski briefed the colonel and the S-3 on what had happened after Team Yankee had crossed the line of departure in its attack on Objective LOG and Hill 214. The Colonel and S-3 would stop them and ask questions about certain aspects of the operation, effects of weapons, where the Team's soldiers seemed to be wanting, how the Soviets reacted, and so on. Jordan recommended that the leadership of Team Yankee prepare a briefing for the officers and NCOs of the battalion. In this way, lessons learned could be passed on. The colonel endorsed the idea. Major Jordan gave Bannon the location where the first sergeant had the rest of Team Yankee, congratulated both him and Uleski on a job well done, and ended the meeting. The colonel also congratulated them and then left with Jordan.

When everyone was gone, Bannon and Uleski sat in the silent room staring at the floor in front of them. Without looking up, Uleski quietly asked, 'Did we really do as well as they said we did?'

Bannon thought for a moment. In the discussion, it had all seemed so easy. It was as if they had been discussing a tactical exercise at Fort Knox, not a battle that had meant life and death for the thirty-five men that had set out to defend Hill 214 yesterday. Their discussion had covered the effects of weapons, the deployment of forces, and the application of firepower. In the cool, quiet setting of the German classroom it all seemed to make sense, to fit together. The dread and fear of dying was missing. The stinging, cutting emotional pain he had felt as the crew of 66 removed Ortelli's shattered body from the burning tank had not been covered. The disgust and anger he had experienced when it seemed that Team Yankee had been wiped out was not important. The battle they had talked about and the one Team Yankee had fought were not the same and never would be. At least not for those who had been there.

Bannon turned to Uleski, 'What do you think, Bob?'

He stared at Bannon for a moment before answering, 'I think we were lucky. Damned lucky.'

'You know, Bob, I think you're right.' With that they left the classroom and went about rebuilding the Team.

For the next three days Team Yankee licked its wounds and pulled itself back together. Their assembly area was a few kilometres from the battalion CP. First Sergeant Harrert had found and claimed it. Soon after arriving Bannon found out why. In the centre there was a small *Gasthaus* where Germans used to stop and eat after taking their long weekend walks through the forest. The old man and woman who ran the place were indifferent to the Team at first but began to become friendly after the first day. By the second day, the old woman was cooking for them and doing their laundry. She said that since she couldn't take care of her son, and since their mothers couldn't take care of them, she would help them. The old man told of his son, a panzer trooper like the men in Team Yankee, and of his own experiences in 'the last war'.

Replacements came in for men, equipment, ammunition, uniforms, weapons, radios, and a myriad of other things modern war required. The first people they got were the infantrymen stripped from the other companies. While the Team didn't get the best, those they did get were usable. When these men came in, Polgar gathered them up and gave them the law according to Polgar. One of the first rules he had established was that they never forget they now belonged to Team Yankee. That struck Bannon as strange at first. In the past, the assignment of a Mech Platoon to the tank company was equated to exile to Siberia. Now it was a matter of pride. In fact, most of the infantry replacements had volunteered to be assigned to the Team. As one of the new men told him, if he had to be in this war, he wanted to be with people who knew how to fight.

The Team was not as fortunate in the replacements they received for the tank crews. Most of them came straight from the advanced individual training course at Fort Knox. Some had never even been in a tank when a round was fired. It seemed that if they could recognise a tank two out of three times, they were shipped. So the Team's number-one priority became training the new men and integrating them into the crews and squads as quickly as possible.

One of the most interesting transitions that had occurred in the Team had taken place in Pfc. Richard Kelp. Before the war he had always been an average soldier, nothing more, nothing less. Since the Team had come off Hill 214, however, he had become a man with a purpose. When they picked up a replacement tank from war stocks, Kelp was the first man on it. Instead of Folk having to keep on Kelp to work, Folk now found it difficult to keep up with him. With the new 66 came a new man. As it is easier to train a loader, Kelp was reassigned as the driver and given the mission of training Pvt. Leo Dowd as the loader. After conducting several hours of crew drills on the second day, Bannon asked Dowd how thing were going for him. He reluctantly answered that he thought that Kelp was being too hard on him. Bannon put on his official company commander's face and told him that Kelp was doing just fine. He added that if Dowd listened to Kelp and did just as Kelp told him, maybe he would make it out of this war alive. After that there were no more complaints.

Along with his new direction in life, Kelp received official recognition for his efforts in the defence of Hill 214. After questioning both privates who had come back from the tank-killing detail that night, Polgar put them in for Silver Stars. As the Dragon gunner who had been killed had led the group for awhile and had taken out the first tank, Bannon added him for a posthumous award. By the time the citations made it to division level, the efforts of the three men took on epic proportions. The story was turned slightly. The killing of the two tanks became the critical event for the battle of Hill 214 that caused the whole Soviet battalion to withdraw. In reality, things weren't that clearcut, but Bannon went along with it since it expedited the awards.

One change that had taken place that was not to Bannon's liking was the outlook on life that Bob Uleski had adopted. His arm had been dislocated during the initial attack on Hill 214. The battalion physician's assistant at the 1st of the 4th Armor's aid station had popped it back into place while the cut on Bannon's face was being cleaned and dressed. They wanted to have Uleski evacuated for a few days to convalesce. But he refused. As the Team was short of officers, Bannon allowed him to stay on as long as he could perform his duties. Despite obvious pain, he performed.

For the most part, he slipped back to his good-natured self. But when it came to training, he was a different man. His personality changed to that of a cold and emotionless being, unable to tolerate the slightest error or any action that was not up to standard. When drilling his crew, he would turn on them with a vengeance if their times were not to his liking. When Bannon approached him on it, he simply shrugged it off as nerves. But there was more to it. Bannon wouldn't ask to replace him simply because he had changed. Everyone had changed. In his case, however, it was not a change for the better. So Bannon watched him closely.

One of the jobs that Bannon had dreaded most began the first night in the assembly area. After the Team had stood down for the night, and only those personnel required for minimal security were posted, he sat alone at a table in the *Gasthaus*. In the quiet of the night, with no noise but the hiss of the coleman lantern, he began to write letters to the families of those who had died.

'Dear Mrs McAlister, I was your son's company commander. You have been informed, I am sure, by this time, of the death of your son, John. While this is small consolation for the grief that you must feel, I want you to know that your son died performing his duties in a manner befitting the fine officer he was. His absence ...'

'Dear Mrs. Ortelli, As you know, I was your husband's company commander and tank commander. You have been informed, I am sure, by this time, of Joseph's death. While this is ...'

'Dear Mr and Mrs Loriet, I was ...'

As he wrote the letters, the images of those who had been lost came back. In his mind's eye he could see 21 hanging on the edge of the ditch, burning and shaking from internal explosions; Ortelli, wrapped in his sleeping bag; Lorriet's eyes that stared and saw nothing; the severed arm belonging to a soldier Bannon didn't even know. Those images were perfectly clear to him. To the responsibility of running the Team, he now added the haunting and frightful baggage of remembering those who had been entrusted to his care and had died. In all his readings, in all the classes he had attended, nothing had prepared him for this. Each commander was left to deal with the images of the dead in his own way.

'Dear Mr and Mrs ...'

On the afternoon of the second day the first sergeant brought 2nd Lt. Randall Avery to the Team's assembly area. Avery had been assigned to take over the 2nd Platoon. As he was hauling his gear out of the first sergeant's vehicle, he noticed Garger going through a sand table exercise with his tank commanders. As the two lieutenants had both been in the same officer basic course at Fort Knox, Avery was thrilled to see the face of an old drinking buddy in this sea of strangers. He called to Garger. But instead of coming over and giving him a hearty greeting and hello, Garger merely acknowledged the new lieutenant's presence with a nod and continued to work with the 3rd Platoon's leaders. Avery could not understand the cold reception. The reception he got from Bannon was even colder.

Bannon and Uleski were sitting at a table on the terrace in front of the *Gasthaus* going over the next day's schedule of training and maintenance when the first sergeant brought Avery over. 'Captain Bannon, this is Lieutenant Avery. He's straight out of Knox and has been assigned to take over the 2nd Platoon.'

With that introduction, Avery came to attention, saluted, and reported. 'Sir, Second Lieutenant Avery reporting for duty.'

Bannon and Uleski looked at each other, and then looked at the first sergeant. With a nod, Bannon acknowledged the lieutenant's salute. For a moment Avery stood there, not sure what to do. 'At ease, Lieutenant. We don't do much saluting in the company area. Where are you coming from?'

'I came over from Fort Knox, where I was attending the motor officer's course after AOB. I was in the same class as Gerry, I mean Lieutenant Garger. We were good friends there, sir.'

Again Bannon and Uleski exchanged glances. 'That's nice. What college did you graduate from?'

'Texas A and M, sir.'

Uleski couldn't resist. He let out three loud whoops. Neither First Sergeant Harrett nor Bannon could keep from breaking out in laughter. Avery stood there at a loss. He didn't appreciate being the butt of the XO's joke. Neither was he in a position to do anything about it. He was totally unprepared for this kind of reception.

Seeing the lieutenant's discomfort, Bannon put his official company commander's face back on. 'You are going to the

2nd Platoon. The man you are replacing was a damned good lieutenant who was killed three days ago. I hope you have better luck. Your platoon sergeant is Sergeant First Class Hebrock. He's been running the platoon since Lieutenant McAlister was killed. Your only hope of surviving is to listen to what that man has to say. I don't know how much time we have before we move out again. You have a lot to learn and not much time, so don't waste any. Is that clear?'

Taken aback by this cheerless how-do-you-do, Avery simply replied, 'Yes, sir' and waited for the next shock.

'Bob, we'll finish this up later during the evening meal. I want you to take the lieutenant down to 2nd Platoon and turn him over to Sergeant Hebrock. Then you best get down to battalion CP and check on the replacement for our FIST track. I damned sure don't want to let battalion let that one slip.'

'OK. You need anything else from battalion while I'm there?'

'Just the usual; mail, if there is such a thing.'

With that, Uleski got up, gathered up his notebook and map and took off at a fast pace. 'Come on, Avery, this way.'

Avery glanced at the XO, turned back to Bannon, gave him a quick salute, then gathered up his gear and took off at a trot to catch up to Uleski who was already thirty metres away. Somehow, Avery had expected something different. His mind was already racing in an effort to figure out what was going to happen next.

It wasn't until the evening meal that Avery had a chance to talk to Gerry Garger. The whole afternoon had been one rude shock after another. The greeting from the Team commander had been warm compared to that received from the platoon. Although Randy Avery was no fool and knew not to expect open arms and warm smiles, he had at least expected a handshake. What he got instead was a reception that ranged from indifferent to almost hostile. Hebrock had been proper but short, following the same line that the Team commander had taken, 'We have a lot to do and not much time, so you need to pay attention, sir.' The sir had been added almost as an afterthought. Hebrock then continued with the training under way.

Sergeant Tessman, the gunner on 21, was less than happy to see the new TC and made little effort to hide it. Even the tank was not what he had expected. Unlike the new 66, which was out of war stocks, the new 21 had belonged to another unit, had been damaged and then repaired, and reissued. Inside the turret there were still burn marks and blackened areas. The welds to repair the damage had been done quickly and crudely and had not been painted. Tessman made a special effort to show his new TC the stains where the former TC had bled all over the tank commander's seat.

Even his good friend, Gerry Garger, appeared to be standoffish. At least Gerry acknowledged him with a hello and a handshake while waiting to eat. But Gerry didn't seem interested in talking while they ate. When asked about the war so far, Garger would give simple, short answers, such as, 'It's hard' or 'It's not like our training at Knox.' By the end of the day, Randall Avery was feeling alone and very confused.

Uleski returned with something that was almost as valuable as news that the war was over: the first letters from families in the States. The announcement that there was news from home stopped everything. Even Bannon could not hide his hopes and apprehensions. Hope that he had a letter, just one letter. Apprehension that it was not there. There was no thought of setting the example of the cool, calm, patient commander. This was too important.

When Uleski handed him his letter, he thanked God, the Postmaster General, the Division Postal Detachment, and anyone he could think of as he turned away and walked to a quiet spot. Bannon did not notice those who still stood there in silence when all the letters had been distributed.

Pat and the children were safe and staying with her parents. He read that line four times before he went on. It was as if nothing else mattered. His family was safe. After having experienced emotional highs and lows in quick succession over the past six days, the elation he felt over this news set an all time high. Not even the ending of the war right now could have boosted him any higher. It was because of that elation that Bannon did not detect the subtle implications in Pat's language until he had read the letter for the sixth time the next day. In reading it more carefully, what she didn't tell him spoke louder than what she had written. Not all was well with her or the children. This realisation dulled his joy and caused new apprehensions. Even though they were safe, something terrible had happened. It would be weeks before Pat was able to bring herself to fully recount the story of their departure from Europe. In that time, the war rolled on, taking new and ominous turns, as wars have a tendency to do.

Chapter Nine

DEEP ATTACK

After two days with Team Yankee, Avery came to realise that the cold reception he had received had not been personal. That is, he had not been the only one who had been received in that manner. All the newly assigned personnel that had been fed into the Team had received the same treatment. At first, he resented this fact. He looked at it as if it were some kind of planned initiation, and he thought that he and the others deserved better. When he commented on this to his friend, Gerry Garger, Garger looked at him, thought about the question, and then told Avery that he had no idea what he was talking about. He told the new platoon leader that as far as he was concerned everyone in the Team got along exceptionally well. He went on to tell Avery that he was being overly sensitive and should settle down to the business at hand. Without so much as a see you later, Garger turned around and walked away from Avery.

Avery began to understand that there was a difference between the newly assigned personnel and the original members of Team Yankee when the CO authorised the tank commanders to paint 'kill rings' on the gun tubes of the Team's tanks. The old German that owned the *Gasthaus* made the suggestion that the Team should do as the German panzer troops had done in World War II: paint a ring on the tank's gun tube for every enemy tank destroyed by that crew. The idea was popular and accepted under certain conditions. The kills had to be confirmed. Only the first sergeant, who didn't have a tank, could authorise the kill rings if, in his opinion, there were sufficient confirmation. The kill rings were to be one-inch black rings, one for each kill, painted on the gun tube just forward of the bore evacuator.

Once the kill rings had been painted on the tanks, the tank commanders and gunners went around to see who the top gun was. To Avery's surprise, it was Garger. His 31 tank had eleven rings on it. The CO's tank, 66, had seven rings. Hebrock told Avery that the CO could have claimed six more kills but instead allowed them to go on 55, the tank that he had been commanding at the time of the kills. Of the ten tanks in Team Yankee, only Avery's tank, 21, had a clean gun tube.

It suddenly dawned upon him that since his arrival in the Team, no one had talked about what he had done in the war. Every time he asked questions about the battles the Team had been in when talking to Garger, his friend would move on to another subject. When the CO, XO, and Polgar gave a class on lessons learned thus far in the war, they gave it in a very impersonal and academic manner. At times, it seemed as if they were talking about another unit. It was as if there was a secret fellowship that only those members of the Team that had been in combat could belong to.

To have bragged about their deeds would have seemed out of place, not right somehow. But the kill rings gave the crews a chance to show what they had done without overtly blowing their own horn. Avery suddenly found himself wanting to go into combat. This revelation shocked him because the first reason that popped into his mind when he thought about it was not to defend freedom or to do his duty in the defence of his country. The reason that drove this desire was a longing to belong to the Team as an equal, to be accepted. Avery wanted kill rings too.

The battalion seemed to have a knack for screwing up breakfasts. On the morning of the fourth day in the assembly area, the eighth of the war, a messenger from battalion came up to the Team with word that there would be an operations order given at battalion headquarters in an hour. All the platoon leaders, the XO, the first sergeant, and the Team's new FIST chief, a second lieutenant by the name of Plesset, were having a working breakfast with Bannon. After finishing green eggs that were once warm, bacon strips that were as crispy as wet noodles, and toast that could have doubled as shingles, they were about to go into the day's training schedule when word of the pending change in mission came.

Bannon promptly cancelled all activities that had been

planned except those involving maintenance and preparation. Instead, the platoon leaders were to conduct precombat inspections and start a sleep plan for the majority of the crews. He had no idea when they would move but the odds were it would be at night, probably tonight. Bannon wanted the Team to be ready and rested.

Uleski and the FIST went to the meeting with Bannon. They arrived a few minutes before the briefing was scheduled to start so that Bannon could talk to the S-3. Major Jordan was at the front of the classroom that served as the battalion's conference room talking to Colonel Reynolds.

The three of them walked up to the front of the room to the operations map. The graphics depicting the new mission were on it, ready for the briefing. A chill went down Bannon's spine when he saw that it was another attack. He and Uleski exchanged glances. Physically, the Team had recovered from the last attack. Mentally, though, Bannon had his doubts. Especially about himself. He wasn't sure if he could deal with another horror show like the last one. Images of the dead and dying flashed through his mind. No, he wasn't ready.

It was an ambitious plan, involving the entire brigade striking deep into East Germany – driving at the heart of the enemy. The arrows depicting the axis of advance that the brigade was to use went through a German panzer grenadier battalion that had already crossed the inter-German boundary, as the border between West and East Germany was called. They were to advance up a narrow valley in the Thuringer Wald, in the direction of Leipzig, north of the Thuringer Wald and on the North German Plain. The arrow showed the brigade going past the city and pointing to an objective to the north. The map the battalion was using was too small to show the ultimate objective they would probably go for. But that wasn't necessary. Berlin, the heart of East Germany and centre of communications, was the objective they were aimed at.

The S-3 saw Bannon studying the map. When he came over, he paused a moment before speaking, 'Well, what do you think?'

'Let's see if I can guess who's leading – C company?'

'Sean, you know damned well who's going to lead the attack, at least initially. Team Yankee is the best company we have, and you have most of our armour. It would be stupid to put anyone else in the lead.'

Bannon looked at the S-3 for a moment, considering his answer. 'Sir, are you attempting to win me over with logic or flattery?'

'A little of both, I guess.'

The battalion XO started the briefing by telling everyone to take their seats. Colonel Reynolds called Bannon to sit next to him. His friendly attitude and smile reminded Bannon of the cat who praised the canary for his beautiful song before eating him. When everyone was settled, the battalion XO gave the briefing sequence and told the S-2 to start.

The last six days of war had done nothing to improve the intel officer's skills in preparing a useful briefing. He started by summarising the progress of the war to date and the gains the Soviets had made in the north. These gains were indeed impressive. Denmark was isolated. Despite the efforts of the NATO allies in the Northern Army Group, the Dutch border had almost been reached. Most of the German sea coast was in Soviet hands. In the central and southern portions of Germany, German, French, and American forces had, for the most part, held the Soviets to minor gains. In one area, a German panzer division found a weak point between two Soviet armies and had driven into East Germany before the drive spent itself. It was this drive that would provide the springboard for the attack the battalion was about to undertake.

The S-3, as usual, provided the meat of the briefing. The entire division would be involved in this effort. Brigade would lead off, widening the breach the Germans had made and going north into the enemy rear. French units deploying from the interior of France were replacing those divisional units still in contact as well as another U.S. division. If the brigade and then the rest of the division were successful in widening the breach, eventually, the attack would grow into a corps-size operation.

The brigade was to advance along two axes, along two valleys running south to north. The 1st of the 98th Mech would lead the attack up one valley to the west while 1st of the 78th Mech, followed by 1st of the 4th Armor, would advance up a valley called the Nebal Valley. The battalion's scheme of manoeuvre called for two company teams to lead the attack, Team Yankee on the right and Team Bravo on the left. The two infantry pure companies, C and D would follow, C company behind Team Yankee. At this point in the briefing, the urge to take a cheap shot at C company was too strong to suppress. Bannon interrupted Major Jordan.

'Excuse me, sir, but I seem to remember trying that before. I don't know if Team Yankee is ready to be supported by C company again.'

There was a moment of silence. Everyone looked at Bannon, then they looked at the battalion commander, waiting for his reaction. Colonel Reynolds exchanged glances with the S-3, then smiled. 'Sean, I can assure you, there will be no rat fucks like the last time. I will personally assure you that C company is where it is supposed to be.' The colonel turned to Cravin, the C company commander, 'Isn't that right, Captain Cravin?' Cravin, smarting from the exchange and visibly upset, simply replied yes in a low voice. Major Jordan winked when he and Bannon exchanged glances, then continued with the order.

The battalion had learned its lessons from the last attack well. While it was moving at night, as before, it would temporarily occupy an assembly area to the rear of the German unit it was to pass through. There they would sort out any last-minute changes, refuel, allow the accompanying artillery time to deploy, and conduct last-minute preparations. They then would be escorted through the German lines by a liaison officer from the German unit. To expedite the actions in the assembly area, the battalion XO would leave at noon with representatives from each company, the battalion's Scout Platoon, and the fuel trucks. The scouts would be used as road guides where needed.

When the S-3 finished, the colonel got up and emphasised certain points that he felt were important. The first one was that the battalion was going for the deep objective, Leipzig. Any resistance that could not be overcome in the first rush was to be bypassed. The second was that he wanted to keep the battalion closed up and tight so that if there was a major fight, the full weight of the battalion could be brought to bear on the enemy rapidly and with maximum violence. The last point he made was that there would be no tolerance for screw-ups as in the last operation. He was looking straight at Cravin as he covered the last point.

As usual, Bannon's mind turned to the new mission as the S-4 and S-1 and all the other staff officers covered their areas. Uleski would catch any important information that they might accidentally put out. Bannon studied the map on his lap and ran a finger along the axis of advance. There would be more than enough room to manoeuvre the Team in the valley they would be moving through. There were a few choke points but nothing of any significance. The biggest threat would come from the hills to the east. He began to draw red goose eggs around those spots that appeared to be ideal for defence or from which a counterattack might come. When this was done, he assigned each one a letter then looked for the best way to move the Team. The ideal formation appeared to be a wedge with the two tank platoons deployed forward and the Mech taking up the rear.

The end of the battalion meeting interrupted his train of thought. He met with Uleski and his FIST, gave each one some items to cover with various staff officers, and then went to the S-3 to clarify some points and make some recommendations. When all questions had been answered, they went back to the Team to prepare the Team order and get ready for the move.

The Team received the news of the new mission with the same dread that Bannon had. While they knew that they could do their part, they had no confidence in the rest of the battalion. The thought of another fight like that for Hill 214 was not a pleasant one to contemplate. Only Avery seemed anxious to get on with the attack. Bannon passed it off as inexperience. No doubt he would lose all enthusiasm the first time he had to collect the dog tags from one of his people. Provided he made it that far.

The rest of the day passed quickly. Bannon issued the Team order just prior to the departure of Uleski at noon. Uleski would go forward to prepare their assembly area along with one man from each tank platoon and an infantry squad for security and to act as guides. He was also to go as far forward as possible. Bannon wanted him to recon the routes through the German lines and co-ordinate with the Germans for fire support and cover during the passage through their lines. He had no doubt that the Soviets saw the danger that the German penetration presented and would be rushing to seal it off or eliminate it. The question now was who would get there first.

After receiving a brief back from each of the platoon leaders on how they were going to perform their assigned tasks and satisfying himself that they were ready, Bannon decided to get some sleep. He went to the *Gasthaus* and borrowed one of the rooms where he could have a few uninterrupted hours. After having slept on the ground for eleven days, the sensation of sleeping between clean sheets on a soft bed was foreign. But it was a sensation that his body adapted to easily.

The easy manner with which the other platoon leaders and Hebrock went about preparing for the attack amazed Avery. They all were going about their business as if this were a tactical exercise at Fort Knox, not an attack that would take them deep into enemy territory. As hard as he tried, he could not settle down. His mind was racing a mile a minute, trying to remember everything that he had learned at the Armor School as he prepared to issue his platoon order.

Not that he had to worry. Hebrock was normally a step ahead of him, issuing orders and checking out the tanks. The two of them went over the order, item by item, crossing out those parts that were not needed and adding things that Avery had overlooked. Hebrock was diplomatic in the manner in which he 'advised' his platoon leader of what he needed to do and say. Even as he issued the order, Avery would occasionally look up at Hebrock for his approval.

When the order had been given and the CO satisfied with the

brief back, Hebrock advised his lieutenant to get some sleep. Only after the platoon sergeant assured him that there was nothing more to be done did Avery make the attempt. Attempt was all that he could manage. His mind was cluttered with thoughts, fears, and problems, real and imagined. Did he cover everything in his order? What if they got lost during the road march? How would he know when they were through the German lines? Would he remember all of his crew and platoon fire commands when they made contact? Would he be alive tomorrow? His mind did not stop. Sleep never came.

The Team began its move at 1800 hours. The old German and his wife watched as they rolled out. First Sergeant Harrert left them two weeks worth of rations, an envelope with dollars and Deutschmarks that he had collected, a first-aid kit, and two cans of gasoline. In order to keep them from having any trouble with German or U.S. authorities, a receipt with Bannon's signature, in English and German, identified those items left as payment in kind for services rendered by the old couple. The old woman cried, and the old man saluted as the tanks went past them. Bannon returned the salute. Watching them as 66 moved off made him think of his own parents. He thanked God that they did not have to suffer as these people did.

As the Team column reached the proper march speed and interval, Garger leaned back in the cupola and relaxed. He considered the last twelve days and the changes that had occurred in him and the Team. The loss of his platoon sergeant was unfortunate. Pierson had taught him a lot and had been very patient with him. Had it not been for Pierson, Garger knew he would have been relieved. The thought of such a disgrace had been more terrifying to him than the prospect of combat.

Garger had not only survived but had found that he had a natural talent for tanking and combat. The panic, the tenseness, the sick feeling in his stomach, the stammering he had experienced at Fort Knox and during his first weeks in the unit were gone. When the firing had started, everything seemed to fall in place. There was no panic, no fear. He had a clarity of mind that he had never experienced before. There was still much he needed to learn and the CO and XO had helped him a great deal while the Team was recovering. Eventually he would learn company tactics and all the ins and outs of staff work, for he knew that he could, and would, master his chosen profession.

The road march to the forward assembly area was a hard and wearing one for Avery. His inability to sleep that afternoon compounded his apprehensions and nervousness. Garger had told him before they left that he was going to have to lighten up or he would have a nervous breakdown before the first Russian got a chance to shoot at him. His friend had meant that as lighthearted but sound advice. Avery had tried to relax but found himself worried now about having a nervous breakdown. That would be disastrous. At least he could live with a wound. Evacuation because of a nervous breakdown before the first battle was a disgrace too terrible to contemplate. Only the sudden realisation that he no longer knew where he was caused Avery to divert his attention from his fears of suffering a nervous breakdown to his fear that he wouldn't be able to find his location again on the map.

Shortly after 2200 hours the Team pulled into the forward assembly area. The movement in and occupation of the marked positions went like clockwork. In peacetime manoeuvres the Team had never had such a smooth road march and assembly area occupation. Bannon greeted Uleski as he dismounted from 66, 'Well, Bob, you've done good. Real good. Have you been able to co-ordinate with the people we'll be passing through?'

'Yes, sir. I was forward this afternoon in their positions and have gone over the route several times. It's a piece of cake.'

'What about the Russians? What have they been up to and does the unit have any information on them?'

'Well, first off, they're not Russians. They're Poles. The Poles hit them just after I arrived there. It appeared that the Russians hadn't told them where the Germans were because they just rolled right up to the Germans in column formation. The German company commander let them come into his positions before he cut loose. The Poles never had much of a chance. They were cut to pieces. The company commander was killed but his XO took over and is still holding. Our battalion XO passed word down to us that the German battalion commander expects them to make another try sometime tonight.'

'What kind of units are we facing?'

'Tanks so far, T-55s. Real second-class stuff.'

'Hey, that's OK by me. I get paid the same amount for blowing away old tanks as I do for tangling with tanks that don't want to die. Tell me, do you have any qualms about going up against your own people, Bob?'

'Sir, those aren't my people. They're as red as the Russians. I'd rather be killing Russian Communists but, if all we have is Polish Communists, they'll do.'

Uleski's cold, unfeeling remark sent a chill down Bannon's spine. The dark side of First Lieutenant Uleski had come out again, the side that worried his commander. Bannon wondered if his hatred would cloud his judgment. He hoped not. For his sake and his crew's, he hoped not.

'Bob, make sure all the people that came with you make it back to where they belong. Then gather up the leadership and have them meet me here.'

The battalion S-3 came into the company area while Uleski was briefing the Team's leaders. Major Jordan waited until the XO was finished before he gave them his information. The battalion was closed up and ready. The 1st of the 4th Armor as well as the artillery battalions would also be in place on time. So far, all had gone well. As far as anyone could tell, the Polish unit didn't know of the battalion's presence. Things would go as planned.

Team Yankee would lead out at 0330 hours. At 0350, two battalions of U.S. and one battalion of German artillery would begin a ten-minute preparation on the Polish forward positions, both identified and suspected. At 0400 hours, Team Yankee's lead element, the 3rd Platoon, would pass through the German positions and begin the attack. If all went well, by early afternoon the battalion would be on the Saale River waiting for the 1st of the 4th Armor to pass through and drive on to Leipzig. This, of course, didn't take into account any Soviet reaction. The Soviets would surely do their damnedest to smash the brigade somewhere along the line. But there was always the possibility that maybe, just maybe, this time the plan might work.

Once all the last-minute details had been covered, and all the questions answered, the meeting broke up. The platoon leaders went back to pass the word on and answer any questions their TCs had. When everyone was gone, Bannon climbed onto 66, and told Folk that they would split guard duty. Jokingly, he told his gunner that since Folk had gotten so much sleep during the road march that he would pull first shift while Bannon would pull second. Without further ado, Bannon rolled out his sleeping bag on top of the turret and went to sleep.

After Avery and Hebrock finished putting out the information they had to the other TCs, Hebrock told his platoon leader to forget about pulling any duty between now and the move-out time and instead go to bed. Avery was too far gone to argue. By now, he had just about worried himself to death. It took all of his effort to keep his eyes open. While the lieutenant leaned against 21 for support, Tessman threw a sleeping bag down to Hebrock who spread it out next to the track. Avery didn't even bother to take his boots off. He simply flopped down, wrapped one side of the sleeping bag over himself, and passed out from exhaustion. He stayed in the same postion until he was roused at 0310 hours.

Team Yankee missed colliding head-on with the expected Polish attack by fifteen minutes. Again the fortunes of war smiled on the Team. Instead of having to go forward and dig out the Polish tank and motorised infantry from their defensive positions, the Poles came out and were smashed by the combined weight of the German defensive fires and the artillery that was already scheduled to fire. In war, one's good fortune is sometimes nothing more than a matter of timing: being at the right place at the right time. Had a staff officer or the brigade commander set the time of attack at 0330, it would have been the Poles enjoying the advantage. As it was, Team Yankee gained a double advantage. Not only did the Poles impale themselves on the German's defences and save the Team the trouble of seeking them out, they allowed the Team to get an extra half hour's sleep.

The sound of the raging battle to their front, the eerie shadows caused by the illumination rounds as they floated down to earth, and the flash from impacting artillery rounds made the crossing of the East German border seem unreal. It was like a scene from a cheap science-fiction movie. Moments like this, when one is not actually involved in the fight but close enough to see and hear it, is when fear reaches a peak. The fear of failure. The fear of being ripped apart by artillery. The fear of death. All these fears run through the mind as a soldier closes to do battle. Once engaged, training and instinct take over. Fear is pushed aside by the necessity to fight or die. But before, when there is still the chance to back out, the rational mind pleads for reason, to stop, to quit before combat is joined. The tank, however, keeps going forward and ignores the rational mind. Combat will be joined, despite reason and one's better judgment.

As Sergeant Polgar's personnel carrier eased down the ramp into the antivehicle ditch that ran along the East German border, he became elated. After being in the Army for sixteen years, something he was doing was making sense. He recalled how, as a private in Vietnam, he and his buddies felt frustrated and betrayed when they had to break off pursuit of the North Vietnamese as soon as they came up to the Vietnamese border. They were never allowed to go all the way in and finish the enemy and the war. He had been in Korea in 1977 when two American officers were hacked to death with axes in broad daylight by North Korean soldiers, and no action was taken to retaliate. He remembered the 444 days of embarrassment when a third-rate nation, Iran, held Americans hostage, and the Army wasn't able to free them. Like others in the military, the half-measures and restrictions placed on the U.S. military didn't make sense to him.

This attack, however, did make sense. For the first time in his military career, he was carrying the war into the enemy's homeland. He and his soldiers were going to be given a chance to strike at the heart of the enemy. No more running up to an imaginary line and then stopping while some politician reflected on what move would come out best on the next public opinion poll; no more letting the enemy run into a safe hole to lick his wounds and come out again at a time and place of his choosing, as in Vietnam. The Army was going to rip out the enemy's heart and drink his blood. That made sense to Polgar. That was the only way to fight a war.

For a moment Colonel Reynolds considered halting the attack to allow the Germans to sort out the situation before the battalion passed. When he called Bannon and told him to be prepared to halt in place, Bannon immediately called back and told him to let the Team go. The Poles were pulling back. This was the ideal time to strike, while they were still confused. The enemy obviously didn't know the battalion was coming; otherwise, they would not have attacked. They had T-55s with old sights. Team Yankee had thermal sights. This was the time to speed up, not slow down. The colonel agreed and told him to go for it. When Bannon dropped to the Team net and ordered Garger to pick up speed, to hit hard, and to keep rolling, all he got back from 3rd Platoon was a simple 'I heard that.'

The 3rd Platoon rolled through the German positions, deploying into a wedge as they went, and engaging the fleeing Poles. The surprise was complete. Some of the Polish tanks attempted to return fire. They had to stop to shoot, however, and this telegraphed their intentions. Garger's people quickly singled them out and destroyed them. Other Polish tanks simply picked up speed and attempted to get out of the way. In this too, they failed. For once, the Americans had better and faster tanks. 3rd Platoon kept up the pursuit and took out the retreating Poles one at a time.

As they were closing in for the kill, Bannon directed the

FIST to shift the artillery fires to the left and the right of the Team's axis of advance and to fire smoke as well as HE. This would keep the Polish infantry still in defensive positions facing the Germans pinned as the Team passed through their front line. Once Team Yankee was in their rear, those Poles still facing the Germans would be obliged to retreat or surrender.

The speed of the 3rd Platoon's attack was causing the Team to become spread out. Bannon was right behind 3rd Platoon and found it difficult to catch up. The 2nd Platoon was behind 66 but still in column. He was sure that the PCs in the Mech Platoon would soon be falling behind. Reluctantly, he ordered the 3rd Platoon to slow down in order to allow the rest of the Team time to deploy. He didn't want to go charging off with only half of the Team, as had happened at Hill 214. He doubted if they would be lucky a second time. Once the tanks in front of 66 began to slow, Bannon had the driver swing 66 over to the left of the 3rd Platoon and ordered the 2nd Platoon to pick up speed and deploy to the left of 66.

The scene before him was incredible. Dante's Inferno could not have been more terrible. In his wildest dreams Avery could not have imagined such chaos and pandemonium. Artillery impacted with no rhyme or reason. The exchange of fire between the lead tanks and the Poles continued. Coloured star clusters were popping overhead. Burning tanks were everywhere. Mortar and artillery illumination rounds cast a sickly pale light on everything. The bucking and jolting of 21 running at full throttle to catch up with the CO's tank tossed him about in the cupola. Then, in the middle of this, the CO came up on the net and in a matter of fact manner ordered the 2nd Platoon to deploy to his left. Avery had no idea where he was and even less idea where the CO was. The best the lieutenant could do was give a 'ROGER // OUT' on the radio and continue to head in the direction that the CO's tank was headed the last time he had seen it.

As 21 crested a hill in search of 66 and the 3rd Platoon, it almost collided with another tank that appeared to its left. Only a quick order to the driver to go right prevented the accident. The TC in the other tank had also seen the near collision at the last minute and had swung to the left some. The two tanks then straightened out and began to run side by side at a distance of twenty metres. Avery was relieved. He had found the CO's tank. As he was about to key the net to order his platoon to begin to deploy, it dawned upon him that the direction of travel of the tank to his left didn't make sense. If the CO's tank was to appear, it should have been to his right, not to the left. He leaned over to take a better look at the tank to his left.

A T-55! It was a *goddamned T-55!* The sudden realisation that he was running side by side with a Polish tank was numbing. It was the sensation or urine running down his leg that galvanised Avery into action. He began to slew the turret and issue his fire command.

'GUNNER // BATTLESIGHT // TANK!'

'UP!'

The target was so near and the thermal sight image so uniformly green that Tessman didn't recognise the object in his sight as a tank. 'CANNOT IDENTIFY!'

The belligerent move by 21 caused the Polish tank commander to give 21 a closer look. He, too, realised his error and began to lay his gun. Tessman repeated his call, 'CANNOT IDENTIFY!'

'FROM MY POSITION // ON THE WAY!'

Avery fired the main gun from his override without bothering to go down to his sight. The report of 21's gun and the impact on target were as one. The T-55 veered off to the left, stopped, and began to burn. For a moment Avery simply stood there and watched the T-55 as 21 continued to roll forward. The loader's report of 'UP!' broke his trance. 'CEASE FIRE.'

The retreat of the Poles had lost all form and formation. They were everywhere. Most of the tanks were gone, destroyed or scattered. Now Garger and his platoon were coming across trucks and personnel carriers. As the platoon crested one knoll, they came face to face with a battery of heavy mortars.

The tanks didn't even break stride. They simply continued to roll forward, firing at the fleeing mortarmen with machine guns, and crushing the mortars under their tracks. Gerry Garger was impatiently awaiting word to move out at top speed again. The whole Polish rear area was in an uproar. He wanted to finish them before they were able to reorganise.

The CO came over the Team net again and ordered the 3rd Platoon into a right echelon. Garger ordered his platoon into the required formation and watched them as they did so. The tanks dropped back and took up their assigned stations, swinging their guns to cover the Team's right flank. It was already becoming light. Garger turned in the cupola and watched 66 come up on his left. Behind 66 he could barely make out the forms of the 2nd Platoon tanks coming on fast. Once they were up, the Team could continue on. Unless something terrible happened, they would be able to reach the Saale River that afternoon with ease.

Finally, 66 was in sight. He hadn't lost the Team. Avery felt relieved. Then, the first humorous thought that he had had since his arrival in Germany ran through his mind: that made the second time that morning that he had been relieved. He thought about the near brush with the T-55 and his reactions. Hip shooting a tank main gun was not in the book, any book. But what the hell, it had worked. Tank 21 had killed the Pole and saved its hide. The platoon had caught up and was deployed to the left of the CO's tank. With the exception of his wet pants, all was working out rather well so far. Avery began to think that maybe he would make it as a platoon leader after all. He was a veteran and 21 had earned its first kill ring.

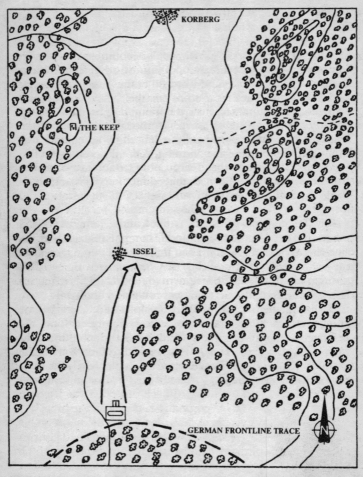

MAP 12: THE ATTACK TO THE SAALE: THE FIRST PHASE

Chapter Ten

RED DAWN

Just prior to dawn, Colonel Reynolds accomplished what the Poles had not been able to, stop Team Yankee. Bannon was sure the colonel would have liked to let the Team keep going if he could have, but that was not possible. The colonel found it necessary to stop them, just as Bannon had been compelled to rein in the 3rd Platoon as it had forged out ahead of the Team. From the reports on the battalion command net, Bannon could tell all was not going well.

While Team Yankee had been able to achieve complete surprise and scatter the Polish units directly to its front, those Poles who had been to the left and right of the penetration did not panic or flee. Instead, they attempted to close off the penetration as soon as Team Yankee and Team Bravo had passed through. Apparently C and D companies' lack of tanks encouraged the Poles to try. Their initial efforts were successful as they greeted the appearance of C company with a deadly crossfire. The garbled and fragmented reports given by Cravin over the battalion net betrayed his confusion and panic.

The battalion XO, who had been following C company, reported the situation and his actions to the colonel. D company was deployed into positions from which they could support C company. The XO was still in contact with the German battalion and was able to get them to add their support to the growing battle. Once a firm base of fire had been established and friendly artillery began to enter the fray, he moved forward to rally C company and reopen the breach.

His efforts, however, were rewarded with a direct hit on his track when it reached the place where C company had gone to ground. The D company commander reported the loss of the battalion XO to Reynolds. He then informed the battalion commander that he was taking over the battalion's rear battle and requested further orders. Unable to contact the C company commander and sensing that the entire operation was in jeopardy, Colonel Reynolds ordered Team Yankee to stop where it was, instructed Major Jordan to stay forward with Team Yankee, and then turned Team Bravo around and led them back to hit the Poles in the rear. The day that had begun so well appeared to be turning against the battalion.

The order to halt and take up hasty defensive positions threw Sergeant Polgar. For a minute he thought that the Team Commander had made a mistake. The 3rd Platoon leader thought the same, for no sooner had Bannon stopped talking, than Lieutenant Garger came back and asked him to repeat his last transmission. A little agitated at being so questioned, Bannon made it a point to repeat his instructions slowly, in such a way as to ensure that they would not be misunderstood.

As each of the platoon leaders responded back to the Team Commander with an acknowledgement, Polgar noted the difference between the two tank platoon leaders. The 3rd Platoon leader was clearly upset with his commander for stopping the mad dash that the 3rd Platoon had been leading. Polgar wanted to get on with the attack himself, especially since they had such a clear advantage over the enemy. But he was an old soldier and realised that Bannon would not have stopped their forward movement unless there was a damned good reason to do so.

The new platoon leader of the 2nd Platoon, on the other hand, sounded as if he were relieved to get the order halting their drive. Not that he could be blamed. The U.S. Army had a tradition of being rough on second lieutenants. It had to be hell on the new lieutenant, being assigned to a unit in the middle of a war and then going right into an attack like this. Polgar couldn't remember the new lieutenant's name, not that it really mattered. He definitely had not impressed anyone so far. The fact was, there was a lottery going around the Team among the enlisted men betting on how long the new lieutenant would last once they went into action. The big money was on two days. Some bet it would be hours. Polgar had been one of the more optimistic. He had his bet riding on three and a half days.

As the Team's tracks settled into positions along an east-west road and cut off their engines, the sun began to rise. Bannon watched the horizon change from black to a deep red. He was reminded of the old saying, 'Red sun at night, sailor's delight. Red sun in the morning, sailor take warning.' The sun that was greeting Team Yankee this morning was blood red. Watching the great red orb rise in the east, he silently prayed that this was not an ill omen.

Once the Team was set, Bannon turned his attention to Team Bravo and their progress as that unit retraced its steps. The colonel prepared to hit the Poles with everything he had available. He called the battalion's artillery fire-support officer and designated targets he wanted hit and when they were to be hit. He instructed the D company commander to get with the Germans and see if they would support the battalion's manoeuvre with fire. Finally, based on information provided by the D company commander, he gave Team Bravo and D company their orders.

His plan was simple. Hold the attention of the Poles to their front with D company and the Germans, pin the Poles with artillery, and hit them from behind with Team Bravo. D company and the Germans played the anvil, the artillery and Team Bravo played the hammer. The plan proved to be as effective as it was simple. The violence that had smashed their initial attack; their failure to destroy C company; the weight of the firepower of D company, the Germans, and the artillery; and the violence of Team Bravo's attack to their rear finally broke the Poles. One of the surviving Poles grimly observed that the Americans and Germans had used so much firepower that even the sun had been hit and was bleeding.

★ Forty kilometres east of Team Yankee's hastily assumed positions, a Soviet tank company commander was about to finish briefing his platoon leaders when he noticed how red the morning sun was. For a brief moment he reflected on its significance. Pointing to the solar orb, he told his gathered platoon leaders that the Great Motherland to the east was sending a red sun as an omen to them. The company commander promised his gathered leaders that if they performed their duties as they had been trained and adhered to the great truths that were the pillars of strength to true Communists, the red dawn that they were witnessing would be the end of the imperialist dreams on Europe and the beginning of a new socialist era. Dismissing them with a salute, the company commander turned away from his platoon leaders and headed for his tank.

As he walked back, he wondered if any of his platoon leaders had believed the line of horseshit he had just served them. He turned for a moment, looked at the red sun, then heaved a great sigh. It wasn't important if they did or not, he thought. The political commissar had been pleased with his outpouring of propaganda. Perhaps that miserable party hack would stay out of his way for the rest of the morning, leaving the serious business of killing Americans in the hands of the professional soldiers. The Soviet captain began to smile. The political commissar is happy, we are finally going to get a chance to kill some Americans, and, if we're lucky, some of those worthless Poles will get in the way, and we can run them down. This truly was shaping up to be a great day.

The end of the Poles did not signal an immediate resumption of the battalion's attack. This had been C company's first time under fire, and the experience had been shattering. The battalion commander informed Major Jordan that it would take anywhere from thirty minutes to an hour to sort out the tangled mess that the three companies had become. In the meantime, the divisional air cavalry troop was going to recon forward to find out what the Soviets were up to. That suited Bannon just fine. He was becoming tired of stumbling around like a blind man waiting for the Soviets to hit the Team. Let the cavalry earn their pay.

As it was now obvious that the Team would be here awhile, he began to scrutinise the lay of the land and the Team's dispositions. Ahead, across the road along which they were deployed was a long valley about ten kilometres wide. Wooded hills rose sharply on either side. Immediately to the Team's left was a small town named Issel. As he looked at the town through his binoculars, Bannon could see no sign that it was occupied. There was the possibility that the Soviets had cleared the village prior to the attack in order to maintain operational security. There also was the possibility that they had left someone behind to observe the area and report on the American advance. It was this second possibility that worried him.

After a quick consultation with Major Jordan on the battalion radio net, Bannon ordered the 2nd Platoon to get into a position from which they could place effective fire onto the town. As they were preparing to do so, he dismounted and walked over to Polgar's track to give him his instructions. With the tanks overwatching his move, Polgar was to take his platoon into the town and check it out. The Mech Platoon really didn't have the manpower to do a thorough job. But at least they could check out the more obvious places and keep anyone who was there busy for awhile. Besides, at least this way some of the Team would be doing something useful. This last point was most appealing to Polgar, who did not like the idea of sitting out in the open waiting for some hotshot Russian pilot to come along and fire up his platoon.

Since there was no chance for surprise, Polgar stormed into the town mounted and with the pedal to the floor. The four PCs rolled into the centre of the town square where the infantry dismounted and began to conduct a systematic search of the buildings. The dismounted infantry worked in three-man groups, one group on each side of a street with their PC following down the middle ready to support them with machine-gun fire if they ran into trouble.

The teams conducting the search all followed the same pattern when they entered a building. One of the soldiers would peep into a window to see if there were any obvious signs of occupants. Once they had done so, the three would converge on the door that they would use for entry. One man would continue to watch the street and the house across the street lest they become so involved in the building they were about to enter that an unseen enemy came up from behind and surprised them. The other two men, one on either side of the door, would prepare themselves for forced entry if necessary.

At first, all the teams tried kicking the doors in. They soon found, however, that this could be a painful experience. Besides, many of the doors had been left unlocked. After bouncing off of a few doors that refused to be kicked in, they all began to try the doorknobs first.

This routine had been going on for thirty minutes when there was a muffled report of a Soviet AK followed by the detonation of a grenade. Polgar ran up to the house where the shots and explosion had originated. He was greeted by two men coming out of the front dragging a third. The PC that had been overwatching this team roared up to the front of the house and began to fire its M2 machine gun at the windows along the second floor. Polgar covered the three men as they made for the rear of the PC, then followed.

Once safely behind the PC, the two men watched for a moment as the medic ripped open their wounded comrade's chemical protective suit and tore away the T-shirt to get at the wound. A quick check showed that the wounded man had taken two rounds in his left shoulder. The wound was painful and bloody, but wouldn't be fatal.

When they were satisfied that their friend was in good hands, they reported to Polgar. The soldier who had been wounded was the point man for the group. They had cleared out the ground floor of this particular house and found nothing. It was when the point man had started up the stairs to check out the second floor that the shooting had started. The first volley hit the point man, sending him tumbling back down the stairs. The two men ran up to help him, one man dragging away the wounded point man, the other throwing a grenade onto the second floor to cover their withdrawal. None of the men had seen anyone or anything.

By this time a squad leader and two other teams had gathered around the PC. Polgar directed the squad leader and one of the teams to circle around back and cover the rear of the house in case someone tried to slip out. He ordered another team to stay with the PC to cover the front of the building. They were also to be prepared to reinforce the team that would clear the house. He would personally lead the two men who had first entered the house back in to deal with the unseen enemy.

After getting a rundown on the layout of the ground floor, the three-man assault party moved back to the front door. As before, two men, one of them Polgar, stationed themselves on either side of the door. This time, however, the third man leaned over and threw a grenade into the opened door. As soon as the grenade went off, Polgar and the man across from him went charging into the house, guns levelled and blazing away. Once inside, the men sought the nearest cover available and waited to see what happened.

When nothing happened, Polgar signalled for the third man to enter and cover him as he approached the stairs. He slowly began to climb the stairs, always peering up to see over onto the second floor. When he was halfway up the stairs, Polgar halted, took a grenade off of his web gear, pulled the pin, and threw it into the room at the head of the stairs. As soon as this grenade detonated, he charged to the top of the stairs, taking two steps at a time and firing as he went. Once he reached the head of the stairs, he threw himself into the room where he had thrown the grenade and, as before, sought cover.

Just as Polgar began to get up, a yell to halt came from his men outside. This was followed by the sound of two M16s firing in the rear of the building. In an instant he realised that the people they were looking for in the house had tried to slip out through the rear and had been caught by the team sent to the back of the house. As the other two men with him came up the stairs and began to check out the other rooms on the second floor, Polgar went to a window overlooking the rear of the house and peered out.

In the small yard, two of his men were standing over the body of a young German boy, sprawled in a small flower bed, bleeding from several wounds. An AK rifle was still in his lifeless hand. For a moment it reminded Polgar of a similar scene in Vietnam some fifteen years earlier. One of his first fire fights had involved a VC unit that consisted mainly of fourteen and fifteen-year-old boys. That experience had been a rude introduction to war, one that often haunted his dreams. He knew what his men were experiencing. 'Is he dead?'

221

One of the soldiers standing over the body looked up and saw Polgar looking down. 'Yeah. He wouldn't stop when I yelled to him to halt. Kind of young to be running around shooting at people, Sarge.'

'Just remember, Patterson, that sorry piece of trash was old enough to put two holes in McGill and would have done the same to you if he had had the chance.'

Patterson looked at his platoon sergeant for a moment, then down at the dead German boy. After another moment of reflection, he reached down, picked up the AK, and went around to the front to continue the house-by-house search.

Polgar's report on the Mech Platoon's contact didn't really surprise Bannon. His only regret was the discovery that the town was populated by a lone fanatic who couldn't have hurt the Team. The price of a casualty hadn't been worth the results.

Impatient and anxious to find out how much longer they were going to sit there, Bannon dismounted and walked over to the battalion S-3's track to find out what Jordan's best guess was. His PC was nestled in a large hedgerow that separated two fields. The troop door on the back ramp was open as was the cargo hatch on top. Bannon stopped at the door and saw Major Jordan seated across from his radios, arms folded and chin resting on his chest. He appeared to be sleeping.

'Must be nice to have a cushy staff job where you can take a nap three times a day.'

Without moving a muscle or opening his eyes, Jordan replied, 'Bannon, someday when you grow up, and I trust you will, you'll appreciate the fact that we old folks need to conserve our energy.'

'Oh, is that what you call it? Conserving energy? Back home we call it sleep.'

'Shit, don't they teach you treadheads anything at Fort Knox?'

'Sure they do, Major. And someday, when Infantry Branch clears you to use words with more than one syllable, I'll tell you all about it.'

'I'm sure there's a reason you came over here other than to

harass me Bannon. Hopefully, it has to do with that shooting in the town you haven't reported to me yet.'

'That was a small affair. Some hyped-up commie high-school kid wanted to play Rambo. He wounded one of Sergeant Polgar's men and got his ass blown away. So far, that's all we've come across. What I really came over here for is to find out when we're going to get this circus moving again. If it's going to be awhile, I want permission to move up onto the high ground to the north-east where we can get under some cover. I'm not thrilled about sitting out here trying to hide my tanks behind these damned bushes.'

'I expect we'll be moving soon. The brigade commander just got off the radio with Colonel Reynolds. Colonel Brunn was all over the Old Man. Told him that if he couldn't get this battalion moving, brigade was prepared to pass the 1st of the 4th through us to continue the attack.'

'Sir, pardon me if I seem like an underachiever, but, if the brigade commander wants to let the 1st of the 4th take the lead, that's fine by me. I could get into playing second team for a while.'

'You don't understand, Bannon. Colonel Brunn damned near relieved Reynolds after the Hill 214 debacle. The only reason he didn't was because there didn't happen to be any spare lieutenant colonels lying around at the time. If the battalion screws the pooch on this operation, the Old Man is gone. The battalion has to succeed.'

'Well, sir, between you, me, and that dumb bush your track is trying to hide in, even if what you say is true, I have no intention of taking any undue risks simply to save someone's reputation. Colonel Reynolds is a good officer and a great guy, but his reputation isn't worth a single unnecessary casualty in Team Yankee.'

'I don't think we need to worry about that. The colonel is too much of a professional to do anything dumb simply to save face.'

'God, I hope you're right, sir.'

They turned to covering the next move. The air cavalry had come across some trucks and reconnaissance vehicles as they roamed out to the front. They scattered the trucks and destroyed the recon vehicles. Unfortunately, the cavalry scouts could not tell if they were Polish or belonged to someone else. A scout helicopter had tried to land near one of the destroyed vehicles to check this out but had drawn fire from an unseen enemy. Not being able to obtain this information and confident that the front would be clear for awhile, Major Jordan requested that the air cav troop shift over to the east and cover the battalion's right flank. The brigade S-3 replied that he would look into that.

Colonel Reynolds, having monitored the reports from the air cav troop, called Jordan on the battalion net and ordered him to get Team Yankee on the move again but at a slower pace. He informed the Major that the rest of the battalion would be moving out momentarily and would be able to catch up provided Team Yankee didn't get carried away again. Major Jordan looked at Bannon, grinned, and told the colonel that he would keep the tankers in check. As soon as the transmission ended, Jordan asked if Bannon had any questions. He replied in the negative; he was to get moving but keep it slow. With that, he went back to 66 and prepared to move the Team.

Orders to stop clearing the town came none too soon as far as Sergeant Polgar was concerned. The house-to-house search was getting old. He didn't want to lose any more of his people to some runny-nosed commie who had not even begun to shave yet. Besides, this kind of work was hard. When he had charged the stairs and thrown himself into the room in the house where the sniper had been, he had landed flat on his chest, forgetting there were still grenades hanging on his web gear. The force of the fall had knocked the wind out of him, and the grenades had dug into his chest. He could feel the bruises forming. As the tracks pulled out of town and headed back to the Team, he decided that he was getting too old to be running around playing John Wayne. In the future, he was going to leave the gung-ho stuff to the young kids in his platoon. He also decided that in the next war, he was going to find himself a nice cushy staff job at the Pentagon, fixing coffee for the generals. His campaigning days were over. War, thought Polgar, belongs to the young and strong.

Avery had mixed feelings about moving again. While sitting in this semi-exposed position was dangerous, moving out into the open again, this time in broad daylight with high ground to both sides of the Team, was more unnerving. The Team commander had ordered him to have his platoon go into a left echelon. This he had done. The 21 was now in the lead with the rest of the platoon trailing off to the left and behind him. The Team commander was off to the right of 21 with 3rd Platoon farther to the right, also in an echelon formation but refusing its right. The Mech Platoon was to the rear in the centre travelling with the XO.

As the Team moved forward, Avery found it difficult to observe his assigned sector, keep track of where they were on the map he had out to his front, control 21's driver, and keep one eye on the platoon and the other on the Team commander. On top of this, 21 was running across a ploughed field against the furrows and an occasional drainage ditch. It seemed that every time he looked down at the map to see where they were, the driver would hit a ditch, catching the young lieutenant by surprise and rattling him around in the cupola. At times, it seemed that he was unable to control 21, let alone the platoon, and that he was only along for the ride. There had to be a way to manage all of this with some degree of efficiency. How to do that, however, was beyond him.

★ The Soviet attack helicopter pilot slowly eased his aircraft into position. With a little luck, their target would be just over the rise to their front. They were lucky to have made it this far. The lead helicopter had barely avoided an enemy scout helicopter on their run in. Although the weapons operator had felt confident that they could have taken out the frail scout, it was not their assigned mission to do so. Someone else would deal with the bothersome scout. They were hunting for tanks.

The two attack helicopters stationed themselves on either side of an ancient keep that they had used as their rally point and for reference. If the reports were correct, when they popped up over the trees, there would be a town to their front and a group of tanks sitting stationary east of it. When the pilot of the lead helicopter signalled that he was set, the attack helicopters began to slowly rise until the weapons operator's field of vision was clear. The pilot, seated behind and a little higher than the weapons operator, saw the town first. Once he had the town in sight, he then began to search to the east of the town for the enemy tanks. He couldn't see them. He ordered the weapons operator to search the area with his powerful sight.

As the weapons operator was searching, something caught the eye of the pilot. There was movement to the north of the town. He turned and looked. Several objects were moving. Over the intercom, he informed the weapons operator of his sighting and turned the aircraft until it was facing almost due east. The weapons operator had no trouble finding his targets. He quickly identified them as M-1 tanks and M-113 personnel carriers. The pilot reported this to his leader who also shifted his orientation to the east and found the targets.

Like great cats preparing to pounce on their prey, the two Soviet MI-24D attack helicopters studied their targets for a moment. The leader called back and asked if the pilot or the weapons operator had observed any anti-aircraft guns or missile launchers. The weapons operator replied in the negative. The pilot checked his radar warning device to ensure that it was functioning and had not detected any enemy search radars before reporting back to his leader. The pilot and weapons operator then continued to track their targets, which were far out of range, while they waited for their leader's orders.

The orders came. Both helicopters would swoop down on the moving tanks at high speed. The leader would go for the far tanks, and the second MI-24D would attack the near tanks. They were not concerned with the personnel carriers. The two attack helicopters would be able to take out two tanks, maybe four, on their first pass. After overflying the target, the two MI-24Ds would turn north, loop around, and attack the tanks head-on. The leader felt confident that they would be able to make two passes on the enemy before any outside help could intervene. After the second run, both helicopters were to rally at the castle keep. They would then decide if they should continue the attack or break it off. Yelling an old Russian battle cry over the radio, the leader signalled the start of the attack.

Avery was hanging on to the machine-gun mount with one hand to steady himself while he ran his finger along his map trying desperately to find a landmark he could use as a reference. The cry of 'HELICOPTERS – NINE O'CLOCK,' followed rapidly by 'MISSILE – MISSILE – MISSILE,' caught him by surprise.

Instinctively he looked up and to his front. There was nothing there. He then turned to his right to look at the Team commander's tank to see what he was doing. For a moment, Avery watched as 66 began to spew out clouds of white smoke from its exhaust and then turn to the right, disappearing behind the smoke. When 66 and the 3rd Platoon began to fire wildly above his head, it suddenly dawned upon him what was happening. Avery turned around just in time to see the hideous attack helicopter bearing down on him, preceded by a round object, growing larger by the second and spewing flames. The impact of the antitank guided missile came before Avery could react.

★ The attack helicopter pilot was surprised at the speed with which the tanks reacted. Almost as one, the tanks had turned and begun to blow huge clouds of white smoke from their engines. The tanks began to weave about and fire. The shooting was wild and totally inaccurate. Still, it was disconcerting to watch the red tracers rise up towards him. A couple of the tanks were even firing their cannons. He had to fight his natural instincts to break off the attack and concentrate on closing on the target.

One of the lead tanks had not turned or cut on its smoke generator. The pilot quickly oriented on this stray and ordered his weapons operator to engage it. Then he launched an antitank guided missile. For several tense moments, the attention of both the pilot and the weapons operator was on the tank as the pilot held the aircraft on course and the weapons operator held his sight on the target. The missile, linked to the weapons operator's sight guidance system by a hair-thin piece of wire, received course corrections and homed in on the targeted tank. Only after the missile impacted on the tank did the pilot jerk his joystick to the left and fly north. He wasn't about to try for a second shot on this run. One hit was good enough.

As the pilot brought the helicopter around, a fast-moving object caught his attention. He looked up to see an American attack helicopter bearing down on him from the north. It must have been with the scout they had seen before. The weapons operator saw it, too, and began to lay his cannon on the closing enemy aircraft. But before the weapons operator could fire, the pilot jerked his joystick to the left again in order to evade. The American, however, was quicker.

The pilot felt his craft shudder, then saw the weapons operator in front of him disappear in a series of small explosions as the American's 20mm cannon shells ripped into the MI-24D. The attack helicopter's canopy was riddled and the cockpit was filled with smoke. The pilot struggled to control his aircraft but couldn't. The MI-24D disappeared in a great ball of fire upon impact with the ground.

'WE GOT 'EM! WE GOT 'EM!'

Bannon turned around to see what Kelp was yelling about. Kelp was hanging onto his machine gun with one hand and pointing to the north with the other. In the distance, Bannon could see a fire and black smoke. Kelp, with a grin from ear to ear, turned back to view the conflagration he was sure he had contributed to. 'Forget him, Kelp. He's gone. Keep your eyes open for the other son-of-a-bitch.'

Bannon ordered the driver to cut the smoke generator off but to be ready to kick it back on. He then called to the platoon leaders for a status report and to find out if anyone saw where the second Hind helicopter had gone. Garger came back with the report that two of his tanks had observed the second Hind disappear to the east, chased by two AH 1 attack helicopters. The two AH 1s were probably from the air cav troop and had just happened to be in the area. For a moment, Bannon reflected on the fact that someone was looking out for the Team.

With the air clear he ordered the platoon leaders to rally their tracks, then rally on him. The air attack had scattered the Team. The smoke and confusion still had not cleared, and it would take a few minutes to sort things out. As they were doing so, Hebrock came up on the Team net and reported that the 21 tank had been hit.

'Damn!' Bannon thought, '2nd Platoon lost another platoon leader.' Not everyone could be lucky. In war someone had to die. But the second lieutenants in the 2nd platoon seemed to be making it a habit. He looked around to see how bad 21 was but was unable to do so because the smoke the tanks had put out still had not dissipated. He called back to find out some more details as 66 came around to head back north. Hebrock reported that as soon as he had any, he'd call back.

As 24 closed on the smoking hulk of the 21 tank, Hebrock was convinced that everyone in the crew was dead. Main gun rounds in the turret ammo compartment were still cooking off, throwing great balls of flame and smoke into the air. The blow-off panels, designed to come off when the ammunition cooked off and vent the force of the explosion up and away from the crew, were lying fifty metres away from where 21 sat. Hebrock brought 24 to within forty metres of 21 and stopped. Both he and his loader watched as the fire died down and smoke slowly rose from the ammo storage compartment on the rear of the turret. Neither man said a word.

Just as he was about to report to the Team commander that 21 was a write off, the loader's hatch on 21 swung open. Hebrock watched for a moment. To his amazement, he saw 21's loader climb out, turn around, then reach down to help someone else. Hebrock ordered his driver to pull up next to 21 and called the first sergeant, telling him they needed the ambulance ASAP.

The air attack had given the rest of the battalion a chance to catch up. Colonel Reynolds called to ask if the Team could continue in the lead or if he needed to pass C company forward. Bannon replied that that wasn't necessary. The platoon leaders had been able to rally their people with no trouble, 2nd Platoon using the shattered 21 as their rally point. Bannon ordered Hebrock to leave the recovery of personnel and 21 to the first sergeant and get his platoon moving.

After he had made the transmission, he thought how cold such an order must seem to an outsider. He had no doubt that every man in the 2nd Platoon wanted to help his buddies in 21. Within the platoons there was a strong personal bond that held the men together. It was natural.

But they were at war. It was unfortunate that lieutenant what's-his-name had been hit and was probably dead. That happens in war. He and his crew would be taken care of, however, by someone else. It was the Team's job, and 2nd Platoon's, to continue the mission. They could not stop each time a tank was hit or a man fell. To do so would be to place the other personnel in the Team in jeopardy. Bannon didn't like the thought of rolling away and leaving 21 on its own, but he had his duty, and the Team had a mission, two very cold and uncompromising words.

Team Yankee, having collected itself, moved forward again. This time, however, they were not alone. Far to the left, Bannon could catch glimpses of some of Team Bravo's tracks. They were now abreast of the Team and moving north. To the rear, he could make out tracks of the battalion command group. He had no doubt that C company was close behind. Satisfied that all was back on track within the Team and the battalion, he turned his attention to the town of Korberg just to the north. That, and the valley to the east of it, would be the next critical point.

As his track and the ambulance closed on 21, First Sergeant Harrett could feel his stomach begin to knot up. He knew that he wasn't going to see anything new. Two tours in Vietnam, training accidents, and the first few days of this war had exposed him to many such scenes. Once he was there and doing something, he would be all right. It was the anticipation that bothered him the most. How bad was it this time? How many? Was there something he could do, or did they simply need the body bags? Did he know them, their wives, their children? Would they be able to identify the bodies? First sergeants are supposed to be detached, able to handle these things without a second thought. But first sergeants are also human.

It was with great relief that First Sergeant Harrert found that there had been only one casualty. Tessman greeted Harrert and led him and the medic to where the lieutenant was lying, face down.

While the medic began to work on Avery, Tessman explained what had happened. Avery had been standing up in the cupola when the missile hit. The force of the explosion from the main gun rounds set off by the missile hit him squarely in the head and back. The lieutenant simply dropped down to the turret floor. Fortunately for the rest of the crew, the ballistic doors that separated the crew from the stored ammunition had been closed. Some flames did get into the crew compartment, but nothing serious. The tank stopped and the halon fire extinguishers activated. After the explosions stopped, they abandoned the tank and did what they could for the lieutenant.

There wasn't much that they, or the medic, could do for Avery. He was in a very bad way with massive wounds and severe burns on his back and head. The medic told the first sergeant that they needed to get him medevacked right away or they would lose him. With the help of the crew, Avery was placed on a stretcher and loaded into the ambulance which took off for the battalion aid station.

With the ambulance gone, the first sergeant and Tessman began to look over 21. They had the driver try to start the engine but to no avail. The 21 would have to be towed back to the rear by the M-88 recovery vehicle. Looking into the turret and the burned out ammo storage compartment, Harrert commented that the tank would probably be back in action within twenty-four hours. Tessman, observing that this was the second time that this tank had been hit, dryly replied that they should retire it and use it for spare parts. Harrett agreed, but noted that the U.S. Army was fast running out of tanks and couldn't afford to throw them away simply because they had had a run of bad luck. To that, Tessman offered 21 to the first sergeant after it had been repaired. The first sergeant had to stop and think about that one. Maybe this tank should be scrapped.

★ The Soviet tank company commander did not like the idea of moving through the woods in single file. He would have preferred to have gone north past the town of Langen. By doing that, the company, and the battalion following it, would have been able to deploy into combat formation before making contact with the Americans. The regimental commander, however, had vetoed that idea because of the activity of American reconnaissance helicopters. To have gone through Langen would have exposed them to observation. Not only would the regiment lose the element of surprise, they would also be open to attack from the air. Instead, the lead tank battalion was winding its way along trails through the woods in order to maintain the element of surprise.

There were few options open to him. Once his tanks began coming out of the woods high on the hill, they would be visible to everyone in the valley. After they had been observed, there would be little time to take advantage of their surprise. Therefore, rather than have the three tanks of his lead platoon, the regiment's combat patrol, go out on its own, he had them pull back with the rest of the company. To succeed, they had to take chances. He gambled that his commander would not find out that he had pulled in the combat patrol, and the company would not stumble into an ambush. Thus the entire company was bunched up as they neared the edge of the woods overlooking the valley. The company would therefore be able to clear the tree line and deploy into a tight battle formation rapidly. It was a good plan, and he was sure that it would work.

The only thing that could possibly go wrong now was an antitank ambush along the trail they were on. If the lead tank was hit, the others would be backed up, unable to bypass or fight. The thought of such a thing gave the tank company commander chills. The sooner he was out of these damned woods and in battle formation, the better, as far as he was concerned.

KORBERG

THE KEEP

ISSEL

GERMAN FRONTLINE TRACE

N

MAP 13: AIR ATTACK

Chapter Eleven

COUNTERATTACK

Air Force Maj. Orrin 'The Snowman' Snow was pissed. As he led his wingman to where their two A-10s were to loiter and wait for good targets, he reflected that the people running Flight Operations had to be morons. He could understand how the Army pukes could screw up. Hell, most of them couldn't tell the difference between their planes and the Russians', let alone what to do with them. But getting the royal weenie from your own people was too much. It was bad enough that they had had to fight their way through enemy flak that wasn't supposed to be there to get at the target. But then to discover that the target wasn't there now, if it ever had been there, was too much.

Now the two A-10s, having barely made it back from behind the enemy lines, were being diverted into a holding pattern where they would wait until a good target was nominated. It made sense. It would have been dumb to send the aircraft back to the air field loaded with ordnance. But Snowman wasn't interested in logic right now. He was madder than hell for wasting their time and being sent on a worthless mission. If someone didn't come up with a good mission fast, he was going to lead the other A-10 to Flight Ops and bomb it, just for the hell of it.

The Team was making good progress, too good. Colonel Reynolds called Bannon and ordered him to slow down. C company was having a hard time keeping up, creating a large gap between Team Yankee and it. The colonel wanted to keep the companies close together. Bannon turned around in the cupola and looked back at the Mech Platoon. They were having no problem keeping up with the tanks. He couldn't imagine what the problem was with C company. Those boys were having a rough morning.

As he prepared to give the necessary orders to slow their rate of advance, the thought occurred to him that the longer he took to give the order, the farther they would go. At their current speed, every second he delayed meant the Team advanced another metre. The faster they went, the less time the Soviets had to throw something at them. A few extra minutes could mean the difference between seizing a bridge over the Salle intact or finding them all destroyed. Of course, speed could work against the Team. If it got far ahead and ran into trouble, the rest of the Battalion might not be able to catch up in time to pull its chestnuts out of the fire. Orders were orders and, as they say, discretion was the better part of valour. Team Yankee slowed down for the third time that morning.

★ As his tanks began to spill out of the woods onto the slope overlooking the valley, the Soviet tank company commander gave one short command. Like the well-drilled machine it was, the company rapidly deployed into a combat line. Once all the tanks were on line, they began to pick up speed and search for targets.

From their vantage point, this was not a difficult task. Before them on the valley floor deployed in a great vee, was a company of armoured personnel carriers and TOW vehicles being led by a small gaggle of three more personnel carriers. A quick count revealed that there were at least fifteen, maybe as many as twenty personnel carriers to their front less than four kilometres away. It had to be an American mechanised infantry company.

The Russian commander watched the advance of his tanks, now moving at a rate of over forty kilometres per hour. The absence of American tanks with the personnel carriers worried him. The fact that the personnel carriers were M-113s and not the new Bradleys pleased him. But there had been reports of tanks. He would have like to have taken out the tanks in the first volley. They were the greatest threat to his company. The M-113s would have been easy to deal with after the tanks. But, without any tanks in sight, the American mechanised company would be dealt with first. Not doubt, once the shooting began, the American tanks would come out of hiding.

Even with his CVC on and 66's engine running, the sharp crack of tank cannons firing was clearly audible to Bannon as the sound reverberated through the valley. Automatically, he straightened up and looked around to see who was under fire. There were no telltale puffs of smoke or dust clouds from tank cannons to the front. A quick scan to the rear revealed nothing. Someone was shooting someone.

'BRAVO 3 ROMEO – THIS IS ROMEO 25 – WHO IS UNDER FIRE AND WHERE'S IT COMING FROM? – OVER.'

Both tank platoons rapidly reported back that they were not under fire. It was the Mech Platoon that provided the answer.

'ROMEO 25 – THIS IS ZULU 77 – I THINK THE PEOPLE THAT WERE FOLLOWING US ARE UNDER ATTACK – I CAN SEE SEVERAL FIRES BEHIND US – OVER.'

Bannon turned completely around in the cupola and stood as high as he could. In the distance, to the rear of the Mech Platoon, he now could clearly see four pillars of black smoke rising into the air. C company had been hit. But from where? By whom? And why no reports from battalion? He dropped down and switched to the battalion net to try to contact the battalion commander. When there was no response, Bannon tried to contact the S-3. Still no luck.

It was the D company commander who told him what was going on. In rapid-fire fragments he reported that C company was under attack from Soviet tanks coming from the east. He went on to report that he was deploying his company into a hasty defence along the road from Issel to Korberg. There was no time to get away. With that, he dropped off the net and stayed off despite Bannon's efforts to contact him. No doubt he was busy running his company.

He then contacted the Team Bravo commander to learn if he was in contact. Lieutenant Peterson reported that he was not in contact but could see the Soviet tanks coming down off the hill to the east. He estimated that there were at least ten, maybe more. He couldn't make out what kind they were but since they were shooting on the move and hitting, he figured that they were T-72s or better.

It was clear that the battalion was in trouble. The battalion commander and the S-3 could not be reached. C company was probably scattered and fighting for its life. D company had checked out of the net as it prepared to greet the Russian onslaught. That left Team Yankee and Bravo with Bannon the senior officer. Suddenly he found himself in the position of being in command of half the battalion and having to come up with a solution to the nightmare or face losing the whole damned battalion. As these thoughts ran through his mind like a runaway locomotive, Team Yankee continued to move north, away from the battle, at a rate of one metre a second.

★ The Soviet tank company commander could feel the adrenaline run through his veins. They were closing on the Americans. Already a half-dozen personnel carriers were burning hulks with the rest scattering to get out of the way. All semblance of order had been lost as the Americans turned and ran. Surprise had been complete. Now they were reaping the benefits that their speed, fire, and shock effect had created.

With curt orders he directed the fire of his platoons. A report that there were more personnel carriers deploying to the west of the road drew his attention to the ten or twelve that were some three kilometres away. These carriers were dropping their ramps to let their infantry dismount. The tank company would have to finish the first enemy company fast and get to the second before they had time to set up a viable defence. Speed was critical! He began to issue new orders to his platoon leaders.

With little chance to think the whole problem out, Bannon began to issue orders. On the battalion net, he ordered Team Bravo to turn east, cross the north-south road, go about a kilometre, then turn south, and take the Soviets under fire in the flank with TOWs and tanks. When Peterson acknowledged those orders, Bannon dropped down to the Team net and ordered the FIST chief to call for all the artillery and close air support he could and to get into position from which he could control it.

He then ordered the Mech Platoon to move to the southeast along the tree line into the gap formed by the two hills to their right. He was sure that the Soviets had come from there and expected more would follow. The Mech Platoon was to set up an anti-armour ambush in the woods and keep the Soviets from reinforcing the company already in the valley. The two tank platoons and the XO were ordered to follow 66.

As 66 turned east and headed up the hill to the tree line, Bannon explained over the Team net what they were going to do. Once they reached the tree line, they would turn south, following the tree line. When they got to the gap, if there were more Soviet tanks already coming out, they would hit them in the flank. If, however, Polgar got to the gap first, the tanks would turn west once they reached the gap and attack the Soviets in the rear. The Mech Platoon would be left to deal with any follow-on Soviets as best they could.

It was all Uleski could do to hang on. The Team commander had his tank roaring along the tree line at full speed, with the rest of the tanks in the Team trying hard to keep up. The Mech Platoon had taken off on its own as soon as it had its orders. To their right they could see the battle in the valley. A dozen burning tracks were scattered about the area. The Soviet tanks were clearly visible as they fired and moved forward. At the ranges the Soviets were firing at, they seldom missed.

Gwent, the gunner, kept his gun laid on the Soviets below. The range was too great even if the Team commander had given them permission to fire. At the rate they were moving, however, that would not be a problem in a few minutes.

Uleski could feel his blood rising as he worked himself into a rage in preparation for the upcoming battle. He stoked the fires of his hatred of the Soviets by recalling how his first driver, Thomas Lorriet, had died. The image of the young soldier's body on the ground that first day pushed aside any last shred of compassion he had for the enemy as he cursed the Russians out loud over the whine of 55's engine.

As his tank raced along behind 66, Garger realised that he was thoroughly enjoying himself. At first, it was frightening.

239

Men were dying there in the valley. In a few minutes he would be in the middle of the fray, adding to the killing and, if his luck ran out, being killed himself. The very idea that he should be enjoying this seemed inappropriate at first.

But there was no denying the feeling. He had never felt so alive. Standing in the turret of 31 as it raced along, the image of the U.S. cavalry riding out to the rescue flashed through his mind. The only things missing from this scene were the troop's guidon and bugler sounding the charge. This was his moment. This was why he had joined the Army. 'To hell with it,' Garger thought, 'This is great! Too bad it can't last.'

★ A frantic and incomprehensible report on the radio was the first indication that the Soviet tank company commander had that his company was under attack. He glanced to his right in time to see a second tank in his company burst into flames. *The enemy tanks! They're on our flank!* As if on cue from the enemy threat to his right, the mechanised infantry company that had deployed along the road began to fire antitank guided missiles. He was trapped. Without a second thought, the tank company commander ordered his tanks to turn left and cut on their smoke generators. They had been lucky, and they had caused a great deal of damage. But the Americans were now gaining the upper hand. It was time to break off this attack and wait for the rest of the battalion before continuing.

Team Bravo was in position and firing before Team Yankee reached the gap and the point where they would turn. As soon as Sergeant Polgar reported that he was in place, Bannon ordered the tanks to execute an action right, form a line, and attack. Following 66's lead, the other tanks cut right and began to advance into the valley. Team Bravo's fire had been effective in forcing the Soviets to break off their attack and had thus relieved the pressure on D company. In a great cloud of smoke created by their smoke generators, the T-72 tanks that had survived disappeared to the south.

Folk switched to the thermal sight and continued to track the Soviet tanks as they fled to the south. It was now a race.

Would the Team be able to catch up to them in time to hit them? Right now, that didn't seem likely. Team Yankee's grand manoeuvre had been a bust. It had, by going too far out in front of the battalion, taken the Team out of the battle.

Then it struck Bannon that this disaster, or at least part of it, had been his fault. Had he obeyed the battalion commander's orders to the letter, Team Yankee would have been closer to C company and able to support it when the Russians hit. A mech company in M-113s on the move was very vulnerable to enemy tanks. Team Yankee should have been able to simply turn around and support the infantry. He had, however, been in a hurry to get out in front and reach the Saale. Now C company and the command group were gone, and the enemy was getting away.

Just as he finished his self-condemnation, the artillery began to impact to the front of the Soviet tanks. The FIST officer Plesset, having seen the enemy turn south, adjusted the incoming artillery to where the enemy was headed. He had wanted the artillery to impact directly on the tanks but had misjudged the enemy's speed and distance. This error caused the Soviets to turn east to avoid the artillery. The rapid change of direction allowed them to escape the artillery, but drove them straight into the Team. The Soviets had either not seen Bannon's tanks and thought their turning east would be safe or they had decided to take on the Team rather than the artillery.

Whatever the reason, the Team now had a chance to finish the job. Without further hesitation, Bannon ordered the tanks to fire at will and issued his fire command as he laid 66's gun on the lead tank coming out of their smoke screen

★ 'ENEMY TANKS TO THE FRONT!'

The Soviet tank company commander snapped his head to the front in response to his gunner's yell. For a moment he was paralysed with fear as he watched a line of M-1 tanks bearing down on him. *It had been a trap. The Americans fooled me and now we are lost.* As improbable as it seemed, that was the only way the tank company commander could explain it. No matter now. There was no time for manoeuvre. No time to make decisions. The only thing left to do was fight it out with the American tanks head-on. The tank company commander ordered his tanks to attack and began to direct his gunner to engage the lead American tank.

The scene was more like a medieval battle between knights than a clash between the most advanced tanks in the world. Like the knights of Middle Ages, the two groups of tanks charged at each other with lowered lances. Team Yankee had the advantage of surprise and numbers, nine against five. The element of surprise allowed the Team to fire first. The volley from Team Yankee stopped three of the T-72s, two of them blowing up and the third only crippled. The return fire from the Soviets claimed a 3rd Platoon tank.

By the time they were ready to fire again, the Team was right on top of the surviving Soviet tanks. Two of 3rd Platoon's tanks drove past the one Soviet tank still running. The turrets of the U.S. tanks stayed locked on the T-72 as they went by. When the two tanks fired on the Soviet at point-blank range, both rounds penetrated, causing the T-72 to stagger to a halt as internal explosions and sheets of flames blew open its hatches.

The crippled T-72 was overwhelmed. The shock of being hit and having so many targets so close was too much for the crew. They were obviously confused in their last seconds. Bannon watched the turret move one way to engage a tank, then in the opposite direction to engage a tank that appeared to be a greater threat, then back to the original tank. As he watched this, he wondered why none of the Team's tanks were firing on it. They had all slowed down by now so as not to bypass it, and most of the tanks had their guns trained on the hapless Soviet tank. Yet no one fired. It was almost as if everyone either felt sorry for this lone survivor or they were enjoying making the Soviets suffer the agony of certain death. Whatever the reason, Bannon ordered Folk to fire. He and four other tank commanders had the same idea at the same instant, giving an effective *coup de grace* to the last tank.

★ Six kilometres to the east on the other side of the hill a Soviet tank battalion commander was in the middle of a raging fit. As the lead tank of his second company raced along the narrow trails to catch up with the company already engaged, it had thrown a track making a sharp turn. Now it blocked the trail.

At first he was not worried. There appeared to be plenty of room for the battalion to bypass to one side. This was ordered. The fourth tank that did so, however, also threw a track. Now the bypass was blocked. As he nervously thumped his fingers on his map, waiting for the path to be cleared, the battalion political officer climbed on board his tank and watched the proceedings from there in silence. The battalion commander tried to ignore the political officer but that was not possible. 'The bastard,' he thought, 'He's come here to intimidate me. He'll not succeed.'

The political officer did, as was his habit, succeed. Both the battalion commander and the political officer heard the report from the lead company that they were being engaged by American tanks in the flank, and the attack had to be broken off. The political officer leaned over and said 'Well, comrade, what are *we* going to do? The attack seems to be failing.'

This was a threat, clear and simple. The political officer was telling the battalion commander that if he didn't take action he, the political officer, would. The commander did not hesitate. At least fighting the Americans gave him a chance. One had no chance with the KGB. The three tanks that had already bypassed were ordered to continue forward to assist the lead company. The battalion commander climbed out of his tank personally to supervise the clearing of the trail. At least the thrashing of arms and yelling would give the appearance of doing something. It was worth a try.

For a moment, Bannon drew a blank. The sight of smashed vehicles and the smell associated with burning tanks was becoming all too familiar. The fact that the battalion's predicament was nowhere near what the plan had called for was not any different from other operations. It was the fact that he had no immediate superior to turn to for orders and assistance that threw him. On Hill 214 he had been alone, but

243

at least he was still able to carry on with the order that had been issued.

This was different. He had one company that had been wiped out and two companies that were facing the wrong way watching the fourth company mill about waiting for him, their commander, to pull his head out and give them some orders. No sooner had the thought 'Why me?' flashed through is mind than the answer followed. 'Because you're it.' For the moment there was no one else, and if he didn't start doing something fast to get this goat screw squared away, the next wave of Russians would finish them.

He ordered Uleski to rally the Team's tanks and stand by for orders. Next he ordered Team Bravo to turn around defensive posture covering the rest of the battalion. The D company commander was ordered to rally his unit and sweep the battlefield to clear it of any Soviet survivors and provide whatever help they could to C company's survivors.

Contacting the battalion S-3 Air, a young captain back at the battalion's main CP, Bannon ordered him to report the battalion's current status to brigade, its location, and the fact that it was halted. Additionally, brigade was to be informed that he had assumed command and would contact the brigade commander personally as soon as possible. With that, Bannon switched back to the Team radio net and contacted Uleski, informing him that he would be leaving the Team net. Until further notice, Uleski would command Team Yankee.

Not wanting to sit out in the middle of the field by himself, Bannon ordered Kelp to follow 55. Dropping down to where the radios were, he flipped through the CEOI, found the radio frequency for the brigade's command net, switched the frequency, and reset the radio's preset frequencies.

While the battalion net had been relatively quiet, brigade's was crowded with a never-ending stream of calls, orders, half-completed conversations, and requests for more information. Bannon entered the net just as the battalion S-3 Air was finishing the report that he had directed him to make. Not surprisingly, most of the information was wrong. Colonel Brunn, the brigade commander, came back and asked the S-3 Air to confirm the battalion's current location.

Before he could respond, Bannon answered and gave the correct location and his assessment of the battalion's current status. He informed the brigade commander that the battalion was no longer capable of continuing the attack. Bannon ran down a list of the reasons why and waited for an answer. When he finished, there was a moment of silence on the brigade net while the grim news sank in. Then, without hesitation or a long-winded discussion, Colonel Brunn contacted the commander of the 1st of the 4th Armor and ordered him to pass through the mech battalion and continue the attack north as the brigade's lead element. Brunn came back to Bannon, ordering him to rally the battalion and to keep the brigade S-3 posted on its status. For the moment, Task Force 1st of the 78th Infantry was out of the war.

As Garger led his platoon through the area where C company and the Soviet tank company had been wiped out, he realised that he was seeing another aspect of war that he had so far missed: the aftermath. Up to this point, all his battles had been at long range. He had taken part in the run through the town of Arnsdorf with the CO during the defence of Hill 214, where they had been eyeball to eyeball with the Russians. But that action was fast, a blur of activity in a heated night action.

This was different. The slow movement of the Team through the battle area offered him ample opportunities to view the debris of battle more closely. There were the smashed vehicles, tanks, and PCs. Some burned fiercely while others showed no apparent damage, almost as if their crews had simply stopped their vehicles. It was the dead and the dying that were most unsettling. Here a tank crewman hung halfway out of a burning tank, his body blackened and burning. Over there a group of dead infantrymen who had abandoned their PC, cut down by the advancing Soviet tanks. Everywhere the lightly wounded were moving about, sorting out those who could be helped and those who were beyond help. Garger didn't want to watch. He wanted to turn away. But that was not possible. The horror of the scene had a fascination that held his attention.

The time span could not have been more than two minutes from when the firing in the valley to the west had stopped and the sound of advancing tanks coming from the east was detected. Polgar heard the squeak of the sprockets just as the forward security team he had sent out reported that there were tanks coming down the trail fast. Polgar had to remind them to report the type and number of tanks they were observing. Sheepishly, the NCO in charge of the security element reported three T-72s moving across an open area in the woods towards where Polgar had deployed the rest of the Platoon.

Instead of defending at the tree line where the security element was located, he had decided to set up deep in the woods where his people would have the greatest advantages and the tanks would be the most vulnerable and helpless. The Dragons would be worthless in this fight. The antitank guided missile they fired needed to fly some distance before the warhead armed. There wasn't enough standoff distance here for that to happen. This fight was going to be strictly man against tank at very close range. For this, the Mech Platoon was ready.

Polgar observed the tanks as they came. The tank commanders were up in the cupolas pushing their tanks forward for all they were worth. They did not seem to be concerned with security. The fact that the lead element had passed through these woods without incident apparently satisfied this group of Russian tankers that the trail was clear. Besides, they were hell-bent to join the lead element as fast as possible. In a twisted bit of humour, Polgar thought to himself as he watched the T-72s advance that all three would very soon be joining their comrades in the valley wherever good Communists go when they die.

Polgar and his men were far more relaxed as they waited to spring this ambush than they had been on Hill 214. The big Soviet tanks could be defeated. The men and the leaders in the Mech Platoon knew this now. They hadn't been too sure the first day or that night on the hill. They were veterans now, however, and knew what they could do. To some it was almost a contest, a challenge of sorts. Infantrymen were always trying to prove to tankers that they could easily do in their archrivals on the battlefield. The detonation of the first antitank mine was their cue to do so again.

As the Platoon went into action, there was nothing for Polgar to do. Every man had been briefed on his role and went into action as planned. Machine gunners and riflemen cut down the tank commanders before they could respond or drop down inside the tanks. Other infantrymen with light antitank rocket launchers, called LAWs, began to fire. One LAW is not enough to kill a tank. Sometimes it would take up to twelve LAWs before the tank died. Because of this Polgar had organised four-man tank killer teams under an NCO. Each man had several LAWs. The NCO would designate the target tank and fire. Each of the men would then fire in turn against the same tank. In this way, the first two tanks were rapidly dispatched.

The third tank, seeing the plight of the first two, began to back up. It didn't get far, however. Two infantrymen, on opposite sides of the trail, pulled a mine attached to a rope onto the trail under the third tank as it backed up. The detonation destroyed the engine but did not kill the crew. The crew began to spray the woods indiscriminately with machine-gun fire in an effort to kill some of their unseen assailants.

A squad leader in charge of this area called for smoke. Several men threw grenades that erupted into billowing clouds of coloured smoke. Once this smoke screen was thick enough to provide cover, the squad leader manoeuvred his tank killer team into position behind the tank where he knew the turret would not be able to be turned on them. For several seconds the LAW gunners waited for the smoke to clear. Once they had a clear shot, the LAW gunners began to fire. First the NCO, then the next man. Then the third. At the range they were engaging from, no one was missing. The LAWs slammed into the crippled tank one after the other at a measured interval. As Polgar watched, he knew the third tank was doomed.

So did the crew of the tank. Deciding that there was no point in dying for the Motherland just for the sake of dying, they surrendered. The tank gunner stuck his hand up out of the commander's hatch and waved a white rag. Both Polgar and the NCO in charge of the LAW gunners ordered a cease-fire.

247

This was something new. They were finally going to meet the enemy. A defeated enemy.

Once the firing stopped, the gunner slowly began to emerge. Looking around, he continued to climb out. When he saw the first American, he stopped and waved the white rag again, just to be sure. The gunner didn't move until the American signalled him to climb down. As he did so, the driver opened his hatch and climbed out and onto the ground.

The Russians were terrified. They were searched at gunpoint, their pistols and anything else that could be used as a weapon were stripped from them. While this search was in progress, an NCO climbed up to check out the tank commander and the rest of the tank. When it was discovered that the tank commander was still alive, two more infantrymen climbed up and gave the NCO a hand, lowering the wounded Russian down and away from the tank while the medic was called. The gunner and driver, seeing this, relaxed. The horror stories their political offcers had told them about Americans killing prisoners were lies. They were safe. They would live.

As he worked on the wounded tank commander, the medic thought how ironic this was. Less than two minutes ago everyone in the platoon was trying to kill this man. Now he was doing his damnedest to save the Russian's life. War was definitely screwed up. The medic hoped that someday someone would explain it all to him. But not right now. There was a man's life to save.

Bannon was in the process of gathering the commanders of Team Bravo and D company when Polgar reported the tanks. As soon as he heard about it, he ordered Uleski to take the Team's tanks up to the Mech Platoon's position. Once there he was to establish a defensive position blocking that trail with one tank platoon and the Mech Platoon and hold another tank platoon back as a reaction force.

His meeting with the other commanders was interrupted by the arrival of Major Jordan. A D company PC making a sweep of the area found the major and the survivors of the command group in a ditch where they had taken cover when their tracks had been hit. Jordan was covered with mud and bloodstains but was physically all right. As soon as he saw the gathered commanders, he smiled, 'Bannon, I never thought that I would be so happy to see those damned tanks of yours as I was when they came rolling down. It was great.' The Major talked fast and appeared hyper. That was not surprising. Given the spot he had just come from, it was to be expected.

'I'm glad to see you, sir. For awhile we thought the whole command group was gone. Did Colonel Reynolds make it?'

'He's been hit, hit bad. The medics have him now. His track and mine were hit in the first volley. That any of us survived is nothing short of a miracle. As it was, we had three dead and five wounded in the command group alone. How did the rest of the battalion do?'

While the Major sat, drinking water and regaining his composure, Bannon went over the current status of the battalion. C company had, for all practical purposes, ceased to exist. Two squads of infantry and their PCs as well as one ITV from C company had joined D company. There were a number of individual stragglers being policed up but many of them were wounded. As all the officers and senior NCOs had been hit or were unaccounted for, it would take awhile to come up with a total casualty count for that unit. D company had lost three PCs and one ITV. Their total casualties included five dead, thirteen wounded, and three missing. Team Bravo hadn't lost anything. Team Yankee had one tank damaged, the 33 tank, with two wounded. In addition to the line companies, the command group had lost all three of their PCs. Overall the battalion had lost fifteen PCs, three ITVs, and one tank during the Soviet counterattack. Even if the three tanks Polgar's people had gotten were counted, the battalion had lost more than it had taken.

The 1st of the 4th began to roll past the major and his gathered commanders on the road headed north. The men of that battalion viewed the devastation on both sides of the road in silence as they went by. When the command group of the 1st of the 4th rolled by, the S-3's track broke out of the column and came down to where Bannon, Jordan and the other commanders were gathered. Major Shell, the battalion S-3, asked for a quick update on what information Major Jordan had so far about activity to the front and flank. Jordan gave him what he had, which wasn't much. Major Shell looked around for a moment, wished him luck, then mounted his track and took off to catch up with the rest of his command group.

Uleski's report that there were more Soviet tanks coming down the trail towards Team Yankee's position broke up the meeting. Bannon asked Jordan if he had any orders for him. Still not completely caught up on the overall picture and somewhat shaken from his experience, Jordan replied, 'No, just hold the flank.' With that, Bannon mounted 66 and moved up to rejoin the Team.

Bob Uleski was still in the process of redeploying the Team when the Soviets appeared. When he had arrived at the position, two of the three tanks the Mech Platoon had hit were burning and giving off clouds of thick black smoke. There was no doubt the next group of Soviets would be able to see the smoke and would put two and two together. The trick of hiding in the woods would not work a second time. After a quick consultation with Polgar, Uleski had 3rd Platoon and his tank deploy on either side of the trail at the tree line where the security element had been watching the open area in the woods. The Mech Platoon, divided into two groups, each with two Dragons, began to deploy to the tree lines on the north and south side of the open area. The plan was for the 3rd Platoon to bar the trail physically while the Mech Platoon hit the Soviets on both flanks. The Mech Platoon was not yet in position, however, when the Soviets started coming.

The lead Soviet tank rolled out into the open and then stopped as soon as he saw the black smoke. It was obvious that the tank commander was reporting and would be able to see the 3rd Platoon sitting in the tree line at a range of six hundred metres. So Uleski ordered Garger to open fire. Two 3rd Platoon tanks quickly destroyed the T-72.

As he watched the T-72 burn, Uleski got Polgar on the radio and told him to get into position fast. It wouldn't be long before the Soviets made their next move. Uleski then entered the battalion net to report, requesting artillery on the trail across the open area from him where the Soviets were probably lined up. It was now a question of who would be ready first.

★ The Soviet battalion commander was not at all happy with his situation. The regimental commander was pushing him to attack and would not listen to reason. The Americans had his battalion bottled up on the trail with almost no room to manoeuvre. When his last appeal to the regimental commander was greeted with a hail of threats and abuse, he gave up. He ordered his remaining tanks, now down to eighteen, to bunch up under cover of the woods. When he gave the order, they were to rush into the open area to their front, deploy on line, and attack the far tree line. He hoped they would be able to overwhelm the enemy with speed and firepower. There was nothing else to do.

Major Snow blew up when he received word to turn around and fly back to attack the target he had just been told was no longer there. Over the air he told his wingman, so that everyone on the net would hear, 'Those people in flight operations have no idea what they're doing! If they wave us off one more time, we're going to go back there and bomb them.' His wingman went along with the abuse of their ground controllers by recommending that they forget the mission and just bomb the controllers. Major Snow simply shook his head and turned back to the heading they had just left. Maybe, just maybe, there was something there this time.

The T-72s began to pour out of the tree line and fanned out to the left and right. Polgar was still not yet in position. With so short a distance and so few tanks to stop the Soviets, Uleski had no doubt that some of the T-72s would make it to them. He knew as they began to fire that it was going to be a hard fight this time.

As the two A-10s came up to the target area, they saw

numerous pillars of black smoke rising up into the sky. To the front left in the valley there was a large amount of smoke. But that wasn't where they had been directed. Further east, in a saddle between two hills there were fewer columns of smoke. That was where they were going. As the A-10s closed on the spot, a clearing crowded with tanks appeared to their front. Neither he nor his wingman knew whose they were. Without an air controller on the ground to help, the only thing left to do was to overfly them and check them out. Commenting to his wingman that this was a hell of a way to do business, Snow dropped down and went in.

One pass was all Major Snow needed. He brought his A-10 up, circled around, and told his wingman to follow him in on the next run. The tanks were Russians. Finally, they were going to get to kill something.

At first Uleski thought the aircraft that buzzed overhead was Soviet. It had come and gone too fast for anyone to see, not that anyone had been looking. The entire clearing was filled with T-72s. The 3rd Platoon was firing as fast as possible and receiving return fire from the advancing Soviets. When he reported the aircraft, the Team's FIST came back and told him that they should be A-10s that had been requested. Not sure, Uleski continued with the business at hand and hoped for the best.

The A-10s came in from behind the Soviets and opened up with their 30mm cannons. In a shower of armour-piercing and HE shells, several T-72s blew up. As the two A-10s overflew the west side of the tree line Snow noticed the American tanks there firing on the Soviets. He cautioned his wingman to watch out for them. There was only two hundred metres between the U.S. and the Soviet tanks. This was truly close air support.

By the time Bannon arrived on the scene it was all over. Coming up next to 55 from behind, he stopped and surveyed the open area. There were at least fifteen T-72s burning to the front. Looking down the tree line he could see that one of the 3rd Platoon tanks was also burning. After making sure that the Soviets had really broken off the attack, Bannon dismounted and ran over to 55. Uleski was just getting over the shock of having been in such a near thing. One Soviet tank had managed to reach a point less than fifty metres from 55. He quickly pulled himself together and reported what had happened and the status of the Team. Satisfied that Uleski had the situation well in hand and that the Soviets wouldn't be coming back this way, Bannon reported to Major Jordan and cancelled the order for 2nd Platoon to come up.

As he waited for new orders, he went over the morning's events in his mind. It wasn't even noon and already the Team had been in four different engagements and had lost three tanks. The mission of the battalion had been changed, and instead of being the lead battalion in the attack, it was now defending the flanks. It was shaping up to be a hell of a day.

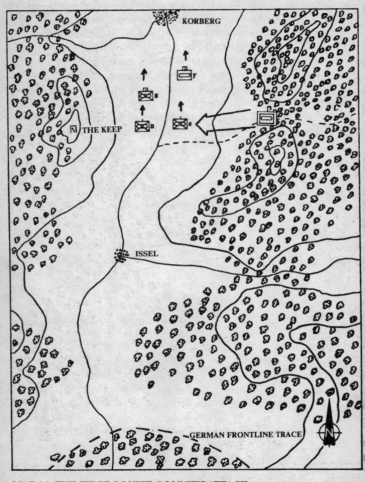

MAP 14: THE FIRST SOVIET COUNTERATTACK

MAP 15: THE BATTALION REACTS

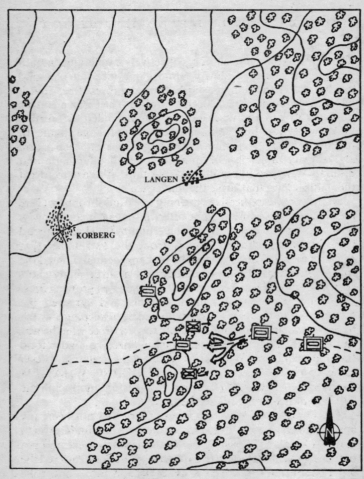

LANGEN

KORBERG

MAP 16: THE SECOND SOVIET COUNTERATTACK

Chapter Twelve

'THEY CAME, IN THE SAME OLD WAY'

The Team sat in its positions, collectively catching its breath and awaiting orders. Slowly, almost unnoticed, a new and unexpected enemy made its appearance: a forest fire. That it happened should not have been a surprise. The tracer elements in the main gun and machine-gun rounds, aided by burning tanks, were more than enough to set the dry foliage aflame. In high-tech fighting machines it is easy to forget that each action and activity affected everything it touched, manmade and natural. Wrapped in a million-dollar tank, it's easy to forget the natural laws that drive the universe.

At first no one noticed the burning trees and shrubbery. Fire had become a common sight after an engagement. Slowly, however, the fire began to grow, as ruptured fuel cells spread their burning contents. Flames from the two tanks that Polgar's men had destroyed in the first engagement ignited the tree branches that hung over them. In a surprisingly short period, the 3rd Platoon found itself between two growing fires.

Bannon stood upright in the cupola and surveyed the growing fire to the rear. Uleski, who had been keeping a watch to the front, saw his commander and turned to see what he was studying so intently. With a single glance, he understood Bannon's concerns. Without using call signs or names, Uleski came up on the Team net, 'YOU THINKING WHAT I'M THINKING? – OVER.' Turning towards 55 and facing the XO, Bannon simply nodded his head yes.

The flames continued to spread. There had not been any appreciable rain for weeks, making the trees and undergrowth grade-A kindling. Knowing the Team had no choice and not bothering to call battalion or explain why, Bannon ordered the 3rd Platoon and the Mech to pack up and move out. Like Uleski, Gerry Garger turned to his rear and immediately realised what was happening.

The move was going to be hazardous. To start, the two

platoons could not back away from the tree line into the woods before turning around. The fire had spread too far for that. Instead, they were going to have to move forward into the open and turn, flanking themselves to any enemy force that might still be to their front. Once clear of that hazard, the tracks had to pick their way slowly through the trees back to the valley. Movement therefore was not only going to be slow, it was going to be potentially dangerous. One error by a driver or TC could cause a tank to lose its track. The crew of 66 already knew about that danger. At the rate the fire was moving, a tank would have little chance of being recovered if it lost a track.

No attempt was made to establish an orderly withdrawal. Bannon ordered the Mech Platoon to move on its own to a rally point where the 2nd Platoon was already sitting in reserve. Uleski and 66 sat overwatching the move of the 3rd Platoon as they began to move. The air, already oppressively hot from the fire and thick with choking smoke from burning wood, diesel, rubber and flesh, was filled with tension as the first of the 3rd Platoon tanks rolled into the open. Folk had his eye glued to his sight as he slowly traversed the turret watching for any hint of movement from the far side of the clearing. Once Bannon was satisfied that there was no one on the other side who would do anything to his command, he signalled Uleski to begin his move. Tank 66 stayed in place for another minute, watching the far tree line, then joined the withdrawal behind 55.

The movement through the woods was agonisingly slow for Garger. Even though the platoon had moved forward into positions by creeping along between trees as they were now, it had taken less time, or so it seemed. He did not like the idea of being caught in the middle of a forest fire in a tank loaded with ammunition and diesel. He really didn't know what would happen if the forest fire engulfed the tank. No one did. That wasn't something they taught you at Fort Knox. He had no intention, however, of finding out. Sticking one's ass out to fight the Russians was one thing. He knew the odds then and could do something about it. Letting yourself get overrun by a forest fire was something else. It was an unnecessary risk that Garger was glad they were going to avoid, provided the tanks reached the valley before the fire reached them.

As 31 crept along, Garger leaned over, watching as the driver carefully picked his way through the woods. Tank 31 was following in the 32 tank's path. As the lead tank, 32 had the task of blazing the trail. The most difficult part for 31's crew was to maintain their calm and not crowd 32. This was easier said than done. When he wasn't watching the drive, Garger was glancing between the approaching fire and 32. He had to restrain himself from egging 32 on over the radio. That would serve no useful purpose other than to make the rest of the platoon more nervous. So he held his tongue and kept watching as 32 plodded ahead at an unnerving three miles an hour.

The whine of M-113s to his right momentarily diverted his attention. The smaller and more agile tracks of the Mech Platoon were making better time. The drivers were running at a good pace, weaving between the trees like skiers dashing between poles in a downhill race. When Polgar went by, he waved to Garger. The lieutenant returned the wave, then pointed at the approaching fire. Polgar acknowledged the lieutenant's problem with a nod and a thumbs up before the M-113s disappeared to the front of the column.

Some say leadership is the art of motivating men to accomplish a mission or do something that they might not otherwise do. That sounds great in a textbook. As 66 slowly inched along behind 55 in an effort to escape the spreading forest fire, Bannon came up with a few new definitions of leadership. The one that appeared to be most appropriate at that particular moment was something along the lines that a leader was the first man in the unit to put his buns out on the line, and the last to pull them in. As 66 continued its maddeningly slow move through the woods, he wondered if those buns weren't going to get overdone this time.

To take his mind off 66's dilemma, he switched the radio to the battalion net and called Major Jordan in order to inform him of the Team's move. Not surprisingly, instead of contacting the major himself, Bannon found himself conversing with a slow-talking radio/telephone operator who answered for the major. Getting an RTO is like getting a new secretary for a major corporation. You know that your message is going to be screwed up even if it finds its way to the right person. His conversation with the major's RTO was a case in point.

First, the man didn't know the proper call signs, insisting that Bannon identify himself fully before letting him proceed with the message. Once he accepted the fact that Bannon really did belong on the battalion net, he couldn't find the major. He had no idea where the major had gone but said that he would take a message and pass it on. Next, Bannon had to repeat the message twice before the RTO got it down. It was no big message. All he had to do was tell the major that a forest fire had forced Team Yankee to move and that the Team was now en route to the 2nd Platoon's location. Simple. When the RTO finally read the message back slowly and correctly, he made Bannon authenticate to make sure that he wasn't the enemy.

This situation, the company commander trying to get a message through a slow-witted RTO, is common and sometimes funny when it is in the past tense. In the present, however, it is extremely frustrating and unnerving. On one end of the radio is a man in danger, wanting to pass a message rapidly or requesting orders or seeking support. On the other end is a class-three moron sitting snug and secure in a command track, learning how to use a radio for the first time and mad because the radio call interrupted his lunch. A leader can know no greater frustration than this.

Bannon had no sooner cleared his mind of the painfully slow radio conversation with the RTO when the same man came back and told him that the request was denied and that the Team was to stay in place until the major came to the position and saw what was wrong. Bannon was livid. How the RTO had managed to screw up the message in less than five minutes was beyond him. He didn't give the RTO another chance. Controlling himself, Bannon told the RTO to get the major and have him call immediately.

By the time he finished with the RTO the second time, 55 was beginning to clear the forest and re-enter the valley. It came none too soon. The 66 came out of the forest just as the fire began to spread above the tank. A few more minutes would have been a few too many. Once again, luck and timing were on Team Yankee's side.

It was early afternoon before Major Jordan made it up to the Team's position. The two platoons that had escaped the fire established themselves in the tree line on either side of 2nd Platoon. The fire had been momentarily stopped by some old fire breaks. The tank positioned nearest the fire, however, had the task of keeping an eye out in that direction for any spread of flames.

The Team spent the time unwinding and taking care of personal needs. It had been on the move or in combat for almost nine hours when it finally pulled in with the 2nd Platoon. The emotional roller-coaster ride and physical efforts of the morning left everyone in a slight stupor. The crews moved at half-speed and with a deliberation that put one in mind of a drunkard. Before the Team could be of any use to anyone, the men, including Bannon, needed a break.

Major Jordan found Bannon sitting against a tree behind 66, eating some dehydrated rations and drinking from a canteen. He was stripped to the waist, his gear in a tangled heap next to him. He remained where he was as Jordan approached. He noted that the major was also suffering from fatigue. When he reached Bannon, he stood and looked down. Then, without a word, Jordan dropped down and took off some of his gear and helmet. Bannon handed him a canteen without a word, and he took it and drank from it without a word. The two sat there in silence for a moment, both with their backs against the tree, watching the men in Team Yankee go about their business.

'Sean, it's been a hell of a day so far. A hell of a day.'

'So far? You got some cheery news that's going to make my day or something?'

'I just got done talking with the brigade commander. He told me that battalion had done a great job and how he was proud to have it in his command. Then he went on to tell me that he had all the confidence in the world that I would do well as its commander.'

'Oh oh. Sounds to me, major, like the Old Man was setting the battalion up for a hummer of a job. You got something you're trying to tell this broken down tanker?'

''Fraid so, Sean. It seems like the tanks we were hit by were only part of a Soviet tank regiment. Division and brigade seem to think that the rest of that regiment is going to try to stop the division's attack again tonight. The brigade commander feels that since we did such a good job with the lead battalion, we should be allowed to finish off the regiment.'

'Bully for us. Did anyone tell you how and where?'

'The where is easy. Everyone thinks they'll attack through the Langen Gap, just north of here. The how is up to us.'

'You got any brilliant ideas yet, sir?'

'Not yet. That's why I came here to talk to you. I figure between the two of us we can come up with something.'

'Thanks for the vote of confidence, sir. My daddy always said misery enjoys company. Lunch, however, has a higher priority. Care to join me?'

'Hell, why not. I need some time to get myself together. After spending the last two hours down in the valley sorting out the rest of the battalion, I know what General Terry felt like when he found Custer and the 7th Cavalry at the Little Bighorn.'

'Well, if it makes you feel any better, I don't envy your position.'

'Sean, save the saddle soap and pass me some food.'

For a few minutes, the events of the morning were allowed to pass as the two officers munched on dehydrated foods. Just as it is necessary for the body to digest a meal, the mind had to be allowed to sort out events and images. For most of Team Yankee, the morning events were not new. If anything, some of the men were becoming a little too casual about the death and destruction that surrounded them. For Major Jordan, however, this morning was his baptism by fire. He was experiencing now what Bannon had gone through during the Hill 214 debacle. Bannon thought that the major had come to the Team to escape the horror show in the valley and to find someone with whom to share his new burden.

The afternoon was passing quietly. Only the distant rumble of artillery and an occasional crack from a tank cannon to the north broke the stillness. The bright day had given way to clouds and a cool wind coming from the west, foreshadowing a coming storm. In the Team area the crews were moving about, checking their tracks, cleaning weapons, or redistributing ammunition between tanks.

There wasn't much talking or shouting. Very little motion was wasted. A casual observer would not be able to determine who was in charge of the Team. Officers and NCOs were just as dirty and just as busy, except for Bannon, as the rest of the crew. The men knew what had to be done and did it. No shouting, no unnecessary rushing about. The Team, through habits born from countless hours of training and drills, was preparing for its next battle.

When they had finished their meal, the major and Bannon unfolded a map and laid it out on the ground. From a prone position, Bannon studied the map as the major went over the information he had received from brigade. The Langen Gap was actually a small valley running from east to west, connecting the main valley the battalion was in and the valley to the east where the Soviet tank regiment was located. The town of Langen itself was in the centre of the gap with high ground to the north and south.

After studying the terrain, they discussed the various ways the Soviets could come. Both were in agreement that they probably would not try sneaking through the woods again. They had already tried that and failed miserably. Odds were, they would try to bull through this time. Hence division's and brigade's belief that they would use the Langen Gap, a conclusion that both Jordan and Bannon concurred with. If the Soviets did come through the gap, they would be forced to go north or south of the village. Thus, the village provided a natural strongpoint if needed.

In the gap itself there were few natural positions, other than Langen, from which the battalion could defend. They couldn't and wouldn't put the whole battalion in the town of Langen itself. From the beginning it was decided that D company, along with the remnants of C company, would defend from Langen. It was the positioning of the two teams that was difficult. If they were deployed on the east slopes of the hills north and south of Langen, they would be out on their own and exposed to Soviet artillery and supporting fires. A team deployed on the southern slope of Hill 358 would be masked by the town of Langen and at too great a range to be of much use. There were very few options.

After some additional discussion, the major decided that they would go with a reverse slope defence. It would be risky but there seemed to be little choice. It was the only way they could protect the force and deploy everyone where the entire battalion would be mutually supporting. Team Yankee, with its eight tanks, the Mech Platoon, and two ITVs would deploy south of Langen on the high ground facing northwest. Team Bravo, with four tanks, a mech platoon, and two ITVs would be situated northeast of Langen facing southwest. Two ITVs would set up on the lower slopes of Hill 358 facing southeast and D company would hold the eastern portion of Langen and face east. In this way, as the enemy force approached Langen and turned either north or south, it would be hit in both flanks. Major Jordan anticipated that the Soviets would turn south, which is why Team Yankee and the majority of the tanks went there. However, Bannon was given a contingency mission to attack into their flank if the Soviets turned north.

In addition to normal artillery fire support, the brigade was allocating several artillery-delivered scatterable minefields to the battalion. The mines, contained in an artillery projectile, were released after firing over a wide area. As soon as the mines landed, they armed automatically. While not powerful enough in most cases to kill a tank, these artillery-delivered mines could easily immobilise them by destroying the tracks, slow others, and cause confusion. The plan was to save the scatterable mines until they knew for certain where the Soviets were going and then drop them right on top of the tanks that were being engaged.

In addition to the teams and D company, the Scout Platoon

with its five Bradleys would be deployed well forward as a combat outpost. The scouts were to engage the Soviets early, stripping away any security elements they might have in front and causing them to deploy early. When the Soviet return fire became too intense, they would pull north into the woods and let the Soviets pass. When the time appeared to be right, they would come back out of hiding and snipe at the Soviet rear or flanks.

After dividing the battalion up into kill zones and doing some initial plotting of artillery, Major Jordan ordered Bannon to recon Team Yankee's position. He was going to call forward the other commanders and have them meet him in Langen. There he would issue their instructions and allow them to recon the area. He wanted the battalion to be in place and ready by 1800 hours. While it would have been possible for Team Yankee and Team Bravo to move then, D company still needed time to sort itself out. Until the battalion was in place, the Scout Platoon would be the only force in the gap.

The move into the Team's positions south of Langen did not take long. By 1700 hours it was settled in and preparing positions. Although the brigade could not provide the battalion with replacements to make good its losses in men and equipment, they sent something to them almost as good. A company of engineers with heavy equipment arrived in Langen shortly after the battalion. The major immediately put them to work digging positions for the two teams and an antitank ditch running from Langen to the northeast. Chances were that it would never be finished, but the visible presence of even a partially completed ditch might be enough to cause the Soviets to shy away from the northern route and go south, where the major wanted them. Besides the digging, a squad of engineers assisted D company in setting up a protective minefield in front of Langen. If used correctly before a battle, a platoon of engineers with heavy equipment can be more valuable than a company of tanks.

The Team was deployed along the tree line south of Langen facing the village. Provided the Soviets obliged them, they would be facing the left flank as the Russians moved to the

265

southwest. The northernmost unit was the Mech Platoon stationed at the northern tip of the forest and hill. They were placed there to protect the Team's blind side and prevent dismounted infantry from rolling up their right flank. Next in line was Uleski in the 55 tank between the Mech Platoon and the 2nd Platoon. The 2nd Platoon was to his left. Bannon placed the 66 tank next and put 3rd Platoon to the left. Garger in the 31 tank was on the Team's far left.

During the afternoon, Major Jordan had done some reshuffling of the battalion's task organisation based on his recon. The two ITVs Team Yankee was supposed to have were taken away. Instead, they were placed on Hill 358. The major felt the ITVs would have better fields of fire from the hill. Because the battalion fire-support officer had been killed when the command group had been hit, Lieutenant Plesset, Team Yankee's FIST, was taken by Major Jordan to fill in as the Battalion's FSO. As in the first battle, Bannon would have to go through battalion to request artillery. This time, however, it would not be as difficult. There was a very limited number of options open to the Team and the Soviets, and all were covered with preplanned target reference points.

The battalion was in place and ready by 1800. Shortly after that a series of showers, hard summer downpours, began. The sky blackened, and the rain came in sheets. At first it was a welcome relief. After twenty minutes, however, it started to become a hindrance. The engineers digging the antitank ditch and positions found themselves fighting mud as well as time. The tedious job of emplacing the minefield became a miserable one as well. The hastily dug foxholes of the Mech Platoon rapidly filled with water, forcing the occupants to abandon them and seek shelter in the PCs when they could.

Everyone who didn't need to be outside sought shelter in the tracks. The infantry company in the town, with the exception of those people working in the minefield, were lucky. They were able to improve their positions in the buildings and remain dry. By the time the last shower passed through at 2000 hours, any joy the men in the battalion had felt over the break in the summer heat had been washed away and replaced by mumbled complaints about the cold, the damp, and the mud.

266

The rain did have one beneficial effect. By coming late in the day it cooled down everything that was not generating heat. This would increase the effectiveness of the thermal sights. The attacking Soviet tanks would be hot and would present clear thermal images against the cool natural backdrop.

While the engineers would continue to work until all light was gone, the battalion was set and as ready as it would ever be. All it had to do now was wait. The tank crews, the infantrymen in the town and on the hills, the scouts, the ITV crewmen, the battalion's heavy mortar men and the numerous staff and support people that kept the battalion going settled in to wait.

The Team, like the rest of the battalion, went to half-manning during the wait. The scouts, deployed in the path of any Soviet advance, would be able to give them at least five minutes warning. Uleski took the first watch for the Team while Bannon got some sleep. At first Uleski found staying awake easy. The cold and the damp coupled with the nervous anticipation kept him alert for the first hour, but boredom and exhaustion soon overtook him. By 2330 hours he was struggling to stay awake and losing. Uleski would shift his weight from one foot to another, shake himself out, and then lean against the side of the turret every five minutes or so. Inevitably, however, he would drop off momentarily, awakening only when his head fell forward and crashed into the M2 machine gun mount.

Just before midnight, he gave up his efforts and roused his gunner to replace him in the cupola. The loader replaced the driver. When Gwent was ready, Uleski told him he was going to check the line, wake up the CO, and come back to get some sleep.

As he moved down the line, starting with Mech Platoon, he was glad to see that the rest of the Team had been able to remain more alert than he had. At each point he was challenged. In the Mech Platoon's area he ran into Sergeant Polgar, who never seemed to sleep. He was always moving around checking on something or someone. Uleski didn't know how he did it. The only way one could tell that Polgar was tired was to listen to him speak. His normal slow southern accent became a little slower when he was tired. When Polgar sounded like a 45 record being played at 33, it was a sure sign that the sergeant was exhausted.

At 66, Uleski found Bannon stretched out on top of 66's turret asleep. Looking at Bannon nestled on top of the camouflage net with the loader's CVC on, Uleski was at first reluctant to wake his commander. He was too tired, however, to be that kind. When Bannon was awake and coherent, Uleski updated him. Not that there was anything to report. Nothing had come over the battalion or team radio nets since radio listening silence had gone into effect. All was quiet.

Bannon was about to tell his XO to go back to his tank and get some rest when a massive volley of artillery rounds impacted in Langen and on the east side of the hill Team Yankee was on. The flash from the impacts lit up the sky. Division and brigade had been right. The Soviets were coming through the gap. In very short order they would find out if the major had guessed right and come up with a winning solution.

The men of the Mech Platoon scrambled into their positions as the Soviet artillery continued to crash into the east side of the hill two hundred metres to their left. The water in their foxholes had long since dissipated, but the mud had not. Wherever the infantrymen made contact with the ground, the mud clung to them and soaked through to their skins.

In spite of the discomfort and fear caused by their environment and imminent attack, they prepared for battle. The riflemen checked their magazines, tapping them against their helmets to ensure that the rounds were properly seated. They loaded their weapons, chambered a round, took their weapons off safe, and placed the barrel on the stake placed along their principal direction of fire. Grenadiers checked the function of their grenade launchers and chambered their first rounds. Machine gunners checked the ammo to ensure that it was clean, dry and ready to feed. Dragon gunners switched on their thermal sights, checked their systems, and began to scan their areas for targets.

Polgar went along the line, stopping at each foxhole. To

each soldier he gave his final instructions. When he came to a squad leader he required him to repeat his orders. The image of their platoon leader, illuminated by the flashes from impacting artillery, squatting above their foxhole as he calmly gave them instructions, served to steady those who were nervous. His confident and businesslike manner was contagious and bound the Platoon into a usable weapon.

The tankers also prepared for their ordeal. The outcome of this fight would be determined by them. The ITVs and the Scout Platoon, firing their TOW antitank guided missiles, and the infantry with their Dragons would contribute. Every gun counted. The fast-firing M68A1 105mm tank cannon, however, would be the prime killer. Capable of firing eight aimed rounds per minute, the tanks would account for eight out of ten kills that night.

The tank and the crew has but one reason to exist. To feed the tank's cannon. All else takes a distant second. Loaders opened their ammo doors to ensure that the rounds were placed in the order they wanted. They would be fighting tanks tonight so the majority of the rounds fired would be the armour-piercing fin-stabilised discarding SABOT rounds with their long needle-like projectiles. Satisfied that the ammo was ready, the loaders closed the doors and checked that the turret floor was clear. In the heat of battle, it would not do to have things clutter the turret. The spent shell casings would be more than enough of a challenge to the loader.

The gunners checked their thermal sights, adjusting the contrast and clarity of the image to obtain the best possible sight picture. They checked their computer settings and functions to ensure the fire-control system was ready and operating. Tank commanders sat perched in their cupolas, alternately watching their crews as they prepared for battle and scanning the tank's assigned sectors. When all was ready, a TC would turn to his wingman and wave until the wingman acknowledged him.

With their weapons ready, the men of Team Yankee prepared mentally for their ordeal, each in his own way. Most said a prayer. Many of the men had forgotten how to do so.

Technology was so much easier to grasp than the concept of a divine being. But war had been a humbling experience, stripping most of the men in the Team of their smug pretenses. The awesome spectacle of war and everpresent death brought each man face-to-face with himself, for many for the first time in their lives. Most found they lacked something; they felt an emptiness. Along the line, men found comfort in beliefs long dormant. In the shadow of death, amidst the violence of the coming attack, simple, heartfelt prayers completed the Team's preparation for battle.

The scouts reported the appearance of the Soviets. They were advancing in company columns, waiting until the last minute to deploy. This made it easy for the scouts to divide up the Soviet formation and engage their tanks without interfering with each other. The scouts began their battle drill, firing, moving, firing, moving. Engaging at maximum range and calling for supporting artillery fires, the scouts began the grim business of the night. The Soviets tried hard to ignore the scouts, for they knew that they were not the main force. To stop and engage the scouts would prevent their reaching the valley and accomplishing their mission.

The scouts were persistent. Just as a single mosquito can keep a full-grown man from sleeping, the Scout Platoon drew some of the Soviets away from their mission. A company of tanks peeled out from the formation and began to engage the scouts. In accordance with their instructions, the scouts fired a few more rounds to draw their attackers farther away from the advancing regiment. Then, they disappeared into the darkness. The Soviets knew that the scouts were still out there. The night betrayed no tell-tale fires from burning tracks. The Soviet commander found himself with ten fewer tanks and the need to keep looking over his shoulder as he began to pass between the two hill masses and turn southwest.

To the men in Team Yankee the Soviet advance was an awesome spectacle. They watched the Soviets pass to their front. The fires started in Langen silhouetted the Soviet tanks as they completed their deployment. The tank regiment was now in columns of companies, each company in line, one behind the other. As the lead company began to pass to the south of Langen, Major Jordan called for the scatterable mine fields.

Amidst the noise of the Soviet artillery fire, the U.S. artillery-delivered mines arrived almost unnoticed. That is, until Soviet tanks began to run over them. The Soviet officers knew about scatterable mines, and they knew their capabilities. There wasn't anything the Soviets didn't know about the American military. But to have knowledge about a weapon system does not always mean that you know what to do about it when you encounter that weapon. The manner in which the Soviets dealt with the scatterable minefields was a case in point.

Tanks began to hit the mines and stop. Commanders at first thought they were under fire but saw no tell-tale gun or missile launcher flash. As more tanks hit the mines, the other tanks began to slow down. A mine field. An unexpected inconvenience but one that the Soviet commanders could deal with. With a single order, the companies began to reform into columns behind the tanks equipped with mine ploughs and rollers. Once the tanks were out of the minefield, they could redeploy and continue as before. Soviet battle drill is good, and it is precise.

It was at this point, when the Soviets were in the midst of redeploying, that Major Jordan ordered the ITVs, D company, and Team Bravo to open fire. The sudden mass volley caught the Soviets off-guard. They had thought that once they had cleared the choke point between the two hills and had begun to bypass Langen, there would be no stopping them. After all, the choke point was the logical place to defend, not after. Confusion, both in the Soviet battle formation caught in the middle of redeploying and in the minds of commanders faced with an unexpected problem, became worse as the Soviet tank company commanders and platoon leaders began to die.

With the Soviets thrashing about in the open, Jordan directed the artillery to switch to firing dual-purpose improved conventional ammunition, or DPICM. Like the scatterable mine, the artillery projectiles were loaded with many small submunitions. The submunitions in DPICM, however, were bomblets that exploded on contact and were designed to penetrate the thin armour covering the top of armoured vehicles. Confusion now began to degenerate into pandemonium. Some tanks simply stopped and began to fire into Langen. Others tried to carry out the last orders given and form into column. Tanks from the second tank battalion of the regiment still in the gap between the hills charged directly towards Langen and ran afoul of the minefields laid by the engineers and infantry. Some tanks simply turned and tried to go back, a few headed towards the woods where Team Yankee was, thinking the silent tree line offered safe haven.

Sensing that the time was right, Major Jordan delivered his *coup de grace*. He ordered Team Yankee to fire. The first volley was devastating. Those Soviets headed towards the Team's positions were dispatched without ever knowing what happened. After the first well-measured volley, the tank crews in Team Yankee began to engage the Soviet tanks in their assigned sectors of responsibility. Firing rapidly, the tanks began to methodically take out the Soviet tanks starting with those closest to the Team's positions. Above the din of battle the shouted orders of tank commanders could be heard: 'FIRE!' 'GUNNER – SABOT – TWO TANKS – FIRE!' 'TARGET – NEXT TANK – FIRE!'

Like a wolf smelling blood on a crippled and dying animal, the Scout Platoon swung around to the rear of the Soviet regiment and began to engage. The people who started the battle rushed forward as the battalion began the final stages of its killing frenzy.

The scene before Bannon was staggering. He stood upright in the turret and watched. Folk no longer needed him, simply continuing to engage anything that appeared in his sight. Folk, the loader, the cannon, and the fire control system were one complete machine, functioning automatically, efficiently, effectively.

Hell itself could not have compared with the scene in the open space to the front of 66. There was the burning village of Langen in the background. Flames, interrupted by the impact of incoming artillery rounds, leaped high above the village and disappeared in low hanging clouds. From the far left of Bannon's field of vision to the far right and beyond, smashed Soviet tanks and tracked vehicles burned, spewing out great sheets of flames as the propellant from onboard ammunition ignited and blew. Burning diesel from ruptured fuel cells formed flaming pools around dead tanks. Tracers and missiles streaked across the field from all directions, causing stunning showers of sparks when a tank round hit a Soviet tank or a brilliant flash as a missile found its mark. Soviet crewmen, some burning, abandoned their tanks only to be cut down as chattering machine guns added their stream of red tracers to the fray. Transfixed by this scene, Bannon received a new understanding of Wilfred Owen's grim poem, 'Dulce et Decorum Est.'

As in all the Team's battles, there was no really clear-cut ending. The deafening crescendo of battle suddenly tapered off as the gunners ran out of targets. It was replaced by random shooting, usually machine guns searching out fugitive Soviet crewmen trying to escape. No order was given to cease fire. There was no need to. As before, Bannon allowed the Team to take out those that had survived the destruction of their vehicles. Mopping up is a useful term for this random killing. Team Yankee and D company continued to mop up for the better part of an hour.

When he was sure that the last of the Soviet tanks had been destroyed, Bannon called for a SITREP from the platoons. From his position he could not see any more of the Team than the tanks to his immediate left and right. In the heat of battle, he and the platoon leaders had become totally absorbed in fighting their tanks. There had been no need to exercise any command or control once the order to fire had been given. It had been a simple case of fire quickly and keep firing. The result was that, although he knew they had stopped the Soviets, Bannon had no idea what it had cost the Team.

The replies he received from the platoons were difficult to believe but welcome. Though several tanks had been hit, the total cost to the Team had been two men killed and four wounded, most of them from the Mech Platoon, as usual, and one tank damaged. The positions dug by the engineers and the fact that Team Yankee had joined the battle last, after the Soviet commanders has lost control of the situation, allowed the Team to come out with relatively light casualties.

Listening to the SITREPs given over the battalion radio net, Bannon learned that D company had suffered far more than Team Yankee due to the Soviet artillery fire and the fact that they were in the middle of things. Even so, that company was still in good shape and could field three slightly understrength platoons.

By the time Major Jordan got around to calling for a SITREP from the Team, Bannon's elation at coming out of this last fight so well with so little damage gave way to cockiness. When the major asked for a report, Bannon gave him the same words Wellington had used when describing the Battle of Waterloo: 'They came in the same old way, and you know, we beat them in the same old way.'

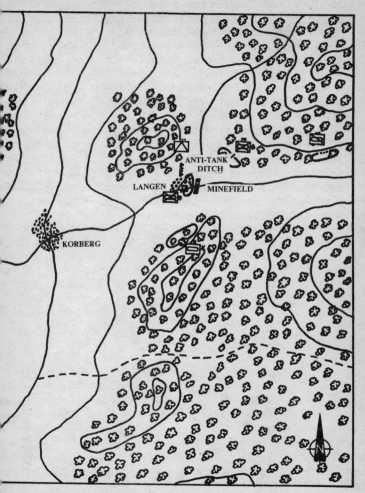

MAP 17: THE DEFENSE OF THE LANGEN GAP

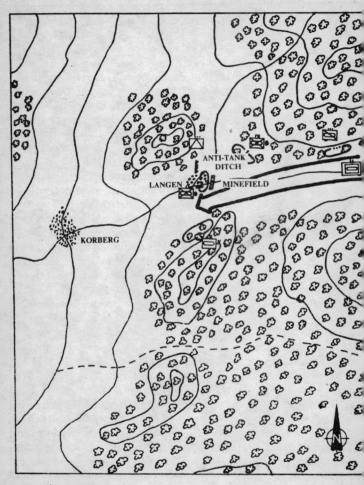

MAP 18: THE NIGHT ATTACK

276

Chapter Thirteen

TO THE SAALE

The creeping dawn of the tenth day of war revealed the full extent of their success. Over eighty Soviet vehicles lay smashed and strewn in the Langen Gap. The largest gaggle of burned-out hulks were between Langen and the Team's positions. A few of the tanks had been less than fifty metres away from Team Yankee when they had been hit and stopped. The battalion had been heavily outnumbered and by all rights should have paid dearly for holding the gap. But it had held and had done so cheaply. The favourable margin of victory had only been achieved through the planning and orchestration of the battle by Major Jordan.

Despite the magnitude of what they had done, there were no visible signs of joy or pride in Team Yankee. The closest thing to emotion displayed by anyone was a look of utter exhaustion. The efforts of the previous day and night, the emotional roller coaster caused by fleeting brushes with death and brief but intense periods of combat had taken their toll. When Bannon trooped the line at dawn, he was greeted with simple nods or stares by those who were still awake. Uleski was lying on top of 55 in a sleep that bordered on death. As there was no need to wake him, Bannon left instructions with Gwent to have him report to 66 when he woke but not later than 1100 hours. Bob Uleski needed his sleep more than Bannon needed him.

In the Mech Platoon area the men were split up evenly, half of them in the foxholes on alert and the rest back at the tracks. The day was starting cool and overcast. Since the mud in the foxholes hadn't begun to dry and wouldn't do so anytime soon, Polgar sent those men who weren't on duty to the tracks to sleep where it was dry. Bannon found him sitting with his back against a tree, his M16 cradled in his arms, asleep. As with Uleski, Bannon didn't bother him but left the same message with the squad leader in charge.

277

The morning passed quietly. The Team simply remained in position and watched the area to its front for any signs of activity. Patrols from D company had begun to sweep the battlefield after the last of the scatterable mines had self-destructed. Occasionally there would be a random shot fired, but no one paid much attention. The patrols were stopping at each Soviet vehicle to check it. When they were satisfied that the vehicle was harmless, the patrol leader would mark it with chalk. Those tracks that were still burning were given wide berth.

The bodies strewn about the field were also checked. Not many Soviet crewmen had managed to abandon their tanks and tracks when they had been hit. Some had, however, and in spite of the machine-gun fire laid down by Team Yankee and D company, some had survived. When a wounded Russian was found the patrol would stop and call for medics. An ambulance track darted from place to place picking up casualties. The patrols even came across a few Russians who had managed to hide or play dead through the night. Those who did not immediately surrender were not given a second chance. There appeared to be no one in a charitable mood on the patrols.

Starting at 1100 hours, word went out to the Platoons to roust everyone and start their maintenance routine, including cleaning and boresighting weapons. When Uleski came around, blurry-eyed and rumpled, Bannon instructed him to compile by noon a complete status of the Team on ammo, fuel, other POL needs, maintenance problems, and personnel needs for each vehicle. At that time Bannon intended to have a short meeting with the platoon leaders to cover their current status and give them any news from battalion that he could come up with. Uleski simply sighed, saluted, and gave a 'Roger – Out' as he began to go about his tasks.

Kelp and Bannon already had a good head start on the task of cleaning up and preparing for the next battle. While they sat and watched D company's patrols during the morning, they had cleaned 66's three machine guns and their own pistols. Although Kelp had matured into a good soldier, he still was excited by some of the more gruesome aspects of war. Sitting on top of the turret, cleaning weapons, he would occasionally yell out, 'There goes another one!' Grabbing the binoculars, he would watch as the patrol stopped to dispatch a Russian who had been hiding and had chosen to evade rather than surrender. After each chase was terminated, he would offer his views and critique the patrol's performance, noting that they were using way too much ammunition to bring down the Russians. When Bannon offered to arrange it so that Kelp could go out there and show the infantry how to do it, he lightened up on his remarks, but continued to watch.

It wasn't until well after noon that Bannon was able to meet with Major Jordan, who had been called to brigade headquarters at 0900 and spent several hours there. On his return, he called all the commanders and staff into Langen for a meeting. He had new orders.

While the battalion's mission hadn't changed, its organisation had. Team Yankee, with all three tank platoons and one mech platoon, was being returned to 1st of the 4th Armor. The 1st of the 78th was to remain at Langen reporting directly to division. Major Jordan explained the reasoning behind all this and the 'Big Picture'.

While the Soviets were busy trying to break into the division's flank through the battalion, they also had thrown other forces directly at the brigade's lead element as they advanced to the Saale River. Despite this, the brigade had been able to continue the advance at a slow, steady, and costly rate. The 1st of the 4th was fought out and in its turn had to be replaced by another battalion while it recouped.

The problem facing the division, and the rest of the U.S. Army in Europe, was that it was running out of equipment. Prepositioned war stocks of tanks, personnel carriers, trucks and all the hardware needed to wage a modern war had run out. Some equipment was arriving from the States but not near enough to replace equipment at the rate at which it was being lost. Even if the Navy could provide the necessary sea lift to carry what was needed, there wasn't enough equipment available in the States anyway. At prewar levels, which most of the factories were still at, the U.S. could only produce a pitifully small number of M-1 tanks a month. The Army in Europe was capable of losing the equivalent of one month's production of tanks in a single day.

The solution to this problem was to strip understrength units and concentrate all resources in those units making the main effort. There wasn't enough to go around so units still capable of carrying out offensive operations or holding critical sectors received priority on everything. The 1st of the 78th was no longer capable of offensive operations. Sitting in Langen, it was now out of the division's main effort. The brigade was still capable of reaching the Saale if all available assets were concentrated to support its two battalions that could still attack. The 1st of the 4th was one of those units, and Team Yankee was one of those available assets that could be sent in.

Major Jordan was not at all pleased to lose the Team. Although nobody at division thought the Soviets would try the Langen Gap again, the 1st of the 78th would be hard pressed to stop them if they did. The battalion was now going to be down to two understrength mech companies. The major didn't discuss this, he didn't have to. The commanders and the staff all knew what could and couldn't be done. The mood of the assembled group was depressed. Everyone also knew, however, that if the war was going to be won, risks had to be taken. The division and brigade were risking that the Soviets would not attack at Langen again. If they did, division was willing to risk the chance of a failure there, hoping that a breakthrough at the Saale would cancel the Soviet threat to the flank. It was the job of division and corps commanders to weigh such risks and make decisions. It was the job of the staff and the commanders of 1st of the 78th to accept those risks and carry out orders.

There was not much fanfare over the Team's departure. The major gave Bannon his instructions on when he was to link up with the 1st of the 4th, where, and route of march. Bannon coordinated with the battalion S-4 for rearming and refuelling before the Team departed that evening. He talked to the Team Bravo commander and told him where the 1st Tank Platoon was to go when it was released back to the Team. Then, with no further business in Langen and much to tend to, he returned to the Team.

News of their return to 1st of the 4th was universally hailed by the Team with the exception of Sergeant Polgar. He said it really didn't matter to him where his platoon went so long as it stayed with Team Yankee. When Bannon thanked him for his vote of confidence he replied that confidence had nothing to do with it. The chow in Team Yankee had always been good, and good food meant he had fewer complaints to listen to from his men.

Second Lieutenant Murray Weiss, the leader of 1st Platoon, was particularly happy to be coming back to the Team. He had the honour of being the company's only Jew, a fact that left him open to a great deal of ethnic humour. Like Bob Uleski, he had almost infinite capacity to absorb incoming jokes and return them, as he had learned to do from an early age. Weiss's decision to make the military his career was a shock to his family. The U.S. Army was not normally something that college-educated Jewish boys were taught to aspire to. But Murray had deep convictions. The Israeli tankers who had fought in the Sinai and on the Golan had been his childhood heroes. While his friends aspired to be doctors or lawyers, he dreamed of being a tanker like Gen. Mordecai Tal. Weiss's performance before and during the war showed he was well on his way.

The Team had much to do. It could not leave before dark. To do so would telegraph to the Soviets the weakness of the Langen Gap. They would find out soon enough that the tanks were gone and there were only two weak companies there. But the Team did not have to help them by flaunting the move in broad daylight. Even with the move several hours off, the leadership and men were busy. Bannon gave Uleski his instructions on organisation, rearming, refuelling and other such details. He also gave him all the information on when the Team was to move, its route, and final destination. Bannon would be taking the first sergeant's track and going to the headquarters of the 1st of 4th to get additional information and, he hoped, an operations order. If he wasn't back in time, the XO was to start the move without him. They were, no doubt, going to be attacking again. The sooner he found out the how and where, the more time he had to plan and get the Team ready.

The trip to the 1st of the 4th's headquarters took him back into the main valley that the Team had advanced into the previous day and through the town of Korberg. The valley had changed overnight. Its emptiness and lack of activity were replaced with the hustle of the division's combat service support elements. Convoys of trucks carrying fuel, munitions, and other supplies forward were passed by empty trucks coming back. There were the grim reminders of the cost of progress. A field hospital was set up outside Korberg, receiving new material in a never-ending flow. Bannon had no doubt that some of the people there were his. Commanders kept doctors busy. He also knew that soon he would be contributing to the flow again.

As he moved farther north he saw more than enough evidence that 1st of the 4th had had no easy time after they had passed through 1st of the 78th. M-1s, PCs, Soviet tanks and smashed trucks attested to the severity of their fight. Maintenance recovery teams were busy retrieving those tanks that could be repaired. As he passed a maintenance collection point he recognised several of the mechanics from 1st of the 4th. They were trying to piece together recovered tracks in an effort to get tanks and PCs ready for the next attack. Were it not for the efforts of these people, many of the units still in the fight, including Team Yakee, would have ceased to exist a long time.

Bannon found both Lieutenant Colonel Hill, the battalion commander, and Major Shell at the battalion TOC. Along with the battalion intelligence officer, Capt. Ken Damato, they were discussing the upcoming operation in front of the intelligence map. Bannon stood in the background for a moment and listened. Apparently, they had already developed the plan and were merely getting an update on enemy units recently reported entering the area of operations and their activities. Damato was pointing out several Soviet battalion-sized units northeast of the Saale that had been located and were being tracked. Across the top of the intelligence map in the area north of the river someone had put in large red letters 'HERE BE RUSSIANS'.

Major Shell saw Bannon first, 'Well, here's the hero himself now. Glad to see the infantry finally let you go.'

Bannon went up to the map where greetings were exchanged. The three officers were haggard and tired. Without any further ado, Colonel Hill asked how much he knew of the upcoming operation. Bannon informed him that other than the fact that he had been told where and when to report, nothing. The colonel told Major Shell and Damato to go over the operation with him. When they were finished, Bannon was then to report to him. The colonel was going to wash up in the meantime.

The operation that Major Shell laid out before Bannon was nothing more than a continuation of the attack towards the Saale. There were a few new twists, but basically it was the same. At that time 2nd of the 94th Mech Infantry was attacking through the Soviets' main defensive belt, which was not nearly as impressive as the Soviet defensive doctrine called for but was enough to grind up the 2nd of the 94th. Progress was slow and the commander and brigade did not believe that battalion would make it to the Saale.

That's where the 1st of the 4th came in. Since being bypassed by the 2nd of the 94th early that morning, 1st of the 4th had been preparing for a river-crossing operation. All available assets were being concentrated in the battalion for this final push. If 2nd of the 94th did not make it to the Saale by nightfall, the plan called for the 1st of the 4th to pass through the 2nd of the 94th and continue the attack. Once at the Saale, 1st of the 4th would make an assault crossing and establish a bridgehead. As soon as the engineers had a bridge in place, the lead elements of the 25th Armored Division, now in reserve, would pass through the battalion and continue the drive on Berlin. The 1st of the 4th would then assume the role of holding the flanks.

The attack of the 1st of the 4th was not the only effort that would be going on that night. The 2nd Brigade would also be attempting to make an assault crossing of the Saale farther to the west. Their mission was identical to 1st of the 4th's; establish a bridgehead, allow the 25th Armored to pass, then protect the flank. It was hoped that both efforts would succeed. The 25th Armored, however, was hedging its bets. They had one brigade following each of the river-crossing efforts. The first one across would become the main effort.

Ken Damato went over the current enemy situation. Until that morning, the Soviets had been trying to stop the division's drive through counterattacks, head-on and in the flanks. The 1st of the 4th had fought the better part of a tank regiment the previous night after a meeting engagement in the valley. While the Soviet tank regiment had been stopped, so had the 1st of the 4th. That is why the 2nd of the 94th was passed through. That battalion had been fighting its way through a series of platoon and company-sized strong points since midnight. Progress had been steady but slow and costly. Reconnaissance of the area immediately south and north of the river showed little indication that the Soviet defence had any depth. The new enemy units identified moving into the area were believed to be fragments of shattered units being thrown in as a last resort. Therefore, the prevailing belief was that, once across the Saale, a clean breakout could be made and there would be little to stop a push to Berlin itself.

Major Shell then got down to the details. The plan was simple. Once 2nd of the 94th had cleared the last of the Soviet positions or could no longer continue, 1st of the 4th would pass through and charge for the river. There would be no finesse, no grandiose schemes of manoeuvre, just a mad dash for the river at the best possible speed. Once at the river, the battalion was not to stop but was to vault across and establish the bridgehead. The idea was to make it to the river and across before the Soviets could do anything about it.

The problem with such a simple plan was that once the battalion started rolling, the Soviets would be able to figure out where it was going and what it intended to do. While they could not keep the Soviets from figuring out its plan, they could confuse and deceive them as to where the main effort was going. The plan called for a reinforced company team to create a diversion and deceive the Soviets as to where the main effort was going to be. Major Shell stopped for a moment, looked at Bannon, and with a blank expression told him that was where Team Yankee came in.

Team Yankee, with three tank platoons, the Mech Platoon and the battalion Scout Platoon attached, would conduct a supporting attack on the battalion's right. It would be the Team's task to give the appearance that Team Yankee was the battalion's main effort by driving for a highway bridge on the Saale. While the Soviets would drop the span before the Team got there, the area near the bridge offered several excellent crossing points. A threat to that area could not be ignored. It was hoped that Team Yankee's attack would draw the Soviets' attention and reserves while the true main effort went on farther to the west. With the exception of the point on the map where Bannon was to orient the Team's effort and instructions to make as much noise as possible, he had a free hand as to how he could go about accomplishing the mission.

Shell stopped for a moment while Bannon looked at the map and considered the task. Bannon asked where they anticipated passing through the 2nd of the 94th. The major showed him a point about twenty kilometres south of the Saale. Bannon asked about fire support and close air support. The major pointed to several target areas that would be hit near the bridge by the Air Force at first light in order to support the deception plan. He also told him that the Team would be supported by the better part of an artillery battalion until the battalion began to cross the river. At that time, Team Yankee would lose most of its support and would have to fend for itself.

Bannon looked at the major, then the map, then back to the major. 'You brought me all the way here to give me this nightmare?'

'Hey, Sean, what are friends for? We're giving you a chance to excel.'

Bannon's reserve of humour was exhausted; he found nothing funny about what the Team was being asked to do.

Again, Team Yankee was going to be on its own, rolling into the unknown. He began to believe that the Light Brigade during the Crimean War had it easy. They only had to do the impossible once. Team Yankee had to do it over and over again. 'If you want to give me something, give me four tanks, a dozen trained infantry replacments, fuel, ammunition, and a four-day rest in the rear. Do you know what kind of shape the Team is in?'

Major Shell sensed the change in mood and became deadly serious, 'Sean, you saw, I'm sure, the burned-out tracks along the battalion's route of advance. We're all in bad shape, and we aren't going to get any stronger. Our war reserves in Europe have been used up and there are no more. It will be another month before the Guard and Reserve units get over here. If we wait for them, the war will be over. We either do it now with what we have or we lose. It's that simple.'

Bannon bent his head down for a moment, looked at his boots, and considered what Major Shell had said before answering, 'I know, I know. Major Jordan went over the same thing with me before I came here. It's just that since the war broke out, the Team has been getting the smelly end of the stick every time we turn around. Everyone, including me, is getting tired of putting his nuts out on the chopping block whenever a new mission comes up. So far we have been lucky, damned lucky. That luck isn't going to last, though. One of these times the Russians are going to come down fast and cut us up. Why can't someone else get a chance to excel?'

'Sean, whether or not you know it, your Team has one hell of a reputation. When the Old Man was given this mission by brigade, Colonel Brunn specifically designated Team Yankee as the force to conduct the supporting attack. Everyone agreed that your Team was the one that could pull it off if anyone could. You're it. You can moan and groan all you want, but in the end, you've got the mission.'

The rest of the meeting was conducted in a curt, businesslike manner. Shell provided additional details, answered Bannon's questions, and asked if there were anything he needed. Bannon pointed out that in the future he could save the saddle soap and come up with easier missions. When they were finished in the

TOC, Bannon went over to the battalion commander and talked with him for a few minutes about the condition of the Team and the mission. There was no point going over arguments for letting someone else take the job. The decision was made, and he wasn't going to get it changed at this late date. All Bannon could do now was give the commander a 'yes, sir, yes, sir, three bags full' and drive on. There was much to be done and not much time.

Before he returned to the Team, Bannon stopped by the assembly area where the Team would pull in before attacking. He found the Scout Platoon already in position. The platoon leader Sergeant First Class Flores, and Bannon discussed the mission and his role. He assigned Flores the task of selecting positions for the rest of the Team in the assembly area and instructed him to provide guides when it arrived. With that taken care of, he started back for Langen and Team Yankee.

The Team never made it to the assembly area. The 2nd of the 94th, in one last push, succeeded in smashing through the Soviet's last defensive belt and destroyed a half-hearted counterattack by an understrength Soviet tank battalion. Orders came down over the Team net to move immediately to the passage point where they were met by the Scout Platoon and ground guides from the 2nd of the 94th. These guides directed Weiss's platoon to a cleared lane through a Soviet minefield that had been breached earlier. Team Yankee was now in the attack and headed for the Saale.

Once clear of the minefield, the 1st Platoon deployed into a wedge and began to pick up speed. From the cupola of his tank, Weiss surveyed the terrain to his front with the aid of his night vision goggles. There was no sign of the enemy. He turned to his left and watched the Scout Platoon, now clear of the minefield, begin to deploy to his right. Like his platoon, it also was forming a wedge. The Mech Platoon would be coming through the minefield now. Before turning to his front, he caught sight of the 66 tank as it pulled into a position between his platoon and the scouts.

Satisfied that all was in order, Murray Weiss leaned back in the cupola and allowed himself to relax for a moment. The entire Team, after spending a relatively peaceful afternoon near Langen, had been on the run ever since the Team commander returned with its new mission. Precombat checks, preparation for the night move, boresighting the tanks, receiving the Team order, and issuing the platoon order had taken up the balance of the afternoon. Immediately after darkness had fallen, the Team moved out for its forward assembly area where it was to wait for the order to pass through the 2nd of the 94th.

Weiss was pleased with the Team's mission and the orders Bannon had issued. The Team was divided into two parts. The XO, with the 2nd and 3rd Platoons, would move along a separate route about one kilometre west of the rest of the Team. Captain Bannon, with the 1st and Scout Platoons followed by the Mech, was to advance towards a bridge on the Saale. The order to bypass all resistance and go hell for leather towards the bridge regardless of the cost pleased both Weiss and Garger. The two lieutenants were tired of being held in check and having to wait for someone else to get their shit together. Although the Team commander tried to dampen their enthusiasm, the lieutenants were thrilled that they finally were going to have a chance to do some no-holds-barred tanking.

The crack of a tank cannon and the blurted contact report from 3rd Platoon jarred Weiss back to the present. The element with the XO had made contact. The enemy was out there. Weiss straightened up in the cupola and began to scan the horizon for them.

No one saw where it had come from. One minute there was nothing. The next minute, there it was. It was as if the BTR-60 had popped up out of the ground less than two hundred metres in front of the platoon. Without breaking pace and with one round, Blackfoot's 32 tank destroyed the BTR. Garger automatically ordered the platoon to refuse its left by going to a left echelon formation. This was done without confusion and with hardly a break in the platoon's stride. After a quick contact report to the XO, Garger turned back to his left and peered into the darkness through his night vision goggles.

There was no further movement for the moment. The lone BTR, now burning, was well to the rear of the platoon as they continued to the Saale.

The 2nd Platoon, to the right, fired next. Garger whipped around to see what they were firing at. Following the tracers from the 2nd Platoon's rounds he saw several forms moving away from the advancing Team. A brilliant flash and shower of sparks followed by an eruption of flames lit up the night. One Soviet tank had been hit and destroyed. A second Russian tank, clearly illuminated by the flames from the hit tank, could be seen fleeing north. It did not make it, however. Another tank in 2nd Platoon fired and dispatched it.

'TANK – TWELVE O'CLOCK – MOVING NORTH!' At first, Garger thought that his gunner was looking at the same tank that he was looking at. Then he realised that the gun tube was still pointed to the left. He dropped down to his sight and saw the tank his gunner had found. For a moment he hesitated. B company, 1st of the 4th, was to their left. He did not want to engage a friendly tank. Garger studied the target in his thermal sight for a moment. He could make out the turret and the tracks. It was definitely moving north. But did it belong to B company or was it Russian? Then he noticed that the rear of the tank was dark. The exhaust from an M-1 tank is vented out the rear, creating a tremendous heat signature. If the tank was an M-1, its rear would have been bright green. The tank was Russian. Without further delay, Garger issued his fire command and dispatched another Soviet tank.

★The young engineer lieutenant was not pleased with his orders nor with having a KGB captain at his side overseeing him. The KGB captain and his people were supposed to be at the bridge to gather up stragglers and control movement. The young lieutenant was smart enough, however, to realise that the squat, stone-faced captain also had the task of ensuring that the people defending the bridge and preparing its destruction followed orders. Why else did the captain follow his every move and question every order the engineer gave?

The 15th Guards Tank Division was in the process of

withdrawing across the Saale. The withdrawal was in great haste and confusion. There seemed to be no rhyme or reason to the order in which units came across. A tank unit was followed by a maintenance detachment, which in turn was followed by an artillery unit with a field hospital mixed in. To add to the confusion, the KGB would halt units at random and demand to see written orders giving them permission to withdraw to the north side of the river. Most of the units did not have these, having received orders over the radio. The KGB knew this but continued to stop units.

The thing that bothered the engineer lieutenant the most was the manner in which the KGB dealt with stragglers. When individuals, officer and enlisted, were found to be crossing without their unit, they were taken over to the side of the road and questioned. At first, the KGB captain was called in to consider each case. After awhile, however, he tired of this and allowed a young and enthusiastic KGB lieutenant to deal with the enlisted stragglers. The captain only wanted to be called in to deal with the officers.

Justice, KGB style, was quick. The engineer, at the insistence of the KGB captain, watched each series of executions. Once a straggler was determined to be a deserter, he was put into a small wooden shed at the south end of the bridge. When the shed was full, the convicted deserters were lined up next to the road, in full view of the troops moving across the bridge. The KGB lieutenant would read a statement outlining the crimes committed against the State and Party before giving the order to fire. The first time he watched, the engineer lieutenant became sick. As he bent over to throw up, the KGB captain slapped him on the back and told him he had nothing to worry about, as long as he carried out his orders. The captain's statement was a promise, not a threat. The engineer lieutenant knew that if he blew the bridge without first receiving permission, the next time the KGB captain slapped his back, there would be a knife in his hand.

The sudden flurry of engagements stopped as rapidly as they had begun. The Team was halfway to the river and making good time. The Soviets encountered by the XO's element had been withdrawing and apparently were not interested in offering resistance. All was going well so far. Things had a nasty habit, however, of changing very rapidly. Six tanks and a couple of well-placed antitank guided missile launchers could raise hell with the Team. Bannon expected to make contact with just such delaying forces momentarily.

The anticipation of such an event was becoming unbearable. An outright shoot-out with the Russians in the open was preferable to this rolling around in the dark waiting to be hit. His mind kept filling with worst case what ifs as the Team came to each point he had marked on his map where the Soviets could take up good delay positions. As the Team approached each point, Bannon could feel his heartbeat quicken as his body prepared for action. But nothing happened. The Team's lead elements would bypass the point and continue rolling north. Just as he managed to calm down, the next critical point would be reached, and he would again tense up in anticipation. They had to either make it to the river soon or make contact with the Russians. It really didn't matter to him. Anything was better than dealing with the stress of the unknown.

Just ahead of the element he was leading was a small town. Bannon would have preferred to bypass it but decided to send the scouts through it. Part of the Team's mission was to be noticed and running through the town was a good way to get noticed. The 1st Platoon and the Mech were ordered to go around the town to the west and the scouts to make a high-speed dash through the centre. If they ran into light resistance, they were to bull through. If the Soviets were present in strength, they were to back out and follow the rest of the Team.

As the 1st Platoon veered off to the left, the scouts formed on the road and raced in at a dead run. The lead scout track had no sooner entered the town when the report of its machine guns came echoing out. Flores sent a quick contact report. He had run into a Soviet recon unit in the town square and was taking it under fire as they rolled through. Bannon reminded him that he was not to become decisively engaged and was to get out of there as soon as possible to rejoin the Team. With the din of battle clearly audible over the radio as he responded,

Flores gave Bannon a curt 'ROGER – OUT' and continued to fight his battle and carry out his orders.

Though concerned that the scouts might not be able to extract themselves, Bannon was pleased, nonetheless, that they had run into the Soviet recon element. No doubt the Soviets would get a report back about the Team's presence, and part of the Team's mission would be accomplished thanks to the Russians themselves.

★ The firing just south of the river startled both the engineer lieutenant and the KGB captain. They looked in the direction of firing, then at each other. For the first time that night, the lieutenant noted a look of concern and uncertainty on the captain's face. They both went to find the motorised rifle company commander who was charged with defending the bridge. They had to find out what was going on.

The firing had also been heard by the soldiers attempting to cross the bridge. Not wanting to be caught on the wrong side when it was dropped by the engineers, they began to push forward. The impatience of the drivers gave way to anger when they felt the people in front were not moving quickly enough. Truck drivers began to blow their horns and bump the vehicles to their front in an effort to speed up the crossing. This did nothing but add to the confusion and push the mass of troops and drivers near the edge of panic.

The Team was now within a few kilometres of the bridge. Bannon decided it was time to start making a lot of noise in an effort to give the appearance that they were going to attempt a crossing. He ordered the Team FIST to fire prearranged artillery concentrations on both the north and south side of the bridge. Since the bridge was gone or soon would be, the artillery fire wouldn't hurt anything. It would, however, appear to the Russians that they were firing a preparatory fire for an assault crossing. The longer and more convincing the deception, the easier it would be for the rest of the battalion.

★ With the first impact of artillery, the KGB captain dropped all pretence of being calm and unconcerned. The idea of facing American combat troops terrified him. He and his men knew what would happen to them if the Americans captured them. Yet he knew they could not leave the bridge without orders. To do so would be considered desertion. After dealing with deserters all night, he knew what would be waiting if he left now. The only hope was to get permission to leave.

Both the engineer lieutenant and the KGB captain tried to make it over to the southern side of the bridge. They were, however, fighting the tide, as everyone on the south side was trying to go north. Vehicular traffic was stopped. Trucks had been hit on both sides of the river, blocking the exit on the north side and the entrance on the south. This jam was compounded by drivers who abandoned their trucks and began to flee on foot.

As they pushed their way against the flow of fleeing troops, both noticed that their men had joined the rout. At first, the lieutenant tried to stop his men and order them back. Few paid any attention as they continued to push their way ahead. The KGB captain tried a different approach. He pulled out his pistol and pointed it at his men. When one of them kept going, he fired several times, dropping the KGB private and two other soldiers who happened to get in the line of fire. This, however, did nothing to stem the tide. The other KGB men simply gave the captain a wide berth as they continued north.

Once on the south side of the river, the lieutenant and the captain found the company commander. The commander was yelling into a radio mike but didn't seem to be getting an answer. When he saw them, he turned to the engineer and told him that the Americans were only a few kilometres away and would be there any minute. The bridge had to be dropped now. The KGB captain asked if they had received orders to do so. The commander replied that he couldn't receive orders because his radio was being jammed. The KGB captain responded that they couldn't drop the bridge until they received permission.

The commander, frustrated now, repeated that the radio was being jammed and that he could not contact anyone to get permission. He reiterated that the bridge had to be dropped now or they would lose it. The engineer joined in, saying that they had to make an immediate decision. The bridge had to go. Both he and the commander stared at the KGB captain. The KGB captain in turn looked at each of them. It was against everything he had been taught. He had been trained from childhood to obey orders, to avoid taking the initiative, to conform. Now, he had to decide on his own. There was no superior to decide for him. There was no one who could share the blame if something went wrong. He had to decide for himself, and he couldn't do it.

Just as the engineer and the commander began to yell at the KGB captain again, demanding permission to drop the bridge, and American 155mm artillery shell ended their debate.

As 11 crested a small rise, Weiss looked down and saw the Saale. In the clear night air, the light from the half-moon reflected from its smooth surface. They had made it. In a few more minutes, their mission would be accomplished.

He scanned the length of the river. All appeared to be calm until he saw the artillery impacts. The rounds were falling among a cluster of vehicles with their headlights on at the bridge they had been heading for. There were still Soviets on the south side of the river. A closer inspection revealed that the vehicles were mostly trucks with only a few personnel carriers mixed in. There seemed to be a great traffic jam at the entrance to the bridge and a great deal of panic. This pleased him. Nothing like an easy kill to finish the attack.

'THE BRIDGE, IT'S STILL UP L. T.!'

Weiss dropped down to his sight extension and looked to see what his gunner was yelling about. It was still there! As 11 rolled down to the river, Weiss traversed the turret, studying the entire length of the bridge. It had not been dropped yet. It suddenly occurred to him that they had a chance to seize the bridge intact.

The report from 1st Platoon was too good to be true. The Team had not only caught some Russians on the wrong side of the river, but the bridge was still up. Suddenly Bannon had to make a snap decision. Did they try for the bridge and risk having it blown up in their face or with some of the Team on it? Or did he simply stop on the south bank and let the Russians blow it up? Whatever he decided, it had to be now. The 1st Platoon was well on its way and would, in a few minutes, decide for him if he didn't.

The Team had been ordered to divert the Soviets' attention from the battalion's main effort. Capturing a bridge intact and establishing a bridgehead here would certainly do that. Without calling battalion, he ordered 1st Platoon to go for the bridge. The scouts, coming up fast after clearing the town, were ordered to follow 1st Platoon across. The Mech Platoon was ordered to drop one squad on the south side to clear any charges on the bridge and send the rest of the Platoon across. Bannon ordered Uleski to get up to the bridge as soon as possible and send the 2nd Platoon across to join Bannon and take charge of the south side of the bridge with the 3rd Platoon and the Mech squad there. Everyone was ordered to hold their fire until they were on top of the Russians.

The 1st Platoon tanks were at point-blank range when Weiss gave the order to fire. The tanks fell in behind 11 and followed it as they all blazed away with machine guns at the fleeing Russians. All semblance of order disappeared as 11 pushed onto the bridge. Going was slow on the bridge as trucks that could not be bypassed were pushed out of the way. Fires sprang up as fuel tanks were ignited by tracers. Russians fled into the night or simply tried to surrender to the charging tanks.

The tanks were not interested in prisoners right then. Neither was the Mech Platoon. As soon as Sergeant Polgar's track reached the south side of the bridge, he stopped and dismounted. The next track in line did likewise, dropping its ramp and disgorging its infantry squad. As the troops came piling out, Polgar yelled to the squad leader to cut all wires to the demolitions. The troops, never having done this, began to rip away at any wire they found. In the rush of the moment, one infantry man tried to cut an electric power line with his bayonet. He nearly electrocuted himself. Despite this, the fire from die-hard Russians, and working in the dark, the infantry managed to keep the bridge from being blown.

Once Uleski had closed up on the south side, the Team went about the task of securing the bridge, dealing with any resistance, and rounding up the Russians who wanted to surrender. Bannon sent the Scout Platoon out as far as he dared to establish a combat outpost line. The 1st Platoon was deployed to the left of the main road in a quarter arc to the river. The 2nd Platoon was deployed to the right, also in an arc from the road to the river. One Mech squad stayed at the bridge's north entrance, one at the south, and the third was deployed forward on the road to set up a road block. Uleski deployed the 3rd Platoon on the south side of the river in a shallow semicircle.

When Bannon reported the seizure of the bridge to battalion, neither the commander nor the S-3 would believe him. They kept asking him to make sure that he was not confusing the Saale River bridge with a small bridge across a stream farther to the south. When he finally convinced them that the Team had in fact seized the main highway bridge, they gave him a wait-out while they conferred on what to do. After a couple of minutes, the battalion commander came on the net and ordered two companies to reinforce Team Yankee at the bridge. The S-3 would continue to drive to the river and conduct the crossing farther to the west as planned. The colonel shifted the main effort to the bridge to prepare for the passage of the 25th Armored Division.

As dawn began to break, Team Yankee found itself momentarily alone and out on a limb again. But there was no sign of fear or apprehension. The men went about preparing for an enemy attack that they expected but would never receive. Unknown to them far beyond the outpost line established by the scouts, men were making decisions and issuing orders that would start the final and potentially most deadly phase of the war.

Chapter Fourteen

THE DAY AFTER

When the battalion commander arrived, he began to expand the bridgehead. Team Yankee elements that were still south of the river were sent north and ordered to move forward and establish a defensive position on high ground four kilometres north east of the bridge. B company was sent to establish a position four kilometres north of the bridge. The scouts were sent farther but had the same mission. Team Charlie was kept south of the river to protect the bridgehead from attack there and to mop up Soviet stragglers still running around.

The only action of the day occurred when a company of Soviet tanks came down the road from the north. The scouts let them pass, reporting their location and allowing B company to prepare for them. It was obvious that the Soviets either didn't know the bridge had fallen or thought that the battalion's positions were farther south. Whatever the reason, B company made short work of them.

By 0700 hours, the lead element of the 25th Armored Division was crossing the river. From their positions, the men in Team Yankee could watch the endless line of vehicles and troops stream north. Once the 25th had passed through B company, B company and Team Yankee were ordered to move to new positions farther east, expanding the bridgehead. Team Charlie did likewise on the south side of the river. By noon the entire battalion, minus Team Charlie, was across the river, reconsolidated and again ordered to move farther to the east.

It was during this last move that word came down from battalion for all the commanders to gather at the battalion CP. When Bannon arrived, he was greeted with a stone-cold silence by the officers who were already there. They were standing around the rear of the command track listening into a conversation the colonel was having on the radio. Bannon stopped and thought to himself, 'Great, some dumb son of a bitch has come up with another nightmare of an operation.'

Coming up closer, he could only catch bits and pieces of the conversation. When the colonel finished, he put down the mike, stood there a moment. Turning to the S-3, he merely said, 'Well, I guess we're fighting a new war now.'

Bannon turned to Frank Wilson, the commander of Team Charlie, 'New war? What's the Old Man talking about? Did someone pop a nuke?'

Frank looked at Bannon, closed his eyes, and nodded his head in the affirmative. They had crossed the nuclear threshold.

Colonel Hall came out of the track followed by Major Shell and stopped in the middle of the officers gathered. 'As some of you heard, the Soviets have initiated nuclear warfare. This morning they launched an attack with a single weapon against a British city, destroying it and causing severe damage to the surrounding area. The United States and Great Britain together retaliated by striking a Soviet city with several weapons. Although there have been no further exchanges, we are to assume that the Soviets will continue to use nuclear weapons, including tactical devices.'

He paused for a moment to let this news sink in before he continued, 'As a result, the battalion will increase the distance between the company positions. Team Yankee will be pulled out of the line and held back as a reserve. The S-3 will provide you with details. I expect you to take all measures necessary to protect your force without losing sight of our mission.'

Major Shell pulled out his map board and pointed out where each company and team was to go. Team Yankee was to pull back into reserve positions. To reduce their vulnerability and present a less lucrative target, the platoons were spread out over a wide area. After some additional instructions, the commanders and staff dispersed and went about adjusting their units and assets to deal with the new threat.

News of the use of nuclear weapons put a pall on all activities and conversations. Up to now, the war had been manageable on a personal level. The Team had been in some very tight spots but had come out in relatively good shape. The men had met the Russians face-to-face and found that they could be defeated. They had confidence in the Team's weapons, its leaders, and the Team itself. They had been sure that they would win.

The initiation of nuclear war, however, was different. Not only was there nothing that the Team could do to stop it, a nuclear war threatened the United States. Their families and friends four thousand miles away were now in as much danger as they were.

It was this fear of the unknown and the feeling of hopeless despair that became Bannon's greatest challenge. As soon as the Team was in its new positions, he went to each of the platoons and gathered the men around, going over what had happened and what it meant. He explained the possible results and what they had to do. For the most part, however, he tried hard to be upbeat in his discussions and point out that they were not entirely helpless. The Team still had a job to do and could still influence the outcome of the war.

By evening he didn't know whether or not his efforts had had any effect. Everyone was in a quiet, reflective mood, the men talking to each other only when necessary. For the most part, each man passed the night alone with his own thoughts and fears.

Bannon too was overcome with a feeling of despair and fear. As a soldier, it was his job to know about the effects of nuclear weapons. He knew national policy and the size of the nuclear arsenals that each side had. For the first time in many days his thoughts kept turning to his family. Nightmare images crept into his mind and destroyed his ability to reason and think. The stress of the last few days, exhaustion, and now fears brought on by the thought of an all-out nuclear war were too much for him to handle. With no one to talk to or share his feelings with, he sought escape through sleep. Like a child faced with a situation beyond his control, he withdrew from the horrors of the real world and drifted into a fitful sleep.

Stand-to the following morning reminded Bannon of the first day. It was as if the Team had gone full circle and was starting anew. In a sense, this was true. Only the distant rumble of an occasional artillery round broke the stillness of the morning. As he greeted the men during his rounds, they responded in a perfunctory manner. Uncertainty and dread underlined everything they did. The lieutenants looked to Bannon, seeking guidance or inspiration or something. They found nothing. He could see this and their disappointment when he could not give them what they needed. Even a hot breakfast, the first cooked meal served in days, did little to raise morale. Something had to be done or he feared they would all go crazy.

After the morning meal was over, Bannon called the platoon leaders in for a meeting. He decided that it would be no use trying to play the cheerleader. Instead, he took the business as usual approach. When the leaders were assembled, he went down a list of protective measures that should have already been put into effect. Such things as every man, including the tank crews, digging foxholes, turning off all but one radio in every platoon, covering all optics when not in use, camouflaging everything, and more. In addition, he warned that the platoons needed to tend to their routine maintenance and personal hygiene.

The platoon leaders at first looked at him with puzzled stares. Since the start of the war they had become loose in some of the areas he wanted to tighten up. He simply returned their stares and told them that each platoon was to inform him when they thought they were ready for inspection. At the conclusion of the meeting he turned them over to the XO and went to battalion to see if there was any news on the progress of the 25th Armored or intelligence updates.

The news at battalion was good. First, there had been no further use of nuclear weapons since the first exchange. It appeared that the Soviets had decided to try to intimidate the Europeans by taking out one of their cities with a nuclear device. Birmingham in England had been chosen for this exercise in terror. The prompt retaliation by both Britain and the U.S. against the city of Minsk was enough to demonstrate the resolve and unity of NATO. The cherished Soviet notion that the U.S. would not risk a nuclear attack on herself to save Europe had been disproved. Just as they had understood the

300

purpose of the Soviet attack, the Soviets understood the meaning of NATO's: NATO would trade blow for blow.

To the north, the 25th Armored Division was making good progress. The Soviets were not able to stop the drive. Furthermore, there were signs that the Warsaw Pact was beginning to break up. Ken Damato gave Bannon a copy of the division's intelligence summary to read. It discussed the breakout of armed insurrection, no doubt aided by U.S. Army Special Forces A teams, in Poland and East Germany. Polish units were no longer attacking. Several Soviet units in Northern Germany had surrendered en masse. Others were on the verge of doing so. Deep strikes by the Air Force were hampering the flow of supplies and the movement of troops. In short, the war was going well for NATO.

Also mentioned in the intel summary was an analysis of the effects of the strike against Minsk. While the loss of Birmingham was a major disaster, it would not interfere with the NATO war effort. The destruction of Minsk, however, was hampering the Soviets by severing a major communications centre. The cold, analytical view of the nuclear exchange was haunting but, at the same time, welcome.

Buoyed by the news at battalion, Bannon went about the day's activities with renewed energy. Maybe things were not as bad as they seemed. As he went from platoon to platoon, he gathered the men around and passed on what news and information he had from the outside world. For the most part, the effect on the Team was about the same as it had been on him. In addition, the return to some type of routine served to keep the men busy and oriented on the job at hand.

In the early evening the battalion was ordered to move farther to the east and establish contact with Soviet forces. A battalion order was prepared and issued to the team commanders at 2100 hours. Team Yankee was to remain in reserve, following the rest of the battalion as it moved forward. Ken Damato expected to make contact about ten to fifteen kilometres to the east of their current front line trace. Time for the movement was 0300 hours.

The news of the new mission was welcomed by just about everyone in the Team. The rest had been good and the reorganisation and maintenance needed. But everyone wanted to get on with it. They knew the sooner they got moving, the sooner the issue would be decided. The Team was as Americans have always been, anxious to avoid a war but when forced to fight, anxious to get on with it and finish it rapidly.

Without an artillery preparation, the lead elements of the battalion moved out. The steady advance was hindered only by Soviet recon units that fired and fled. Dawn of the thirteenth day of war found the battalion still moving to the east. After an advance of fifteen kilometres they were ordered to halt. While they had not made contact with the Soviets' main forces yet, division did not want to go too far. The main effort was still aimed for Berlin. There were few forces available to protect the flanks of that drive and there was no need to spread them too thin.

The battalion was again dispersed over as wide an area as possible so as to reduce its vulnerability to a nuclear attack. Team Yankee stayed in reserve. Once the Team was in its position, it settled in and prepared for another day. Foxholes were dug, camouflage placed, fighting and hide positions improved, platoon fire plans prepared and numerous other tasks accomplished. By noon, they were ready and went to half-manning. When Bannon was satisfied that all was in order, he lay down in the first sergeant's PC and went to sleep.

At 1700 hours, First Sergeant Harrert woke him to tell him that he was wanted at the battalion CP immediately. As Bannon stumbled around, still half-asleep, he asked if the first sergeant knew what was up. The first sergeant replied negative. The S-3 wouldn't tell him. The only message was to get up to the CP ASAP.

His feeling of dread dispersed as soon as he walked into the farmhouse where the CP was located. Everyone was going around the room shaking each other's hands as if it was an alumni reunion. Bannon went up to Frank Wilson and asked what was going on.

'Haven't you been told? The Soviets have declared a cease-fire effective midnight tonight. They're throwing in the towel. It's over.'

He stood there for a moment. Just like that, the war was over. It was too good to be true. Something had to be wrong. 'You mean they are surrendering? Now? Without our even touching the Soviet Union?'

'Something like that. We don't have all the details yet but from what we heard, the Soviet leadership has changed and they want an immediate end to the war.'

The colonel entered the room followed by the S-3 and the battalion XO. The XO called the meeting to order. Colonel Hill went over the information he had and what he thought. He tried hard to be cautious and keep from becoming carried away by commenting that the cease-fire wasn't in effect yet and that things could change rapidly. But he, like the commanders and staff assembled, was optimistic and overjoyed with the prospect of peace.

He was followed by Ken Damato, the S-2 who gave a brief summary on the current enemy situation and pointed out some of the dangers they had to guard against once the cease-fire was in effect. The biggest one was from sabotage and espionage from line crossers and local populace. They were, he reminded them, still in Communist East Germany.

Major Shell followed and explained the rules of engagement that were to be placed into effect once the cease-fire became official. Warsaw Pact forces were not to come any closer to NATO positions than 1000 metres. If they continued to advance, they were to be engaged. All NATO soldiers had the right to protect themselves and return fire if fired upon. Effective at midnight, NATO forces were not to move any farther than the front line trace they had achieved as of that time. The NATO commander had ordered that all operations currently in progress were to continue until then. Communications with any Warsaw Pact forces were forbidden unless permission was obtained. The S-3 finished by saying that copies of the rules of engagement for distribution down to platoon level would be ready soon.

The colonel finished the meeting by cautioning everyone

against becoming too optimistic and especially against letting down their guard. They were still at war and the cease-fire could fail at any moment.

The sun was beginning to settle in the west as Bannon rolled back to the Team's area. At his back the sky was alive with brilliant reds and purples. The beauty of the lush green German landscape, unfolding before him, coupled with the spectacle of the setting sun and the quiet early night air lifted Bannon's spirit to a height that he had not experienced in months. The driver knew the way back, leaving him free to reflect on the joy of the moment. It was over. His worst nightmare was over and he had survived. There would be a tomorrow and he would see it. With nothing more weighty on his mind than such thoughts, he relaxed and enjoyed the beauty of the countryside he had not seen before.

The leadership of Team Yankee was waiting at the Team CP when he came rolling in. They had become accustomed to his returning from battalion with grim news or word of a new mission. They had become practised at remaining calm while their commander explained how the Team was about to risk the lives of its men to execute its new orders. This time, like all the times before, they expected no less.

The were taken aback, therefore, when Bannon approached with a smile on his face. Bob Uleski, sensing that something was afoot, turned to the first sergeant. 'Well, Sergeant, either it's good news or the pressure had gotten to him and the Old Man has finally slipped the track.'

As hard as he tried, Bannon couldn't downplay his joy as the colonel had. After all they had been through, he couldn't hold back, 'Men, unless we receive information to the contrary, effective midnight tonight, a cease-fire will take effect along the entire front. Unless something terrible happens, the war is over.'

Epilogue

Nothing terrible did go wrong. The cease-fire held. Over the next few days the Team stayed in place, maintaining its vigilance and preparing for a possible continuation of hostilities. While they were careful not to let their guard down, life began to improve. Regular hot meals became available, as did mail service. The men began to catch up on their personal needs, from bathing to clean laundry. Even the weather improved as they moved from the heat of summer into the cool days of early September.

It was during the first week of September that the division was replaced by a National Guard unit recently arrived from the States. The job of disarming the Soviets went to them and other units. Division was temporarily moved back into West Germany, where it received some replacements of equipment and personnel. By then the Soviet regime that had started the war was dismantled, and the chances of a new war were nonexistent.

With the crisis over, the Army bureaucrats began to reassert themselves. Those people who had lived in government quarters in Germany before the war were being sent back to conduct an inventory of their property, if it were still there, and to prepare a claim for any damages. The decision as to whether personal property that survived would be sent back to the States or families brought back to Germany hadn't been made yet.

It was strange returning to the military community the battalion had left a little over a month earlier. So much had changed. The community looked the same, empty of people but otherwise unchanged. The MP who escorted Bannon's group verified their names and quarters' addresses before letting each of them into their quarters. Bannon, like most of the others, had lost his keys somewhere along the way.

When he walked into his quarters, Bannon was overcome by a feeling of relief and joy. For the first time, he knew that it was all over. The horrors, though they would never be forgotten, were now relegated to the past. He looked around the quarters. Everything was as it had been when he had left. He was home.

He picked up the family album and sat on the sofa, just as he had that night in early August. As he leafed through it, he realised how much he missed his family. Looking at the pictures of his children, he was secure in the knowledge that they had a future free of the fears both he and his wife had grown up with. Again, Americans had been called on to pay for their freedom. And again, they had met the challenge, paid the price and prevailed. Bannon prayed this would be the last time.

But he knew better.

THE MAFIA KILLED PRESIDENT KENNEDY

David E. Scheim

On November 24, 1963, Dallas gangster Jack Ruby fatally shot Lee Harvey Oswald, JFK's accused assassin. The motive, Ruby explained, was patriotic fury.

But leading European journalists proposed another scenario. The Mafia, enraged by the Kennedys' anti-crime crusade, had murdered the President and then ordered Oswald silenced to cover its trail. This suspicion was supported years later by aging Mafia don Johnny Roselli, who admitted that Ruby was 'one of our boys'. Soon after, in 1976, Roselli's body was found floating in Miami's Biscayne Bay. In 1979, following a two-year probe, the House Select Committee on Assassinations reached a similar shocking conclusion.

Current Affairs/History
£6.99 Net

Available from all good Book Shops

KAHAWA

Donald E. Westlake

In Swahili, Kahawa means coffee. In East Africa in 1977 it spells a way of striking an audacious body blow against the corrupt regime in Uganda led by Idi Amin.

'Sheer delight'
Daily Telegraph

'Terrific'
Daily Mail

'A remarkable novel'
Robert Ludlum

'A well-written reminder of the unspeakable horror of Amin's regime'
Sunday Telegraph

Thriller
£3.99 Net

Available from all good Book Shops